Captain W. E. Johns was born in Hertfordshire in 1893. He flew with the Royal Flying Corps in the First World War and made a daring escape from a German prison camp in 1918. Between the wars he edited *Flying* and *Popular Flying* and became a writer for the Ministry of Defence. The first Biggles story, *Biggles: the Camels are Coming* was published in 1932, and W. E. Johns went on to write a staggering 102 Biggles titles before his death in 1968.

www.**randomhousechildrens**.co.uk

# BIGGLES STORIES AVAILABLE

## FIRST WORLD WAR
*Biggles Learns to Fly*
*Biggles Flies East*
*Biggles: the Camels are Coming*
*Biggles of the Fighter Squadron*
*Biggles in France*
*Biggles and the Rescue Flight*

## BETWEEN THE WARS
*Biggles and Cruise of the Condor*
*Biggles and Co.*
*Biggles Flies West*
*Biggles Goes to War*
*Biggles and the Black Peril*
*Biggles in Spain*

## SECOND WORLD WAR
*Biggles Defies the Swastika*
*Biggles Delivers the Goods*
*Biggles Defends the Desert*
*Biggles Fails to Return*

# BIGGLES
## ADVENTURE DOUBLE

### BIGGLES LEARNS TO FLY &
### BIGGLES: THE CAMELS ARE COMING

## CAPTAIN W. E. JOHNS

DOUBLEDAY

BIGGLES ADVENTURE DOUBLE
BIGGLES LEARNS TO FLY & BIGGLES THE CAMELS ARE COMING
A DOUBLEDAY BOOK 978 085 7532060

This edition published 2012 in Great Britain by Doubleday,
an imprint of Random House Children's Publishers UK
A Random House Group Company

1 3 5 7 9 10 8 6 4 2

*Biggles Learns to Fly*
First published in Great Britain by Boy's Friend Library, London 1935
Copyright © W. E. Johns (Publications) Ltd, 1935

*Biggles: the Camels are Coming*
First published in Great Britain by John Hamilton, London 1932
Copyright © W. E. Johns (Publications) Ltd, 1932

The right of W. E. Johns to be identified as the author of this work has been asserted
in accordance with the Copyright, Designs and Patents Act 1988.

The Random House Group Limited supports the Forest Stewardship Council (FSC®), the
leading international forest certification organization. Our books carrying the FSC label
are printed on FSC®-certified paper. FSC is the only forest certification scheme endorsed
by the leading environmental organizations, including Greenpeace. Our paper
procurement policy can be found at www.randomhouse.co.uk/environment.

RANDOM HOUSE CHILDREN'S PUBLISHERS UK
61–63 Uxbridge Road, London W5 5SA

www.**randomhousechildrens**.co.uk
www.**totallyrandombooks**.co.uk
www.**randomhouse**.co.uk

Addresses for companies within The Random House Group Limited
can be found at: www.randomhouse.co.uk/offices.htm

THE RANDOM HOUSE GROUP Limited Reg. No. 954009

A CIP catalogue record for this book is available from the British Library.

Printed and bound in UK by Clays Ltd, St Ives plc

# CONTENTS

# BIGGLES
## LEARNS to FLY

# CONTENTS

# Author's Note

The printing of this book is the answer to those who have asked when and where Biggles learned to fly. It was written many years ago, while the events were fresh in the author's mind, long before there was any talk of Hitler and a Second World War. The sons of some of the boys who read it then now fly jets. Time marches on—and in aviation it has marched very fast indeed. But this was the beginning, and the beginning of Biggles.

To readers of the modern Biggles books these early adventures may seem strange, both in the terms used and in the style of conversation. But Biggles was very young then. So was the Air Service. In fact, there was no air service. Fighting planes were flown by officers seconded from the Army (the R.F.C.) and the Navy (Royal Naval Air Service).

When Biggles (and the author) learned to fly, aeroplanes and equipment, by modern standards, were primitive. Combat tactics, as they are understood today, were unknown. Every pilot had his own method and, if he lived long enough, picked up a few tricks from the old hands. Once in the air he could more or less do as he pleased, for he was out of touch with the ground except by simple visual signals.

Communication between aircraft, or between pilot and gunner, was also by hand signals. Crossed fingers meant an enemy aircraft. First finger and thumb in the form of a circle meant British aircraft. Thumbs up meant all was well. Thumbs down—well, not so good. One also signalled the approach of enemy aircraft by rocking one's wings.

As the reader may guess, the writer's own experiences were much the same as those described herein. A few flights, and off you went solo. A few hours solo, and off you went to war, to take your luck. Casualties, of course, were grim; but all the same, happy-go-lucky were those days that have now become history. The mystery is that anyone survived, for apart from the risks of battle, structural failure was common, and there were no parachutes. On the other hand, the machines being slow, and made of wood, wire and fabric, one had a better chance in a crash than in the modern high-performance fighter.

The word 'Hun', as used in this book, was the common generic term for anything belonging to the enemy. It was used in a familiar sense, rather than derogatory. Witness the fact that in the R.F.C. a hun was also a pupil at a flying training school.

# Chapter 1
# First Time Up!

One fine late September morning in the war-stricken year of 1916, a young officer, in the distinctive uniform of the Royal Flying Corps, appeared in the doorway of one of the long, low, narrow wooden huts which, mushroom-like, had sprung up all over England during the previous eighteen months. He paused for a moment to regard a great open expanse that stretched away as far as he could see before him in the thin autumn mist that made everything outside a radius of a few hundred yards seem shadowy and vague.

There was little about him to distinguish him from thousands of others in whose ears the call to arms had not sounded in vain, and who were doing precisely the same thing in various parts of the country. His uniform was still free from the marks of war that would eventually stain it. His Sam Browne belt still squeaked slightly when he moved, like a pair of new boots.

There was nothing remarkable, or even martial, about his physique; on the contrary, he was slim, rather below average height, and delicate-looking. A wisp of fair hair protruded from one side of his rakishly tilted R.F.C. cap; his eyes, now sparkling with pleasurable anticipation, were what is usually called hazel. His features were finely cut, but the squareness of his chin and the firm line of his mouth revealed a certain doggedness, a tenacity of purpose, that denied any suggestion of weakness. Only his hands were small and white, and might have been those of a girl.

His youthfulness was apparent. He might have reached the eighteen years shown on his papers, but his birth certificate, had he produced it at the recruiting office, would have revealed that he would not attain that age for another eleven months. Like many others who had left school to plunge straight into the war, he had conveniently 'lost' his birth certificate when applying for enlistment, nearly three months previously.

A heavy, hair-lined leather coat, which looked large enough for a man twice his size, hung stiffly over his left arm. In his right hand he held a flying-helmet, also of leather but lined with fur, a pair of huge gauntlets, with coarse, yellowish hair on the backs, and a pair of goggles.

He started as the silence was shattered by a reverberating roar which rose to a mighty crescendo and then died away to a low splutter. The sound, which he knew was the roar of an aero-engine, although he had never been so close to one before, came from a row of giant structures that loomed dimly through the now-dispersing mist, along one side of the bleak expanse upon which he gazed with eager anticipation. There was little enough to see, yet he had visualized that flat area of sandy soil, set with short, coarse grass, a thousand times during the past two months while he had been at the 'ground' school. It was an aerodrome, or, to be more precise, the aerodrome of No. 17 Flying Training School, which was situated near the village of Settling, in Norfolk. The great, darkly looming buildings were the hangars that housed the extraordinary collection of

8

hastily built aeroplanes which at this period of the first Great War* were used to teach pupils the art of flying.

A faint smell was borne to his nostrils, a curious aroma that brought a slight flush to his cheeks. It was one common to all aerodromes, a mingling of petrol, oil, dope**, and burnt gases, and which, once experienced, was never forgotten.

Figures, all carrying flying-kit, began to emerge from other huts and hurry towards the hangars, where strange-looking vehicles were now being wheeled out on to a strip of concrete that shone whitely along the front of the hangars for their entire length. After a last appraising glance around, the new officer set off at a brisk pace in their direction.

A chilly breeze had sprung up; it swept aside the curtain of mist and exposed the white orb of the sun, low in the sky, for it was still very early. Yet it was daylight, and no daylight was wasted at flying schools during the Great War.

He reached the nearest hangar, and then stopped, eyes devouring an extraordinary structure of wood, wire, and canvas that stood in his path. A propeller, set behind two exposed seats, revolved slowly. Beside it stood a tall, thin man in flying-kit; his leather flying-coat, which was filthy beyond description with oil stains, flapped open, exposing an equally dirty tunic, on the breast of which a device in the form of a small pair of wings could just be seen. Under them was a

* The First World War 1914–18. Principal contenders, the Allies: Britain, France, Russia, Italy, Serbia, Belgium, Japan (1915), Romania (1916), USA (1917). Against the Central Powers: Germany, Austria-Hungary, Turkey and Bulgaria (1915).
** Liquid similar to varnish, applied to the fabric surfaces to stiffen and weatherproof them.

tiny strip of the violet-and-white ribbon of the Military Cross.

To a fully fledged pilot the figure would have been commonplace enough, but the young newcomer regarded him with an awe that amounted almost to worship. He knew that the tall, thin man could fly; not only could he fly, but he had fought other aeroplanes in the sky, as the decoration on his breast proved. At that moment, however, he seemed merely bored, for he yawned mightily as he stared at the aeroplane with no sign of interest. Then, turning suddenly, he saw the newcomer watching him.

'You one of the fellows on the new course?' he asked shortly.

'Er—er—yes, sir,' was the startled reply.

'Ever been in the air?'

'No, sir.'

'What's your name?'

'Bigglesworth, sir. I'm afraid it's a bit of a mouthful, but that isn't my fault. Most people call me Biggles for short.'

A slow smile spread over the face of the instructor.

'Sensible idea,' he said. 'All right, Biggles, get in.'

Biggles started violently. He knew that he had come to the aerodrome to learn to fly, but at the back of his mind he had an idea that there would be some sort of ceremony about it, some preliminary overtures that would slowly lead up to a grand finale in which he would take his place in an aeroplane before the eyes of admiring mechanics. And now the instructor had just said 'Get in!' as if the aeroplane were a common motor-car. Mechanics were there, it is true, but they were getting on with their work, taking not the slightest notice of the thrilling exploit about to be enacted. Only one, a corporal, was standing near the nose of the machine looking round the sky with a half-vacant expression on his face.

In something like a daze, Biggles donned his flying-kit. It was the first time he had worn it, and he felt that the weight of it would bear him to the ground. Stiffly he approached the machine.

'Look out!'

He sprang back as the shrill warning came faintly to his ears through the thick helmet. The instructor was glaring at him, his face convulsed with rage.

'What are you trying to do?' he roared. 'Break my propeller with your head? Come round to the front!'

'Sorry, sir,' gasped Biggles, and hurried as fast as his heavy kit would permit to the front of the machine. He raised his foot and clutched at a wire to help him up.

'Not there, you fool! Take your foot off that wing before you burst the fabric!' shouted the instructor from his seat.

Biggles backed away hastily—too hastily; his foot caught in one of the many wires that ran in all directions. He clutched wildly at the leading edge of the lower 'plane to save himself, but in vain, and the next instant he had measured his length on the ground.

The instructor looked down at him with such withering contempt that Biggles nearly burst into tears. The corporal came to his assistance. 'Put your left foot in that hole—now the other one in there—now swing yourself up. That's right!'

To Biggles the cockpit seemed hopelessly inadequate, but he squeezed himself into it somehow and settled down with a sigh of relief. Something struck him smartly on the back of the head, and he jumped violently.

'Strap in,' said a hard voice, 'and keep your hands and feet off the controls. If you start any nonsense I'll lam you over the back of the skull with this!'

With some difficulty Biggles screwed his head round to see what 'this' was. A large iron wrench was thrust under his nose; at the same moment the machine began to move forward, slowly at first, but with ever-increasing speed.

Something like panic seized him, and he struggled wildly to buckle up the cumbrous leather belt that he could see on either side of him. It took him a minute to realize that he was sitting on it. 'If he loops the loop or something I'm sunk!' he muttered bitterly, as he fought to pull it from under him. The machine seemed to lurch suddenly, and he grabbed both sides of the cockpit, looking down as he did so. The hangars were just disappearing below.

The next few minutes, which seemed an hour, were a nightmare. The machine rose and fell in a series of sickening movements; every now and then one of the wings would tip up at an alarming angle. He was capable of the one thought only: 'I shall never fly this thing as long as I live—never. I must have been crazy to think I could.'

Woods, fields, and houses passed below in bewildering succession, each looking like its fellow. Had the pilot told him they were over any county in the United Kingdom, he would have believed him.

'We must have gone fifty miles away from the aerodrome,' he thought presently; but the nose of the machine tilted down, and he saw the hangars leaping up towards him. For a moment he really did not believe they were the hangars; he thought it was a trick of the imagination. But there was a sudden grinding of wheels, and before he really grasped what was happening, the machine had run to a standstill in exactly the same spot from which it had taken off. He surveyed the apparent miracle with wonderment, making no effort to move.

'Well, how did you like it?' said a voice in his ear.

Biggles clambered awkwardly from his seat and turned to the speaker. The instructor was actually smiling.

'Grand!' he cried enthusiastically. 'Top hole.'

'Didn't feel sick?'

'Not a bit.'

'It's a wonder. It's bumpy enough to make anyone sick; we shall have to pack up flying if it doesn't get better. Let's go and mark your time up on the board. Enter up your log-book. "First flight. Air experience five minutes." '

'Five minutes!' cried Biggles incredulously. 'We were only up five minutes? I thought we were at least half an hour.'

The instructor had stopped before a notice-board headed ' "A" Flight,' below which was a list of names.

'What did you say your name was?' he asked, a frown lining his forehead.

'Bigglesworth, sir.'

'What flight are you in?'

'Flight? I don't know, sir.'

'You don't know?' snarled the instructor. 'Then what the dickens do you mean by wasting my time? What were you loafing about here for? These are "A" Flight sheds.'

Biggles stepped back quickly in his nervousness; his

heel struck a chock, and he grabbed wildly at a passing officer to save himself from falling.

'Hi! Not so much of the clutching hand!' growled a voice. 'This is a flying ground, not a wrestling school.'

'Sorry!' cried Biggles, aghast, detaching himself.

'Your name isn't Bigglesworth, by any chance, is it?' went on the officer, a short, thick-set man with a frightful scar on his face that reached from the corner of one eye to his chin.

'Why, yes, sir,' replied Biggles hesitatingly.

'Then what are you doing down here? You're in my flight, and you've kept the class waiting.'

'I've been flying, sir,' protested Biggles.

'You've been what?'

'He's right!' grumbled the first instructor. 'He was down here, so I naturally thought he was one of my fellows. I wish you'd look after your own pupils!'

Biggles waited for no more, but hurried along the tarmac to where a little group of officers—all pupils, judging by their spotless uniforms—stood at the door of a hangar.

'Where have you been?' cried one. 'Nerky's been blinding you to all eternity!'

'Nerky?'

'Captain Nerkinson. We call him Nerky because he's as nerky as they make 'em! He's crashed about ten times, so you can't blame him. Look out, here he comes!'

'Well, don't let us waste any more time,' began the instructor. 'Gather round this machine while I tell you something about it.'

The pupils formed a respectful semi-circle round the machine he had indicated.

'This aeroplane,' he began, 'is called a Maurice

Farman Shorthorn, chiefly because it hasn't any horns, short or otherwise. Some people call it a Rumpity. Others call it a birdcage, because of the number of wires it has got. The easiest way to find out if all the wires are in their places is to put a canary between the wings; if the bird gets out, you know there is a wire missing somewhere.

'Always remember that if this machine gets into a spin, it never gets out of it; and if it gets into a dive, the wings are apt to come off. Presently I shall take you up in it, one at a time; if anybody doesn't like it, he has only to say so, and he can transfer to the infantry.'

His voice trailed away to a whisper as a faint whistling sound reached their ears. All eyes were staring upwards at a machine that was coming in to land. It was a Rumpity, and it seemed to be descending in short jerks, as if coming down an invisible staircase; the pilot could seen sitting bolt upright in his seat.

A deep groan burst from the instructor's lips, as if he had been suddenly smitten with a violent pain.

'That's Rafferty, I'll bet my hide!' he muttered. 'I thought I'd cured him of that habit. Watch him, everybody, and you'll see the answer to the question why instructors go mad!'

Everybody on the tarmac was watching the machine, Biggles with a curious mixture of fear and fascination. A motor-truck, with a dozen mechanics carrying Pyrene fire-extinguishers hanging on to it, was already moving out on to the aerodrome in anticipation of the crash.

The pilot of the descending machine continued to swoop downwards in a series of short jerks. At the last moment he seemed to realize his danger, and must

15

have pulled the joystick back into his stomach, for the machine reared up like a startled horse and then slid back, tail first, to the ground. There was a terrific crash of breaking woodwork and tearing fabric, and the machine collapsed in a cloud of flying splinters. The pilot shot out of his seat as if propelled by an invisible spring, and rolled over and over along the ground like a shot rabbit. Then, to the utter astonishment of everybody, he rose to his feet and rubbed the back of his head ruefully. A shout of laughter rose into the air from the spectators.

Captain Nerkinson nodded soberly.

'You have just seen a beautiful picture,' he said, 'of how not to land an aeroplane!'

# Chapter 2
# Landed—But Lost

A week later, a Rumpity landed on the aerodrome, and Captain Nerkinson swung himself to the ground. Biggles, in the front cockpit, was about to follow, but the instructor stopped him.

'You're absolutely O.K.,' he said, 'except that you are inclined to come in a bit too fast. Don't forget that. Off you go!'

'Off I what?' cried Biggles, refusing to believe his ears.

'You heard me. You're as right as rain—but don't be more than ten minutes.'

'I won't—by James I won't, you can bet your life on that!' declared Biggles emphatically. He took a last lingering survey of the aerodrome, as when a swimmer who has climbed up to the high diving-board for the first time looks down. Then, suddenly making up his mind, he thrust the throttle open with a despairing jerk and grabbed at the weird, spectacle-like arrangement that served as a joy-stick in the Rumpity.

The machine leapt forward and careered wildly in a wide circle towards the distant hedge. For a moment, as the machine started to swing, Biggles thought he was going to turn a complete circle and charge the hangars; but he kept his head, and straightened it.

The tail lifted, and he eased the joy-stick back gently. To his surprise the machine lifted as lightly as a feather, but the needle on the air-speed indicator ran back alarmingly. He shoved the joy-stick forward again with a frantic movement as he realized with a heart-palpitating shock that he had nearly stalled through climbing too quickly. Settling his nose on the horizon and holding the machine on an even keel, he soon began to gather confidence.

A nasty 'bump' over the edge of a wood brought his heart into his mouth, and he muttered 'Whoa, there!' as if he was talking to a horse. The sound of his own voice increased his confidence, so from time to time he encouraged himself with such comments as 'Steady, there! Whoa, my beauty!' and 'Easy does it!'

Presently it struck him that it was time he started turning to complete a circuit that would bring him back to the aerodrome. He snatched a swift glance over his left shoulder, but he could not see the hangars. He turned a little farther and looked again. The aerodrome was nowhere in sight. It had disappeared as completely as if the earth had opened and swallowed it up. Perspiration broke out on his brow as he quickened his turn and examined every point of the compass in quick succession; but there was no aerodrome.

It took him another few seconds to realize that this miracle had actually taken place.

'No matter,' he muttered. 'I've only got to go back the way I came and I can't miss it.' In five minutes he was looking down on country that he knew he had never seen before.

His heart fluttered, and his lips turned dry as the full shock of the fact that he was completely lost struck him. Another 'plane appeared in his range of vision, seeming to drift sideways like a great grasshopper in that curious manner other machines have in the air, and he followed it eagerly. It might not be going to his aerodrome, but that did not matter; any aerodrome would suit him equally well. His toe slipped off the rudder-bar, and he looked down to adjust it.

When he looked up again his machine was in an almost vertical bank; he levelled out from a sickening side-slip, with beads of moisture forming inside his goggles. He pushed them up with a nervous jerk, and looked around for the other machine. It had gone. North, south, east and west he strained his eyes, but in vain. His heart sank, but he spotted a railway line and headed towards it.

'It must be the line that goes to Settling,' he thought, and he started to follow it eagerly. He was quite right— it was; but unfortunately he was going in the wrong direction.

After what seemed an eternity of time, a curious phenomenon appeared ahead. It seemed as if the land stopped short, ending abruptly in space, so to speak. He pondered it for a moment, and had just arrived at the conclusion that it was a belt of fog, when something else caught his eye, and he stared at it wonderingly. The shape seemed familiar, but for a moment or two he could not make out what it was. It looked like a ship, but how could a ship float in fog? Other smaller ones came into view, and at last the truth dawned on him. He was looking at the sea. It seemed impossible. As near as he could judge by visualizing the map, the coast was at least forty miles from Settling.

'This is frightful!' he groaned, and turned away from the forbidding spectacle. A blast of air smote him on the cheek, and objects on the ground suddenly grew larger. He clenched his teeth, knowing that he had side-slipped badly on the turn. He snatched a quick glance at the altimeter, and noted that it indicated four hundred feet, whereas a moment before the needle had pointed to the twelve hundred mark.

'Good heavens, this won't do!' he told himself angrily. 'What was it Nerky had said? "Never lose your head!" That was it.' He pulled himself together with an effort and looked at his watch. He had been in the air an hour and a half, and Nerky had told him not to be more than ten minutes.

He wondered how much longer his petrol would last, realizing with fresh dismay that he did not know how much petrol had been in the tanks when he started. The light was already failing; presently it would be dark, and what hope would he have then of finding his way? He remembered that he had a map in his pocket, but what use was that if he did not know where he was? He could only find that out by landing and asking somebody.

'It's the only way!' he told himself despairingly. 'I might go on drifting round in circles for the rest of my life without finding the aerodrome.'

He began to watch the ground for a suitable field on which to land.

He flew for some time before he found one. It was an enormous field, beautifully green, and he headed the machine towards it. At the last moment it struck him that there was something queer about the grass, and he pulled up again with a jerk, realizing that he had nearly landed on a field of turnips.

Another quarter of an hour passed, and another large field presented itself; it looked like stubble, which could do the machine no harm; but he approached it warily. Only when he was quite sure that it was stubble did he pull the throttle back. The sudden silence as the engine died away almost frightened him, and he watched the ground, now seeming to come towards him, longingly.

In the next few seconds of agonizing suspense he hardly knew what he did, and it was with unspeakable relief and surprise that he heard his wheels trundling over solid earth. The machine stopped, and he surveyed the countryside, scarcely able to believe that he was actually on the ground.

'I've landed!' he told himself joyfully. 'Landed without breaking anything! How did I do it? Good old aeroplane!' he went on, patting the wooden side of the cockpit. 'You must have done it yourself—I didn't. But the thing is, where are we?'

He stood up in the cockpit and looked around. Not a soul was in sight, nor was there any sign of human habitation.

'I would choose the only place in England where there aren't any roads, houses or people!' he thought bitterly. 'If I've got to walk to the horizon looking for somebody, it will be pitch dark before I get back. Then I should probably lose myself as well as the aeroplane!' he concluded miserably.

He sprang up as the sound of an aero engine reached his ears. It was a Rumpity, and, what was more, it was coming towards him. It almost looked as if the pilot intended landing in the same field.

'Cheers!' muttered Biggles. 'Now I shall soon know where I am!'

He was quite right; he was soon to know.

The Rumpity landed. The pilot jumped to the ground and strode towards him; there seemed to be something curiously familiar about his gait.

'Can it be?' thought Biggles. 'Great jumping fish, it is. Well, I'm dashed!'

Captain Nerkinson, his brows black as a thunder-cloud, was coming toward him. 'What game d'you think you're playing?' he snarled.

'Game?' echoed Biggles, in amazement. 'Playing?'

'Yes, game! Who told you you could land outside the aerodrome?'

'I told myself,' replied Biggles truthfully. 'I wanted to find out where I was. I lost myself, and I knew I had got so far away from the aerodrome that I—'

'Lost! What are you talking about? You've crossed the aerodrome three times during the last hour. I saw you!'

'I crossed the aerodrome?'

'You've just flown straight over it! That's why I chased you.'

'Flown over it!' Biggles shut his eyes, and shook his head, shuddering. 'Then it can only be a few miles away,' he exclaimed.

'A few miles! It's only a few yards, you young fool—just the other side of the hedge!'

Biggles sank down weakly in his seat.

'All right, let's get back,' went on the instructor. 'Follow close behind, and don't take your eyes off me.'

He hurried back to his machine and took off. Biggles followed. The leading machine merely hopped over the hedge and then began to glide down again at once, and Biggles could hardly believe his eyes when the aerodrome loomed up; it did not seem possible that he could have missed seeing those enormous sheds.

He started to glide down in Captain Nerkinson's wake. He seemed to be travelling much faster than the leading machine, for his nose was soon nearly touching its tail. He saw the instructor lean out of his seat and look back at him, white-faced. He seemed to be yelling something.

'He thinks I'm going to ram him,' thought Biggles. 'And so I shall if he doesn't get out of my way; he ought to know jolly well that I can't stop.'

The instructor landed, but he did not stop; instead, he raced madly across the ground towards the far side of the aerodrome, Biggles following close behind.

'I'm not losing you,' he declared grimly.

Captain Nerkinson swung round in a wide circle towards the sheds, and then, leaping out of the machine almost before it had stopped, sprinted for safety.

Biggles missed the other machine by inches; indeed, he would probably have crashed into it but for half a dozen mechanics, who, seeing the danger, dashed out and grabbed his wings.

'Are you trying to kill me?' Captain Nerkinson asked him, with deadly calm. He was breathing heavily.

'You said I wasn't to lose you.'

'I know I did, but I didn't ask you to ram me, you lunatic!'

The instructor recovered himself, and pointed to the hangar. 'Go and enter up your time,' he said sadly. 'If you stick to the tails of the Huns as closely as you stuck to mine, you should make a skyfighter.'

Three days later a little group collected around the notice-board outside the orderly-room.

'What is it?' asked Biggles, trying to reach the board.

'Posting,' said somebody.

Biggles pushed his way to the front and ran his eye down the alphabetical list of names until he reached his own, and read:

*2nd Lieut. Bigglesworth, J., to No. 4 School of Fighting, Frensham.*

The posting was dated to take effect from the following day.

He spent the evening hurriedly packing his kit, and, in company with four other officers who had been posted to the same aerodrome, caught the night train for his new station.

It was daylight the following day when they arrived, for although the journey to the School of Fighting, which was situated on the Lincolnshire coast, was not a long one, it involved many changes and delays. A tender met them at the station and dropped them with their kits in front of the orderly-room.

Biggles knocked at the door, entered, and saluted.

'Second-Lieutenant Bigglesworth reporting for duty, sir,' he said smartly.

The adjutant* consulted a list. 'The mess secretary will fix you up with quarters, Bigglesworth,' he said. 'Get yourself settled as soon as you can and report to "A" Flight—Major Maccleston.' He nodded, and then went on with his work.

Biggles dumped his kit in the room allotted to him, and then made his way to the sheds, where he was told that Major Maccleston was in the air.

He was not surprised, for the air was full of machines—Avros, B.E.s, F.E.s, Pups, and one or two types he did not recognize. Most of them were circling at the far side of the aerodrome and diving at something on the ground. The distant rattle of machine-guns came to his ears.

---

* An officer responsible for assisting the Commanding Officer with correspondence and paperwork.

Later on he learned that the far side of the aerodrome ran straight down into the sea, a long, deserted fore-shore, on which old obsolete aeroplanes were placed as targets. Scores of officers stood on the tarmac, singly or in little groups, waiting for their turns to fly.

A Pup* taxied out to take off, and he watched it with intense interest, for it was the type that he ultimately hoped to fly. An F.E. was just coming in to land, and he stiffened with horror, knowing that a collision was inevitable.

He saw the gunner in the front seat of the F.E. spring up and cover his face with his arms; then the Pup bored into it from underneath with a dreadful crash of splintering woodwork. For a moment the machines clung together, motionless in mid air; then they broke apart, each spinning into the ground with a terrible noise which, once heard, is never forgotten. A streak of fire ran along the side of one of them, and then a sheet of flame leapt high into the air. An ambulance raced towards the scene, and Biggles turned away, feeling suddenly sick. It was the first real crash he had seen.

A flight-sergeant was watching him grimly. 'A nasty one, sir,' he said casually, as if he had been watching a football match in which one of the players had fallen. 'You'll soon get used to that, though,' he went on, noting Biggles' pale face. 'We killed seven here last week.'

Biggles turned away. Flying no longer seemed just a thrilling game; tragedy stalked it too closely. He was glad when an instructor landed, turned out his passen-

* Sopwith Pup. A single seat fighter with one fixed machine-gun synchronised to allow the bullets to pass between the propeller blades.

ger, and beckoned him to take his place. Biggles took his seat in the cockpit, noting with a thrill that it was fitted with machine-guns.

'We're going to do a little gunnery practice,' said the instructor, and took off.

Three days later, Biggles was called to the orderly-room.

'What's up?' he asked a sober-faced officer, who was just leaving.

'Heavy casualties in France,' was the reply. 'They're shoving everybody out as fast as they can.'

Biggles entered and saluted. The adjutant handed him a movement order and a railway warrant.

'A tender will leave the mess at six forty-five to catch the seven o'clock train,' he said. 'You will proceed direct to France via Newhaven and Dieppe.'

'But I haven't finished my tests yet, sir!' exclaimed Biggles, in surprise.

'Have you got your logbook and training transfer-card?'

Biggles placed them on the desk.

The adjutant filled in the tests which had not been marked up, signed them, and then applied the orderly-room stamp.

'You've passed them now,' he said, with a queer smile. 'You may put up your "wings"!'

Biggles saluted, and returned to the aerodrome in a state of suppressed excitement. Two thoughts filled his mind. One was that he was now a fully fledged pilot, entitled to wear the coveted 'wings', and the other that he was going to France.

The fact that he had done less than fifteen hours' flying, dual and solo, did not depress him in the least.

# Chapter 3
# The Boat for France

There are some people who say that the North Pole is
the most desolate spot on the face of the globe. Others
give the doubtful credit to the middle of the Sahara
Desert. They are all wrong.

Without the slightest shadow of doubt the most
dismal spot on the face of the earth is that depressing
railway terminus known as Newhaven Quay, on the
south coast of England, where the passenger for the
Continent gets out of a train, walks across a platform,
and steps on to the cross-Channel boat. At normal
times it is bad enough, but during the First World War
it was hard to find words to describe it.

So thought Biggles, who crouched rather than sat on
a kit-bag in a corner of the platform. His attitude
dripped depression as plainly as the dark silhouette of
the station dripped moisture.

He was not alone on the platform. At intervals along
the stone slabs, dark, ghostly figures loomed mysteri-
ously, in ones and twos, and in little groups. At the far
end, a long line of men in greatcoats, with unwieldy-
looking bundles on their backs, filed slowly into view
from an indistinguishable background. The only
sounds were vague, muffled orders, and the weird
moaning of the biting north-east wind through the rig-
ging of a ship that rested like a great vague shadow
against the quay. Not a light showed anywhere, for
German submarines had been reported in the Channel.

Once, a low laugh echoed eerily from the shadows, and the unusual sound caused those who heard it to turn curiously in the direction whence it came, for the occasion of the departure of a leave-boat for France was not usually one for mirth.

Biggles moved uneasily and seemed to sink a little lower into the greatcoat that enveloped him. He did not even move when another isolated figure emerged slowly from the pillar behind which it had been sheltering from the icy blast, and stopped close by.

'Miserable business, this messing about doing nothing,' observed the newcomer. His voice sounded almost cheerful, and it may have been this quality that caused Biggles to look up.

'Miserable, did you say?' he exclaimed bitterly. 'It's awful. There isn't a word bad enough for it. I'm no longer alive—I'm just a chunk of frozen misery.'

'They say we shall be moving off presently.'

'I've been hearing that ever since I arrived!'

'They say it's a U-boat in the Channel that's holding us up.'

'What about it? Surely to goodness it's better to drown quickly than sit here and freeze to death slowly. Why the dickens don't they let us go on board, anyway?'

'Ask me something easier. Is this your first time over?'

Biggles nodded. 'Yes,' he said grimly, 'and if it's always like this, I hope it will be the last.'

'It probably will be, so you needn't worry about that.'

'What a nice cheerful fellow you are!'

The other laughed softly. 'I see you're R.F.C. What squadron are you going to?'

'I've no idea. My Movement Order takes me as far as the Pool* at St Omer.'

'Splendid! We shall go that far together: I'm in Two-six-six.'

Biggles glanced up with fresh interest. 'So you've been over before?' he queried.

'Had six months of it; just going back from my first leave. By the way, my name's Mahoney—we may as well know each other.'

'Mine's Bigglesworth, though most people find that rather a mouthful and leave off the "worth." You fly Pups in Two-six-six, don't you?'

'We do—they're nice little Hun-getters.'

'I hope to goodness I get to a scout squadron, although I haven't flown a scout yet.'

'So much the better,' laughed Mahoney. 'If you'd been flying scouts they'd be certain to put you on bombers when you got to France. Fellows who have been flying two-seaters are usually pitched into scout squadrons. That's the sort of daft thing they do, and one of the reasons why we haven't won the war yet. Hallo! It looks as if we're going to move at last.'

A gangway slid from the quay to the ship with a dull rattle, and the groups of officers and other ranks began to converge upon it.

'Come on, laddie; on your feet and let's get aboard,' continued Mahoney. 'Where's the rest of your kit?'

'Goodness knows! The last I saw of it, it was being slung on to a pile with about a thousand others.'

'Don't worry. It will find you all right. How much flying have you done?'

* A depot to which officers were posted until assigned to an active service squadron.

29

'Fifteen hours.'

Mahoney shook his head. 'Not enough,' he said. 'Never mind, if you get to Two-six-six, I'll give you a tip or two.'

'You can give me them on the journey, in case I don't,' suggested Biggles. 'I've been waiting for a chance to learn a few things first-hand from someone who has done it.'

'If more chaps would take that view there would be fewer casualties,' said Mahoney soberly, as they crossed over the narrow gangway.

Two days later a Crossley tender pulled up on a lonely, poplar-lined road to the north of St Omer, and Biggles stepped out. There was nothing in sight to break the bleak inhospitality of the landscape except three many-hued canvas hangars, a cluster of wooden huts, and three or four curious semi-circular corrugated iron buildings.

'Well, here you are, Biggles,' said Mahoney, who had remained inside the vehicle. 'We say good-bye here.'

'So this is One-six-nine Squadron,' replied Biggles, looking about him. 'My word! I must say it doesn't look the sort of place you'd choose for a summer holiday!'

'It isn't. But then you're not on a holiday!' smiled Mahoney. 'Don't worry; you'll find things cheerful enough inside. It's too bad they wouldn't let you go to a scout squadron; but F.E.'s* aren't so bad. They can fight when they have to, and the Huns know it, believe me. I suppose they're so short of pilots that they are just bunging fellows straight to the squadrons where

* Two-seater biplane with the engine behind the pilot, the gunner just in front of him. See cover illustration.

pilots are most needed. Well, I must get along; Two-six-six is only seven or eight miles farther on, so we shall be seeing something of each other. Come over to our next guest night. Remember what I've told you—and you may live until next Christmas. Cheerio, laddie!'

'Cheerio!' replied Biggles, with a wave of farewell as the car sped on to its destination. He picked up his valise and walked towards a square wooden building near the hangars, which he rightly judged to be the squadron office. He tapped on the door, opened it in response to a curt invitation to enter, and saluted briskly.

'Second-Lieutenant Bigglesworth, sir,' he said.

An officer who sat at a desk strewn with papers, rose, came towards him, and offered his hand. 'Pleased to meet you, Bigglesworth,' he said. 'And if you can fly, everyone here will be more than pleased to see you. We are having a tough time just at present. I'm Todd—more often known as "Toddy"—and I'm simply the Recording Officer. The C.O. is in the air, but he'll want a word with you when he gets back. You'll like Major Paynter. Wing 'phoned us that you were on the way, so you'll find your quarters ready in Number Four Hut. Get your kit inside, and make yourself comfortable; then go across to the mess. I'll be along presently. By the way, how many hours' flying—solo—have you done?'

'Nearly nine hours.'

Toddy grimaced. 'What on?' he asked.

'Shorthorns and Avros.'

'Ever flown an F.E.?'

'Not solo. I had a flight in one at Frensham, but an instructor was in the other seat.'

'Never mind; they're easy enough to fly,' answered Toddy. 'See you later.'

Biggles departed to his quarters. The work of unpacking his kit occupied only a few minutes, and then he made his way slowly towards the officers' mess*. He was still a little distance away, when the sound of an aero-engine made him glance upwards. An aeroplane was heading towards the aerodrome, a type which he did not recognize. But, unwilling to betray his ignorance before possible spectators in the mess, he paid no further attention to it and continued on his course. He then noted with some surprise that Toddy was behaving in a very odd manner. The Recording Officer began by flinging open the door of the squadron office and racing towards the mess. When he had reached about half-way, however, he appeared to change his mind, and, turning like a hare, took a flying leap into a sort of hole.

Biggles next noticed the faces of several officers at the mess window; they seemed to be very excited about something, waving their arms wildly. It did not occur to him for a moment that the signals were intended for him. The first indication he received that something unusual was happening was a curious whistling sound; but even then the full significance of it did not strike him. The whistle swiftly became a shrill howl, and thinking he was about to be run down by a speedy car, he jumped sideways. The movement probably saved his life, for the next instant the world seemed to explode around him in a brilliant flash of flame. There was a thundering detonation that seemed to make the very earth rock, and he was flung violently to the ground. For

* The place where officers eat their meals and relax together.

a moment he lay quite still, dazed, while a steady downpour of clods, stones, and loose earth rained about him.

The steady rattle of machine-guns in action penetrated his temporarily paralysed brain, and he rose unsteadily to his feet. He noted that the aeroplane had disappeared, and that a little crowd of officers and mechanics were racing towards him.

'What the dickens was that?' he asked the officers who ran up.

The question seemed to amuse them, for a yell of laughter rose into the air.

Biggles flushed. 'Do you usually greet new fellows like that?' he inquired angrily.

There was a renewed burst of laughter.

'Jerry* does, when he gets the chance. Our friends over the Line must have heard that you had arrived, so they sent their love and kisses,' replied a tall, good-looking officer, with a wink at the others. 'Don't you know an L.V.G.** when you see one?' he added.

'An L.V.G.! A Hun!' cried Biggles.

The other nodded. 'Yes. Just slipped over to lay the daily egg. You're lucky,' he went on. 'When I saw you strolling across the aerodrome as if you were taking an airing in the park, I thought we should be packing up your kit by this time. You're Bigglesworth, I suppose; we heard you were coming. My name is Mapleton, of A Flight. This is Marriot—Lutters—Way—McAngus. We're all A Flight. The others are in the air. But come across to the mess and make yourself at home!'

'But what about that L.V.G.?' cried Biggles. 'Do you let him get away with that sort of thing?'

* Slang: Germans
** A German two-seater, the product of Luft Verkehrs Ges'ellschaft.

'He's half-way home by now; the best thing we can hope for is that the Line archies* give him a warm time. Hallo, here comes the patrol! What—'

A sudden hush fell upon the group as all eyes turned upwards to where two machines were coming in to land. Biggles noticed that Mapleton's face had turned oddly pale and strained. He noticed, too, for the first time, that there were three stars on his sleeves, which indicated the rank of captain.

'Two!' breathed the man whom Captain Mapleton had named Marriot. 'Two!' he said again. And Biggles could feel a sudden tension in the air.

'Come on!' said Mapleton. 'Let's go and meet them. Maybe the others have stayed on a bit longer.'

Together they hurried towards the now taxi-ing machines.

The events of the next few minutes were to live in Biggles' mind for ever. His whole system, brought face to face with the grim realities of war, received a shock which sent his nerves leaping like a piece of taut elastic that has been severed with scissors. He was hardly conscious of it as the time, however, when, with the others, he reached the leading machine. He merely looked at it curiously. Then, instinctively, he looked at the pilot, who was pushing up his goggles very slowly and deliberately.

One glance at his face and Biggles knew he was in the presence of tragedy. The face was drawn and white, but it was the expression on it—or, rather, the absence of expression on it—that made Biggles catch his breath. There was no fear written there, but rather a look of weariness. For perhaps two minutes he sat thus, staring

---

* Anti aircraft gun batteries close to the front line of battle.

34

with unseeing eyes at his instrument-board. Then, with a movement that was obviously an effort, he passed his hand wearily over his face and climbed stiffly to the ground. Still without speaking he began to walk towards the mess, followed by two or three of the officers.

A low, muttered exclamation made Biggles half-turn to the man next to him. It was Lutters.

'Just look at that kite!' Lutters said. 'The Old Man* must have been through hell backwards.'

'Old Man?' ejaculated Biggles questioningly.

'Yes—the C.O. There must be two hundred bullet holes in that machine; how it holds together beats me!'

Biggles' attention had been so taken up with the pilot that he had failed to notice the machine, and now he caught his breath as he looked at it. There were holes everywhere; in several places pieces of torn canvas hung loosely, having been wrenched into long, narrow streamers by the wind. One of the interplane struts was splintered for more than half its length, and a flying wire trailed uselessly across the lower 'plane.

He was about to take a step nearer, when a cry made him look towards the second machine. Two mechanics were carefully lifting a limp body to the ground.

'You'd better keep out of the way,' said McAngus brusquely, as he passed; but Biggles paid no attention. He knew that McAngus was right, and that the sight was hardly one for a new pilot; but the tableau drew him irresistibly towards it.

When he reached the machine they had laid the mortally wounded pilot on the ground. His eyes were

---

* Slang for the person in authority, Commanding Officer, often shortened to C.O.

open, but there was an expression in them that Biggles had never seen before.

'Jimmy—how's Jimmy?' the stricken man was muttering; and then: 'Look after Jimmy!'

Biggles felt himself roughly pushed aside.

It was the C.O., who had returned. 'Get him to hospital as fast as you can,' he told the driver of the motor-ambulance which had pulled up alongside. Then, 'How's Mr Forrester?' he asked a mechanic, who was bending over the front cockpit of the machine.

'I'm afraid he's dead, sir,' was the quiet reply.

'All right—get him out!' said the C.O. briefly.

Biggles watched two mechanics swing up to the forward cockpit of the F.E. Slowly, and with great care, they lifted the body of the dead observer and lowered it into waiting hands below.

Biggles caught a glimpse of a pale, waxen face, wearing a curious, fixed smile, and then he turned away, feeling that he was in the middle of a ghastly dream, from which he would presently awaken. He was overwhelmed with a sense of fantastic unreality.

Again the drone of an aero-engine rose and fell on the breeze, and at the same instant a voice cried: 'Here's another!' He swung round and stood expectant with the others as the machine reached the aerodrome, roared low over their heads as it came round into the wind, and then landed. A large white letter U was painted on the nose.

'It's Allen and Thompson!' cried several voices at once.

The machine taxied up quickly. The observer leaped out as soon as it stopped, and started buffing his arms to restore the circulation. The pilot joined him on the ground, flung open his flying-coat and lit a cigarette.

Biggles saw there were several bullet-holes in this machine, too, but neither pilot nor observer paid any attention to them. In fact, the pilot, a stockily built, red-faced youth, was grinning cheerfully, and Biggles stared in amazement at a man who could laugh in the shadow of death.

'Love old Ireland!' observed Thompson, the observer. 'Isn't it perishing cold! Give me a match, somebody. What a day!' he went on. 'The sky's fairly raining Huns. The Old Man got a couple—did he tell you? Poor Jimmy's gone, I'm afraid, and Lucas. We ran into the biggest bunch of Huns over Douai that I ever saw in my life.'

He turned and walked away towards the mess, the others following, and Biggles was left alone with the mechanics, who were now pulling the machines into the hangars with excited comments on the damage they had suffered. He watched them for a few minutes, and then, deep in thought, followed the other officers towards the mess, feeling strangely subdued. For the first time he had looked upon death, and although he was not afraid, something inside him seemed to have changed. Hitherto he had regarded the War as 'fun'. But he now perceived that he had been mistaken. It was one thing to read of death in the newspapers, but quite another matter to see it in reality.

He was passing the squadron office when Toddy called him. 'The C.O. wants to have a word with you right away,' he said.

Several officers were in the room when Biggles entered, and he felt rather self-conscious of his inexperience; but the C.O. soon put him at ease.

'I'm afraid you've come at rather a bad moment,' he began, shaking hands. 'I mean for yourself,' he added quickly. 'We hope it will be a good one for us. I'm posting you to A Flight; Captain Mapleton will be your flight-commander. We like to keep pilots and observers together, as far as we can, but it's not always possible. I believe Way is without a regular pilot, isn't he, Mapleton? So Bigglesworth might pair off with him.'

Captain Mapleton nodded. 'Yes, sir,' he said. 'He's my only observer now without a regular pilot.'

'Good! Then your Flight is now up to establishment,' continued the major, turning again to Biggles. 'Don't let what you've seen to-day depress you. It was an unfortunate moment for you to arrive; that sort of thing doesn't happen every day, thank goodness!' He hesitated and went on, 'I want you always to remember that the honour of the squadron comes first. We are going through rather a difficult time just now, and we may have a lot of uphill work ahead of us, so we're all doing our best. Trust your flight-commander implicitly, and always follow his instructions. In the ordinary way I should give you a week or two to get your bearings before letting you go over the Line, but we've had a bad run of casualties, and I need every officer I can get hold of. It's rather bad luck on you, but I want you to do the best you can in the circumstances. Study the map and the photographs in the map-room; in that way you will soon become acquainted with the area. All right, gentlemen, that's all.'

As the officers filed out, a deeply tanned, keen-eyed young officer tapped Biggles on the arm. 'I'm Mark Way,' he said. 'It looks as if we shall be flying together, so the sooner we know each other the better.'

'That's true,' said Biggles. 'Have you been out here long?'

'Nearly three months,' replied Mark simply. 'But I saw a bit of active service with the infantry before I transferred to the R.F.C. I came over with the New Zealand contingent; my home is out there.'

'Sporting of you to come all this way to help us. Who have you been flying with?'

'Lane.'

'Where is he now?'

Mark gave Biggles a sidelong glance. 'He's gone topsides,' he said slowly. 'He died in hospital last week—bullet through the lungs.'

Biggles was silent for a moment, feeling rather embarrassed.

'You'll like Mapleton,' went on Mark. 'He's a good sort. By the way, we call him Mabs; I don't know why, but he was called that when I came here. Marble is his observer—his real name is Mardell, but Marble is a good name for him. He's as cold as ice in a dog-fight,* and knows every inch of the Line. They're a jolly good pair, and I'd follow them anywhere. Allen is O.C.** B Flight. It's best to keep out of his way; he's a bad-tempered brute. Perhaps it isn't quite fair of me to say that, because I don't think he means to be nasty; he's been out here a long time, and his nerves are all to pieces. Rayner has C Flight. He's all right, but a bit of a snob, although personally I think it's all affectation. His brother was killed early in the war, and all he really thinks about is revenge. He's got several Huns. He takes on Huns wherever he finds them, regardless of numbers, and he gets his Flight into pretty hot water; but they can't complain, because he's always

* An aerial battle rather than a hit-and-run attack.
** Officer commanding B Flight

39

in the thick of it himself. I don't think his luck can last much longer. I wouldn't be his observer for anything! Marriot and McAngus are the other two pilots in A Flight. Conway flies with Marriot, and Lutter is Mac's observer; they're a good crowd. Hallo, here comes Mabs. What does he want?'

'Bigglesworth,' began the flight-commander, coming up, 'I don't want to rush you, but I'm taking a Line patrol up this afternoon. I think it will be pretty quiet, or I wouldn't let you come, even if you wanted to. But the fact is, everybody has been flying all hours, and it will mean extra flying if someone has to make a special journey to show you the Lines. And it isn't as if we were flying single-seaters; you've always got Mark with you to put you right if you get adrift. So if you care to come this afternoon it will serve two purposes. You'll get a squint at the Line and a whiff of archie, and it will give McAngus a rest. He's looking a bit knocked up.'

'Certainly I'll come,' replied Biggles quickly.

'That's fine! I thought you wouldn't mind. It's all for your own good, in the long run, because the sooner you get used to archie the better. But for goodness' sake keep close to me. You keep your eye on him, Mark. We take off at three o'clock, but be on the tarmac a quarter of an hour before that, and I'll show you our proposed course while the engines are warming up.'

# Chapter 4
# Battle

It was under a cold, grey sky, that Biggles sat in his cockpit the same afternoon, waiting for the signal to take off. He had made one short flight over the aerodrome immediately after lunch to accustom himself to his new machine, and he had satisfied himself that he was able to fly it without difficulty. The F.E.2b. was not a difficult machine to fly; it had no vicious habits, which was, perhaps, the reason why those who flew it were unstinted in its praise.

The patrol was made up of three machines. Captain Mapleton, of course, was leading. Marriot and his gunner, 'Con' Conway, were on the right, and Biggles, with Mark Way in the front seat, on the left.

The machine was fitted with two machine-guns, one firing forward and the other backwards over the top 'plane, both operated by the gunner. A rack containing drums of ammunition was fitted to the inside of the cockpit.

Biggles felt a thrill of excitement run through him as the flight-commander's machine began to move forward; he heard Marriot's engine roar, and then the sound was drowned in the bellow of his own as he opened the throttle. Together the three machines tore across the damp aerodrome and then soared into the air, turning slowly in a wide circle.

A quarter of an hour later they were still over the aerodrome, but at a height of seven thousand feet, and Biggles, who had settled down into the long turn, dashed off at a tangent as the leader suddenly straightened out and headed towards the east. A sharp exclamation from the watchful Mark warned him of his error, which he hastened to rectify, although he still remained at a little distance from the other two machines.

'Try to keep up!' yelled Mark, turning in his seat and smiling encouragingly. 'It's easier for everybody then.'

Biggles put his nose down a little to gain extra speed, and then zoomed back into position, a manœuvre which Mark acknowledged with an approving wave. For some time they flew on without incident, and then Mark began to move about in his cockpit, looking towards every point of the compass in turn, and searching the sky above and the earth below with long, penetrating stares.

Once he reached for his gun, and caused Biggles' heart to jump by firing a short burst downwards. But then Biggles remembered that Mark had said he would fire a burst when they reached the Line, to warm the guns, which would reduce the chance of a jam.

Following the line of the gun-barrel, he looked down and saw an expanse of brown earth, perhaps a mile in width, merging gradually into dull green on either side. Tiny zig-zag lines ran in all directions. Must be the Lines, he thought, with a quiver of excitement, not unmixed with apprehension, and he continued to look down with interest and awe.

'Hi!'

He looked up with a guilty start; Mark was yelling at him, and he saw the reason—he had drifted a good hundred yards from his companions.

'My hat!' he mused. 'I shall never see anything if I can't take my eyes off them without losing them.'

But Mark was pointing with outstretched finger over the side of the cockpit, and, following the line indicated, he saw a little group of round, black blobs floating in space. Automatically he counted them; there were five—no, six. He blinked and looked again. There were eight. 'That's queer!' he muttered, and even as the truth dawned upon him there was a flash of flame near his wing-tip, and a dull explosion that could be heard above the noise of the engine.

The swerve of the machine brought his heart into his mouth, but he righted it quickly and looked around for the other two. They had disappeared. For a moment he nearly panicked, but Mark's casual nod in the direction of his right wing restored his confidence, and, peering forward, he perceived them about fifty yards or so to his right. He turned quickly into his proper place, receiving a nod of approval from his gunner as he did so.

The black archie bursts were all around them now, but Mark did not appear to notice them; he had reached for his gun and held it in a position of readiness. Suddenly he tilted it up and fired a long burst: then, as quick as lightning, he dragged it to the other side and fired again.

Biggles nearly strained his neck trying to see what Mark was shooting at, but seeing nothing but empty air decided that he must be warming up his guns again. He looked across at the machine on his right, and noticed that Conway was shooting, too. As he watched him he ceased firing and looked down over the side of his cockpit for a long time; then he looked across at Mark and held up his fist, thumb pointing upwards.

'There seems to be a lot of signalling going on!' thought Biggles. 'I wonder what it's all about?'

The time passed slowly, and he began to feel bored and rather tired, for it was the longest flight he had ever made. This seems a pretty tame business, he pondered. I should have liked to see a Hun or two, just to get an idea of what they look like. 'Hallo!'

Mark was standing up again, trying to point his gun straight down, and for the first time he seemed to be excited. Casually Biggles leaned over the side to see what it was that could interest his gunner to such an extent. There, immediately below him, not fifty yards away, was a large green swept-back wing, but that which held his gaze and caused his lips to part in horrified amazement were the two enormous black Maltese crosses, one on each end. His skin turned to goose flesh and his lips went dry. He saw a man standing in the back seat of the machine pointing something at him; then, for no reason that he could discover, the man fell limply sideways, and the green wing folded up like a piece of tissue paper. It turned over on its side and the man fell out.

In a kind of paralysed fascination Biggles watched the brown, leather-clad body turning slowly over and over as it fell. He thought it would never reach the ground.

He was brought to his senses with a jerk by a shrill yell. The other two machines were turning—had nearly completed the turn. He swung round after them in a frantic bank, skidding in a manner that made Mark clutch at the side of his cockpit. He could see no other German machines in sight, so he decided that the time allotted for their patrol had expired.

'My word, now he has decided to go home, he is

certainly going in a hurry!' thought Biggles, as the leading machine nearly stood on its nose as it dived full out towards the ground. He thrust his joy-stick forward, and with difficulty restrained a yell of delight.

The shriek of the propeller, the howl of the wind in the wires, seemed to get into his blood and intoxicate him. He wondered vaguely why Mark was looking back over his shoulder instead of looking where they were going and enjoying the fun, and he was almost sorry when the flight-commander pulled out of the dive and commenced to glide down.

He watched the ground closely, noting such land-marks as he thought he would be able to recognize again, until the aerodrome came into view, when he concentrated on the business of landing.

A green Very light* soared upwards from the leading machine, and then dropped swiftly; it was the 'wash-out' signal, meaning that the machines were to land independently. He allowed the others to land first, and then, with exultation in his heart, he followed them down and taxied up to the hangars.

Mark gave him a queer smile as he switched off the engine. 'Pretty good!' he said cheerfully. 'That's one on the slate for me on Lane's account.'

'You mean that green Hun underneath us?' cried Biggles. 'My gosh! It gave me a queer feeling to see that fellow going down.'

'Great Scott, no! Conway got him. I got the blue-and-yellow devil.'

'What!' exclaimed Biggles, in amazement. 'What blue-and-yellow devil?'

* A coloured flare fired as a signal, from a special short-barrelled pistol.

45

'Didn't you see him diving down on us from in front? He was after you.'

'No, I didn't, and that's a fact,' admitted Biggles soberly. 'I didn't see you shoot at him.'

'I couldn't at first, because I was busy plastering the black fellow who was peppering us from underneath.'

Biggles blinked and shook his head. 'Black, blue, green! How the dickens many of them were there?' he muttered, in a dazed voice.

'Seven altogether. We got three of them between us.'

Biggles sat down limply. 'And I only saw one!' he groaned. 'What on earth would have happened to me if I'd been alone?'

Mark laughed. 'Don't worry, you'll soon get the hang of spotting 'em,' he said. 'You saw that mob coming down on us at the finish?'

Biggles shook his head, eyes wide open. He couldn't speak.

'You didn't? You ought to have seen those—there must have been more than a dozen of 'em. Mabs spotted them the instant they shoved their ugly noses out of the mist, and like a sensible fellow he streaked for home.'

'Thank goodness he did!' muttered Biggles weakly. 'And I thought he was merely hurrying home!'

'That's just what he was doing,' observed Mark dryly. 'But let's go and get some tea—I can do with it!'

# Chapter 5
# Plots and Plans

Biggles landed his F.E. after a short test flight and glanced in the direction of the sheds, where Mabs and the rest of the flight were standing watching him.

A week had elapsed since his first never-to-be-forgotten flight over the Lines. He had done at least one patrol every day since, and was already beginning to feel that he was an old hand at the game. He had picked up the art of war flying with an aptitude that had amazed everyone, particularly his flight-commander, who had reported to Major Paynter, the C.O., that young Biggles seemed to have a sort of second sight where enemy aircraft were concerned.

He jumped down now from the cockpit and with a brief 'She's running nicely!' to his fitter, walked quickly towards the flight shed, where the others were apparently waiting for him.

'Come on!' announced Mabs, with a curious smile. 'There's a little party on, and we knew you wouldn't like to be left out.'

'You're right!' agreed Biggles. 'What's it about? I like parties.'

'You may not like this one,' said Mabs. 'Stand fast while I get it off my chest. You know, of course, that headquarters have been shouting for days about a report they want making on the railway junction and sidings at Vanfleur?'

'You mean the show that Littleton and Gormsby went on?'

'That's right. As you know, they didn't come back. Neither did Blake nor Anderson, who went yesterday. Both the other flights have had a shot at it, and now it's our turn. The Old Man says I'm not to go, otherwise I shouldn't be here telling you about it. That means that either you or Marriot or McAngus will have to go.'

'I'd already worked that out,' replied Biggles. 'Nothing wrong with that, is there?'

'Nothing! I'm just telling you, that's all. You can settle amongst yourselves who's going, or if there's any argument about it I shall have to detail someone for the job. I'm not going to ask for volunteers, because you'd all volunteer on principle, and nothing would be decided. But there's two things you've got to remember. In the first place, it's no use going all the way to Vanfleur and coming back without learning something. It means counting every wagon and truck in the siding, and noting any dumps in the vicinity. In other words, the information has got to be correct. It's no use guessing or imagining things, because incorrect information is misleading, and does more harm than good. The other thing is, it's going to be a stick show for the man who goes. Vanfleur is forty miles over the Line, if it's an inch. You don't need me to tell you that there are more Hun scouts at Douai than any Boche* aerodrome on the front. Rumour says that Richthofen** and his crowd have just moved to Douai, and maybe that's

---

* Derogatory term for the Germans.
** Manfred Von Richthofen 'the Red Baron' – German ace who shot down a total of 80 Allied aircraft. Killed in April 1918.

why the other fellows didn't get back. Well, there it is. Tell me in five minutes who's going.'

'I'll go!' said Biggles promptly.

'No, you don't!' replied Mabs quickly. 'I'm not letting anyone commit suicide just because he thinks it's the right thing to do. I suggest you toss for it—odd man goes—that's the fairest way, and then whatever happens there can be no reproaches about it.'

Biggles took a coin from his pocket and the others did the same. 'Spin,' he said, and tossed the coin into the air. The three coins rang on the concrete.

'Heads,' said Biggles, looking at his own coin.

'Tails,' announced Marriot.

'Same here,' said McAngus.

'That means I'm the boob!' grinned Biggles. 'When do I start?'

'When you like—the sooner the better. I should think first thing in the morning might be the best time,' suggested Mabs.

'Why do you think that?'

'Well, that's the time these shows are usually done.'

'That's what I thought—and the Huns know that as well as we do. I'll go this afternoon, just by way of a change, if it's all the same to you. What do you think, Mark?'

'Suits me!'

'That's that, then!' said Mabs. 'You'd better come with me and tell the Old Man you're going. He'll want to have a word with you first. And you'd better come along, too, Mark.'

The C.O. looked up from his desk when they entered the squadron office. 'Ah, so it's you, Bigglesworth, and Way. I had an idea it might be.' He rose to his feet and walked over to them. 'Now look here, you fellows,' he went on. 'There isn't much I can say, but remember that these shows are not carried out just for the fun of it, or to find us jobs of work. They are of the greatest possible importance to H.Q., as they themselves are beginning to admit.' He smiled whimsically, recalling the days when the military leaders had laughed at the idea of aeroplanes being of practical value for reconnoitring. 'I want you to pay particular attention to the rolling stock in the sidings,' he resumed. 'Also, have a good look at these places I've marked on the map. Study the last set of photographs we got of the area—you'll find them in the map-room. You know what to look out for; make a note of any alterations in the landscape.

'If you see a clump of bushes growing where there were none last week, when the photos were taken, it probably means that it is a camouflaged battery. Watch for "blazes" on the grass, caused by the flash of the guns, and cables leading to the spot. You will not be able to see telephone wires, of course, but you may see the shadows cast by the poles, or a row of dots—the newly turned earth at the foot of each pole. You may see a track joining the dots—the footmarks and beaten-down grass caused by the working party. It's easier still to pick out an underground cable. If the trench has not been filled in, it shows as a clear-cut line; if it has been filled in, it reveals itself as a sort of woolly line, blurred at the edges. If you see several such lines of communication converging on one spot it may mean that there is an enemy headquarters there.

'Quantities of fresh barbed wire means that the enemy is expecting to be attacked, and has prepared new positions upon which to retire. On the other hand, new trenches, saps, dug-outs, and, more particularly, light railways, means that he is preparing an offensive. But there, you should have learned about these things by now so there's no need for me to go over them again. When have you decided to go?'

'After lunch, sir,' replied Biggles.

'I thought you'd start in the morning: that's the usual time.'

'Yes, sir; that's why we decided to go this afternoon.'

The C.O. frowned, then a smile spread over his face. 'Good for you!' he said, nodding approval. 'That's the worst of being out here a long time; we get into habits without knowing it. Little points like the one you've just mentioned have been staring us in the face for so long that we can't see them. All right, then. Good luck!'

'Come on, Mark!' said Biggles, when they had left the office. 'Let's get the machine ready. Then we can sit back and think things over until it's time to go.'

It was exactly two o'clock when they took off. The distance to their objective was, Mabs had said, a full forty miles, and as they expected to be away at least three hours, they dared not start later, as it began to get dark soon after four.

For twenty minutes Biggles climbed steeply, crossing and recrossing the aerodrome as he bored his way upwards, knowing that the higher they were when they crossed the Lines the less chance there would be of their being molested; so he waited until the altimeter was nearly on the eight thousand feet mark before striking out for the Lines.

A few desultory archie bursts greeted them as they passed over, and for the next half-hour they had the sky to themselves. It was a good day for their purpose from one point of view, but a bad day from another aspect.

Great masses of wet clouds were drifting sluggishly eastwards at various altitudes—6,000, 8,000 and even at 10,000 feet—and while this might afford cover in the event of their being attacked, it also provided cover for prowling enemy scouts to lie in wait for them. Again, while it concealed them from the gunners on the ground, it limited their range of vision and prevented them from seeing many of the landmarks they had decided to follow. Moreover, if their objective was concealed by cloud, they would either have to return with their mission unfulfilled, or they would have to descend very low, a dangerous performance so far over enemy territory. Nevertheless, Biggles had decided that unless enemy interference made the project hopeless, he would go down to a thousand feet, if necessary, rather than return with a blank report, which, rightly or wrongly, would be regarded as failure by headquarters.

They were now approaching the objective, and Biggles began to hope that they might achieve their object without firing a single shot. But the atmosphere rapidly thickened, and he realized with annoyance that a blanket of mist hung over the very spot they had come so far and risked so much to view. He shut off his engine and began a gentle glide.

'I'm going down!' he roared to Mark, who stood up in his seat, guns ready for action, scanning the atmosphere anxiously in all directions.

At six thousand feet they sank into the billowing mist, and Biggles turned his eyes to his instruments, every nerve tense. 5,000—4,000—3,000 feet, and still there was no break, and he knew he would never be able to climb up through it again without losing control of the machine. He hoped desperately that he would find a hole, or at least a thin patch, in the cloud, after their work was accomplished. At two thousand feet he emerged into a cold, cheerless world, and looked about anxiously for the railway line. 'There it is!' he yelled, pointing to the right, at the same time opening up his engine and heading towards it. Mark had seen the junction at the same instant, and, leaving his guns, grabbed his note-book and prepared to write.

*Whoof, whoof, whoof,* barked the archie; but the enemy gunners were shooting hurriedly, and the shots went wide. Other guns joined in, and the bursts began to come closer as the gunners corrected their aim. But Biggles kept the machine on even keel as he watched the sky around them, while Mark counted the railway trucks, jotting down his notes as well as his cold hands and the sometimes swaying machine would permit.

Biggles made a complete circuit around the railway junction, which was as choc-a-bloc with traffic as only a railway junction of strategical importance could be in time of war.

Four long trains were in the station itself; two others—one consisting of open trucks, carrying field artillery—stood in a siding, with steam up and ready to move. Shells were being loaded in the other from a great dump.

'Have you finished?' yelled Biggles.

'Go round once more!' bellowed Mark.

Biggles frowned, but proceeded to make another circuit, twisting and turning from time to time to dodge the ever-increasing archie and machine-gun bullets. Wish I had a bomb or two, he thought, as he eyed the great ammunition dump. But there, no doubt the bombers will arrive in due course, when we've made our report.

Without warning the archie stopped abruptly. Mark

dropped his pencil, shoved his writing-pad into his pocket, and grabbed his gun. 'Look out!' he yelled.

But Biggles had already seen them—a big formation of straight-winged planes sweeping up from the east. There was no need to speculate as to their nationality.

'What a mob!' he muttered, and swung round for home. But an icy hand clutched his heart as he beheld yet another formation of enemy machines racing towards the spot from the direction of the Lines. They were cut off.

We stayed too long, he thought bitterly. The people at the station must have rung up every squadron for miles, and they're not going to let us get our report home if they can prevent it. 'Well, I can't fight that lot!' he muttered desperately, and, turning his nose to the north-west, raced away in the only direction open to him.

Fortunately there was a lot of broken cloud on the horizon, apart from a big mass overhead, and this, he hoped, would help him to throw the wolves off his trail.

Mark suddenly crouched low behind the gun that fired backwards over the top 'plane, and began firing in short, sharp bursts. Biggles winced as a bullet bored through his instrument-board with a vicious thud. He began side-slipping gently to and fro to throw the enemy pilots off their mark—a tip that had been given him on the boat coming over. A faint rattle reached his ears above the noise of the engine. They're overtaking us, he thought. Mark signalled frantically to him to climb. He put his nose down for an instant to gather speed, and then zoomed upwards. The cold, grey mist enveloped them like a blanket.

'Must be twenty of 'em—Albatripes*!' yelled Mark.

* Albatros, German single seater fighter with two fixed machine guns.

But Biggles was busy fighting to keep the machine on even keel. The bubble of the inclinometer* was jumping from one side to the other in a most alarming way, and the needle of his compass was swinging violently. 'It's no use—I'll have to go down!' he yelled. A blast of air struck him on the side of the face, and he knew he was side-slipping; he rectified the slip, but, as usual in such cases, he overdid it, and the draught struck his other cheek. He shot out of the cloud with one wing pointing straight to the ground.

He picked the machine up while Mark clambered to his feet, searching the atmosphere behind them. Biggles, snatching a glance behind him, saw enemy machines scattered all over the sky to the south-east, still effectually barring their return. No sooner did the lone F.E. appear than they turned in its direction and began overhauling it.

'I don't know where we're getting, but I can't face that lot,' shouted Biggles, still heading north-west. 'We must be miles off our course.'

The black-crossed machines were closing the gap between them quickly, so he pushed his nose down and raced towards the low clouds, now only a short distance away. He reached them just as a burst of fire from the rear made the F.E. quiver from propeller-boss to tail-skid, and he plunged into the nearest mass of white, woolly vapour in something like a panic. He came out on the other side, banked vertically to the left, and plunged into another.

And so he went on, twisting and turning, sometimes through and sometimes around the clouds. He dived

---

* An instrument similar to a spirit level, for showing the angle of the aircraft relative to the ground

below them and then zoomed up again through them. He knew he was hopelessly lost, but even that, he decided, was better than facing the overwhelming odds against them.

Mark, still standing up, was examining the sky behind them; then he held up his fists, thumbs pointing upwards.

'O.K.! We've lost them!' he bellowed.

Biggles breathed a sigh of relief and began to glide down through the cloud, hoping to pick up some outstanding landmark that might be recognized from his map. The F.E. emerged once more into clear air, and he looked down anxiously. He stared, blinked, and stared again as a dark green expanse of foam-lashed water met his horrified gaze.

There could be no mistake. He was looking down at the sea. The clouds, as so often happens, ended abruptly at the coast-line, which revealed itself as a white, surf-lashed line just behind him. In front of him the sky was a clear, pale blue as far as he could see.

He thought quickly, feeling for his map, guessing what had happened. In their long rush to the northwest they had actually reached the Belgian coast, so he turned to the south, knowing that sooner or later they were bound to reach France again.

Mark, too, examined his map as Biggles began following the coast-line.

'We shall be all right if the petrol holds out, and if it doesn't get dark before we can see where we are,' he shouted, and then settled back in his seat, to resume the eternal task of watching the sky for enemy machines. Slowly the blue of the sky turned to misty grey with the approach of dusk, and Biggles came lower in order not to lose the coast-line.

Suddenly Mark sprang to his feet and swung his gun round to face the open sea. Biggles, following the line of the gun, saw an Albatros diving on them out of the mist. Something, it may have been pure instinct, made him glance in the opposite direction—a second Albatros was coming in on their left, the landward side. Two scouts, evidently working together, were launching a dual attack.

The events of the next thirty seconds followed each other so swiftly that they outraced Biggles' capacity for thinking. Mark was shooting steadily at the first scout, which had now opened fire on them; Biggles was watching the second, which was also shooting. The pilots of both enemy scouts, evidently old hands at the game, thrust home their attack so closely that Biggles instinctively zoomed to avoid collision; but they both swerved at the last moment in the same direction. They met head-on just below and in front of the F.E. with a crash that made Biggles jump. At the same instant his engine cut out dead, and a pungent, almost overpowering stench of petrol filled his nostrils. Automatically he put his nose down towards the shore. Out of the corner of his eye he saw the fragments of the two German scouts strike the water with a terrific splash.

# Chapter 6
# Late for Dinner

In the now failing light the coast-line, although fairly close, was not much more than a dark, indistinct mass, with a strip of pale orange sand, lashed with white foam, running along the edge.

We shall never reach it!' thought Biggles, as he glanced at his altimeter. It registered one thousand feet.

Mark was standing up, calmly divesting himself of his leather coat and flying-boots. He tore off the two top pages of his writing-pad and folded the precious report carefully into a leather wallet, which he thrust into his breeches pocket.

He lifted the guns off their mountings and tossed them overboard, and Biggles knew that he did this for two reasons. Firstly, to prevent them falling into the hands of the enemy, and secondly, to lighten the machine, and thus give them a better chance of reaching the shore.

Then Mark looked at Biggles, and, cupping his hands round his mouth, shouted: 'Get your clothes off. It looks as if we shall have to swim for it!'

With some difficulty, first holding the joy-stick with one hand and then the other, Biggles managed to get his coat off and throw it overboard. Cap, goggles and sheepskin flying-boots followed.

At the last moment, just as he thought they might reach the beach, a slant of wind caught them and they dropped swiftly. He held the machine off as long as he could, but as it lost flying speed it wobbled and then flopped bodily into the water. A wave lifted the doomed F.E. like a feather and rushed it towards the beach; then, as it grated harshly on the sand, they jumped clear and struck out for the shore.

Half drowned, Biggles felt a wave roll him over and over. It dropped him on all fours on solid ground, and he dug his fingers into the sand as he felt the backwash sucking him back again. Mark, who was heavier, grabbed him by the collar and clung to him desperately until the wave had receded. Crawling, swaying, stumbling and falling, they managed to reach the beach, gasping and spitting out mouthfuls of sea-water.

'My hat, isn't it cold!' muttered Biggles through chattering teeth.

'Come on, get on your feet—they'll be here any minute. They must have seen us come down!' snapped Mark; and at a reeling gait in their water-logged clothes they hurried towards the wide sand dunes which line that part of the Belgian coast.

'What's the hurry?' panted Biggles.

'The Huns will be here any minute—we're still the wrong side of the Lines!'

Hardly had they plunged into the bewildering valleys of the dunes than they heard the sound of harsh, guttural voices coming towards them.

'Down!' hissed Mark, and they flung themselves flat in the coarse, scrubby grass that grew in patches on the sand. It was now nearly dark, so there was still just a chance that they might escape observation.

Biggles clenched his teeth tightly in order to restrain their chattering, which he thought would betray them, while the voices passed not more than ten yards away and receded in the direction of the shore.

For twenty minutes or more they lay while dark figures loomed around them, going towards or returning from the beach. One party came so close that Biggles held his breath, expecting to feel a heavy boot in the small of his back at any moment.

'What are we going to do? I shall freeze to death if we stay here much longer!' he whispered as the footsteps receded.

'So shall I if it comes to that,' muttered Mark. 'I'm dead from the feet up. But our only chance is to lie still and hope that they'll think we were drowned. They must have seen the two Albatripes attack us, and for all they know we might have been wounded. There are bound to be people on the beach for some time watching for the bodies of those two Boche pilots. We shall have to put up with the cold for a minute or two while people are moving about. When it gets a bit darker we'll crawl to the top of a dune and see if we can see what's going on.'

Another quarter of an hour passed, and at last it was really dark, except for the feeble light of a crescent moon low in the sky. With a whispered 'Come on!' Mark began crawling up the sloping side of the nearest sand dune, and Biggles followed, glad to be moving at last. Side by side they reached the top, and, raising their heads slowly, peered round. Not a soul was in sight except on the beach, where a small group of figures could just be made out watching the remains of the F.E being pounded to pieces by the surf. Some debris had evidently been salved, for it lay in a pile just beyond the reach of the waves.

'They must think we were drowned or there'd be

more activity,' breathed Mark. 'Our only chance now is to work our way along the coast. It might be better if we waited a bit longer, but we can't do that or we shall be frozen to death. Anyway, we've got to be round the wire before morning or we shall certainly be spotted.'

'Wire—what wire?' asked Biggles.

'The barbed wire between the Lines. I'm not absolutely certain but I think I saw it as we came down; I was on the look-out for it. If I'm right, it's only about a mile farther along. Confound those two Huns; in another five minutes we should have been well over the Lines.'

'Shall we be able to get through the wire, do you think?' asked Biggles.

'We shall not. I hear they have tightened things up a good deal along here lately, owing to escaped prisoners working their way back along the coast. Somebody told me they've got little bells hung all along the wire, and you can't touch it without ringing them. In any case, we should need rubber gloves because the Huns are electrifying their wire. No, I'm afraid we shall have to go round it.'

'Round it!'

'Yes, by swimming round it. It's been done before and it's our only chance.'

Biggles groaned. 'Fancy having to get into that water again! I'd sooner face the biggest formation of Huns that ever took the air. I had no idea water could be so cold. I nearly joined the Navy once; I'm thundering glad I didn't!' he grumbled.

'Don't grouse—we're lucky to be alive!' muttered Mark. 'Come on, now, no noise!'

Crouching and crawling, they began to wind their

way through the dunes, taking a peep over the top whenever an opportunity presented itself in order to keep direction, which lay parallel to the shore. Sometimes they were able to walk a few yards, but on other occasions they had to worm their way like snakes across open spaces. Once they had to lie flat as a squad of troops, evidently a working party, passed within a few yards of them.

At last Mark raised himself up and peered forward. 'I think I can see the wire just ahead,' he breathed, 'but we can't get any farther along here. There must be a trench just in front, because I can hear people talking. We'd better get down to the water.'

'Lead on,' breathed Biggles. 'I can't be any colder than I am already!'

Dragging themselves along on their stomachs, often stopping to listen, they wormed their way to the water's edge.

'How far can you swim?' whispered Mark.

'I don't know,' admitted Biggles. 'I've never found it necessary to find out.'

'You'll have to chance it, then. I can swim pretty well any distance, but not when it's as cold as this. I was brought up by the sea. If you feel your strength giving out, hang on to my collar and we'll get round— or sink together. We shall have to get out just beyond the breakers, and then swim parallel to the coast. As soon as we see our own wire we'll come ashore. If we don't see it, we'll swim as far as we can. But the Lines can't be very far apart—come on!'

They plunged into the icy water and struck out through the blinding spray. Biggles paid little or no attention to the direction, but simply fixed his eyes on the black head bobbing in front of him and followed it.

How long they swam he did not know, but it seemed to be an eternity and he was just about to call out that he could go no farther when Mark turned shorewards. Biggles made one last despairing dash through the surf, and then lay panting and gasping like a stranded fish.

Mark seized him by the collar and dragged him out of the reach of the waves. 'Get up!' he snapped.

'Wait—a minute—let me—get—breath!' panted Biggles.

Mark dragged him roughly to his feet. 'Run!' he said. 'We shall have to start our blood moving, or we shall both be down with pneumonia. I think we're round both lots of wire; if we aren't then we're unstuck, that's all about it.'

Without waiting for any more he set off at a steady trot along the sand, Biggles reeling behind him, their clothes squelching and discharging water at every step.

'*Halte la*\*!'

They pulled up with a jerk as the challenge rang out.

'Friend—ami!' yelled Biggles desperately, but joyfully, for he knew the language was not German.

'*Attendez!*' called the voice, and they heard the jangle of military equipment. A dark figure, closely followed by several others, loomed up in the darkness in front of them, rifles and bayonets held at the ready.

'You do the talking!' growled Mark. 'I can't speak the lingo!'

'*Je suis—nous ont—Anglais*', began Biggles in his best French. '*Aviateurs—aviateurs Anglais.*'

There was a sharp intake of breath, and a flashlight

---

\* French: halt! wait! I am—we have—English. Aviators. English aviators.

stabbed the darkness. The figures closed around them and they were hurried a short distance into a trench, and then into a dugout, where an officer in a blue uniform sat writing.

Quickly, in a strange mixture of English and broken French, Biggles told his story to the Belgian officer. He eyed them suspiciously at first, but at the end of the story he made a brief telephone call which seemed to satisfy him.

The dripping clothes were stripped off the two airmen, blankets were produced, and boiling soup, in great basins, thrust into their hands.

An hour later a British staff officer stepped into the dugout.

'Who are you?' he asked curtly, obviously suspicious. But suspicion quickly gave way to friendliness as the two airmen told their story.

Mark handed over his report, which, although wet, was still legible. 'I wish you'd get that back as quickly as you can, sir,' he said. 'We've been through some trouble to get it!'

'You can bring it yourself,' the officer told him. 'I have a car waiting a little way back. But you'll have to borrow some clothes if our Belgian friends can provide them. You can't put those wet ones on again!'

Dinner was in progress when Biggles and Mark, attired in mixed Belgian uniforms, arrived at their aerodrome. They opened the mess door, and amid dead silence, with all eyes on them, they marched stiffly to the head of the table, where the C.O. sat, and apologized for being late for dinner.

The C.O. stared at them, while a babble of voices broke out, punctuated with laughs, that finally swelled into a roar in which everyone joined. Mark, who had seen such a scene before, knew that the laughter was simply the British way of expressing relief after they had been given up for lost.

But Biggles turned a pained face to the room.

'What's the joke?' he cried hotly. 'Do you think we're all dressed up for the fun of it?'

A fresh burst of laughter greeted his words.

'Everyone's glad to see you back, that's all!' said the C.O. 'And that's the chief thing. Did you get a report on the junction?'

'Yes, sir,' replied Mark.

'That's splendid! Sit down and have your dinners. You can tell us all about it afterwards!'

# Chapter 7
# A Daring Stunt

'I'm not going to pretend that I know much about it, but it seems to me that if the Huns are going to mass their squadrons—as apparently they are—we shall have to do the same or else be wiped out.' Biggles, having ventured an opinion for the first time since he joined the squadron, glanced up, half-expecting a remark about his inexperience.

'He's right!' exclaimed Mabs emphatically. 'I've been saying the same thing for the last month. Richthofen, they say, has grouped three squadrons together, including all the best pilots in the German Air Force. And, whether he has or not, we know for a fact that he's sailing up and down the Lines with thirty triplanes* tagged on behind him. Who's going to face that bunch? Who's going to take on that little lot, I'd like to know? What chance has an ordinary Line patrol of three planes got if it bumps into that pack?'

'Rot!' snapped Captain Rayner, of C Flight. 'The more the merrier! Dive straight into the middle of them and the formation will go to pieces. It will take them all their time to avoid collision.'

'Don't kid yourself!' declared Captain Allen of B Flight. 'They've got this game weighed up nicely. They

---

* Fokker aeroplane with three wings and two forward-firing machine guns. Often referred to as a tripe or tripehound.

didn't wait for us to bump into them this morni
they bumped into us and we jolly soon knew about i

There was silence for a moment, due to the fact that B Flight had lost two machines that very morning through the menace they were discussing.

'I think it's a logical conclusion that if we start sending big patrols of twenty or thirty machines against them they'll start flying in fifties or more. Whatever we do, they will maintain numerical superiority, and at the finish formations will be flying in hundreds. A nice sort of game that will be!' declared Marriot disgustedly.

'Well, it may come to that some day, but if it does I hope I'm not here to see it,' observed Allen coldly. 'I—'

The ante-room door opened and an orderly appeared. 'Major Paynter's compliments, and will all officers please report to the squadron office at once?'

There was a general move towards the door.

The Major was in earnest conversation with Toddy, the Recording Officer, when they arrived, but he broke off and turned to face them as they entered.

'Well, gentlemen,' he said, 'I've some news for you, though whether you'll regard it as good or bad I don't know. Will all those officers who have had any experience of night-flying please take a pace to the front?'

Mabs, a pilot of B Flight, and a pilot and observer of C Flight stepped forward.

'That's worse than I expected,' said the Major. 'Never mind; this is the position. Whether we like it or not, Wing have decided to carry out certain operations that can best be done at night. As you know, enemy scout squadrons have been concentrated opposite this sector of the Front, and our machines have neither the performance nor numerical strength of theirs. In these s we are going to try to cripple them on t is thought that night raids will adversely norale, to say nothing of the damage we n their machines or aerodromes. It's pro-ry out the first raid on a very big scale; other squadrons will participate and keep the ball rolling all night. In order to put as large a number of machines in the air as possible, this squadron will take part in the raid, which will be on Douai Aerodrome, the headquarters of the Richthofen group.

'Fortunately, our machines are well adapted for night-flying, so for the next two nights I shall want all officers to put in as much practice in the air as possible. It's up to everyone to make himself proficient in the new conditions. Flares will be put out, and lectures will be arranged, which must be attended by all officers on the station. Has anyone any questions to ask?'

'I take it that the attack will be in the form of a bomb raid, sir?' said Biggles.

'We shall attack with all arms—heavy bombs, Cooper bombs, baby incendiaries*, and machine-guns. Naturally, it is in our own interest to make a good job of the show; if things go according to plan, we shall meet with less opposition when we resume daylight patrols. That's all.'

'Well, that's the answer to the question!' observed Mark brightly, when they were outside.

'What question?'

'The thing we were talking about in the mess when

* Heavy bombs 112lb and Cooper bombs 20lb were both carried under the aircraft. Baby incendiaries (sometimes abbreviated as BI's) were fire bombs thrown by hand from the cockpit—a dangerous game.

the C.O. sent for us—the big Boche formations. We're going to swipe them on the ground!'

'Well, it may be all right,' replied Biggles thoughtfully, 'but we could have wiped them out in daylight shows if it comes to that. I'm thinking that there is one thing the staff people may have overlooked.'

'What's that?'

'You don't imagine for one moment that the Huns will take this night-strafing business lying down, do you? If I know anything about 'em they'll soon be showing us that it's a game two can play. You mark my words, they'll be over here the next night, handing us doses of our own medicine—in spoonfuls. I hope I'm mistaken, but I reckon things will be getting warmish here presently!'

'Well, the staff won't mind that; they won't be here,' observed Mark bitterly. 'I must say I don't fancy being archied at night; the flashes look ghastly. I've been told that they are a nice bright orange when they are close to you, and a beautiful dull crimson when they're some distance away.'

'We shall soon be able to see for ourselves whether your information is correct,' returned Biggles. 'As long as they're not pink with blue spots on 'em I don't mind!'

The weather on the night decided for the first raid was all that could be desired, considering the time of the year. There was no wind, and a new moon shone brightly in a clear, frosty, star-spangled sky, against which the hangars loomed as black silhouettes.

By the C.O.'s orders not a light gleamed anywhere, for every step was being taken to prevent information of the impending raid from reaching the enemy through the many spies whose duty it was to report such operations.

An engine roared suddenly in the darkness, and the end machine of a long line that stood in front of the hangars began to waddle, in the ungainly fashion of aeroplanes on the ground, towards the point allocated for the take-off; a dark red, intermittent flame, curled back from the exhaust-pipe.

'There goes Mabs,' said Biggles, who, with Mark his gunner, was standing by their machine.

The planes were to leave at five-minute intervals, which gave each aircraft a chance to get clear before the next one took off, and so lessened the chances of a collision either on the ground or in the air.

'Marriot goes next, and then McAngus, so we've got a quarter of an hour to wait,' went on Biggles. 'It's going to be perishing cold if I know anything about it,' he remarked, glancing up at the frosty sky. 'But there, we can't have it all ways. We shall at least be able to see where we are, and that's a lot better than groping our way in and out of clouds; that's bad enough in the day-time! Hallo! There goes Marriot!'

A second machine taxied out and roared up into the darkness.

'Mabs has got to the Line—look!' said Mark, pointing to a cluster of twinkling yellow lights in the distant sky. 'That's archie!'

Lines of pale green balls seemed to be floating lazily upwards.

'Look at the onions,' he added, referring to the well-known enemy anti-aircraft device commonly known as flaming onions.

A third machine taxied out and vanished into the gloom.

'Well, there goes McAngus; we'd better see about getting started up,' said Biggles tersely.

They climbed into their cockpits, and mechanics ran to their wings and propeller.

'Switch off!'

'Off!'

The engine hissed and gurgled as the big propeller was dragged round to suck the gas into the cylinders.

'Contact!' cried the mechanic.

'Contact!' echoed Biggles.

There was a sharp explosion as the engine came to life; then it settled down to the musical purr peculiar to the Beardmore type.

For a few minutes they sat thus, giving the engine time to warm up; then Biggles opened the throttle a trifle and pointed to his right wing—the signal to the mechanics that he wanted it held in order to slew the machine round to the right. While a machine is on the ground with the engine running all orders are given by signals, for the human voice would be lost in the noise of the engine; even if it was heard, the words might not be distinguished clearly, and an accident result.

With his nose pointing towards the open aerodrome, Biggles waved both hands above his head, the signal to the mechanics to stand clear. The F.E. raced across the aerodrome, and then roared up into the starry night.

He did not waste time climbing for height over the aerodrome, but headed straight for the Lines, climbing as he went. Peering below, he could see the countryside about them almost as plainly as in day-time; here and there the lighted windows of cottages and farms stood out brightly in the darkness; far ahead he could see the

71

track of the three preceding machines by the darting flashes of archie that followed them.

A British searchlight flashed a challenge to him as he passed over it, but Mark was ready, and replied at once with the colour of the night—a Very light that first burnt red and then changed to green. 'O.K.—O.K.,' flashed the searchlight in the Morse code, and they pursued their way for a time unmolested.

Biggles crouched a little lower in his seat as the first archies began to flash around them. It reached a crescendo as they crossed the Line, augmented by the inevitable flaming onions that rose up vertically from below like white-hot cannon-balls; but the turmoil soon faded away behind them as they sped on through the night over enemy territory, the Beardmore engine roaring sullen defiance. From time to time he peered below to pick up his landmarks, but for the most part he stared straight ahead, eyes probing the gloom for other machines.

The planes, of course, carried no lights, and although the chances of collision were remote, with machines of both sides going to and fro all the time, it was an ever-present possibility. In night raids it was usual for the machines taking part to return by a different route, or at a higher altitude to the one taken on the outward journey, and while machines adhered to this arrangement, collision was impossible.

Biggles was, of course, aware of this, but he kept an anxious eye on his line of flight in case an enemy machine had decided to take the same route as himself, but in the opposite direction, or in case Marriot or McAngus had got off their course.

Mark suddenly rose to his feet and pointed with outstretched finger. Far away, almost on the horizon, it seemed, a shaft of flame had leapt high into the air; the sky glowed redly from the conflagration, and Biggles knew that one of the machines preceding him had either reached its destination and set fire to the hangars, or had itself been shot down in flames.

The fire, however, served one good purpose, for it acted as a beacon that would guide them direct to their objective. It continued to blaze fiercely as they approached it, and presently the crew of the F.E. were able to see that it was actually on Douai Aerodrome. It looked like one of the hangars. Keeping on a line that would bring him right over it Biggles throttled back and began gliding down.

Orders had stated that machines should descend as low as five hundred feet, if necessary, to be reasonably sure of hitting the target; but the thrill of the game was in his blood, and he no longer thought of orders. At five hundred feet he shoved the throttle open wide, and, pushing the stick forward, swept down so low that Mark, in the front seat, stared back over his shoulder in amazement.

The instant he opened his throttle an inferno seemed to break loose about the machine. Anti-aircraft guns and even field-guns situated on the edge of the aerodrome spat their hate; machine-guns rattled like casta-nets, the tracer bullets cutting white pencil lines through the darkness. Out of the corner of his eye Biggles saw Mark crouch low over his gun and heard it break into its staccato chatter.

He grabbed the bomb-toggle as the first hangar leapt into view, and, steadying the machine until the ridge of the roof appeared at the junction of his fuselage and the leading edge of the lower plane, he jerked it upwards—one, two.

Two 112-pound bombs swung off their racks, and the machine wobbled as it was relieved of their weight. Straight along over the hangars the F.E. roared, while Mark stood up and threw the baby incendiaries overboard.

When they came to the end of the line, Biggles zoomed up in a wide turn and tore out of the vicinity, twisting and turning like a wounded bird. Only when the furious bombardment had died away behind them did he lean over the side of his cockpit and look back at the aerodrome. His heart leapt with satisfaction, for two hangars were blazing furiously, the flames leaping high into the sky and casting a lurid glow on the surrounding landscape.

A body of men was working feverishly to get some aeroplanes out of one of the burning hangars; a machine that had evidently been standing outside when the attack was launched had been blown over on its back; several figures were prone on the ground, and one man was crawling painfully away from the heat of the fire.

'Well, that should make things easy for the others; they can't very well miss that little bonfire!' mused Biggles with satisfaction. Shells started bursting again in the air on the far side of the aerodrome, and he knew that Captain Allen, in the leading machine of B Flight, was approaching to carry on the good work.

'If our people are going to keep that up all night, those fellows down there will have nasty tastes in their mouths by the morning!' called Biggles, smiling; but the next instant the smile had given way to a frown of anxiety as a new note crept into the steady drone of the engine.

Looking back over his shoulder his heart missed a

beat as he saw a streamer of flame sweeping aft from one of the cylinders. Mark had seen it, too, and was staring at him questioningly, his face shining oddly pink in the glow.

Biggles throttled back a trifle and the flame became smaller, but the noise continued and the machine began to vibrate.

'It feels as if they've either blown one of my jampots* off or else a bullet has knocked a hole through the water jacket,' he yelled. 'If it will last for another half-hour, all right! If it doesn't, we're in the soup!'

With the throttle retarded he was creeping along at a little more than stalling speed, so he tried opening it again gently. Instantly a long streamer of fire leapt out of the engine, and the vibration became so bad that it threatened to tear the engine from its bearers. With a nasty sinking feeling in the pit of his stomach he snatched the throttle back to its original position, and shook his head at Mark as the only means he had of telling him that he was unable to overcome the trouble.

The noise increased until it became a rattling jar, as if a tin of nails was being shaken. A violent explosion behind caused him to catch his breath, and he retarded the throttle still farther, with a corresponding loss of speed. He had to tilt his nose down in order to prevent the machine from stalling, and he knew that he was losing height too fast to reach home.

He moistened his lips and stared into the darkness ahead, for it had been arranged that a 'lighthouse' should flash a beam at regular intervals to guide the bombers back to their nest. Watching, he saw a glow on the skyline wax and wane, but it was still far away.

* Slang: engine cylinders

He looked at his altimeter; it registered two thousand five hundred feet. Could he do it? He thought not, but he could try.

The rattle behind him and the vibration grew rapidly worse; it became a definite pulsating jolt that threatened to shake the machine to pieces at any moment. But he could see the Lines in the distance now, or rather, the trench system, where the patrols on either side were watching or trying to repair their barbed wire.

Two loud explosions in quick succession and a blinding sheet of flame leapt from the engine and made him throttle right back with frantic haste.

'Well, if we're down, we're down!' he muttered savagely. 'But I'm not going to sit up here and be fried to death for anybody; the Huns can shoot us if they like when we're on the ground, and that's better than being roasted like a joint of meat on the spit.'

Looking behind him he could see flames from the engine playing on his tail unit, and he knew that if he tried to remain in the air it was only a matter of seconds before the whole thing took fire. He switched off altogether and began gliding down through the darkness, straining his eyes in an effort to see what lay beneath.

In the uncanny silence he could hear the reports of the guns on the ground, and even hear the rattle of machine-gun fire. A searchlight probed the sky like a trembling white finger, searching for him, and archie began to illuminate the surrounding blackness.

Mark, the ever-practical, was calmly preparing for the inevitable end, and even in that desperate moment Biggles wondered if there was anything that could shake Mark out of his habitual calmness. He picked up the machine guns, one after the other, and threw them overboard; the Huns would be welcome to what was left of them after their eight-hundred-foot fall. The ammunition drums followed. He tore up his maps, threw them into the air and watched them swirl away aft.

Biggles felt in the canvas pocket inside the cockpit, then took out his own maps, ripped them across, and sent the pieces after Mark's. He thrust his loaded Very pistol into his pocket in readiness to send a shot into the petrol tank of the machine as soon as they were on the ground—providing they were not knocked out in the crash.

The destruction of his machine to prevent it falling into the hands of the enemy is the first duty of an airman who lands in hostile territory.

The sky around them became an inferno of darting flames and hurtling metal. Several pieces of shrapnel struck the machine, and it quivered like a terrified horse. Once the F.E. was nearly turned upside down by a terrific explosion under the port wing-tip. 400—300—200 feet ran the altimeter. Mark was leaning over the side staring into the blackness below them.

Biggles could distinguish nothing; the earth looked like a dark indigo stain, broken only by the flashes of guns and the intermittent spurts of machine-guns. He no longer looked at his altimeter, for he knew he was too low for it to be of any assistance; he could only keep his eyes glued below and hope for the best.

Suddenly, the shadow that was the earth swept up to meet him. He pulled the joy-stick back until the machine was flying on even keel. It began to sink as it lost flying speed, then staggered like a drunken animal. He lifted his knees to his chin, covered his face with his arms, and waited for the end. For a moment there was silence, broken only by the faint hum of the wires and the rumble of the guns.

Crash! With a crunching, tearing, rending scream of protest, the machine struck the ground and subsided in a heap of debris. The nacelle, in which the crew sat, buried its nose into the earth, reared up, then turned turtle.

Biggles soared through space and landed with a dull squelch in a sea of mud, but he had scrambled to his feet in an instant, wiping the slime from his eyes with the backs of his gauntlets.

'Mark—Mark!' he hissed. 'Where are you, Mark? Are you hurt, old man?'

'Hold hard, I'm coming! Don't make such a row, you fool!' snarled Mark, dragging himself clear of the debris and unwinding a wire that had coiled around his neck.

*Rat-tat-tat-tat. Rat-tat-tat-tat.*

A Very light soared upwards, and half a dozen machine-guns began their vicious stutter somewhere near at hand; bullets began splintering into the tangled wreck of the machine and zipping into the mud like a swarm of angry hornets.

'Come on, let's get out of this!' gasped Mark. 'Run for it; the artillery will open up any second!'

'Run! Where to?' panted Biggles.

'Anywhere—to get away from here!' snapped Mark, slithering and sliding through the ooze.

*Whee-e-e—Bang!* The first shell arrived with the noise of an express train and exploded with a roar like the end of the world. Biggles took a flying leap into a shell-hole and wormed his way into the mud at the bottom like a mole. He grunted as Mark landed on top of him.

'Why—the dickens—don't you look—where you're

going!' he spluttered, as they squelched side by side in the sludge; while the shell-torn earth rocked under the onslaught from the artillery.

'We're all right here,' announced Mark firmly. 'They say a shell never lands in the same place twice.'

'I wish I knew that for a fact,' muttered Biggles. 'This is what comes of night-flying. Night birds, eh? Great jumping mackerel, we're a couple of owls all right; an owl's got enough sense to stay—'

'Shut up!' snarled Mark, as the bombardment grew less intense, and then suddenly died away. 'Let's see where we are,' he whispered, as an eerie silence settled over the scene.

'See where we are? Have you any idea where we are?'

'Hark!'

They held their breaths and listened, but no sound reached their ears.

'I thought I heard someone coming,' breathed Mark. 'This is awful, not knowing which side of the lines we're on!'

They crept up to the lip of the shell-crater and stared into the surrounding darkness. A Very light soared upwards from a spot about a hundred yards away. Biggles, peering under his hand in the glare, distinctly saw a belt of barbed wire a few yards away on their left. Mark, who was looking in the other direction, gripped his arm in a vice-like clutch.

'Huns!' he whispered. 'There's a party of them coming this way. I could tell them by the shape of their helmets. Come on, this way!'

They started crawling warily towards the wire, but when they reached it, finding no opening, they commenced crawling parallel with it, freezing into a death-like stillness whenever a Very light cast its weird glow over the scene.

'Those Huns were coming from the opposite direction, so this should be our side,' muttered Mark.

'Don't talk,' whispered Biggles, 'let's keep going — this looks like a gap in the wire.'

By lying flat on the ground so that the obstruction was silhouetted against the sky, they could see a break in the ten feet wide belt of barbed wire, where it had evidently been torn up by shell-fire. They crawled through the breach, then paused to listen with straining ears.

'I can hear someone talking ahead of us; they must be in a trench,' whispered Mark.

'So can I; let's get closer,' whispered Biggles. 'Ssh — there it is! I can see the parapet. We shall have to go carefully, or we may be shot by our own fellows.' He raised himself on his hands and was about to call out — in fact, he had opened his mouth to do so — when a sound reached their ears that seemed to freeze the blood in their veins.

It was a harsh, coarse voice, speaking in a language they did not understand, but which they had no difficulty in recognizing as German. It came from the parapet a few yards in front of them.

A line of bayonets and then a body of men rose up in the darkness at the edge of the trench; there was no mistaking the coal-scuttle helmets.

Neither of the airmen spoke; as one man they sank to the ground, forcing themselves into the cold mud, and lay motionless. Heavy footsteps squelched through the mud towards them; a voice was speaking in a low undertone. Nearer and nearer they came, until Biggles felt the muscles of his back retract to receive the stabbing pain of a bayonet-thrust. He nearly cried out as a heavy foot descended on his hand, but his gauntlet and the soft mud under it saved the bones from being broken. The German stumbled, recovered, half-glanced over his shoulder to see what had tripped him; but, seeing what he supposed to be a corpse, turned and walked quickly after the others.

'Phew!' gasped Biggles, as the footsteps receded into the distance.

'Let's get out of this!' muttered Mark. 'They may be back any moment. Another minute and we should have walked straight into their trench. Hark!'

The hum of an F.E. reached their ears, and although they could not see it they could follow its path of flight by the archie bursts and the sound. It was coming from the direction of the German trench. It passed straight over them; the archie died away, and presently the sound faded into the night.

'That's one of our fellows going home, so it gives us our direction if we can only find a way through our own wire. If there isn't a gap, we're sunk; so we might crawl along this blinking wire to Switzerland!'

'Ssh!'

Once more the sound of footsteps reached them from somewhere near at hand, but they could see nothing.

'I can't stand much more of this!' growled Biggles. 'It's giving me the creeps. I've just crawled over some-body—or something that was somebody.'

Bang! They both jumped and then lay flat as another Very light curved high into the air; in its dazzling light Biggles distinctly saw a group of German soldiers, evidently a patrol, standing quite still, not more than fifty yards away. Suddenly he remembered something. He groped in his pocket, whipped out his own Very pistol, took careful aim, and fired. The light in the air went out at the same moment. The shot from Biggles' pistol dropped in the mud a hundred yards away, where it lay hissing in a cloud of red smoke that changed gradually to a ghastly, livid green.

'You fool, what are you at?' snarled Mark. 'I thought I was shot.'

'Didn't you see those Huns? I bet I've made them jump!'

'They'll probably make us jump in a minute!' retorted Mark.

'Would have done if I hadn't fired that Very light at 'em, you mean!' retorted Biggles. 'Nothing like getting in the first shot. Makes the other fellow scary. We've been walked over by one crowd and treated as bloomin' doormats. I don't want a second dose of that!'

'You'll get a dose of something else if those Huns poodle along here to inquire what the fireworks are for!' replied Mark.

'If!' jeered Biggles. 'I'll bet those chaps are legging it for home for all they're worth. An' I don't blame 'em. I'd do the same myself if I jolly well knew where home was.'

'You'll never live to see home again if you don't stop playing the silly ass!' growled Mark. 'And now shut up and listen. See if you can hear anybody talking in a language we understand.'

For some time the two airmen remained still, lying on the ground and listening intently for the sound of voices. But they could hear nothing save the occasional banging of rifles. At last Biggles grew impatient.

'Well, I'm not going to stay messing about here any longer!' he snapped. 'We'll settle things one way or the other. I will start to get light presently, and then we're done for. I believe that's our wire just in front of us. What about letting out a shout to see if our fellows are within earshot?'

'The Huns will hear us, too.'

'I can't help that. Hold tight, I'm going to yell. Hallo, there!' he bellowed. 'Is anybody about?'

A reply came from a spot so close that Biggles instinctively ducked.

'What are you bleating abart?' said a Cockney voice calmly. 'You come any closer to me and I'll give you something to holler for. You can't catch me on that hop!'

*Bang*! A rifle blazed in the darkness, not ten yards away, and a bullet whistled past Biggles' head.

'Hi! That's enough of that!' he shouted. 'We're British officers, I tell you—fliers. We crashed outside the wire and can't get through. Come and show us the way!'

'Why didn't you say so before?' came the reply. 'You might 'ave got 'urt. 'Old 'ard a minute! But you keep your 'ands up, and no half-larks!'

Silence fell.

'He's either coming himself, or he's gone to fetch someone,' muttered Mark. 'We can't blame him for being suspicious. He must have been in the listening-post, which is where people shoot first and ask questions afterwards. The Huns get up to all sorts of tricks.'

'Where are you, you fellow?' suddenly said a quiet voice near them.

'Here we are!' answered Biggles.

'Stand fast—I'm coming.'

An officer, revolver in hand, closely followed by half a dozen Tommies wearing the unmistakable British tin helmets, loomed up suddenly in the darkness.

'How many of you are there?' said the voice.

'Two,' replied Biggles shortly.

'All right, follow me—and don't make a row about it.'

Squelching through the ooze, they followed the officer through a zigzag track in the wire. The Tommies closed in behind them. A trench, from which projected a line of bayonets, lay across their path, but at a word from their escort the rifles were lowered, and the two airmen half-slipped and half scrambled into the trench. The beam of a flash-lamp cut through the darkness and went slowly over their faces and uniforms.

'You look a couple of pretty scarecrows, I must say,' said a voice, with a chuckle. 'Come into my dugout and have a rest. I'll send a runner to headquarters with a request that they ring up your squadron and tell them you're safe. What have you been up to?'

'Oh—er—night flying, that's all. Just night flying!' said Biggles airily.

# Chapter 8
# The Dawn Patrol

Biggles opened his eyes drowsily as a hand shook his shoulder respectfully but firmly. At the back of his sleep-soaked mind he knew it was his batman* calling him.

'Come on, sir!' said the voice. 'It's six o'clock! Patrol leaves at half-past!'

Second-Lieutenant Bigglesworth (Biggles for short) stared at the man coldly. 'Push off!' he said, and nestled lower under the bedclothes.

'Come on, now, sir, drink your tea!' The batman held out the cup invitingly.

Biggles swung his legs over the side of the bed, shivering as the cold air struck his warm limbs, and took tea.

'What's the weather like?' he asked.

'Not too good, sir, lot of cloud about, but no rain as yet!' Satisfied that his officer was really awake, the batman departed.

Biggles stood up and pulled his sweater on. He glanced across the room at Mark Way, who had already been called, but was fast asleep again and snoring gently. He picked up his pillow and heaved it at the peaceful face of his flying partner.

Instead of hitting the slumbering Mark, it swept a row of ornaments from the shelf above his head. There was a fearful crash as they scattered in all directions.

* An attendant serving an officer. A position discontinued in today's Royal Air Force.

85

Mark leapt up in bed as if impelled by an invisible spring.

'What th—' he began, looking about him wildly.

Biggles, who was brushing his hair in front of a cracked mirror, side-stepped quickly to avoid the pillow as it came back, hurled by a vigorous arm. It caught the half-empty tea-cup and swept it into the middle of his bed. He looked at the marksman in disgust.

'Rotten shot!' he said. 'Your shooting on the ground is worse than it is in the air, and that's saying something!'

'Can't you fellows get up without making such an infernal din?' snarled an angry voice from the far end of the room. 'This place is like a madhouse when A Flight are on an early show. You two should save your energy; you'll need it presently, when Rayner gets going.'

'Rayner—what's Rayner got to do with me?' asked Biggles, in surprise, as he pulled on his sheepskin boots.

'Mapleton is going to have a tooth drawn this morning, so he has had to report sick. I heard him talking to the Old Man about it last night. Rayner is going to lead your show this morning.'

'I see,' said Biggles. 'Well, it'll be a change for him to find his Flight sticking to his tail instead of scattering all over the sky when a Hun heaves into sight.'

He ducked to avoid a cake of soap hurled by a member of C Flight, of which Captain Rayner was in command, and departed.

He hurried to the sheds and started the engine of his F.E.2b two-seater plane. Mark came out of the armoury carrying his gun, which he proceeded to test, and Captain Rayner appeared at the corner of A Flight hangar.

'It's right, then!' Biggles muttered to Mark. 'Mabs isn't doing the show—here's Rayner!'

'What about it?' grunted Mark, from the cockpit, where he was carefully arranging his ammunition drums.

'I suppose he'll try to show us what a hot-stuff merchant he is, that's all. And it's a bit too early in the morning for fireworks,' answered Biggles.

Captain Rayner climbed into his machine, looked around to see that the others were in place, taxied out on to the aerodrome, and roared into the air. The three other machines that were to form the dawn patrol took off behind him, heading towards the distant trenches of the western battlefront.

The grey light of early morning grew stronger, and before the Lines were reached the sun was shining brightly. A strong wind was blowing from the west, bringing with it masses of cloud like great white cauliflowers, gleaming with gold and yellow at the top, merging into dark blue and purple at the base. Here and there the ground was still obscured by long grey blankets of ground mist, through which the earth showed in pale greens and browns.

The patrol climbed for some time before approaching the Lines, the leader making his way towards one of the strips of blue sky that here and there showed through the mass of cloud. They entered the opening at five thousand feet, and then corkscrewed upwards, climbing steeply as though through a hollow tube to the top side of the cloud. Then the four machines levelled out and headed eastward.

Biggles, looking over the side, could see mile after mile of rolling white clouds, like great masses of cotton-wool, stretching away to the infinite distance where they cut a hard line against the blue sky. Below them, their four grey shadows, each surrounded by a complete rainbow, raced at incredible speed over the top of the gleaming vapour.

As far as he could see there were no other machines in the sky, although he was not quite certain if they had actually crossed the Lines yet. But Rayner seemed to be flying on a steady course, and Biggles could not help admiring the confident manner in which the leader flew. He seemed to know exactly where he was and what he was doing.

For some time they flew on, climbing gently, rounding mighty fantastic pyramids of cloud that seemed to reach to high heaven. Compared with them the four F.E.s were so small as to be negligible—'like gnats flying round the base of snow-covered mountains,' Biggles thought.

For twenty minutes or so Rayner headed straight into German territory, turning neither to right nor left, a proceeding which caused Mark to look round at his pilot with a sour grimace.

Biggles knew well enough what his gunner was thinking. The distance they had covered, with the wind behind them, could not be less than twenty miles; it would take them a long time to return with the wind in their teeth. He wished there were some gaps in the clouds so that he might see the Lines if they were in sight. They formed a barrier between the known and the unknown. On one side lay home, friends, and safety; on the other, mystery, enemies, and death!

From time to time round, whirling balls of black smoke stained the cloudscape; they increased in size, becoming less dense as they did so, and then drifted into long plumes before they were finally dispersed by the wind. Archie—otherwise anti-aircraft gunfire! Biggles eyed it moodily, for although he no longer feared it, he never failed to regard it with suspicion. After all, one never knew—

Mark stood up, and, with a reassuring smile at Biggles, fired a short burst downwards from his gun, to warm it up and make sure it was in working order. From time to time the other observers did the same.

Biggles was glad when at last Rayner changed his direction and began to fly north-west on a course nearly parallel with the Lines, a course that Biggles estimated would bring them back to the Lines some thirty miles above where they had crossed.

The clouds seemed to increase in size in their new direction, until they assumed colossal proportions. The patrol was now flying at nine thousand feet, but the summits of the clouds seemed to tower as far above them as the bases were below. Biggles had no idea that clouds could be so enormous.

They had been in the air for more than an hour, and so far they had not seen a single other machine, either friend or foe. Several times Mark stood up—as did the other gunners—and squinted at the blinding sun between his first finger and thumb.

'This is too tame to be true,' thought Biggles, as he wiped the frozen breath from his windscreen with the back of his glove, and worked his lips, which felt as if they were getting frostbitten in the icy wind. He noticed that Rayner was leading them to the very top of a stupendous pile of cloud that lay directly in their path.

'He's going over it rather than round it—got an idea there's something on the other side, I suppose,' thought Biggles, watching both sides of the gleaming mass.

The gunners were suspicious, too, for they all stood

up as the machines approached it, guns at the 'ready.' Mark looked round and grinned, although his face was blue with cold.

'Yes, this is where we strike the rough stuff!' said Biggles to himself. He did not know why he thought that. On the face of it, there was no more reason to suppose that this particular cloud would conceal enemy aircraft any more than the others they had already passed. It may have been the amazing instinct which he was beginning to develop that warned him. At any rate, something inside him seemed to say that hostile machines were not far away.

Rayner was immediately over the top of the cloud-pile now, and Biggles could see him, and his gunner, looking down at something that was still invisible to the others.

'There they are!' thought Biggles. And he no longer thought of the cold, for Rayner's machine was wobbling its wings. A red Very light soared into the air from the gunner's cockpit—the signal that enemy aircraft had been sighted.

Rayner was banking now, turning slowly, and the other three machines swam into the spot where the leader had been a few moments before.

Biggles looked over the side, and caught his breath sharply as he found himself looking into a hole in the clouds, a vast cavity that would have been impossible to imagine. It reminded him vaguely of the crater of a volcano of incredible proportions.

Straight down for a sheer eight thousand feet the walls of opaque mist dropped, turning from yellow to brown, brown to mauve, and mauve to indigo at the basin-like depression in the remote bottom. The precipitous sides looked so solid that it seemed as if a man might try to climb down them, or rest on one of the shelves that jutted out at intervals.

He was so taken up with this phenomenon that for a brief space of time all else was forgotten. Then a tiny movement far, far below caught his eye, and he knew he was looking at that which the eagle-eyed flight-commander had seen instantly.

A number of machines—how many, he could not tell—were circling round and round at the very bottom of the yawning crater, looking like microscopic fish at the bottom of a deep pool in a river. Occasionally one or more of them would completely disappear in the shadows, to reappear a moment later, wings flashing faintly as the light caught them.

They were much too far away to distinguish whether they were friends or foes, but Rayner seemed to have no doubt in the matter. A tiny living spark of orange fire, flashing diagonally across the void, told its own story. It was a machine going down in flames, and that could only mean one thing—a dog-fight was in progress in that well of mystery.

Then Rayner went down, closely followed by the others.

Biggles never forgot that dive. There was something awe-inspiring about it. It was like sinking down into the very centre of the earth. There was insufficient room for the four machines to keep in a straight dive, as the cavity was not more than a few hundred yards across, so they were compelled to take a spiral course.

Down—down—down they went. Biggles thought they would never come to the end. The wind howled and screamed through struts and wires like a thousand demons in agony, but he heeded it not. He was too engrossed in watching the tragedy being enacted below.

Twice, as they went down in that soul-shaking dive, he saw machines fall out of the fight, leaving streamers of black smoke behind them, around which the others continued to turn, and roll, and shoot. There were at least twenty of them: drab biplanes with yellow wings, and rainbow-hued triplanes—red, green, blue, mauve, and even a white one.

Soon the dawn patrol was amongst the whirling machines, and it was every man for himself.

Biggles picked out a group of triplanes with black-crossed wings that were flying close together. They saw him coming, and scattered like a school of minnows when a pike appears. He rushed at one of them, a blue machine with white wing-tips, and pursued it relentlessly. Mark's gun started chattering, and he saw the tracer-bullets pouring straight into the centre of the fuselage of the machine below him.

The Hun did not burst into flames as he hoped it would. Instead, it zoomed upwards, turned slowly over on to its back, and then, with the engine still on, spun down out of sight into the misty floor of the basin.

Biggles jerked the machine up sharply, and swerved just in time to avoid collision, with a whirling bonfire of struts and canvas. His nostrils twitched as he hurtled through its smoking trail.

Mark was shooting again, this time at a white machine. But the pilot of it was not to be so easily disposed of. He twisted and turned like a fish with a sea-lion after it, and more than once succeeded in getting in a burst of fire at them.

This was the hottest dog-fight in which Biggles had as yet taken part. One thought was uppermost in his mind, and that was—that he must inevitably collide with somebody in a moment. Already they had missed machines—triplanes, F.E.s, and Pups, which he now perceived the British machines to be—by inches. But the thought of collision did not frighten him.

He felt only a strange elation, a burning desire to go on doing this indefinitely—to down the enemy machines before he himself was killed, as he never doubted that he would be in the end. There was no thought in his mind of retreat or escape.

Mark's gun was rattling incessantly, and Biggles marvelled at the calm deliberation with which he flung the empty drums overboard after their ammunition was exhausted, and replaced them with new ones.

Something struck the machine with a force that made it quiver. The compass flew to pieces, and the liquid that it contained spurted back, half blinding him. Mechanically, he wiped his face with the back of his glove.

Where was the white Hun? He looked around, and his blood seemed to turn to ice at the sight that met his gaze. An F.E.—a blazing meteor of spurting fire—was roaring nosedown across his front at frightful speed!

A black figure emerged from the flames with its arm flung over its face, and leapt outwards and downwards. The machine, almost as if it was still under control, deliberately swerved towards the white triplane that was whirling across its front.

The Hun pilot saw his danger, and twisted like lightning to escape. But he was too late. The blazing F.E. caught it fair and square across the fuselage. There was a shower of sparks and debris, and then a blinding flash of flames as the triplane's tanks exploded. Then the two machines disappeared from Biggles's field of view.

For a moment he was stunned with shock, utterly unable to think, and it was a shrill yell from Mark that brought him back to realities. Where was he? What was he doing? Oh, yes, fighting! Who had been in the F.E.? Marriot? Or was it McAngus? It must have been one of them. A yellow Hun was shooting at him.

With a mighty effort he pulled himself together, but he felt that he could not stand the strain much longer. He was flying on his nerves, and he knew it. His flying was getting wild and erratic.

Turning, he swerved into the side of the cloud, temporarily blinding himself, and then burst out again, fighting frantically to keep the machine under control. Bullets were crashing into his engine, and he wondered why it did not burst into flames.

Where were the bullets coming from? He leaned over the side of the cockpit and looked behind. A yellow Hun was on his tail. He turned with a speed that amazed himself. Unprepared for the move, the Hun overshot the F.E. Next instant the tables were turned, Biggles roaring down after the triplane in hot pursuit.

Rat-tat-tat-tat! stuttered Mark's gun. At such short range it was impossible to miss. The yellow top wing swung back and floated away into space, and the fuselage plunged out of sight, a streamer of flame creeping along its side.

For a moment Biggles watched it, fascinated, then he looked up with a start. Where were the others? Where were his companions? He was just in time to see one of them disappear into the side of the cloud, then he was alone.

At first he could not believe it. Where were the Huns? Not one of them was in sight. Where, a moment or two before, there had been twenty or more machines, not one remained except himself—Yes, one; a Pup was just disappearing through the floor of the basin.

A feeling of horrible loneliness came over him and a doubt crept into his mind as to his ability to find his way home. He had not the remotest idea of his position. He looked upwards, but from his own level to the distant circle of blue at the top of the crater there was not a single machine to be seen. He had yet to learn of the suddenness with which machines could disappear when a dog-fight was broken off by mutual consent.

He had hoped to see the F.E. that he had seen disappear into the mist come out again, but it did not.

'I'll bet that Pup pilot knows where he is; I'll go after him,' he thought desperately, and tore down in the wake of the single-seater that had disappeared below. He looked at his altimeter, which had somehow escaped the general ruin caused by the bullets. One thousand feet, it read. He sank into the mist and came out under it almost at once. Below lay open country— fields, hedges, and a long, deserted road. Not a soul was in sight as far as he could see, and there was no landmark that he could recognize.

He saw the Pup at once. It was still going down, and he raced after it intending to get alongside in the hope of making his predicament known to the pilot. Then, with a shock of understanding, he saw that the Pup's propeller was not turning. Its engine must have been put out of action in the combat, and the pilot had no choice but to land.

As he watched the machine, he saw the leather-helmeted head turn in the cockpit as the pilot looked back over his shoulder. Then he turned again and made a neat landing in a field.

Biggles did not hesitate. He knew they were far over

hostile country—how far he did not like to think—and the Pup pilot must be rescued. The single-seater was blazing when he landed beside it, and its pilot ran towards the F.E., carrying a still smoking Very pistol in his hand.

Biggles recognized him at once.

'Mahoney!' he yelled.

The Pup pilot pulled up dead and stared.

'Great smoking rattlesnakes!' he cried. 'If it isn't young Bigglesworth!'

'Get in, and buck up about it!' shouted Biggles.

'Get in here with me,' called Mark. 'It'll be a bit of a squash, but it can be done.'

Mahoney clambered aboard and squeezed himself into the front cockpit with the gunner.

'Look out,' he yelled. 'Huns!'

Biggles did not look. He saw little tufts of grass flying up just in front of the machine, and he heard the distant rattle of a gun. It told him all he needed to know, and he knew he had no time to lose.

The F.E. took a long run to get off with its unusual burden, but it managed it. Fortunately, its nose was pointing towards the Lines, and there was no need to turn. The machine zoomed upwards and the mist enfolded them like a blanket.

For a few minutes Biggles fought his way through the gloom, then he put the nose of the machine down again, for he knew he could not hope to keep it on even keel for very long in such conditions. The ground loomed darkly below; he corrected the machine, and then climbed up again.

'Do you know where we are?' he yelled.

Mahoney nodded, and made a sign that he was to keep straight on.

Biggles breathed more comfortably, and flew along just at the base of the clouds. Suddenly he remembered the blazing F.E.

'Who was in that F.E.?' he bellowed to Mark.

'Rayner!' was the reply.

So Rayner had gone at last—gone out in one of the wildest dog-fights he could have desired. Sooner or later it was bound to happen, Biggles reflected, but it was tough luck on poor Marble, his observer.

Poor old Marble. Two hours before they had drunk their coffee together, and now—What a beastly business war was!

It must have been Marble whom he had seen jump. And Rayner had deliberately rammed the Hun, he was certain of it.

'Well, I only hope I shall have as much nerve when my time comes!' he mused. 'Poor old Rayner, he wasn't such a bad sort!'

Biggles pulled himself together and tried to put the matter from his mind, but he could not forget the picture. He knew he would never forget it.

An archie burst blossomed out just in front of him and warned him that they were approaching the Lines. Two minutes later they were in the thick of it, rocking in a wide area of flame-torn sky. The gunners, knowing to an inch the height of the clouds, were able to make good shooting, yet they passed through unscathed, letting out a whoop of joy as they raced into the sheltered security of their own Lines.

Mahoney guided the F.E. to his own aerodrome, which Biggles had seen from the air, although he had never landed on it, and after a rather bumpy landing, it ran to a standstill in front of No. 266 Squadron sheds, where a number of officers and mechanics were watching.

'I believe I've busted a tyre,' muttered Biggles, in disgust. But a quick examination revealed that the damage had not been his fault. The tyre had been pierced from side to side by a bullet.

There was a general babble of excitement, in which everybody talked at once. Biggles was warmly congratulated on his rescue work, which everyone present regarded as an exceptionally good show.

'Does anyone know what happened to the other two F.E.s?' asked Biggles.

'Yes, they've gone home,' said several voices at once. 'They broke off the fight when we did, and we all came home together!'

'Thank goodness!' muttered Biggles. 'I thought they had all gone west. How did the show start?'

'We saw the Huns down in that hole, and we went in after 'em; it looked such a nice hole that we thought it ought to be ours,' grinned Mahoney. 'There were seven of us, but there were more of them than we thought at first. We had just got down to things when you butted in. I didn't see you until you were amongst us. Which way did you come in?'

'Through the front door—at the top!' laughed Biggles.

'Well, it was a fine dog-fight!' sighed Mahoney. 'The sort of scrap one remembers. Hallo, here's the C.O.!' he added. 'Here, sir, meet Bigglesworth, who I was telling you about the other day. He picked me up this morning in Hunland after a Boche had shot my engine to scrap iron.' He turned to Biggles again. 'Let me introduce you to Major Mullen, our C.O.,' he said.

'Pleased to meet you, Bigglesworth,' said Major

98

Mullen, shaking hands. 'You seem to be the sort of fellow we want out here. I shall have to keep an eye on you with a view to getting you transferred to 266.'

'I wish to goodness you could fix that, sir,' replied Biggles earnestly. 'I shall not be happy until I get in a scout squadron—although I should be sorry to leave Mark,' he added quickly.

'Don't worry about me,' broke in Mark. 'My application's in for training as a pilot, so I may be leaving you, anyway.'

'Well, I can't promise anything, of course, but I'll see what can be done about it,' Major Mullen told him.

'What are you two going to do now?' asked Mahoney.

'I think we'd better be getting back,' answered Biggles.

'Won't you stay to lunch?'

'No, thanks. We'll leave the machine here, if you'll have that tyre put right and can lend us transport to get home. We'll come back later on to fly the machine home.'

'Good enough!' declared Mahoney. 'I'll ask the C.O. if you can borrow his car. I shan't forget how you picked me up. Maybe it will be my turn to lend a hand next time!'

'Well, so long as you don't ask me to squeeze into the cockpit of a Pup with you I don't mind!' laughed Biggles. 'See you later!'

# Chapter 9
# Special Mission

'Beg pardon, sir, but Major Paynter wishes to speak to you, sir.'

Biggles glanced up, folded the letter he was reading, and put it in his pocket. 'On the 'phone, do you mean?' he asked the mess waiter, who had delivered the message.

'No, sir, in his office. Mr Todd rang up to say would you go along right away.'

'All right, Collins, thanks.' Biggles picked up his cap as he went through the hall and walked quickly along the well-worn path to the squadron office. Two people were present in addition to the C.O. when he entered— one a red-tabbed staff-officer, and the other, a round-faced, cheerful-looking civilian in a black coat and bowler hat. Biggles saluted.

'Just make sure the door is closed, will you, Biggles-worth?' began the C.O. 'Thanks. This is Major Raymond, of Wing Headquarters.'

'How do you do, sir?' said Biggles to the staff officer, wondering why the C.O. did not introduce the civilian, and what he was doing there.

'I want to have a few words with you, Bigglesworth, on a very delicate subject,' went on the C.O. rather awkwardly. 'Er—I, or I should say the squadron, has been asked to undertake an—er—operation of the greatest importance. It is a job that will have to be done single-handed, and I am putting the proposition to you first because you have shown real enthusiasm in your work since you've been with us, and because you have extricated yourself from one or two difficult situations entirely by your own initiative. The job in hand demands both initiative and resource.'

'Thank you, sir.'

'Not a bit. Now, this is the proposition. The operation, briefly, consists in taking an—er—gentleman over the Lines, landing him at a suitable spot, and then returning home. It is probable that you will have to go over the Lines again afterwards, either the same night or at a subsequent date, and pick him up from the place where you landed him.'

'That does not seem diffi—'

Major Paynter held up his hand.

'Wait!' he said. 'Let me finish. It is only fair that I should warn you that in the event of your being forced down on the wrong side of the Lines, or being captured in any way, you would probably be shot. Even if you had to force-land in German territory on the return journey, with no one in the machine but yourself, it is more than likely that the enemy would suspect your purpose and subject you to rigorous interrogation. And if the enemy could wring the truth from you—that you had been carrying a Secret Service agent—they would be justified in marching you before a firing squad.'

'I understand. Very good, sir. I'll go.'

'Thank you, Bigglesworth! The gentleman here with Major Raymond will be your passenger. It would be well for you to meet him now, as you will not see him again in daylight, and you should be able to identify each other.'

Biggles walked over to the civilian and held out his hand. 'Pleased to meet you!' he said.

The spy—for Biggles had no delusion about the real nature of the work on hand—smiled and wrung his hand warmly. He was a rather fat, jovial-looking little man with a huge black moustache; in no way was he like the character Biggles would have expected for such work.

'Well, I think that's all for the present, Raymond,' went on the C.O. 'Let me know the details as soon as you can. I'll have another word with you, Bigglesworth, before you go.'

Biggles saluted as the staff officer departed with his civilian companion, and then turned his attention again to Major Paynter, who was staring thoughtfully out of the window.

'I want you to see this thing in its true perspective,' resumed the C.O. 'We are apt to think spying is rather dirty work. It may be, from the strictly military point of view, but one should not forget that it needs as much nerve—if not more—than anything a soldier is called upon to face. A soldier may be killed, wounded, or made prisoner. But a spy's career can only have one ending if he's caught—the firing squad! He does not die a man's death in the heat of battle; he is shot like a dog against a brick wall. That's the result of failure. If he succeeds, he gets no medals, honour or glory. Silence surrounds him always.

'And most of these men work for nothing. Take that man you've just seen, for instance. He is, of course, a Frenchman. In private life he's a schoolmaster at Aille, which is now in territory occupied by the enemy. He worked his way across the frontier into Holland, and then to France, via England, to offer his services to his country. He asks no reward. There's courage and self-sacrifice, if you like. Remember that when he's in your machine. His knowledge of the country around Aille makes his services particularly valuable. If he gets back safely this time—he has already made at least one trip—he will go again. And so it will go on, until one day he will not come back.

'As far as you're concerned as his pilot, you need have no scruples. Most of the leading French pilots have taken their turns for special missions, as these affairs are called. For obvious reasons, only the best pilots, those of proven courage, are chosen for the work. Well, I think that's all. I'll let you know the details, the date and time, later on. Don't mention this matter to anybody, except, of course, your flight-commander, who will have to know.'

Biggles bumped into Mapleton, his flight-commander, just outside the office.

'What's on?' asked Mabs quietly. 'Special mission?'

Biggles nodded.

'I thought so. For the love of Mike be careful! You've only got to make one bloomer at that game, and all the king's horses and all the king's men couldn't save you. I did one once, and that was enough for me. No more, thank you!'

'Why, did things go wrong?' inquired Biggles, as they walked towards the mess.

'Wrong! It was worse than that. In the first place, the cove refused to get out of the machine when we got there; his nerves petered out. He couldn't speak English, and I can't speak French, so I couldn't tell him what I thought of him. When I tried to throw him out he kicked up such a row that it brought all the Huns for miles to the spot. I had to get off in a hurry, I can tell you, bringing the blighter back with me. But some of these fellows have been over no end of times, and they have brought back, or sent back, information of the greatest importance. They have to carry a basket of pigeons with them, and they release one every time they get information worth while. How would you like to walk about amongst the Boche with a pigeon up your coat? It's only got to give one coo and you're sunk. The French do a lot of this business; most of the leading French pilots have had a go at it. Vedrines, the pre-war pilot, did several shows. When the War broke out the French expected great things of him, and when he just faded into insignificance they began saying nasty things about him. But he was doing special missions, and those are things people don't talk about.'

'Well, if my bowler-hatted bird starts any trouble I'll give him a thick ear!' observed Biggles.

'Oh, he'll be all right, I should think!' replied Mabs. 'The landing is the tricky part. The Huns know all about this spy-dropping game, and they do their best to catch people in the act by laying traps in likely landing-fields, such as by digging trenches across the field and then covering them up with grass so that you can't see them. When you land—zonk! Another scheme is to stretch wire across the field, which has a similar result.'

'Sounds cheerful! And there are no means of knowing whether a trap has been laid in the field that you have to land on?'

'Not until you land,' grinned Mabs.

'That's a fat lot of good!' growled Biggles. 'Well, we shall see. Many thanks for the tips!'

'That's all right. My only advice is, don't let them catch you alive, laddie. Remember, they shoot you as well as the fellow you are carrying if you're caught. They treat you both alike!'

'They'll have to shoot me to catch me!' replied Biggles grimly.

The hands of the mess clock pointed to the hour of nine when, a few evenings later, Biggles finished his after-dinner coffee, and, collecting his flying kit from its peg in the hall, strolled towards the door.

Mark Way, who had followed him out of the room, noted these proceedings with surprise. 'What's the idea?' he asked, reaching for his own flying kit.

'I've a little job to do—on my own. I can't talk about it. Sorry, old lad!' replied Biggles, and departed. He found Major Raymond and his civilian acquaintance waiting on the tarmac. In accordance with his instructions to the flight-sergeant, his F.E.2b had been wheeled out and the engine was ticking over quietly.

'Remember, he's doing the job for us, not for the French,' Major Raymond told him quietly. 'He's going to dynamite a bridge over the Aisne near the point that I told you about yesterday,' he went on, referring to a conversation on the previous day at which the details had been arranged. 'He's asked me to tell you not to worry about his return. He's quite willing for you to leave him to work his own way back across the frontier, although naturally he'd be glad if you would pick him up again later on.'

'How long will he be doing this job, sir?' asked Biggles.

'It's impossible to say. So much depends on the conditions when he gets there—whether or not there are guards at the bridge, and so on. If it is all clear, he might do the job in half an hour, or an hour. On the other hand, he may be two or three days, waiting for his opportunity. Why do you ask?'·

'I was thinking that if he wasn't going to be very long, I might wait for him?'

The major shook his head. 'It isn't usually done that way,' he said. 'It's too risky!'

'The risk doesn't seem to be any greater than making another landing.'

'Wait a minute and I'll ask him,' said the major.

He had a quick low conversation with the secret agent, and then returned to Biggles.

'He says the noise of your engine would attract attention if you waited, and it would not be advisable for you to switch off,' he reported. 'All the same, he asked me to tell you that he'd be very grateful if you would pick him up a few hours afterwards—it would save him three weeks' or a month's anxious work getting through Holland. He suggests that you allow him as much as possible, in case he's delayed. If you'll return at the first glimmer of dawn he'll try to be back by then. If he's not there, go home and forget about him. He suggests dawn because it may save you actually landing. If you can't see him in the field, or on the edge of the field, don't land. If he is there, he'll show himself. That seems to be a very sensible arrangement, and a fair one for both parties.'

'More than fair,' agreed Biggles. 'If he's got enough nerve to dodge about amongst the Huns with a stick of dynamite in one pocket and a pigeon in the other, I ought to have enough nerve to fetch him back!'

'Quite! Still, he's willing to leave it to you.'

· Biggles strolled across and shook hands with the man, who did not seem in the least concerned about the frightful task he was about to undertake. He was munching a biscuit contentedly.

'It is an honour to know you,' Biggles said. And he meant it.

'It is for *La France*,' answered the man simply.

'Well, I'm ready when you are!'

'*Bon*. Let us go,' was the reply. And they climbed into their seats.

Biggles noted with amazement that his passenger did not even wear flying kit. He wore the same dark suit as before, and the bowler hat, which he jammed hard on. He carried two bundles, and Biggles did not question what they contained; he thought he knew. Pigeons and dynamite were a curious mixture, he thought, as he settled himself into his seat.

He could hardly repress a smile as his eye fell on the unusual silhouette in the front cockpit. There was something queer about going to war in a bowler hat. Then something suspiciously like a lump came into his throat at the thought of the simple Frenchman, unsoldierly though he was in appearance, risking his all to perform an act of service to his country. He made up his mind that if human hands could accomplish it, he would bring his man safely back.

'I am ready, my little cabbage. Pour the sauce*!' cried the man. And Biggles laughed aloud at the command to open the throttle. There was something very likeable about this fellow who could start on a mission of such desperate peril so casually.

'Won't you be frozen?' asked Biggles.

'It is not of the importance,' replied the Frenchman. 'We shall not be of the long time.'

'As you like,' shouted Biggles, and waved the wingtip mechanics away. The engines roared as he opened

* French slang for 'open the throttle'

the throttle, and a moment later he was in the air heading towards the Lines. In spite of the cold the little man still stood in his seat, with his coat-collar turned up, gazing below at the dark shadow of his beloved France.

Presently the archie began to tear the air about them. It was particularly vicious, and Biggles crouched a little lower in his seat. The spy leaned back towards him, and cupped his hands around his mouth. 'How badly they shoot, these Boche!' he called cheerfully.

Biggles regarded him stonily. The fellow obviously had no imagination, for the bombardment was bad enough to make a veteran quail.

'He can't understand, that's all about it! Great jumping cats, I'd hate to be with him in what he would call good shooting!' he thought, and then turned his attention to the task of finding his way to the landing-ground they had decided upon. For his greatest fear was that he would be unable to locate it in the darkness, although he had marked it down as closely as he could by means of surrounding landmarks.

He picked out a main road, lying like a grey ribbon across the landscape, followed it until it forked, took the left fork, and then followed that until it disappeared into a wood. On the far side of the wood he made out the unmistakable straight track of a railway line, running at right angles to it. He followed this in turn, until the lights of a small town appeared ahead. Two roads converged upon it, and somewhere between the two roads and the railway line lay the field in which he had been instructed to land.

He intended to follow his instructions to the letter, knowing that the authorities must have a good reason for their choice. Possibly they knew from secret agents who were working, or had worked, in the vicinity, that the field had not been wired, or that it had not even fallen under the suspicion of the enemy. He dismissed the matter from his mind and concentrated upon the task of finding the field and landing the machine on it.

He cut the engine and commenced a long glide down. He glided as slowly as he could without losing flying speed so that possible watchers on the ground would not hear the wind vibrating in his wires, which they might if he came down too quickly. The spy was leaning over the side of the cockpit, watching the proceedings with interest. Then, as Biggles suddenly spotted the field and circled carefully towards it, the Frenchman picked up his parcels and placed them on the seat with no more concern than a passenger in an omnibus or railway train prepares to alight.

Biggles could see the field clearly now—a long, though not very wide strip of turf. He side-slipped gently to bring the F.E. dead in line with the centre of the field, glided like a wraith over the tops of the trees that bounded the northern end, and then flattened out.

The machine sank slowly, the wheels trundled over the rough turf—with rather a lot of noise, Biggles thought—the tail-skid dragged, and the machine ran to a stop after one of the best landings he had ever made in his life. He sank back limply, realizing that the tension of the last few minutes had been intense.

'Thank you, my little cabbage!' whispered the Frenchman, and glided away into the darkness.

For a moment or two Biggles could hardly believe that he had gone, so quietly and swiftly had he disappeared. For perhaps a minute he sat listening, but he could hear nothing, save the muffled swish of his idling propeller. He stood up and stared into the darkness on all sides, but there was no sign of life; not a light showed anywhere. As far as his late passenger was concerned, the ground might have opened and swallowed him up.

'Well, I might as well be going!' he decided.

There was no need for him to turn in order to take off. He had plenty of 'run' in front of him, and the engine roared as he opened the throttle and swept up into the night. He almost laughed with relief as the earth dropped away below him.

It had been absurdly easy, and the reaction left him with a curious feeling of elation—a joyful sensation that the enemy had been outwitted. 'These things aren't so black as they're painted!' was his unspoken thought as he headed back towards the Lines. He crossed them in the usual flurry of archie, and ten minutes later taxied up to his flight hangar and switched off. He glanced at his watch. Exactly fifty minutes had elapsed since he and his companion had taken off from the very spot on which the machine now stood, and it seemed incredible that in that interval of time he had actually landed in German territory and unloaded a man who, for all he knew, might now be dead or in a prison cell awaiting execution. He hoped fervently that the second half of his task might prove as simple. He climbed stiffly to the ground and met Mabs and Mark, who had evidently heard him land.

'How did you get on?' asked Mabs quickly.

'Fine! If I'd known you were waiting I'd have brought you a bunch of German primroses; there were some growing in the field.'

'You'd better turn in and get some sleep,' Mabs advised him.

'Yes, I might as well—for a bit.'

'For a bit? What do you mean?'

'I'm going over again presently to fetch my bowler-hatted pal back!'

Biggles condemned the spy, the authorities in general, and the Germans in particular, to purgatory when, at the depressing hour of five o'clock the following morning, his batman aroused him from a deep, refreshing sleep.

It was bitterly cold, and the stars were still twinkling brightly in a wintry sky; a thick layer of white frost covered everything and wove curious patterns on the window-panes. It was one of those early spring frosts that remind us that the winter is not yet finished.

'What an hour to be hauled out of bed!' he grumbled, half-regretting his rash promise to fetch his man. But a cup of hot coffee and some toast put a fresh complexion on things, and he hummed cheerfully as he strode briskly over the crisp turf towards the sheds. He had told the flight-sergeant to detail two mechanics to 'stand by,' and he found them shivering in their greatcoats, impatiently awaiting his arrival. 'All right, get her out,' he said sharply, and between them they dragged the F.E. out on to the tarmac. 'Start her up,' he went on, tying a thick woollen muffler round his neck and then pulling on his flying kit.

Five minutes later he was in the air again, heading towards the scene of action.

The sky began to grow pale in the east, and, following the same landmarks that he had used before, he had no difficulty in finding his way. The first flush of dawn was stealing across the sky as he approached the field, but the earth was still bathed in deep blue and purple shadows.

He throttled back and began gliding down, eyes probing the shadows, seeking for the field and a little man. He picked out the field, but the spy was nowhere in sight, and Biggles' heart sank with apprehension, for he had developed a strong liking for him. He continued to circle for a few minutes, losing height slowly, eyes running over the surrounding country. Suddenly they stopped, and remained fixed on the one spot where a movement had attracted his attention. Something had flashed dully, but for a second he could not make out what it was.

A fresh turn brought him nearer, and then he saw distinctly—horses—mounted troops—Uhlans*. A troop of them was standing quietly under a clump of leafless trees near the main road, not more than a couple of hundred yards away from the field. He saw others, and small groups of infantry, at various points around the field, concealing themselves as well as the sparse cover would permit.

His lips turned dry. No wonder the little man was not there. For some reason or other, possibly because the mission had been successful, the whole countryside was being watched. Yet, he reasoned, the very presence of the troops suggested that the little man had not been caught. If he had been taken there would be no need for the troops—unless they were waiting for the plane. Well, the little man was not there, so there was no point in landing. He might as well go home. He had no intention of stepping into the trap.

He was within two hundred feet of the ground, and actually had his hand on the throttle to open his engine again, when a figure burst from the edge of the field

* German cavalrymen

112

and waved its arms. Biggles drew in his breath with a sharp hiss, for the Uhlans had started to move forward. He flung the control-stick over to the left, and, holding up the plane's nose with right rudder, dropped like a stone in a vertical sideslip towards the field.

Never in his life had his nerves been screwed up to such a pitch. His heart hammered violently against his ribs but his brain was clear, and he remained cool and collected. He knew that only perfect judgment and timing could save the situation. The Uhlans were coming at a canter; already they were in the next field.

With his eyes on the man he skimmed over the tops of the trees, put the machine on even keel, and began to flatten out. Then a remarkable thing happened—an occurrence so unexpected and so inexplicable that for a moment he was within an ace of taking off again. A second figure had sprung out of the ditch behind the man in the field and started to run towards him. The new-comer wore a black coat and bowler hat. He did not run towards the machine, but raced towards the man who had been waving, and who was now making for the F.E.

Up to this moment it had not occurred to Biggles for one instant that the man who had been waving was not his little man, and when the second figure appeared his calculations were thrown into confusion. The man in the bowler hat was the spy, there was no doubt of that, for he was now close enough for his face and figure to be recognized. Who, then, was the other?

The Frenchman seemed to know, for as he closed on him he flung up his right hand. There was a spurt of flame. The other flung up his arms and pitched forward on to his face.

Biggles began to see daylight. The thing was an

artfully prepared trap. The first man who had showed himself was a decoy, an imposter to lure him to his death. The real spy had been lying in the hedge bottom, not daring to show himself with so many troops about, hoping that he, Biggles, would not land, which would have been in accordance with their plans.

From his position the spy had seen the decoy break cover, and knew his purpose. So he had exposed himself to warn his flying partner, even at the expense of his own life.

The knowledge made Biggles still more determined to save him, although he could see it was going to be a matter of touch-and-go. The decoy lay where he had fallen, and the little Frenchman, still wearing his bowler, was sprinting as fast as his legs could carry him towards the now taxi-ing machine.

But the Uhlans were already putting their horses at the hedge, not a hundred yards away. Shots rang out, the sharp whip-like cracks of cavalry carbines splitting the still morning air. Bullets hummed like angry wasps, one tearing through the machine with a biting jar that made Biggles wince.

'Come on!' he roared, unable to restrain himself, and he opened the throttle slightly.

The little man's face was red with exertion, and he was puffing hard. He took a flying leap at the nose of the F.E. and dragged himself up on to the edge of the cockpit. '*Voila*! We have made it, my little mushroom!' he gasped. And then, as Biggles jammed the throttle wide open, he pitched head first inside.

The Uhlans were galloping towards them, crouching low on the backs of their mounts, and spurring them to greater efforts. There was no time to turn. Biggles did the only thing possible. He shoved the joy-stick forward and charged. He caught a glimpse of swerving horses and flashing carbines straight in front of him; then he pulled the stick back into his stomach, flinching from what seemed must end in collision.

He relaxed limply as the F.E. zoomed upwards, and shook his head as if unable to believe that they were actually in the air. For the last two or three minutes he had not been conscious of actual thought. He had acted purely on instinct, throwing the whole strain on his nerves.

A round, good-humoured face appeared above the edge of the forward cockpit. The spy caught his eye and grinned. '*Bon*! he shouted. 'That's the stuff, my little cabbage!'

Major Raymond was watching on the tarmac when they landed. His face beamed with delight when he saw they were both in the machine.

'How did it go?' he asked the little Frenchman quickly.

'*Pouf*! Like that!' said the spy. 'The bridge is no more, and, thanks to my little specimen here, I can now have my coffee at home instead of with the pigs-heads over the way.'

'Have a close call, Bigglesworth?' asked the major, becoming serious.

'We did, sir!' admitted Biggles. 'I think I shall fly in a bowler hat in future—they seem to be lucky!'

'Ah! But those Boches are cunning ones!' muttered the Frenchman. 'They hunt for me, but I am in the ditch like a rabbit. They know the aeroplane will come, so they find another man to make my little artichoke land. He lands—so. I think furiously. *La, la*, it is simple. I shoot, and then I run. My Jingoes, how I run! Pish.

We win, and here we are. I think we will go again some day, eh?' He beamed at Biggles.

'Perhaps!' agreed Biggles, but without enthusiasm. 'I've had all I want for a little while, though!'

'Pish!' laughed the spy. 'It was nothing! Just a little excitement to—how you say?—warm the blood.'

'Warm the blood!' exclaimed Biggles. 'When I want to do that I'll do it in front of the mess-room fire, thanks! Your sort of warm gets me overheated!'

# Chapter 10
# Eyes of the Guns

Biggles' face wore a curious expression as he gazed down upon the blue-green panorama four thousand feet below. The day was fine and clear, and recent rain had washed the earth until roads and fields lay sharply defined to the far horizon. Ponds and lakes gleamed like mirrors in the sun, and ruined villages lay here and there like the bones of long-forgotten monsters. At intervals along the roads were long, black caterpillars that he knew were bodies of marching men, sometimes with wagons and artillery. There was nothing unusual about the scene, certainly nothing to cause the look of distaste on the pilot's face. It was an everyday scene on the Western Front.

The truth of the matter was he was setting out on a task that he expected would be wearisome to the point of utter boredom. He had never been detailed for this particular job before, but he had heard a good deal about it, and nothing that was pleasant. The work in question was that known throughout the Royal Flying Corps by those two mystic syllables 'art obs'—in other words, artillery observation.

There were certain squadrons that did nothing else but this work—ranging the guns of our artillery on those of the enemy; sometimes, however, the target was an ammunition dump, a bridge, or a similar strategical point that the higher command decided must be destroyed.

It was by no means as simple as it might appear, and the crew of the machine told off for the task were expected to remain at their post until each gun of the battery for which it was working had scored a hit, after which, without altering the range, they might continue to fire shot after shot at the target until it was wiped out of existence.

If the pilot was lucky, or clever, and the battery for which he was spotting good at its work, the job might be finished in an hour—or it might take three hours; and during the whole of that period the artillery aeroplane would have to circle continuously over the same spot, itself a target for every archie battery within range, and the prey of every prowling enemy scout.

Whether the task was more monotonous for the pilot, who had to watch his own battery for the flash of the gun and then the target for the bursting shell, signalling its position by the Morse code, or for the observer, whose duty it was not to watch the ground (as might reasonably be supposed) but the sky around for danger while the pilot was engrossed in his work, is a matter of opinion.

In any case, Biggles neither knew nor cared, but of one thing he was certain; circling in the same spot for hours was neither amusing nor interesting. Hence the unusual expression on his face as he made his way eastwards towards the Lines, to find the British battery for which he was detailed, and the enemy battery which the British guns proposed to wipe out. This being his first attempt at art obs, he was by no means sure that he would be able to find either of them, and this may have been another reason why he was not flying with his usual enthusiasm.

Now, in order that the operation known as art obs

should be understood, a few words of explanation are necessary, although the procedure is quite simple once the idea has been grasped. Biggles, like all other R.F.C. officers, had been given a certain amount of instruction at his training school, but as he had hoped to be sent to a scout squadron, which never did this class of work, he had not concentrated on the instruction as much as he might have done.

Briefly, this was the programme, for which, as a general rule, wireless was used, although occasionally a system of Very lights was employed. Wireless, at the time of which we are speaking, was of a primitive nature. The pilot, by means of an aerial which he lowered below the machine, could only send messages; he could not receive them. The gunners, in order to convey a message to the pilot, had to lay out strips of white material in the form of letters. The target was considered to be the centre of an imaginary clock, twelve o'clock being due north. Six o'clock was therefore due south, and the other cardinal points in their relative positions. Imaginary rings drawn round the target were lettered A, B, C, D, E, and F. These were 50, 100, 200, 300, 400, and 500 yards away respectively.

When the gunners started work, if the first shell dropped, say, one hundred yards away and due north of the target, all the pilot had to do was to signal B 12. 'B' meant that the shell burst one hundred yards away, and the '12' meant at twelve o'clock on the imaginary clock face. Thus the gunners were able to mark on their map exactly were the shell had fallen, and were therefore able to adjust their gun for the next shot. As another example, a shell bursting three hundred yards to the right of the target would be signalled D 3, or three hundred yards away at three o'clock. In this way the pilot was saved the trouble of tapping out long messages.

Briefly, while the 'shoot', as it was called, was in progress, the pilot continued to correct the aim of the gunners until they scored a hit. The first gun was now ranged on the target. The second gun was ranged in the same way, and so it went on until every gun in the battery was ranged on the target. Then they fired a salvo (all guns together) which the pilot would signal 'mostly O.K.', and thereafter the battery would pump out shells as fast as it could until the enemy guns were put out of action.

This is what Biggles had to do.

Approaching the Line, he quickly picked out the battery of guns for which he was to act as the 'eyes', and after a rather longer search he found the enemy battery, neatly camouflaged, and quite oblivious to the treat in store for it. He reached for his buzzer, which was a small key on the inside of his cockpit, and sent out a series of letter B's in the Morse code, meaning 'Are you receiving my signals?'

This was at once acknowledged by the battery, which put out three strips of white cloth in the form of a letter K—the recognition signal.

Biggles was rather amused, not to say surprised, at this prompt response. It struck him as strange that by pressing a lever in the cockpit he could make people on the ground do things. In fact, it was rather fun. He reached for his buzzer again, and sent K Q, K Q, K Q, meaning 'Are you ready to fire?' (All signals were repeated three times) Biggles, of course, could not hear his own signals; they were sent out by wireless, which was picked up on a small receiving set at the battery's listening-post.

The white strips of cloth on the ground at once took the form of a letter L, meaning 'ready.'

'G—G—G, buzzed Biggles. G was the signal to fire. Instantly a gun flashed, and Biggles, who was becoming engrossed in his task, turned his machine, eyes seeking the distant objective to watch the shell burst.

'Hi!'

The shrill shout from Mark Way, his observer, made him jump. Mark was pointing. Falling like a meteor from the sky was an Albatros, silver with scarlet wingtips. The sun flashed on the gleaming wings, turning them into streaks of fire, on the ends of which were two large black crosses.

Biggles frowned and waved his hand impatiently. 'Make him keep out of the way!' he yelled, and turned back to watch the shell burst. But he was too late. A faint cloud of white smoke was drifting across the landscape near the target, but it was already dispersing, so it was impossible to say just where the shell had burst.

'Dash it!' muttered Biggles, turning and feeling for his buzzer. 'Now I've got to do it again.' G—G—G, he signalled.

There was a moment's pause before the gun flashed again, the gunners possibly wondering why he had not registered their first shot. Biggles turned again towards the target, but before the shell exploded the chatter of a machine-gun made him look up quickly. The Albatros had fired a burst at them, swung up in a climbing turn, and was now coming back at them.

'You cock-eyed son of a coot!' Biggles roared at Mark, as he turned to meet the attack. At this rate the job would never be done. 'And I'll give you something to fling yourself about for, you interfering hound!' he growled at the approaching Albatros. Curiously, it did not occur to him that their lives were in any particular danger, a fact which reveals the confidence that was coming to him as a result of experience. He was not in the least afraid of a single German aeroplane. However, he had still much to learn.

His windscreen flew to pieces, and something whanged against his engine. Again the Hun pulled up in a wonderful zoom, twisting cunningly out of the hail of lead that Mark's gun spat at him. He levelled out, turned, and came down at them again.

For the first time it dawned on Biggles that the man in the machine was no ordinary pilot; he was an artist, a man who knew just what he was doing. Further, he had obviously singled him out for destruction. Well, the battery would have to wait, that was all.

Biggles brought his machine round to face the new attack, pulling his nose up to give Mark the chance of a shot. But before he could fire, the Hun had swerved in an amazing fashion to some point behind them, and a steady stream of bullets began to rip through the wings of the British machine. Again Biggles turned swiftly—but the Hun was not there.

*Rat-tat-tat-tat-tat*—a stream of lead poured up from below, one of the bullets jarring against the root of the joystick with a jerk that flung it out of his hand.

'You artful swipe!' rasped Biggles, flinging the F.E. round in such a steep turn that Mark nearly went overboard.

'Sorry!' Biggles' lips formed the words, but he was pointing at the Hun, who had climbed up out of range, but was now coming down again like a thunderbolt, guns spurting long streams of flame. Mark was shooting, too, their bullets seeming to meet between the two machines. The Albatros came so close that Biggles could distinctly see the tappets of the other's engine working, and the pilot's face peering at them over the side of his cockpit. Then he swerved, and Biggles breathed a sigh of relief.

But he was congratulating himself too soon. The Albatros twisted like a hawk, dived, turned as he dived, and then came up at them like a rocket. To Biggles this manœuvre was so unexpected, so seemingly impossible, that he could hardly believe it, and he experienced a real spasm of fright. He no longer thought of the battery below; he knew he was fighting the battle of his life, his first real duel against a man who knew his job thoroughly.

During the next five minutes he learnt many things, things that were to stand him in good stead later on, and the fact that he escaped was due, not to his ability, but to a circumstance for which he was duly grateful. Twice he had made a break, in the hope of reaching the Lines. For during the combat, as was so often the case, the wind had blown them steadily over enemy country, but each time the enemy was there first, cutting off his escape. Mark had not been idle, but the wily German seldom gave him a fair chance for even a fleeting shot, much less a 'sitter*.'

The Hun seemed to attack from all points of the compass at once. Biggles turned to face his aggressor in a new quarter—the fellow was always in the most unexpected quarter—and dived furiously at him; too furiously. He overshot, and, before he could turn, the Hun was behind him, pouring hot lead into his engine.

* A target moving directly away from the gunner and therefore a relatively easy target.

He knew that he was lost. Something grazed his arm, and with horror he saw blood running down Mark's face. He crouched low as he tried to turn out of the hail of lead. The bullets stopped abruptly as he came round, glaring wildly. The Hun had gone. Presently Biggles made him out, dropping like a stone towards the safety of his own territory. He could hardly believe his eyes. He had been cold meat* for the enemy pilot, and he knew it. Why, then—But Mark was pointing upwards, grinning.

Biggles' eyes followed the outstretched finger, and he saw a formation of nine Sopwith Pups sweeping across the sky five thousand feet above them. He grinned back, trembling slightly from reaction.

'By gosh, that was a close one! I'll remember that piece of silver-and-red furniture, and keep out of his way!' he vowed, inwardly marvelling, and wondering how the Boche pilot had been able to concentrate his attack on him in the way that he had, and yet watch the surrounding sky for possible danger. He knew that if there had been a thousand machines in the sky he would not have seen them, yet the Hun had not failed to see the approaching Pups when they were miles away. 'Pretty good!' he muttered admiringly. 'I'll remember that!'

And he did. It was his first real lesson in the art of air combat. His pride suffered when he thought of the way the Hun had 'made rings round him,' and he was not quite as confident of himself as he had been, yet he knew that the experience was worth all the anxiety it had caused him.

* Slang: an easy victim

But what about the enemy battery? He looked down, and saw that he had drifted miles away from it.

He snorted his disgust at the archie that opened up on him the instant the Hun had departed, and made his way back to his original rendezvous. The calico 'L' was still lying on the ground near the battery. Although he did not know it, the gunners had watched the combat with the greatest interest, and were agreeably surprised to see him returning so soon after the attack.

G—G—G, he buzzed. The gun flashed, and the F.E. rocked suddenly, almost as if it had been shaken by an invisible hand.

Biggles started, and looked at his altimeter. In the fight he had, as usual, lost height, and he was now below three thousand feet. He knew that the great howitzer shell had passed close to him, so he started climbing as quickly as possible to get above its culminating point. The archie smoke was so thick that he had great difficulty in seeing the shell burst. It was a good five hundred yards short. F6—F6—F6 he signalled; and then, after a brief interval: G—G—G. He watched with interest for the next shell to burst, but it was farther from the mark than the first one had been.

'If they don't improve faster than that we shall still be here when the bugles blow "Cease fire!" ' he muttered in disgust.

The next shot was better, but it was a good four hundred yards beyond the mark and slightly to the right. D1—D1—D1 he tapped out as he turned in a wide circle and then back again towards the target on a course which, had he been a sky-writer, would have traced a large figure eight—the usual method of the artillery spotting 'plane, which allowed the pilot to see both his own battery and the target in turn. It also kept the archie gunners guessing which way he was going next.

An hour later Biggles was still at it, and the first gun had got no closer than two hundred yards to its mark. The fascination of the pastime was beginning to wear off; indeed it was already bordering on the monotonous. 'This is a nice game played slow,' he shouted. 'Why don't those fellows learn to shoot?'

He was falling into a sort of reverie, sending his signals automatically, when he was again brought back to realities by a yell from Mark. He looked round sharply, and fixed his eyes on a small, straight-winged machine that was climbing up towards them from the east. The German anti-aircraft gunners must have seen it, too, for the archie died away abruptly as they ceased fire rather than take the risk of hitting their own man. There was no mistaking the machine. It was the red-and-silver Albatros.

Biggles was not to be caught napping twice. He turned his nose towards home and dived, only pulling out when he felt he was a safe distance over the Lines. He turned in time to see his late adversary gliding away into a haze that was forming over the other side of the Lines.

Once more he returned to his post, and signalled to the gunners to fire, but even as the gun flashed, he heard the *rat-tat-tat-tat* of a machine-gun, and the disconcerting *flac-flac-flac* of bullets ripping through his wings.

'You cunning hound!' he grated, seething with rage as he caught a glimpse of the red-and-silver wings of his old adversary as it darted in from the edge of the haze in which it had taken cover. It was another tip in the art of stalking that he did not forget. At the moment he was concerned only with the destruction of his persistent tormentor, and he attacked with a fury that he had never felt before. He wanted to see the Albatros crash—he wanted to see that more than he had ever wanted to see anything in his life. Completely mastered by his anger, he made no attempt to escape, but positively flung the F.E. at the black-crossed machine. This was evidently something the Hun did not expect, and he was nearly caught napping.

Mark got in a good burst before the Hun swerved out of his line of fire. Biggles yanked the F.E. round in a turn that might have torn its wings off, and plunged down on the tail of the Albatros. He saw the pilot look back over his shoulder, and felt a curious intuition as to which way he would turn. He saw the Hun's rudder start to move, which confirmed it, and, without waiting for the Albatros actually to answer to its controls, he whipped the F.E. round in a vertical bank.

The Hun had turned the same way, as he knew he must, and he was still on its tail, less than fifty yards away. It was a brilliant move, although at the time he did not know it; it showed anticipation in the moves of the games that marked the expert in air combat. He thrust the stick forward with both hands until he could see the dark gases flowing out of his enemy's exhaustpipe; saw the pilot's blond moustache, saw the goggled eyes staring at him, and saw Mark's bullets sewing a leaden seam across his fuselage.

The Hun turned over on to its back and then spun, Biggles watching it with savage satisfaction that turned to chagrin when, a thousand feet from the ground, the red-and-silver machine levelled out and sped towards home. The pilot had deliberately thrown his machine out of control in order to mislead his enemy—another trick Biggles never forgot.

'We've given the blighter something to think about, at any rate!' he thought moodily, as he turned to the battery.

The gunners were waiting for him, but, to his annoyance and disgust, the first shot went wide; it was, in fact, farther away from the target than the first one had been.

'This is a game for mugs!' he snarled. 'As far as I can see, there's nothing to prevent this going on for ever. Don't those fellows ever hit what they shoot at?'

He was getting tired, for they had now been in the air for more than three hours, and, as far as he could see, they were no nearer the end than when they started. The archie was getting troublesome again, and he was almost in despair when an idea struck him.

'H.Q. want that Hun battery blown up, do they?' he thought. 'All right, they shall have it blown up—but I know a quicker way of doing it than this.' He turned suddenly and raced back towards his aerodrome, sending the C H I signal as he went. C H I in the code meant 'I am going home.' He landed and taxied up to the hangars.

'Fill her up with petrol and hang two 112-pounder bombs on the racks—and make it snappy!' he told the flight-sergeant. Then he hurried down to the mess and called up on the telephone the battery for which he had been acting.

'Look here,' he began hotly, 'I'm getting tired, trying to put you ham-fisted—What's that? Colonel? Sorry, sir!' He collected himself quickly, realizing that he had made a bad break. The brigade colonel was on the other end of the wire. 'Well, the fact is, sir,' he went on, 'I've just thought of an idea that may speed things up a bit. The target is a bit too low for you to see, I think, and—well, if I laid an egg on that spot it would show your gun-layers just where the target is. What's that, sir? Unusual? Yes, I know it is, but if it comes off it will save a lot of time and ammunition. If it fails I'll go on with the shoot again in the ordinary way. Yes, sir—very good, sir—I'll be over in about a quarter of an hour.'

He put the receiver down, and, ignoring Toddy's cry of protest, hurried back to the sheds. Mark looked at him in astonishment when he climbed back into his seat. 'Haven't you had enough of it, or have you got a rush of blood to the brain?' he asked coldly.

'Brain, my foot!' snapped Biggles. 'I'm going to give those Huns a rush of something. I've done figures of eight until I'm dizzy. Round and round the blinking mulberry-bush, with every archie battery for miles practising on me. I'm going to liven things up a bit. You coming, or are you going to stay at home? Things are likely to get warmish.'

'Of course I'm coming!'

'Well, come on, let's get on with it.'

He took off, and climbed back to the old position between the batteries, but he sent no signal. He did not even let his aerial out. He began to circle as if he was going to continue the 'shoot,' but then, turning suddenly, he jammed his joystick forward with both hands and tore down at the German gunpits. For a few moments he left the storm of archie far behind, but as the gunners perceived his intention, it broke out again with renewed intensity, and the sky around him became an inferno of smoke and fire.

Crouching low in his cockpit, his lips pressed in a

straight line, he did not swerve an inch. It was neck or nothing now, and he knew it. His only hope of success lay in speed. Any delay could only make his task more perilous, for already the artillery observers on the ground would be ringing up the *Jagdstaffeln* (German fighter squadrons), calling on them to deal with this Englander who must either be mad or intoxicated.

He could see his objective clearly, and he made for it by the shortest possible course. Twice shells flamed so close to him that he felt certain the machine must fall in pieces out of his hands. The wind screamed in his wires and struts and plucked at his face and shoulders. A flying wire trailed uselessly from the root of an inter-plane strut, cut through as clean as a carrot by shrapnel, beating a wild tattoo on the fabric.

Mark was crouching low in the front cockpit, blood oozing from a flesh wound in his forehead, caused by flying glass.

It is difficult to keep track of time in such moments. The period from the start of his dive until he actually reached the objective was probably not more than three minutes—four at the most—but to Biggles it seemed an eternity. Time seemed to stand still; trifling incidents assumed enormous proportions, occurring as they did with slow deliberation. Thus, he saw a mobile archie battery, the gun mounted on a motor-lorry, tearing along the road. He saw it stop, and the well-trained team leap to their allotted stations; saw the long barrel swing round towards him, and the first flash of flame from its muzzle. He felt certain the shot would hit him, and wondered vaguely what the fellows at the squadron would say about his crazy exploit when he did not return.

The shell burst fifty feet in front of him, an orange

spurt of flame that was instantly engulfed in a whirling ball of black smoke. He went straight through it, his propeller churning the smoke to the four winds, and he gasped as the acrid fumes bit into his lungs.

He saw the gun fire again, and felt the plunging machine lurch as the projectile passed desperately close. He did not look back, but he knew his track must be marked by a solid-looking plume of black smoke visible for miles. He wondered grimly what the colonel to whom he had spoken on the telephone was thinking about it, for he would be watching the proceedings.

Down—down—down, but there was no sensation of falling. The machine seemed to be stationary, with the earth rushing up to meet him. At five hundred feet the enemy gun-crew, who could not resist the temptation of watching him, bolted for their dug-outs like rabbits when a fox-terrier appears. Perhaps they had thought it impossible for the British machine to survive such a maelstrom of fire. Anyway, they left it rather late.

Not until he was within a hundred feet of the ground did Biggles start to pull the machine out of its dive, slowly, in case he stripped his wings off as they encountered the resistance of the air. Mark's gun was stuttering, bullets kicking up the earth about the gunpits in case one of the German gunners, bolder than the rest, decided to try his luck with a rifle or machine-gun.

The end came suddenly. Biggles saw the target leap towards him, and at what must have been less than fifty feet, he pulled his bomb toggle, letting both bombs go together. Then he zoomed high.

Such was his speed that he was back at a thousand feet when the two bombs burst simultaneously; but the blast of air lifted the F.E. like a piece of tissue paper. He fought the machine back under control, and, without waiting to see the result of the explosion, tore in a zigzag course towards his own battery.

At three thousand feet he levelled out and looked back. He had succeeded beyond his wildest hopes, and knew that he must have hit the enemy ammunition dump. Flames were still leaping skyward in a dense pall of black smoke.

With a feeling of satisfaction, he lowered his aerial. His fingers sought the buzzer key and tapped out the letters G—G—G. The British gun flashed instantly. The gun-layer was no longer firing blind, and the shot landed in the middle of the smoking mass.

O.K.—O.K.—O.K. tapped Biggles exultantly.

The second gun of the battery sent its projectile hurtling towards the Boche gunpits. It was less than one hundred yards short, but with visible target to shoot at it required only two or three minutes to get it ranged on the target. The others followed.

G—D—O, G—D—O, G—D—O, tapped Biggles enthusiastically, for G—D—O was the signal to the gunners to begin firing in their own time. The four guns were ranged on the target, and they no longer needed his assistance. With salvo after salvo they pounded the enemy gunpits out of existence, Biggles and Mark watching the work of destruction with the satisfaction of knowing their job had been well done.

Then they looked at each other, and a slow smile spread over Biggles's face. C H I, C H I, C H I (I am going home) he tapped, and turned towards the aerodrome. Instantly his smile gave way to a frown of annoyance. What were the fools doing? A cloud of white archie smoke had appeared just in front of him. White archie!

Only British archie was white! Why were they shooting at him? The answer struck him at the same moment that Mark yelled and pointed. He lifted up his eyes. Straight across their front, in the direction they must go, but two thousand feet above them, a long line of white archie bursts trailed across the sky. In front of them, always it seemed just out of their reach, sped a small, straight-winged plane, its top wings were slightly longer than the lower ones.

Two thoughts rushed into Biggles' mind at once. The first was that the gunners on the ground had fired the burst close to him to warn him of his danger, and the second was that the German machine was an Albatros. There was no mistaking the shark-like fuselage. Something, an instinct which he could not have explained, told him it was their old red-and-silver enemy. He was right—it was. At that moment it turned, and the sun revealed its colours. It dived towards the British machine, and the archie gunners were compelled to cease fire for fear of hitting the F.E.

There was no escape. Biggles would have avoided combat had it been possible, for he was rather worried about the damage the F.E. might have suffered during its dive. Mark glowered as he turned his gun towards the persistent enemy, and then crouched low, waiting for it come into effective range.

But the Hun had no intention of making things so easy. His machine had already been badly knocked about in the last effort, an insult which he was probably anxious to avenge, and intended to see that no such thing occurred again. At two hundred feet he started shooting, and Biggles pulled his nose up to meet him. From that position he would not swerve, for it was a point of honour in the R.F.C. never to turn away from a frontal attack, even though the result was a collision.

Just what happened after that he was never quite sure. In trying to keep his nose on the Hun, who was still coming down from above, he got it too high up, with the result that one of two courses was open to him. Either he could let the F.E. stall, in which case the Hun would get a 'sitting' shot at him at the moment of stalling—a chance he was not likely to miss—or he could pull the machine right over in a loop. He chose the latter course.

As he came out of the loop, he looked round wildly for the Hun. For a fleeting fraction of an instant he saw him at his own level, not more than twenty or thirty feet away, going in the opposite direction. At the same moment he was nearly flung out of his seat by a jar that jerked him sideways and made the F.E. quiver from propeller boss to tail skid. His heart stood still, for he felt certain that his top 'plane, or some other part of the machine, had broken away, but to his utter amazement it answered to the controls, and he soon had it on an even keel.

Mark was yelling, jabbing downwards with his finger. Biggles looked over the side of his cockpit. The Hun was gliding towards his own Lines.

There seemed to be something wrong with the Albatros—something missing; and for the moment Biggles could not make out what it was. Then he saw. It had no propeller! How the miracle had happened he did not know, and he had already turned to follow it to administer the knock-out when another yell from Mark made him change his mind—quickly. A formation of at least twenty Huns were tearing towards the scene.

Biggles waited for no more. He put his nose down for home and not until the aerodrome loomed upon the horizon did he ease the pace. He remembered his aerial, and took hold of the handle of the reel to wind in the long length of copper wire with its lead plummet on the end to keep it extended.

The reel was in place, but there was no aerial, and he guessed what had happened. He should have wound it in immediately he had sent the C H I signal, and he knew that if he had done so he would in all probability by now be lying in a heap of charred wreckage in No Man's Land. He had forgotten to wind in, and to that fact he probably owed his life. When he had swung round after his loop, the wire, with the plummet on the end, must have swished round like a flail and struck the Boche machine, smashing its propeller!

The C.O. was waiting for them on the tarmac when they landed. There was a curious expression on his face, but several other officers who were standing behind him were smiling expectantly.

'You were detailed for the art obs show to-day, I think, Bigglesworth,' began Major Paynter coldly.

'That is so, sir,' said Biggles.

'Wing has just been on the telephone to me, and so has the commander of the battery for whom you were acting. Will you please tell me precisely what has happened?'

Briefly Biggles related what had occurred. The major did not move a muscle until he had finished. Then he looked at him with an expressionless face. 'Far be it from me to discourage zeal or initiative,' he said, 'but we cannot have this sort of thing. Your instructions were quite clear—you were to do the shoot for the artillery. You had no instructions to use bombs, and your action might have resulted in the loss of a valuable machine. I must discourage this excess of exuberance,' went on the C.O. 'As a punishment, you will return this afternoon to the scene of the affair, taking a camera with you. I shall require a photograph of the wrecked German battery on my desk by one hour after sunset. Is that clear?'

'Perfectly, sir.'

'That's all, then. Don't let it happen again. The artillery think we are trying to do them out of their jobs; but it was a jolly good show, all the same!' he concluded, with something as near a chuckle as his dignity would permit.

# Chapter 11
# The Camera

There was no hurry. Major Paynter, the C.O., had not named any particular hour for the 'show'. He had said that the photographs must be delivered to him by one hour after sunset and there were still five hours of daylight.

With Mark, Biggles made his way to the mess for a rest, and over coffee they learned some news that set every member of the squadron agog with excitement. Toddy, the Recording Officer, divulged that the equipment of the squadron was to be changed, the change to take effect as quickly as possible. In future they were to fly Bristol Fighters.*

It transpired that Toddy had been aware of the impending change for some time, but the orders had been marked 'secret,' so he had not been allowed to make the information public. But now that ferry pilots were to start delivering the new machines, there was no longer any need to keep silent. They might expect the Bristols to arrive at any time, Toddy told them, and A Flight, by reason of its seniority, was to have the first.

Biggles, being in A Flight, was overjoyed. He had grown very attached to his old F.E. which had given him good service, but it had always been a source of irritation to him, as the pilot, that the actual shooting

* Two-seater biplane fighter with remarkable manoeuvrability.

had perforce been left to Mark. In future they would both have guns, to say nothing of a machine of higher performance.

In the excitement caused by the news the time passed quickly, and it was nearly two-thirty when they walked towards the sheds in order to proceed with the work for which they had been detailed.

Biggles' shoulder had been grazed by a bullet in the morning's combat with the red-and-silver Albatros, but it caused him no inconvenience, and he did not bother to report it. Neither had Mark's wound been very severe, not much more than a scratch, as he himself said, and it did not occur to him to go 'sick' with it. It was a clean cut in his forehead about an inch long, caused by a splinter of flying glass. He had washed it with antiseptic, stuck a piece of plaster over it, and dismissed it from his mind. On their way to the hangars they met the medical officer on his way back from visiting some mechanics who were sick in their huts. They were about to pass him with a cheerful nod when his eyes fell on the strip of court-plaster on Mark's forehead. He stopped and raised his eyebrows. 'Hallo, what have you been up to?' he asked.

'Up to?' echoed Mark, not understanding.

'What have you done to your head?'

'Oh—that! Nothing to speak of. I stopped a piece of loose glass in a little affair with a Hun this morning,' replied Mark casually.

'Let me have a look at it.' The M.O. removed the piece of court-plaster and examined the wound critically. 'Where are you off to now?' he inquired.

'I've got a short show to do with Bigglesworth.'

'Short or long, you'll do no more flying to-day, my boy; you get back to your quarters and rest for a bit.

Too much cold air on that cut, and we shall have you down with erysipelas. I'll speak to the C.O.'.

'But—' began Mark, in astonishment.

'There's no "but" about it,' said the M.O. tersely. 'You do as you're told, my lad. Twelve hours' rest will put you right. Off you go!'

Mark looked at Biggles hopelessly.

'Doc's right, Mark,' said Biggles, nodding. 'I ought to have had the sense to know it myself. I'll bet your skull aches even now.'

'Not it!' snorted Mark.

'That's all right, doc, I'll find another partner,' asserted Biggles. 'See you later, Mark.'

He made his way to the Squadron Office and reported the matter to Toddy.

'You wouldn't like to take one of the new fellows, I suppose?' suggested Toddy, referring to two new observer officers who had reported for duty the previous evening. 'I think they're about somewhere.'

'Certainly I will,' replied Biggles. 'Someone will have to take them over some time, so the sooner the better. It's only a short show, anyway.'

Toddy dispatched an orderly at the double to find the new officers, and Biggles awaited their arrival impatiently. He had already spoken to them, so they were not quite strangers, but they were of such opposite types that he could not make up his mind which one to choose. Harris was a mere lad, fair-haired and blue-eyed, straight from school. He had failed in his tests as a pilot, and was satisfied to take his chances as an aerial gunner rather than go into the infantry. Culver, the other, was an older man, a cavalry captain who had seen service in the Dardanelles before he had transferred to the R.F.C.

They came in quickly, anxious to know what was in the wind. Briefly, Biggles told them and explained the position. 'Toss for it,' he suggested. 'That's the fairest way. All I ask is that whoever comes will keep his eyes wide open and shoot straight, if there is any shooting to be done.'

Harris won the toss, and with difficulty concealed his satisfaction, for although Biggles was unaware of it, he—Biggles—had already achieved the reputation of being one of the best pilots in the squadron.

'Good enough. Get into your flying kit and get a good gun,' Biggles said shortly. 'I'll go and start up.'

He was satisfied but by no means enthusiastic about taking the new man over. Few experienced pilots felt entirely happy in the company of men new to the job and who had not had an opportunity of proving themselves. It was not that cowardice was anticipated. Biggles knew what all experienced flyers knew; that a man could be as plucky as they make them when on the ground—might have shown himself to be a fearless fighter in trench warfare—but until he had been put to the test it was impossible to say how he would behave in his first air combat; how he would react to the terrifying sensation of hearing bullets ripping through spruce and canvas.

As a matter of fact, it was worse for an observer than it was for a pilot. It needed a peculiar kind of temperament, or courage, to stand up and face twin machine-guns spouting death at point-blank range; not only to stand up, but calmly align the sights of a Lewis gun and return the fire.

There was only one way to find out if a man could do it and that was to take him into the air. There were some who could not do it, in the same way that there were cases of officers who could not face 'archie.' And after one or two trips over the Line this was apparent to others, even if it was not admitted. And it needed a certain amount of courage to confess. But it was better for an officer to be frank with his C.O. and tell the truth, rather than throw away his life, and an aeroplane. Officers reporting 'sick' in this way were either transferred to ground duties or sent home for instructional work.

Biggles wore a worried frown, therefore, as he walked up to the sheds. He realized for the first time just how much confidence he had in Mark, and the comfort he derived from the knowledge that he had a reliable man in the observer's cockpit.

They took their places in the machine, and after Biggles had given Harris a reassuring smile he took off and headed for the strafed* German battery. He would gain all the height he needed on the way to the Lines, for he proposed to take the photographs from not higher than five thousand feet. A good deal of cloud had drifted up from the west, which was annoying, for it was likely to make his task more difficult. It would not prevent him reaching his objective, but the C.O. would certainly not be pleased if he was handed a nice photograph of a large white cloud.

He crossed the Lines at four thousand, still climbing, and zigzagged his way through the archie in the direction of the wrecked German battery. He noted with satisfaction that his new partner took his baptism of anti-aircraft fire well, for he turned and smiled cheerfully, even if the smile was a trifle forced. He was rather

* To strafe: to bombard a target with gunfire, artillery shells or machine-gun fire.

pale, but Biggles paid no attention to that. There are few men who do not change colour the first time they find themselves under fire.

The sky seemed clear of aircraft, although the clouds formed good cover for lurking enemy scouts, and he began to hope the job might be done in record time. He skirted a massive pile of cloud, and there, straight before him, lay the scene of his morning exploit. A grin spread over his face as he surveyed the huge craters that marked the spot where the enemy battery had once hidden itself; the job had been done thoroughly, and headquarters could hardly fail to be pleased.

After a swift glance around he put his nose down and dived, and then, swinging upwind, he began to expose his plates. In five minutes he had been over the whole area twice, covering not only the actual site of the battery, but the surrounding country. With the satisfaction of knowing that his job had been well done, he turned for home. 'Good!' he muttered. 'That's that!'

Swinging round another towering mass of opaque mist he ran into a one-sided dog-fight with a suddenness that almost caught him off his guard. A lone F.E. was fighting a battle with five enemy Albatroses.

Now, according to the rules of war flying, this was no affair of Biggles'. Strictly speaking, the duty of a pilot with a definite mission was to fulfil that mission and return home as quickly as possible; but needless to say, this was not always adhered to. Few pilots could resist the temptation of butting into a dog-fight, or attacking an enemy machine if one was seen. To leave a comrade fighting overwhelming odds was unthinkable.

Biggles certainly did not think about it. The combat was going on at about his own altitude, and although the F.E. had more than one opportunity of dodging into the clouds and thereby escaping, the pilot had obviously made up his mind to see the matter through.

Biggles' lips parted in a smile and he barged into the fight. Then, to his horror, he saw that his gunner was not even looking at the milling machines. He had not even seen them. It seemed incredible. But there it was. And Biggles, remembering his own blindness when he was a beginner, forgave him. Harris was gazing at the ground immediately below with an almost bored expression on his face.

'Hi!' roared Biggles, with the full power of his lungs. 'Get busy!'

Harris' start of astonishment and horror as he looked up just as a blue Albatros dashed across his nose was almost comical; but he grabbed his gun like lightning and sent a stream of lead after the whirling Hun.

Biggles dashed in close to the other F.E. to make his presence known. A swift signal greeting passed between the two pilots, and then they set about the work on hand.

The fight did not last many minutes, but it was red-hot while it lasted. One Albatros went down in flames; another glided down out of control with its engine evidently out of action. The other three dived for home. Biggles straightened his machine and looked around for the other F.E., but it had disappeared. He had not seen it go, so whether it had been shot down, or had merely proceeded on its way, he was unable to ascertain.

Harris was standing up surveying their own machine ruefully, for it had been badly shot about. Biggles caught his eye and nodded approvingly. 'You'll do!' he told himself; for the boy had undoubtedly acquitted himself well. Then he continued on his course for the aerodrome.

He reached it without further incident and taxied in, eyes on a brand new Bristol Fighter that was standing on the tarmac. The photographic sergeant hurried towards him to collect the camera and plates, in order to develop them forthwith. Biggles jumped to the ground, and was about to join the group of officers admiring the Bristol when a cry from the N.C.O. made him turn.

'What's the matter?' he asked quickly.

'Sorry sir, but look!' said the sergeant apologetically.

Biggles' eyes opened wide as they followed the N.C.O.'s pointing finger, and then he made a gesture of anger and disgust. The camera was bent all shapes, and the plate container was a perforated wreck. There was no need to wonder how it had happened; a burst of fire from one of the enemy machines had reduced the camera to a twisted ruin.

He could see at a glance that the plates were spoilt. His journey had been in vain. Looking over the machine thoroughly for the first time he saw that the damage was a good deal worse than he had thought. Two wires had been severed and one of the hinges of his elevators shot off. The machine had brought him home safely, but in its present condition it was certainly not safe to fly.

'What's the matter?' asked Mapleton, his flight-commander, seeing that something was wrong.

Briefly, Biggles explained the catastrophe.

'What are you going to do about it?' asked Mabs.

'I'll have to do the show again, that's all about it!' replied Biggles disgustedly. 'The Old Man was very decent about this morning's effort. He's waiting for these photos; I can't let him down.'

'You can't fly that machine again today, that's a certainty.'

'So I see.'

'Would you like to try the Bristol?'

Biggles started. 'I'd say I would!'

'You can have it if you like, but for the love of Mike don't hurt it. It's been allotted to me, so it's my pigeon. She's all O.K. and in fighting trim. I was just off to try her out myself.'

'That's jolly sporting of you,' declared Biggles. 'I shan't be long, and I'll take care of her. Come on, Harris, get your guns—and get me another camera, sergeant; look sharp, it will soon be dark.'

In a few minutes Biggles was in the air again, on his way to the enemy battery for the third time that day. He had no difficulty in flying the Bristol, which was an easy machine to fly, and after a few practice turns he felt quite at home in it.

He noticed with dismay that the clouds were thickening, and he was afraid that they might totally obscure the objective. Twice, as he approached it, he thought he caught sight of a lurking shadow, dodging through the heavy cloud-bank above him, but each time he looked it had vanished before he could make sure.

'There's a Hun up there, watching me, or I'm a Dutchman,' he mused uneasily. 'I hope that kid in the back seat will keep his eyes skinned.' He shot through a small patch of cloud and distinctly saw another machine disappear into a cloud just ahead and above him. It was an Albatros, painted red and silver. 'So it's you, is it?' he muttered, frowning, for the idea of taking on his old antagonist with a comparatively untried gunner in the back seat did not fill him with enthusiasm. With Mark it would have been a different matter.

He turned sharply into another cloud and approached the objective on a zigzag course, never flying straight for more than a few moments at a time. He knew that this would leave the watcher, if he were still watching, in doubt as to his actual course, but it was nervy work, knowing that an attack might be launched at any moment.

As he expected, he found the battery concealed under a thick layer of grey cloud, but he throttled back and came out below it at two thousand feet. Instantly he was the target for a dozen archie batteries, but he ignored them and flew level until he had exposed all his plates. He was feeling more anxious than he had ever felt before in the air, not so much for his own safety as for the safety of Mab's machine, so it was with something like a sigh of relief that he finished his task, jammed the throttle wide open, and zoomed upwards through the opaque ceiling.

The instant he cleared the top side of the cloud the rattle of a machine-gun came to his ears and the Bristol quivered as a stream of lead ripped through it. He whirled round just in time to see the red-and-silver 'plane zoom over him, not twenty feet away. Why hadn't Harris fired? Was he asleep, the young fool? With his brow black as thunder Biggles twisted round in his seat and looked behind him. Harris was lying in a crumpled heap on the side of his cockpit.

Biggles went ice-cold all over. The corners of his mouth turned down. 'He's got him!' he breathed, and then exposing his teeth, 'You hound!' he grated, and dragged the Bristol round on its axis and in the direction of the Albatros, now circling to renew the attack.

If the Boche pilot supposed that the British machine would now seek to escape he was mistaken. Unknowingly, he was faced with the most dangerous of all opponents, a pilot who was fighting mad. A clever, calculating enemy, fighting in cold blood, was a foe to be respected; but a pilot seeing red and seething with hate was much worse. For the first time, the war had become a personal matter with Biggles, and he would have rammed his adversary if he could have reached him.

The pilot in the black-crossed machine seemed to realize this, for he suddenly broke off the combat and sought to escape by diving towards the nearest cloud. Biggles was behind him in a flash, eye to the Aldis sight. Farther and yet farther forward he pushed the control-stick, and the distance rapidly closed between them.

The Hun saw death on his tail and twisted like an eel, but the Bristol stuck to him as if connected by an invisible wire. A hundred feet—fifty feet—Biggles drew nearer, but still he did not fire. The glittering arc of his propeller was nearly touching the other's elevators. The cross-wires of the Aldis sight cut across the tail, crept along the fuselage to the brown-helmeted head in the cockpit.

Biggles knew that he had won and was filled with a savage exultation. He was so close that every detail of the Boche machine was indelibly imprinted on his brain. He could see the tappets of the Mercedes engine working, and the dark smoke pouring from its exhaust. He could even see the patches over the old bullet holes in the lower wings. His gloved hand sought the Bowden lever, closed on it, and gripped it hard. Orange flame darted from the muzzle of his gun and the harsh metallic clatter of the cocking handle filled his ears. The Albatros jerked upwards, the Bristol still on its tail. A tongue of scarlet flame licked along its side, and a cloud of black smoke poured out of the engine. The pilot covered his face with his hands.

Biggles turned away, feeling suddenly limp. He seemed to have awakened with a shock from a vivid dream. Where was he? He did not know. He saw the Hun break up just as it reached the lower stratum of cloud, and he followed it down to try to pick up some landmark that would give him his position. It was with real relief that he was able to recognize the road near where the wreck of the Albatros had fallen, and he shot upwards again to escape the ever-present archie.

For the first time since the fight began he remembered Harris, and raced for home. He tried to persuade himself that perhaps he was only wounded, but in his heart of hearts he knew the truth. Harris was dead. Four straight-winged 'planes materialized out of the mist in front of him, but Biggles did not swerve. The feeling of hate began to surge through him again. 'If you're looking for trouble you can have it!' he snarled, and tore straight at the Albatroses.

They opened up to let him go through, and then closed in behind him. He swerved round a fragment of cloud, and then, with the speed of light, flung the Bristol on its side with a sharp intake of breath. It was perhaps only because his nerves were screwed up to snapping point that he had caught sight of what seemed to be a fine wire standing vertically in the air.

Without even thinking, he knew it was a balloon cable. Somewhere above the clouds an enemy observation balloon was taking a last look round the land-scape, or as much of it as could be seen, before being wound down for the night. Then an idea struck him, and he swerved in the opposite direction.

The leading Hun, with his eyes only on the Bristol was round in a flash to cut across the arc of the circle and intercept him, and Biggles witnessed just what he hoped would happen—the picture of a machine collid-ing with a balloon cable. It was a sight permitted to very few war pilots, although it actually happened several times.

The cable tore the top and bottom port wings off the Albatros as cleanly as if they had been sheared through with an axe. The machine swung round in its own length, and the pilot was flung clean over the centre section. He fell, clutching wildly at space. Biggles saw that the cable had parted, and that the other machines were hesitating, watching their falling leader. Then they came on again. They overtook him before he reached the Lines, as he knew they would. A bullet splashed into his instrument-board, and he had no alternative but to turn and face them.

With a steady gunner in the back seat he would have felt no qualms as to the ultimate result of the combat, but with his rear gun silent he was much worse off than the single-seaters, as he had a larger machine to handle. To make matters worse, the Lewis gun, pointing up to the sky in the rear cockpit, told its own story. The enemy pilots knew that his gunner was down, and that they could get on his tail with impunity.

The three Boche pilots were evidently old hands, for they separated and then launched an attack from three directions simultaneously. The best that Biggles could do was to take on one machine at a time, yet while he was engaging it his flanks and tail were exposed to the attacks of the other two.

Several bullets struck the Bristol, and it began to look as if his luck had broken at last. He fought coolly, without the all-devouring hate that had consumed him when he attacked the red-and-silver Albatros. These methods would not serve him now.

He tried to break out of the circle into which they had automatically fallen, in order to reach the shelter of the clouds, but a devastating blast of lead through his centre section warned him of the folly of turning his back on them. He swung round again to meet them. A shark-like aircraft, painted dark green and buff, circled to get behind him; the other two were coming in from either side. His position, he knew, was critical.

Then a miracle happened, or so it seemed. The circling Hun broke into pieces and hurtled earthwards. Biggles stared, and then understood. A drab-coloured single-seater, wearing red, white, and blue ring markings, swept across his nose. It was a Sopwith Pup. He looked around quickly for others, but it was alone.

Its advent soon decided matters. The black-crossed machines dived out of the fight and disappeared into the clouds. Biggles waved his hand to the single-seater pilot and they turned towards the Lines. The Pup stayed with him until the aerodrome loomed up through the gloom, and then disappeared as magically as it arrived.

Biggles felt for his Very pistol and fired a red light over the side. The ruddy glow cast a weird light over the twilight scene. He saw the ambulance start out almost before his wheels had touched the ground, and he taxied to meet it. Mabs and Mark were following it at a brisk trot; the C.O. was standing in the doorway of the squadron office.

Mark, with a bandage round his head, caught Biggles' eye as two R.A.M.C men gently lifted the dead observer from his seat. Biggles did not look; he felt that tears were not far away, and was ashamed of his weakness. He taxied up to the sheds and climbed wearily to the ground.

'How did the Bristol go?' asked Mabs awkwardly.

'Bristol? Oh, yes—fine, thanks!'

The photographic sergeant removed the camera.

'See that the prints are in the squadron office as quickly as you can manage it,' Biggles told him.

'Lucky for me the doc made me stay at home,' observed Mark.

Biggles shrugged his shoulders. 'Maybe. On the other hand, it might not have happened if you'd been there.'

'How did it happen?' asked the C.O., coming up.

Briefly Biggles told him.

'Anyway, it's some consolation that you got the Hun,' said the C.O.

'Yes, I got him!' answered Biggles grimly.

'And the photos?'

'You'll have them in time, sir.'

'Cheer up, whispered Mark, as they walked slowly towards the mess. 'It's a beastly business, but it's no good getting down-hearted.

'I know,' replied Biggles. 'It's the sort of thing that's liable to happen to any of us—will happen, I expect, before we're very much older. But it was tough luck for Harris. He'd only been here about five minutes, and now he's gone—gone before he fully realized what he was up against. It's ghastly.'

'It's a war!' retorted Mark. 'Try to forget it, or we'll have you getting nervy. The other Bristols will be here in the morning,' he added, changing the subject.

'Mahoney, of 266, is on the 'phone asking for you,' shouted Toddy, as they passed the squadron office. 'He asked me who was in the Bristol, and when I told him it was you he said he'd like to have a word with you.'

Biggles picked up the receiver. 'Hallo, Mahoney!' he said.

'You'll be saying hallo to the Flanders poppies if you don't watch your step, my lad!' Mahoney told him seriously.

Biggles started. 'What do you know about it?' he asked quickly.

'Know about it? I like that,' growled Mahoney, over the wire. 'Is that all the thanks I get—?'

'Was that you in the Pup?' interrupted Biggles, suddenly understanding.

'What other fool do you suppose would risk being fried alive to get a crazy Bristol out of a hole? You ought to look where you're going. Have you bought the sky, or something?'

'Why, have you sold it?' asked Biggles naïvely.

There was a choking noise at the other end of the wire. Then: 'You watch your step, laddie! We want you in 266. The Old Man has already sent in an application for your transfer, but it looks to me as if he's wasted his time. You'll be cold meat before—'

'Oh, rats!' grinned Biggles. 'I'm just beginning to learn something about this game. You watch your perishing Pup!'

'Well, we're quits now, anyway,' observed Mahoney.

'That's as it should be,' replied Biggles. 'Meet me

tonight in the town and I'll stand you a dinner on the strength of it.'

'I'll be there!' Mahoney told him briskly. 'Bring your wallet—you'll need it!'

# Chapter 12
# The 'Show'

Biggles had just left the fireside circle preparatory to going to bed when Major Paynter entered the officers' mess.

'Pay attention, everybody, please!' said the major, rather unnecessarily, for an expectant hush had fallen on the room. 'A big attack along this entire section of Front has been planned to come into operation in the near future. If weather conditions permit, it may start tomorrow morning. As far as this squadron is concerned, every available machine will leave the ground at dawn, and, flying as low as possible, harass the enemy's troops within the boundaries you'll find marked on the large map in the squadron office. Each machine will carry eight Cooper bombs and work independently, concentrating on preventing the movement of enemy troops on the roads leading to the Front. Every officer will do three patrols of two and a half hours each, daily, until further notice.

'The greatest care must be exercised in order that pilots and observers do not fire on our own troops, who will disclose their positions, as far as they are able, with Very lights and ground strips. Their objective is the high ridge which at present runs about two miles in front of our forward positions. These are the orders, gentlemen. I understand that all British machines not actually engaged in ground strafing will be in the air, either bombing back areas or protecting the low-flying machines from air attack. I need hardly say that the higher command relies implicitly on every officer carrying out his duty to the best possible advantage; the impending battle may have very decisive results on the progress of the War. I think that's all. All previous orders are cancelled. Officers will muster on the tarmac at six-fifty, by which time it should be light enough to see to take off. Good night, everybody.'

A babble of voices broke out as the C.O. left the mess.

'That's the stuff!' declared Mark Way, enthusiastically.

Mabs eyed him coldly. 'Have you done any trench strafing?' he asked. 'I don't mean just emptying your guns into the Lines as you come back from an O.P.*, but as a regular job during one of these big offensives?'

Mark shook his head. 'As a matter of fact, I haven't,' he admitted.

Mabs grinned sarcastically. 'Inside three days you'll be staggering about looking for somewhere to sleep. But there won't be any sleep. You're going to know what hard work it is for the first time in your life. I was in the big spring offensive last year, and the Hun counter-attack that followed it, and by the time it was over I never wanted to see another aeroplane again as long as I lived. You heard what the Old Man said— three shows a day. By this time tomorrow you won't be able to see the ground for crashes, and those that can still fly will have to do the work of the others as well as their own.'

'You're a nice cheerful cove, I must say!' said Biggles.

* Offensive Patrol – actively looking for enemy aircraft to attack.

'Well, you might as well know what we're in for,' returned Mabs, 'and it won't come as a surprise! When you've flown up and down a double artillery barrage for a couple of hours you'll know what flying is.' He rose and made for the door. 'I'm going to hit the sheets,' he announced. 'Get to bed, officers of A Flight, please. It may be the last chance you'll get for some time!'

There was a general move towards the door as he disappeared.

'Tired or not, I've got an appointment with a steak and chips in Rouen tomorrow night,' declared Curtiss, of B Flight, yawning, little dreaming that he was going to bed for the last time in his life.

The tarmac, just before daybreak the following morning was a scene of intense activity. Nine big, drab-coloured Bristol Fighters stood in line in front of the flight sheds, with a swarm of air mechanics bustling about them, adjusting equipment and fitting Cooper bombs on the bomb racks. Propellers were being turned round and engines started up, while the *rat-tat-tat-tat* of machine-guns came from the direction of the gun-testing pits. Biggles' fitter was standing by his machine.

'Everything all right?' asked Biggles.

'All ready, sir,' was the reply.

'Suck in, then!' called Biggles, as he climbed into his cockpit. 'Suck in' was the signal to suck petrol into the cylinders of the engine.

Mark, his gunner, disappeared for a few moments, to return with a Lewis gun, which he adjusted on the Scarff mounting round the rear seat. A mechanic handed up a dozen drums of ammunition.

The engine roared into pulsating life, and Biggles fixed his cap and goggles securely as he allowed it to warm up. Mabs' machine, wearing streamers on wingtips and tail, began to taxi out into position to take off. The others followed. For a minute or two they waddled across the soaking turf like a flock of ungainly geese. Then, with a roar that filled the heavens, they skimmed into the air and headed towards the Lines. They kept no particular formation, but generally followed the direction set by the leader. The work before them did not call for close formation flying.

A watery sun, still low on the eastern horizon, cast a feeble and uncertain light over the landscape, the British reserve trenches, and the war-scarred battle-fields beyond. Patches of ground mist still hung here and there towards the west, but for the most part the ground lay fairly clear. Signs of the activity on the ground were at once apparent. Long lines of marching men, guns, horses, and ammunition wagons were winding like long grey caterpillars towards the Front. A group of queer-looking toad-like monsters slid ponderously over the mud, and Biggles watched them for a moment with interest. He knew they were tanks, the latest engines of destruction.

The ground was dull green, with big bare patches, pock-marked with holes, some of which were still smoking, showing where shells had recently fallen. A clump of shattered trees, blasted into bare, gaunt spectres, marked the site of what had once been a wood. Straight ahead, the green merged into a dull brown sea of mud, flat except for the craters and shell-holes, marked with countless zigzag lines of trenches in which a million men were crouching in readiness for the coming struggle.

Beyond the patch of barren mud the green started again, dotted here and there with roofless houses and shattered villages. In the far distance a river wound like a gleaming silver thread towards the horizon. Spouting columns of flame and clouds of smoke began to appear in the sea of mud; the brown earth was flung high into the air by the bursting shells.

It was a depressing sight, and Biggles, turning his eyes upwards, made out a number of black specks against the pale blue sky. They were the escorting scouts. In one place a dog-fight was raging, and he longed to join it, but the duty on hand forbade it. He nestled a little lower in his cockpit, for the air was cold and damp, so cold that his fingers inside the thick gauntlets were numbed. They had nearly reached the Lines now, so he turned his eyes to Mabs' machine, watching for the signal Very light that would announce the attack. It came, a streak of scarlet flame that described a wide parabola before it began to drop earthwards. Simultaneously the machine from which it had appeared roared down towards the ground. The open formation broke up as each pilot selected his own target and followed.

Biggles saw the welter of mud leaping up at him as he thrust the control-stick forward, eyes probing the barren earth for the enemy. Guns flashed like twinkling stars in all directions. He saw a Pup, racing low, plunge nose-first into the ground to be swallowed up by an inferno of fire.

Charred skeletons of machines lay everywhere, whether friend or foe it was impossible to tell. Lines of white tracer bullets streamed upwards, seeming to move quite slowly. Something smashed against the engine cowling of the Bristol and Biggles ducked instinctively.

*Rat-tat-tat-tat*! Mark's gun began its staccato chatter, but Biggles did not look round to see what he was shooting at; his eyes were on the ground. The sky above would have to take care of itself. The needle of his altimeter was falling steadily; five hundred feet, four hundred, yet he forced it lower, throttle wide open, until the ground flashed past at incredible speed.

He could hear the guns now, a low rumble that reminded him of distant thunder on a summer's day. He heard bullets ripping through the machine somewhere behind him, and kicked hard on right rudder, swerving farther into enemy country. He could still see Mabs' machine some distance ahead and to the left of him, nose tilted down to the ground, a stream of tracer bullets pouring from the forward gun.

Something tapped him sharply on the shoulder and he looked round in alarm. Mark was pointing. Following the outstretched finger he picked out a mud-churned road. A long column of troops in field-grey were marching along it, followed by guns or wagons, he could not tell which.

He swung the Bristol round in its own length, noting with a curious sense of detachment that had he continued flying on his original course for another two seconds the machine must have been blown to smithereens for a jagged sheet of flame split the air; it was too large for an ordinary archie and must have been a shell from a field-gun. Even as it was, the Bristol bucked like a wild horse in the blast.

He tilted his nose down towards the German infantry and watched them over the top of his engine cowling. His hand sought the bomb-toggle. There was a rending clatter as a stream of machine-gun bullets made a colander of his right wing; a wire snapped with a sharp twang, but he did not alter his course.

A cloud of smoke, mixed with lumps of earth, shot

high into the air not fifty yards away, and again the machine rocked. He knew that any second might be his last, but the thought did not worry him. Something at the back of his mind seemed to be saying: 'This is war, war, war!' and he hated it. This was not his idea of flying; it was just a welter of death and destruction.

The enemy troops were less than five hundred yards away, and he saw the leaders pointing their rifles at him. He drew level with the head of the column, and jerked the bomb-toggle savagely. Then he kicked the rudder-bar hard, and at the same time jerked the control-stick back; even so, he was nearly turned upside-down by the force of the explosions, and clods of earth and stones dropped past him from above.

He glanced down. The earth was hidden under a great cloud of smoke. Again he swept down, tore straight along the road, and released the remainder of his bombs. Again he zoomed upwards.

The air was filled with strange noises; the crash of bursting shells, the clatter of his broken wire beating against a strut, and the slap-slap-slap of torn fabric on his wings. Mark's gun was still chattering, which relieved him, for it told him that all was still well with his partner. He half-turned and glanced back at the place where he had dropped his bombs.

There were eight large, smoking holes, around which a number of figures were lying; others were running a away. It struck him that he was some way over the Lines, so he turned again and raced back towards the conspicuous stretch of No Man's Land, across which figures were now hurrying at a clumsy run. Nearer to him a number of grey-coated troops were clustered around a gun, and he sprayed them with a shower of lead as he passed.

He reached the Line, and raced along it, keeping well over the German side to make sure of not hitting any British troops who might have advanced. Burst after burst he poured into the trenches and at· the concrete pill-boxes in which machine-guns nestled.

He passed a Bristol lying upside-down on the ground, and a scout seemingly undamaged. Mark tapped him on the shoulder, turned his thumbs down and pointed to his gun, and Biggles knew that he meant that his ammunition was finished.

'I'll finish mine, too, and get out of this!' he thought. 'I've had about enough.' He took sights on a group of men who were struggling to drag a field-gun to the rear, and they flung themselves flat as the withering hail smote them. Biggles held the Bowden lever* of his gun down until the gun ceased firing, then turned and raced towards his own side of the Lines.

Some Tommies waved to him as he skimmed along not fifty feet above their heads. Mark returned the salutation. The Bristol rocked as it crossed the tracks of heavy shells, and Biggles breathed a sigh of relief as they left the war zone behind them.

Five machines, one of which was Mabs' had already returned when they landed, their crews standing about on the tarmac discussing the 'show.'

'Well, what do you think of it?' asked the flight-commander as Biggles and Mark joined them.

'Rotten!' replied Biggles buffing his arms to restore circulation. He felt curiously exhausted, and began to understand the strain that low flying entails.

'Get filled up, and then rest while you can. We leave the ground again in an hour!' Mabs told them. 'The

---

* The 'trigger' to fire the machine-guns.

enemy are giving way all along the sector and we've got to prevent them bringing up reinforcements.'

'I see,' replied Biggles, without enthusiasm. 'In that case we might as well go down to the mess. Come on, Mark.'

# Chapter 13
# Dirty Work

For three days the attack continued. The squadron lost four machines; two others were unserviceable. The remainder were doing four shows a day, and Biggles staggered about almost asleep on his feet. Life had become a nightmare. Even when he flung himself on his bed at night he could not sleep. In his ears rang the incessant roar of his engine, and his bed seemed to stagger in the bumps of bursting shells, just as the Bristol had done during the day. Mabs had gone to hospital with a bullet through the leg, and new pilots were arriving to replace casualties.

On the fourth morning he made his way, weary and unrefreshed, to the sheds; Mark, who was also feeling the strain, had preceded him. They seldom spoke. They no longer smiled. Mark eyed him grimly as he reached the Bristol and prepared to climb into his seat. 'Why so pale and wan, young airman, prithee why so pale?' he misquoted mockingly.

Biggles looked at him coldly. 'I'm sick and I'm tired,' he said, 'and I've got a nasty feeling that our turn is about due. Just a hunch that something's going to happen, that's all,' he concluded shortly.

'You'll make a good undertaker's clerk when this is over, you cheerful Jonah!' growled Mark.

'Well, come on, let's get on with it. Personally, I'm beyond caring what happens,' replied Biggles, climbing into his seat.

He was thoroughly sick of the war; the futility of it appalled him. He envied the scouts circling high in the sky as they protected the flow-flying trench strafers; they were putting in long hours, he knew, but they did at least escape the everlasting fire from the ground. Above all he sympathized with the swarms of human beings crawling and falling in the sea of mud below.

He took off and proceeded to the sector allotted to the squadron, and where four of its machines now lay in heaps of wreckage. For some minutes he flew up and down the Line, trying to pick out the new British advance posts, for the enemy were still retiring; it would be an easy matter to make a mistake and shoot up the hard-won positions that a few days before had been in German hands.

Archie and field-guns began to cough and bark as he approached the new German front Line, and machine-guns chattered shrilly, but he was past caring about such things. There was no way of avoiding them; they were just evils that had to be borne. One hoped for the best and carried on.

The battle was still raging. It was difficult to distinguish between the British and German troops, they seemed so hopelessly intermingled, so he turned farther into German territory rather than risk making a mistake.

He found a trench in which a swarm of troops were feverishly repairing the parapet, and forced them to seek cover. Then he turned sharp to the right and broke up another working-party; there were no more long convoys to attack, but he found a German staff car and chased it until the driver, taking a corner too fast in his efforts to escape, overturned it in a ditch.

For some minutes he worried a battery of field-guns

that were taking up a new position. Then he turned back towards the Lines—or the stretch of No man's Land that had originally marked the trench system.

He was still half a mile away when it happened. Just what it was he could not say, although Mark swore it was one of the new 'chain' archies—two phosphorus flares joined together by a length of wire that wrapped itself around whatever it struck, and set it on fire. The Bristol lurched sickeningly, and for a moment went out of control.

White-faced, Biggles fought with the control-stick to get the machine on even keel again, for at his height of a thousand feet there was very little margin of safety. He had just got the machine level when a wild yell and a blow on the back of his head brought him round, staring.

Aft of the gunner's cockpit the machine was a raging sheet of flame, which Mark was squirting with his Pyrene extinguisher, but without visible effect. As the extinguisher emptied itself of its contents he flung it overboard and set about beating the flames with his gauntlets.

Biggles did the only thing he could do in the circumstances; he jammed the control-stick forward and dived in a frantic effort to 'blow out' the flames with his slipstream. Fortunately his nose was still pointing towards the Lines, and the effort brought him fairly close, but the flames were only partly subdued and sprang to life again as he eased the control-stick back to prevent the machine from diving into the ground.

The Bristol answered to the controls so slowly that his wheels actually grazed the turf, and he knew at once what had happened. The flames had burnt through to his tail unit destroying the fabric on his elevators, rendering the fore and aft controls useless. He knew it was the end, and, abandoning hope of reaching the Lines, he concentrated his efforts on saving their lives. He thought and acted with a coolness that surprised him.

He tilted the machine on to its side, holding up his nose with the throttle, and commenced to slip wing-tip first towards the ground. Whether he was over British or German territory he neither knew nor cared; he had to get on to the ground or be burnt alive.

A quick glance behind revealed Mark still thrashing the flames with his glove, shielding his face with his left arm. Twenty feet from the ground Biggles switched off everything and unfastened his safety belt. The prop stopped. In the moment's silence he yelled 'Jump!'

He did not wait to see if Mark had followed his instructions, for there was no time, but climbed quickly out of his cockpit on to the wing just as the tip touched the ground. He had a fleeting vision of what seemed to be a gigantic catherine wheel as the machine cartwheeled over the ground, shedding struts and flaming canvas, and then he lay on his back, staring at the sky, gasping for breath.

For a ghastly moment he thought his back was broken, and he struggled to rise in an agony of suspense. He groaned as he fought for breath, really winded for the first time in his life.

Mark appeared by his side and clutched at his shoulders. 'What is it—what is it?' he cried, believing that his partner was mortally hurt.

Biggles could not speak, he could only gasp. Mark caught him by the collar and dragged him into a nearby trench. They fell in a heap at the bottom.

'Not hurt—winded!' choked Biggles. 'Where are we?'

Mark took a quick look over the parapet, and then jumped back, shaking his head. 'Dunno!' he said laconically. 'Can't see anybody. All in the trenches, I suppose.'

Biggles managed to stagger to his feet. 'We'd better lie low till we find out where we are!' he panted. 'What a mess! Let's get in here!' He nodded towards the gaping mouth of a dugout.

Footsteps were squelching through the mud towards them, and they dived into the dugout, Biggles leading. He knew instantly that the place was already occupied, but in the semi-darkness he could not for a moment make out who or what it was. Then he saw, and his eyes went round with astonishment. It was a German, cowering in a corner.

'*Kamerad! Kamerad*\*!' cried the man, with his arms above his head.

'All right, we shan't hurt you,' Biggles assured him, kicking a rifle out of the way. 'It looks as if we're all in the same boat, but if you try any funny stuff I'll knock your block off!'

The German stared at him wide-eyed, but made no reply.

There was a great noise of splashing and shouting in the trench outside; a shell landed somewhere close at hand with a deafening roar, and a trickle of earth fell from the ceiling.

Mark grabbed Biggles' arm as a line of feet passed the entrance; there was no mistaking the regulation German boots, but if confirmation was needed, the harsh, guttural voices supplied it. They both breathed

* German: Friend! Friend!

more freely as the feet disappeared and the noise receded.

'It looks as if we've landed in the middle of the war,' observed Biggles, with a watchful eye on the Boche, who still crouched in his corner as if dazed—as indeed he was.

'What are we going to do? We can't spend the rest of the war in here,' declared Mark.

'I wouldn't if I could,' replied Biggles. 'But it's no use doing anything in a hurry.'

'Some Boche troops will come barging in here in a minute and hand us a few inches of cold steel; they're not likely to be particular after that hullaballoo outside.'

Hullaballoo was a good word; it described things exactly. There came a medley of sounds in which shouts, groans, rifle and revolver shots and the reports of bursting hand-grenades could be distinguished.

'It sounds as if they're fighting all round us,' muttered Mark anxiously.

'As long as they stay round us I don't mind,' Biggles told him. 'It'll be when they start crowding in here that the fun will begin!'

Heavy footsteps continued to splash up and down the communication trench. Once a German officer stopped outside the dugout and Biggles held his breath. The Boche seemed to be about to enter, but changed his mind and went off at a run.

Then there came the sound of a sharp scuffle in the trench and a German N.C.O. leapt panting into the dugout. He glanced around wildly as the two airmen started up, and broke into a torrent of words. He was splashed with mud from head to foot, and bleeding from a cut in the cheek. He carried a rifle, but made no attempt to use it.

'Steady!' cried Biggles, removing the weapon from the man's unresisting hands. The Boche seemed to be trying to tell them something, pointing and gesticulating as he spoke.

'I think he means that his pals outside are coming in,' said Biggles with a flash of inspiration. 'Well, there's still plenty of room.'

'Anybody in there?' cried a voice from the doorway.

Before Biggles could speak the German had let out a yell.

'Just share this among you, but don't quarrel over it!' went on the same voice.

'This' was a Mills bomb* that pitched on to the floor between them.

There was a wild stampede for the door; Biggles slipped, and was the last out. He had just flung himself clear as the dugout went up with a roar that seemed to burst his eardrums. He looked up to see the point of a bayonet a few inches from his throat; behind it was the amazed face of a British Tommy.

The soldier let out a whistle of surprise. More troops came bundling round the corner of the trench, an officer among them. 'Hallo, what's all this?' he cried, halting in surprise.

'Don't let us get in your way,' Biggles told him quickly. 'Go on with the war!'

'What might you be doing here?'

'We might be blackberrying, but we're not. Again, we might be playing croquet, or roller-skating, but we're not. We're just waiting.'

* Hand grenade.

'Waiting! What for?'

'For you blokes to come along, of course. I've got a date with a bath and a bar of soap, so I'll be getting along.'

'You'd better get out of this,' the other told him, grinning, as he prepared to move on.

'That's what I thought!' declared Biggles. 'Perhaps you'd tell us the easiest and safest way?'

The other laughed. 'Sure I will,' he said. 'Keep straight on down that sap* we've just come up and you'll come to our old Line. It's all fairly quiet now.'

'So I've noticed,' murmured Biggles. 'Come on, Mark, let's get back to where we belong.'

'What about the Bristol?' asked Mark.

'What about it? Are you thinking of carrying it back with you? I didn't stop to examine it closely, as you may have noticed, but I fancy that kite, or what's left of it, will take a bit of sticking together again. We needn't worry about that. The repair section will collect it, if it's any good. Come on!'

Three hours later, weary and smothered with mud, they arrived back at the aerodrome, having got a lift part of the way on a lorry.

Mabs, on crutches, was standing at the door of the mess. 'Where have you been?' he asked.

'Ha! Where haven't we!' replied Biggles, without stopping.

'Where are you off to now in such a hurry?' called Mabs after him.

'To bed, laddie,' Biggles told him enthusiastically. 'To bed, till you find me another aeroplane.'

---

* Part of the trench system to protect moving troops from enemy gunfire.

# Chapter 14
# The Pup's First Flight

When the time came for Biggles to leave his old squadron and say good-bye to Mark Way, his gunner, he found himself a good deal more depressed than he had thought possible; he realized for the first time just how attached to them he had become. Naturally, he had been delighted to join a scout squadron, for he had always wanted to fly single-seaters. The presence of his old pal, Mahoney, who was flight-commander, prevented any awkwardness or strangeness amongst his new comrades, and he quickly settled down to routine work.

The commanding officer, Major Mullen, of his new squadron, No. 266, stationed at Maranique, allowed none of his pilots to take unnecessary risks if he could prevent it. So he gave Biggles ten days in which to make himself proficient in the handling of the single-seater Pup that had been allocated to him.

Biggles was told to put in as much flying-time as possible, but on no account to cross the Lines, and he found that the enforced rest from eternal vigilance did him a power of good, for his nerves had been badly jarred by his late spell of trench strafing.

By the end of a week he was thoroughly at home with the Pup, and ready to try his hand at something more serious than beetling up and down behind his own Lines. He had noted all the outstanding landmarks around Maranique, and once or twice he accompanied

Mahoney on practice formation flights. His flight-commander had expressed himself satisfied, and Biggles begged to be allowed to do a 'show.'

His chance came soon. Lorton was wounded in the arm and packed off to hospital, and Biggles was detailed to take his place the following morning. But the afternoon before this decision took effect he had what he regarded as a slice of luck that greatly enhanced his reputation with the C.O., and the officers of the squadron, as well as bringing his name before Wing Headquarters.

He had set off on a cross-country flight to the Aircraft Repair Section at St Omer, to make inquiries for the equipment officer about a machine that had gone back for reconditioning, when he spotted a line of white archie bursts at a very high altitude—about 15,000 feet, he judged it to be.

He was flying at about 5,000 a few miles inside the Lines at the time, and he knew that the archie was being fired by British guns, which could only mean that the target was an enemy aircraft. It seemed to be flying on a course parallel with the Lines, evidently on a photographic or scouting raid.

Without any real hope of overtaking it he set off in pursuit, and, knowing that sooner or later the German would have to turn to reach his own side he steered an oblique course that would bring him between the raider and the Lines. In a few minutes he had increased his height to 10,000 feet, and could distinctly see the enemy machine. It was a Rumpler two-seater*. He had no doubt that the observer had spotted him, but the

* German two-seater biplane used for general duties as well as fighting.

machine continued on its way as if the pilot was not concerned, possibly by reason of his superior altitude.

Biggles began to edge a little nearer to the Lines, and was not much more than a thousand feet below the Hun, when, to his disgust, it turned slowly and headed off on a diagonal course towards No Man's Land.

The Pup was climbing very slowly now, and it was more with hope than confidence that Biggles continued the pursuit. Then the unexpected happened. The enemy pilot turned sharply and dived straight at him, but opened fire at much too great a range for it to be effective, although he held the burst for at least a hundred rounds. Biggles had no idea where the bullets went, but he saw the Hun, at the end of his dive, zoom nearly back to his original altitude, and then make for home at full speed. But he had lingered just a trifle too long.

Biggles climbed up into the 'blind' spot under the enemy's elevators, and although the range was still too long for good shooting, he opened fire. Whether any of his shots took effect he was unable to tell, but the Hun was evidently alarmed, for the Rumpler made a quick turn out of the line of fire. It was a clumsy turn, and cost him two hundred precious feet of height at a moment when height was all-important. Moreover, it did not give the gunner in the back seat a chance to use his weapon.

Biggles seized his opportunity and fired one of the longest bursts he ever fired in his life. The German gunner swayed for a moment, then collapsed in his cockpit. Then, to his intense satisfaction, Biggles saw the propeller of the other machine slow down and stop, whereupon the enemy pilot shoved his nose down and dived for the Lines, now not more than two or three miles away.

It was a move that suited Biggles well, for the Rumpler was defenceless from the rear, so he tore down in hot pursuit, guns blazing, knowing that the Hun was at his mercy. The enemy pilot seemed to realize this for he turned broadside on and threw up his hands in surrender.

Biggles was amazed, for although he had heard of such things being done it was his first experience of it. He ceased firing at once and took up a position on the far side of the disabled machine; he did not trust his prisoner very much, for he guessed that he would, if the opportunity arose, make a dash for the Lines—so near, and yet so far away. Biggles therefore shepherded him down like a well-trained sheep-dog bringing in a stray lamb.

He could not really find it in his heart to blame the enemy pilot for surrendering. The fellow had had to choose between being made prisoner and certain death, and had chosen captivity as the lesser of the two evils. 'Death before capture,' is no doubt an admirable slogan, but it loses some of its attractiveness in the face of cold facts.

The German landed about four miles from Maranique and was prevented by a crowd of Tommies from purposely injuring his machine. Biggles landed in a near-by field and hurried to the scene, arriving just as the C.O. and several officers of the squadron, who had witnessed the end of the combat from the aerodrome, dashed up in the squadron car. It was purely a matter of luck that Major Raymond, of Wing Headquarters, who had been on the aerodrome talking with Major Mullen, was with them.

He smiled at Biggles approvingly. 'Good show!' he said. 'We've been trying to get hold of one of these machines intact for a long time.'

Biggles made a suitable reply and requested that the crew of the Rumpler should be well cared for. The pilot, whose name they learnt was Schmidt, looked morose and bad-tempered—as, indeed, he had every cause to be; the observer had been wounded in the chest and was unconscious.

They were taken away under escort in an ambulance, and that was the end of the affair. Biggles never learned what happened to them.

The offensive patrol for which he had been detailed in place of Lorton turned out to be a more difficult business. It began quite simply. He took his place in a formation of five machines, and for an hour or more they cruised up and down their sector without incident, except, of course, for the inevitable archie. Then the trouble started around a single machine.

Several times they had passed a British machine— an R.E.8*—circling over the same spot, obviously engaged in doing a 'shoot' for the artillery, and Biggles was able to sympathize with the pilot. He watched the circling 'plane quite dispassionately for a moment or two, glanced away, and then turned back to the R.E.8. It was no longer there.

He stared—and stared harder. Then he saw it, three thousand feet below, plunging earthwards in flames. Screwing his head round a little farther he made out three German Albatros streaking for home. They must have made their attack on the two-seater under the

* British two-seater biplane designed for reconnaissance and artillery observation purposes.

175

very noses of the Pups, and, well satisfied with the result of their work, were removing themselves from the vicinity without loss of time. But they were well below the Pups, and Mahoney, who was leading, tore down after them in a screaming dive, closely followed by the rest of the formation.

As they went down, something—he could not say what—made Biggles, who was an outside flank man, look back over his shoulder. There was really no reason why he should but the fact that he did so provided another example of the uncanny instinct he was developing for detecting the presence of Huns.

The sight that met his gaze put all thought of the escaping Albatroses clean out of his head. A German High Patrol of not fewer than twenty Triplanes were coming down like the proverbial ton of bricks.

Biggles' first idea was to warn Mahoney of the impending onslaught, but, try as he would, he could not overtake his leader. Yet he knew that if the Huns were allowed to come on in a solid formation on their tails, most of them would be wiped out before they knew what had hit them. He could think of only one thing to do, and he did it, although it did not occur to him that he was making something very much like a deliberate sacrifice of his own life. That he was not killed was due no doubt to the very unexpectedness of his move, which temporarily disorganized the Hun circus*. He swung the Pup round on its axis, cocked up his nose to face the oncoming Huns, and let drive at the whole formation.

The leader swerved just in time to avoid head-on

* Formations of German fighter aircraft usually named after their leader e.g. Richthofen circus.

collision. His wing tip missed Biggles by inches. The lightning turn threw the others out of their places, and they, too, had to swerve wildly to avoid collision with their leader.

Biggles held his breath as the cloud of gaudy-coloured enemy machines roared past him, so close that he could see the faces of the pilots staring at him. Yet not a bullet touched his machine. Nor did he hit one of them—at least, as far as he could see.

The Huns pulled up, hesitating, to see if their leader was going on after the other Pups or staying to slay the impudent one. At that moment, Mahoney, missing one of his men, looked back. In that quick flash it must have seemed to him that Biggles was taking on the entire German Air Force single-handed, and he hung his Pup on its prop as he headed back towards the mêlée.

He knew what Biggles himself did not know; that the German formation was the formidable Richthofen circus, led by the famous Baron himself, his conspicuous all-red Fokker triplane even then pouring lead at the lone Pup.

Biggles could never afterwards describe the sensation of finding himself in the middle of Germany's most noted air fighters. He was, as he put it, completely flummoxed. He merely shot at every machine that swam across his sights, wondering all the while why his Pup did not fall to pieces.

The reason why it did not was probably that put forward by Captain Albert Ball, V.C., in defence of his method of plunging headlong into the middle of an enemy 'circus'. Such tactics temporarily disorganized the enemy formation, and the pilots dared not shoot as freely as they would normally for fear of hitting or colliding with their own men. Be that as it may, in the opening stage of the uproar Biggles' Pup was hit less than a dozen times, and in no place was it seriously damaged.

By the time the Huns sorted themselves out Mahoney and the other three Pups were on the scene. Even so, the gallant action of the leader in taking on such overwhelming odds would not have availed had it not been for the opportune arrival of a second formation of Pups and a squadron of Bristols—Biggles' old squadron, although he did not know it. That turned the tide.

The huge dog-fight lost height quickly, as such affairs nearly always did, and was soon down to five thousand feet. It was impossible for any pilot to know exactly what was happening; each man picked an opponent and stuck to him as long as he could. If he lost him he turned to find another.

That was precisely what Biggles did, and it was utterly out of the question for him to see if he shot anyone down. If a machine at which he was shooting fell out of the fight, someone else was shooting at him before he could determine whether his Hun was really hit or merely shamming.

He saw more than one machine spinning, and two or three smoke-trails where others had gone down in flames. He also saw a Bristol and a triplane that had collided whirling down together in a last ghastly embrace.

At four thousand feet he pulled out, slightly dizzy, and tried to make out what was happening. He picked out Mahoney by his streamers, not far away, and noted that the fight seemed to be breaking up by mutual consent. Odd machines were still circling round each other, but each leader was trying to rally his men.

Mahoney, in particular, was trying frantically to attract the attention of the surviving members of his patrol, for the fight had drifted over German territory and it was high time to see about getting nearer the Lines.

Biggles took up position on Mahoney's flank, and presently another Pup joined them. Of the other two there was no sign.

The Bristols were already streaming back towards home in open formation and Mahoney followed them. They passed the charred remains of the R.E.8 that had been the cause of all the trouble, gaunt and black in the middle of No Man's Land. They reached the Lines and turned to fly parallel with them.

Their patrol was not yet finished, but all the machines had been more or less damaged, so after waiting a few minutes to give the other two Pups a chance of joining them if they were still in the air, they turned towards the aerodrome. It was as well they did, for Biggles' engine began to give trouble, although by nursing it he managed to reach home.

They discovered that the squadron had already been informed of the dog-fight, artillery observers along the Line reporting that five British and seven German machines had been seen to fall. There seemed little chance of the two missing Pups turning up. The surviving members of the patrol hung about the tarmac for some time, but they did not return. That evening they were reported 'missing'.

# Chapter 15
# Caught Napping

'How often do you run into shows as big as that?'
Biggles asked Mahoney, at lunch.

'Oh, once in a while! Not every day, thank goodness!'
replied Mahoney. 'Why?'

'I was just wondering.' Biggles ruminated a minute
or two. 'You know, laddie, we do a lot of sneering at
the Huns, and say they've no imagination.'

'What about it?'

'Well, I'm not so sure about it, that's all.'

'What! You turning pro-Hun, or something?'

'But it seems to me they're using their brains more
than we are.'

'How?'

'We just fly and fight, and that's all we think about.'

'What do you mean?'

'Well, in the first place, the Huns mostly stay over
their own side of the Lines, knowing that we'll go over
to them. How often do you see a big formation of Hun
scouts over this side? Mighty seldom. That isn't just
luck. That's a clever policy laid down by the German
higher authority.

'Then there's this grouping of their hot-stuff pilots
into "circuses". And the way that bunch arrived this
morning wasn't a fluke—you can bet your life on that.
It was all very neatly arranged. Can't you see the idea?
The old R.E.8 was the meat; three Huns go down after
it just when they knew we were about due back, and

that we were certain to follow them—go down after them. It pans out just as they expected, and off they go, taking us slap under the big mob who were sitting up topsides waiting for us. Although I say it as shouldn't, it was a bit of luck I happened to look back. As it turned out, the Hun plan went off at half-cock, but it might not have done. That's why I say these tripe-hound merchants are flying with their heads.'

'Well, I can't stop 'em, if that's what you mean.'

'I never suggested you could, did I? But there's nothing to prevent us exercising our grey matter a bit, is there?'

'You're right, kid,' joined in Maclaren, another flight-commander, who had overheard the conversation. 'You're absolutely dead right!'

'I think I am,' replied Biggles frankly. 'War-flying is too new for strategy to be laid down in the text-books; we've got to work it out for ourselves.'

'What's all this?' asked Major Mullen, who had entered the room and caught the last part of the conversation.

Briefly, Maclaren gave him the gist of the conversation. The C.O. nodded as he listened, then he looked at Biggles.

'What do you suggest?' he asked.

'Well, sir, it seems to me we might have a word with the other scout squadrons about it, and work out a scheme. At present we all do our shows independently, so to speak, but if we could work out a plot together— an ambush, if you like, like the Huns did this morning—we might give the tripe merchants over the way something to think about. If we did happen to catch them properly it would have the effect of making them chary about tackling odd machines for a bit. They'd always be worried for fear they were heading into a trap.'

'That sounds like common-sense to me,' agreed the C.O. 'All right, Bigglesworth, you work out the plot and submit it to me, and I'll see what can be done about it. But we shall have to keep it to ourselves. If Wing heard about it they'd probably knock it on the head, on the ground that such methods were irregular, although perhaps I shouldn't say that.'

'We all know it, sir, without you saying it, anyway!' grinned Biggles.

After dinner he sat down with a pencil and paper to work out his 'plot', and before he went to bed he had the scheme cut and dried. It was fairly simple, as he explained to the others in the morning, and based upon the methodical habits of the enemy, and the assumption that the other scout squadrons would co-operate.

'From my own personal observation,' he explained, 'the Huns—by which I mean the big circuses, particularly the Richthofen crowd which is stationed at Douai—do two big shows a day. Sometimes, when things are lively, they do three. They always do a big evening show, one that finishes about sunset, just before they pack up for the night. Very well. It gets dark now about half past six. That means that the Huns must leave the ground on their last show between four and four-thirty. Now, if they have a dog-fight they don't all go home together, but do the same as we do—trickle home independently, in twos and threes. They did that this morning. I saw them. Now, I reckon that the last place they'd expect big trouble would be on the way home, near their own aerodrome, and that's where I propose to spring the surprise packet.

'To carry out my idea with maximum safety, it would

need three squadrons—four would be even better. This is the way of it: at four o'clock one squadron pushes along to some prearranged sector of the Line, and makes itself a nuisance—shooting up the Hun trenches, or anything to make itself conspicuous. The Hun artillery observers will see this, of course, and are almost certain to ring up the Richthofen headquarters to say there is a lot of aerial activity on their bit of Front. It stands to reason that the circus will at once make for that spot; give them their due they don't shirk a rough-house. Right-ho. The squadron that is kicking up the fuss keeps its eyes peeled for the Huns. It'll pretend not to see them until they're fairly close. Then they scatter, making towards home. The Huns are almost bound to split up to chase them, and our fellows can please themselves whether or not they stay and fight. But they must remember that their job is to split up the Huns.

'As soon as this business is well under way, the other two—or three—squadrons will take off, climb to the limit of their height, and head over the Lines on a course that'll bring them round by Douai. Get the idea? The Huns will think the show's over and come drifting home in small parties, without keeping very careful watch. We shall be there to meet them, and we shall have height of them. Huns on the ground may see us, but they won't be able to warn the fellows in the air. In that way, if the scheme works out as I've planned it, we shall catch these pretty birds bending when they're least expecting it. That's all. If the worst comes to the worst we should be no worse off than we are on an ordinary show, when we always seem to be outnumbered. At the best, we shall give the Huns a shock they'll remember for some time. What do you think about it, sir?'

'I certainly think there is a good deal to be said for it,' agreed the major. 'I'll speak to the other squadrons. Perhaps your old squadron would oblige by kicking up the fuss with their Bristols. Then, if 287, with their S.E.s, and 231, and ourselves, get behind the Huns we shall at least be sure of meeting them on even terms, even if they do happen to keep in one formation. All right; leave it to me. I'll see what I can do.'

It took nearly a week of conferences to bring the scheme to a stage where it was ready to be tried out, but at last, burning with impatience and excitement, Biggles made his way to the sheds with the others for the big show.

Watches had been carefully synchronized on the instrument boards of all pilots taking part, and every possible precaution taken to prevent a miscarriage of plans. Major Paynter, of Biggles' old squadron, had agreed to send every Bristol he could raise into the air, to make itself as obnoxious as possible at a given spot, at the arranged time.

The others were to rendezvous over Maranique in 'layer' formation (machines flying in tiers) at four-thirty—No. 266 Squadron at ten thousand feet, 231 Squadron at thirteen thousand feet, and 287 Squadron at sixteen thousand feet. Major Mullen was leading the whole show on a roundabout course that would bring them behind the enemy, assuming, of course, that the enemy circus would concentrate in the area where the Bristols were to lure them.

Three-quarters of an hour later, Major Mullen swung round in a wide circle that brought them actually within sight of Douai, the headquarters of the most famous fighting scouts in the German Imperial Air Service. Biggles never forgot the scene. The sun was low in the west, sinking in a crimson glow. A slight mist was rising, softening the hard outlines of roads, woods, hedges, and fields below, as though seen through a piece of lilac-tinted gauze. To the east, the earth was already bathed in deep purple and indigo shadows.

No enemy aircraft were in sight, not even on the ground, as they turned slowly over the peaceful scene to seek the enemy in the glowing mists of the west. They had not long to wait.

Biggles saw two Triplanes, flying close together, slowly materialize in the mist, like goldfish swimming in a pale milky liquid. The enemy pilots were gliding down, probably with their eyes on the aerodrome, and it is doubtful if they even saw the full force of British machines that had assembled to overwhelm them. Biggles felt almost sorry for them as Major Mullen shook his wings, as a signal, and the nine Pups roared down on the unsuspecting Triplanes.

It was impossible to say which machine actually scored most hits. One Triplane broke up instantly. The other jerked upwards as if the pilot had been mortally wounded, turned slowly over on to its back, plunged downwards in a vicious spin with its engine full on and bored into the ground two miles below.

The Pups resumed formation and returned to their original height and course. Another Triplane emerged from the mist, but something evidently caught the pilot's eye—perhaps the sun flashing on a wing—and he looked upwards. He acted with the speed of light and flung his machine into a spin to seek safety on the ground. The Pups did not follow, for the Triplane was far below them and they would not risk getting too low so far over the Line.

A few minutes later a straggling party of seven machines appeared, followed at a distance by five more. It was obvious from the loose formation in which they were flying that they considered themselves quite secure so near their nest. They, too, must have been looking at the ground, and Biggles was amazed at the casual manner in which they continued flying straight on with death literally raining on them from the sky.

He picked out his man and poured in a long burst of bullets before the pilot had time to realize his peril. A cloud of smoke, quickly followed by flame, burst from the Triplane's engine. Biggles zoomed upwards and looked back. The seven machines had disappeared. Two long pillars of smoke marked the going of at least two of them.

How many had actually fallen he was unable to tell. Away to the left the other five Triplanes were milling around in a circle, hotly pursued by the second squadron of Pups, whilst the S.E.s were sitting slightly above, waiting to pounce on any enemy machine that tried to leave the combat.

It was the last real surprise of the day, not counting a lonely straggler that they picked up near the Lines and which they had sent down under a tornado of lead. Biggles quite definitely felt sorry for that pilot. Two or three more machines had appeared while the main combat was in progress, but the dog-fight had lost height, and they saw it at once, so were able to escape by spinning down.

The engagement really resolved itself into the sort of show that Biggles had anticipated. The enemy had been caught napping, and many of them had paid the penalty. The three squadrons of British machines reached the Line at dusk, without a single casualty and almost unscathed. One machine only, an S.E.5 of 287b Squadron, had to break formation near the Lines with a piece of archie shrapnel in its engine. Except for that, the Pups and S.E.s returned home in a formation as perfect as when they started.

Congratulations flew fast and furious when Major Mullen's squadron landed, for it had unquestionably been one of the most successful 'shows' ever undertaken by the squadron. A quick comparison of notes revealed that seven Triplanes had been destroyed for certain, either having been seen to crash or fall in flames. How many others had been damaged, or enemy pilots wounded, they had, of course, no means of knowing.

But the most successful part of the issue was that not a single British machine had been lost. Major Mullen thanked Biggles personally and congratulated him on his initiative, in the Squadron Office, in front of the other pilots.

'Well, I'm glad it has turned out as I hoped it would, sir. We've given the Huns something to talk about in mess tonight. Maybe they won't be quite so chirpy in future!' observed Biggles modestly.

The party was about to break up when Watt Tyler, the Recording Officer, hurried into the room waving a strip of paper above his head; his eyes were shining as he laid it on the C.O.'s desk.

Major Mullen read the signal, and a grim smile spread over his face. 'Gentlemen,' he said, 'I am glad to be able to tell you that we shall be able to give the Huns something else to think about before long; the squadron is to be equipped with the long-secret super-scout at last. Our Pups are to be replaced by Sopwith Camels*.'

A moment's silence greeted this important announcement.

It was broken by Biggles. 'Fine!' he said. 'Now we'll show the Huns what's what!'

* Single seater fighter aircraft, with two fixed machine guns firing through the propeller. A more powerful development of the Pup but tricky to fly.

# Chapter 16
# The Yellow Hun

No. 266 Squadron, R.F.C., at Maranique, had been equipped with Sopwith Camels for nearly a month, and with the improved equipment the pilots were showing the enemy—as Biggles had put it—what was what. Except for two pilots who had been killed whilst learning to fly the very tricky Camels, things had gone along quite smoothly, and Biggles had long ago settled down as a regular member of the squadron. Indeed, he was beginning to regard himself as something of a veteran.

It was a warm spring afternoon, and as he sat sunning himself on the veranda after an uneventful morning patrol he felt on good terms with himself and the world in general. 'Where's the Old Man?' he suddenly asked Mahoney, who had just returned from the sheds, where he had been supervising the timing of his guns.

'Dunno,' was the reply. 'I think he's gone off to Amiens, or somewhere, for a conference. Oh, here he comes now. He looks pretty grim. I'll bet something's in the wind!'

The C.O. joined them on the veranda. He looked at Biggles as if he were about to speak, but he changed his mind and looked through the open window into the ante-room, where several other officers were sitting. He called to them to come outside.

'I've a bit of news—or perhaps I should say a story,' he began, when everyone had assembled. 'It will be of particular interest to you, Bigglesworth.'

Biggles stared. 'To me, sir?' he cried in surprise.

'Yes. You haven't been over to your old squadron lately, have you?'

Biggles shook his head. 'No, sir, I haven't!' he said wonderingly.

'Then you haven't heard about Way?'

'Mark Way!' Biggles felt his face going white. Mark had been his gunner and great friend when they were together in 169 Squadron. 'Why, he isn't—?' He could not bring himself to say the fatal word.

'No, he isn't dead, but he'll never fly again,' said the C.O. quitely.

Biggles' lips turned dry. 'But how—what?' he stammered.

'I've just seen him,' went on the C.O. 'I had to attend a conference in Amiens, and I ran into Major Paynter, who was going to the hospital to see Way. He told me about it. Way is now en route for England. He'll never come back.'

'But I don't understand!' exclaimed Biggles. 'He was due to go home when I came here; he was going to get his pilot's wings. In fact I thought he'd actually gone.'

'That's right,'said the C.O. 'He packed up his kit and set off, but apparently he was kept hanging about the port of embarkation for some time. Then the Huns made their big show, and he with everyone else who was waiting to go home was recalled to his squadron.'

'But why didn't he let me know?' cried Biggles.

'He hadn't time. He arrived back just in time to be sent on a show with Captain Mapleton. They didn't return, and were posted missing the same day. Way arrived back yesterday, having crawled into our front line trench, minus his right hand and an eye.'

'Good heavens!'

'He asked to be remembered to you, and said he would write to you as soon as he was able, from home.'

'But what happened, sir?'

'I'm coming to that. In point of fact, what I'm about to say was intended for you alone—his last message—but I think it is a matter that concerns everyone, so I shall make no secret of it.' The C.O.'s face hardened. 'This is what he told me,' he continued. 'As I said, he was flying with Mapleton—'

'Where's Mapleton now?' broke in Biggles.

'Mapleton was killed. But let me continue.'

Biggles gripped the rail of the veranda, but said nothing.

'He was, I say, acting as gunner for Mapleton,' went on the C.O. 'They were attacked by a big bunch of enemy machines, near Lille. By a bit of bad luck they got their engine shot up in the early stages of the fight, and had to go down, and the Hun who had hit them followed them down, shooting at them all the time. Their prop had stopped, and they waved to him to show that they were going to land, but he continued shooting at them while they were, so to speak helpless.'

A stir ran through the listeners.

'It was at this juncture that Way was struck in the eye by a piece of glass; but he didn't lose consciousness. Mapleton made a perfect landing in spite of the damage the machine had suffered and it looked as if they would both escape with their lives—as indeed they should have done. But the Hun thought differently. Thank Heaven they are not all like him. He deliberately shot them up after they had landed—emptied his guns at them.'

'The unspeakable hog!' Biggles ground the words out through clenched teeth.

'Mapleton fell dead with a bullet through his head. Way's wrist was splintered by an explosive bullet, and his hand was subsequently amputated in a German field hospital. Three days ago, on the eve of being transferred to a prison camp, he escaped, and managed to work his way through the Lines. He arrived in a state of collapse, and Major Paynter thinks that it was only the burning desire to report the flagrant breach of the accepted rules of air fighting, and the passion for revenge, which he knew would follow, that kept him on his feet. The Hun seems to have been a Hun in every sense of the word; he actually went and gloated over Way in hospital.'

'Mark didn't learn his name, by any chance?' muttered Biggles harshly.

'Yes. It's Von Kraudil, of Jagdstaffel Seventeen.'

'What colour was his kite?' asked Biggles, his hands twitching curiously.

'Yes, that's more important, for by this we shall be able to recognize him.' The C.O. spoke softly, but very distinctly. 'He flies a sulphur-yellow Albatros with a black nose, and a black diamond painted on each side of the fuselage.'

'I've seen that skunk!' snarled McLaren, starting up. 'Yellow is a good colour for him. I'll—'

The C.O. held up his hands as a babble of voices broke out. 'Yes, I know,' he said quickly. 'Most of us have seen this machine; it's been working on this part of the Front for some time, so I hope it is still about.'

'I'll nail his yellow hide up in the ante-room!' declared Mahoney.

'Such methods would have been in order a few hundred years ago, but we can hardly do that sort of thing to-day,' smiled the C.O. 'All the same, a piece of yellow fuselage might look well—'

'Leave that to me, sir!' interrupted Biggles. 'Mark Way was my—'

'Not likely! No fear!' a chorus of protests from the other pilots overwhelmed him, and the C.O. was again compelled to call for silence. 'It's up to everyone to get him,' he went on. 'And the officer who gets him may have a week's leave!'

'I'll get that leave—to go and see Mark!' declared Biggles.

'All right, gentlemen, that's all,' concluded the C.O.

'He says that's all!' muttered Biggles to Mahoney. 'It isn't, not by a long shot!'

Under the influence of his cold fury his first idea was to rush off into the air and stay there until he had found the yellow Hun. Instead, he controlled himself, and made his way to his room to think the matter over. He was in a curious state of nerves, for the news had stirred him as nothing had ever done before. He was depressed by the tragic end of the man whom he still regarded as he best friend, and with whom he had had so many thrilling adventures. And tears actually came into his eyes when he thought of his old flight-commander, Mapleton, whom they all called Mabs, one of the most brilliant and fearless fighters in France.

He was suffering from a mild form of shock, although he did not know it, and behind it all was the burning desire for vengeance. That by his cold-blooded action the yellow Hun had signed his own death warrant Biggles did not doubt, for not a single member of either his old squadron or his present one would rest until Mabs had been avenged. But Biggles wanted to shoot the man down himself. He wanted to see his tracer bullets boring into that yellow cockpit. The mere fact that the Hun had fallen under the guns of someone else would not give him the same satisfaction. In fact, as he pondered the matter, he began to feel afraid that someone else might shoot the Hun down before he could come to grips with him.

The matter was chiefly his concern, after all, he reasoned. Mark had been his friend, and Mabs his flight-commander. No doubt machines were already scouring the sky for the murderer—for that was almost what the action of shooting at a machine on the ground amounted to.

'Well,' he muttered at last, 'if I'm going to get this hound I'd better see about it!'

He rose, washed, picked up his flying kit, and made his way to the sheds. 'Where's everybody?' he asked Smyth, the flight-sergeant.

'In the air, sir.'

'Ah, I might have known it,' breathed Biggles. He was so accustomed to the sound of aero engines that he had hardly noticed the others taking off. But he knew only too well why the aerodrome was deserted, and he hastened to his own machine.

Within five minutes he was in his Camel, heading for the Lines. He hardly expected to find Von Kraudil cruising about the sky alone; that would be asking too much. He would certainly be flying with a formation of single-seaters. If that were so, he, Biggles, would stand a better chance of finding his man by flying alone, as the Huns would certainly attack the lone British machine if they saw him, whereas they might refuse to engage the others if they were flying together.

In any case, a wide area would have to be combed, for the enemy machines operated far to the east and west of their base. So in order to expedite matters, Biggles deliberately asked for trouble by thrusting deep into the enemy country. Ground observers could hardly fail to see him, and would, he hoped, report his presence to the nearest squadrons, in accordance with their usual practice.

Far and wide he searched, but curiously enough the sky appeared to be deserted. Once he saw a formation of three Camels, and a little later three more, but he did not join them. Never had he seen the sky so empty.

At the end of two hours he was forced to return to the aerodrome without having seen an enemy aircraft of any sort, and consequently without firing a shot. On the ground he learned that the other machines had already returned, refuelled, and taken off again.

Then he had a stroke of luck—or so he regarded it. His tanks had been filled, and he was about to take off again, when Watt Tyler rushed out of the Squadron Office and hailed him. 'You're looking for that yellow devil, I suppose?' he inquired shortly.

'Who else do you suppose I'd be looking for?' replied Biggles coldly.

'All right, keep your hair on! I was only going to tell you that forward gunner observers have just reported that a large enemy formation has just crossed our Lines in pursuit of two Camels.'

'Where?'

'Up by Passchendaele.'

Biggles did not stop to thank Watt for the information. He thrust the throttle open, and his wheels left the ground he soared upwards in a steep climbing turn in the direction of the well-known town.

He saw the dog-fight afar off. At least, he saw the archie bursts that clustered thickly about the isolated machines, and he roared towards the spot on full throttle, peering ahead round his windscreen to try to identify the combatants. Presently he was able to make out what had happened, for the two Camels that had been pursued had turned, and were now hard at it, assisted by half a dozen Bristols. There seemed to be about twelve or fourteen Huns, all Albatroses. He guessed that they had chased the Camels over the Line, and, on turning, found their retreat cut off by the Bristols. That, in fact, was exactly what had happened.

The enemy machines were still too far away for their colours to be distinguished, but as he drew nearer he saw one, dark blue in colour, break out of the fight some distance below him and streak for the Line.

'Not so fast!' growled Biggles, as he altered his course slightly and tore down after the escaping Hun. The enemy pilot, who did not even see him, was leaning out of his cockpit on the opposite side of the fuselage, looking back at the dogfight as if he expected the other machines to follow, and wondered why they did not. For a few seconds he omitted to watch the sky around him and paid the penalty for that neglect—as so many pilots did, sooner or later.

Biggles fired exactly five rounds at point-blank range, and the Hun's petrol tank burst into flames. Biggles zoomed clear, amazed at the effectiveness of his fire, for hitherto he had fired many rounds before such a thing had happened. His first shot must have gone straight through the tank. He glanced down, to see the Hun still falling, the doomed pilot leaning back in his cockpit with his arms over his face. It crashed in a sheet of flame near a British rest camp, and Biggles turned again to the dog-fight, which had now become more scattered over a fairly wide area.

Several Huns had broken out of the fight and were racing towards the Lines. But, as far as Biggles could see, there was not a yellow one amongst them, although he wasted some precious time chasing first one and then another in the hope of recognizing the particular one he sought. He turned back towards the spot where several machines were still circling, and as he drew nearer he saw something that would normally have given him satisfaction, but on this occasion brought a quick frown to his forehead. With a quick movement of his left hand he pushed up his goggles to make quite certain that he was not mistaken. But there was no mistake about it.

A bright yellow Hun had broken clear of the fight, but was being furiously attacked by a Camel—which Biggles instantly recognized by its markings as the one belonging to Mahoney. He had never seen a Camel handled like it before, and he sensed the hatred that possessed the pilot and inspired such brilliant flying.

The Hun hadn't a ghost of a chance; it was out-manœuvred at every turn. Once, as if to make suspicion a certainty, it turned broadside on towards Biggles, who saw a large black diamond painted on its yellow wooden side. That the Hun would fall was certain. It was only a matter of time, for the Camel was glued to its tail, guns spouting tracer bullets in long, vicious bursts. The pilot of the yellow machine seemed to be making no effort to retaliate but concentrated his efforts in attempting to escape, twisting and turning like a fish with an otter behind it.

Biggles had no excuse for butting-in, and he knew it. Mahoney was quite capable of handling the affair himself, and his presence might do more harm than good. If he got in the way of the whirling machines, the two Camel pilots would certainly have to watch each other to avoid collision, and in the confusion the Hun might escape.

That was a contingency Biggles dared not risk, much as he would have liked to take a hand. So he kept clear, and, circling, watched the end of a very one-sided duel. Suddenly in a last frantic effort to escape, the Hun spun, came out, and spun again; but the Camel had spun down behind it and was ready to administer the knock-out. Mahoney let drive again, but the Hun did not wait for any more. Once again he spun, only to pull out at the last minute, then drop in a steep sideslip to a rather bad landing in a handy field.

Biggles, who had followed the fight down, beat the side of his cockpit with his clenched fist in impotent rage. 'The yellow skunk!' he grated. 'He's got away with it. Never mind, this is where Mahoney treats him to a spot of his own medicine.'

But Mahoney did nothing of the sort, as Biggles, in his heart, knew he would not. The Flight-Commander simply could not bring himself to shoot at a man who was virtually unarmed.

The knowledge that he, Biggles, could not either, made him still more angry, and with hate smouldering in his eyes, he dropped down and landed near Mahoney who had already put his machine on the ground not far from the Hun.

As they jumped from their cockpits and raced towards the yellow machine Biggles was afraid that Von Kraudil would set fire to his Albatros before they could reach him; but the Boche had no such intention, either because he forgot to do so, or because he was too scared.

'I got him!' roared Mahoney as they ran.

'All right, I know you did. I'm not arguing about it, am I?' answered Biggles shortly. The fact that his flight-commander had shot down the yellow machine, the pilot of which, had after all escaped just retribution, was rather a bitter pill for him to swallow. He slowed down while still some yards away, for the German pilot certainly did not look the sort of man Biggles imagined he would be. He had taken off his cap and goggles and was leaning against the fuselage flaxen-haired and blue-eyed—eyes now wide open with apprehension. A trickle of blood was running down his ashen cheek, and he endeavoured to stem it with a handkerchief while he looked from the two pilots to a crowd of Tommies who, with an officer at their head, were coming at the double across the field.

Mahoney eyed his prisoner coldly, but said nothing.

'What's your name?' snapped Biggles, eyes bright with hostility.

The German shook his head, making it clear that he did not understand.

Biggles pointed at the man. 'Von Kraudil?' he asked.

'*Nein, nein!*' was the reply.

Biggles looked at Mahoney, and Mahoney looked at Biggles.

'I don't believe it's him after all!' declared Biggles. 'This kid doesn't look like a murderer to me. I say,' he went to the infantry officer, who now joined them, 'do you, or any of your fellows, happen to speak German?'

'I know a bit,' admitted the youthful, mud-splashed subaltern.

'Then would you mind asking him his name?' requested Biggles.

The officer put the question to the Boche, and turned back to Biggles.

'He says his name is Schultz.'

'Ask him for his identification disc; I have special reasons for not wanting to make any mistake about this.'

Again the infantry officer addressed the German, who groped under his tunic and produced a small, round piece of metal.

'He's telling the truth,' went on the subaltern, after a quick glance at it. 'Here's his name right enough— Wilhelm Schultz.'

'Then ask him if he's flying Von Kraudil's machine.'

'No!' came the prompt reply from the subaltern, who had continued the interrogation. 'He says this used to be Von Kraudil's machine, but it was handed over to him the other day; Von Kraudil has a new one—a blue one.'

Biggles stared.

'Blue, did you say?'

The Hun stared from one to another as the question was put to him, evidently unable to make out what the questions were leading up to.

'Yes. He says Von Kraudil's machine is blue, with a white diagonal bar behind the cross on the fuselage.'

'So that was Von Kraudil, eh?' mused Biggles softly.

'Why do you say "was"?' asked Mahoney.

'Because I got him after all!' cried Biggles exultantly. 'I got a machine answering to that description ten minutes ago! Come on, let's go and confirm it!'

'How did you manage to get mixed up in this affair?' asked Mahoney, as Biggles led the way to where the blue machine had crashed in flames. 'You were missing when the rest of us took off—asleep in your room or something.'

'Asleep, my foot!' snorted Biggles. 'I was doing a

spot of thinking—wondering what was the best way to get at that yellow Hun. It was sheer luck I heard about your dog-fight. I was making for my machine when Watt Tyler gave me the news that a formation of Huns was chasing two Camels. He gave me the direction so I beetled along. I saw the blue machine break away from the fight as I came up, went after it, and sent it down a flamer.'

'How about the pilot?' asked Mahoney. 'Did he manage to jump clear of his machine? If he didn't, we're going to have a job proving that Von Kraudil was flying it. We've only that other pilot's word for it that it was Von Kraudil's machine, you know.'

'H'm!' grunted Biggles. 'I hadn't thought of that. I certainly didn't see him jump, but he may have been flung clear when his machine crashed. Anyway,' he added, as the still smoking remains of the blue machine came into view, 'we'll soon know.'

A crowd of officers and men from the near-by rest camp were clustered around the remains. Forcing their way through the crowd, Mahoney and Biggles approached as near as they could to the hot debris of the machine. It was a terrible jumble of fused and twisted wires, utterly unrecognizable as an aeroplane.

'Gosh! What a mess!' muttered Biggles.

It was impossible to search the hot debris for the body of the pilot, and from the distance it was impossible to distinguish any sign of human remains. Mahoney turned to one of the officers. 'Can you tell me what happened to the pilot of this machine?' he asked.

'Why, yes,' replied the other. 'We found his body lying some distance away. He must have been killed when he was thrown out, but he had been badly burned beforehand. We took the body to the camp.'

'We want to find out his name,' said Mahoney. 'So we'll go along to the camp.'

'No need to do that,' said the officer. 'His name was Von Kraudil. I examined the identity disc.'

'Then it was our man, after all!' exclaimed Biggles. 'Come on; let's get back and report. I think I'll take that week's leave the Old Man spoke about—and go and see Mark.'

# BIGGLES

## *The* CAMELS
## ARE COMING

# CONTENTS

# Foreword

Captain James Bigglesworth is a fictitious character, yet he could have been found in any R.F.C.* mess during those great days of 1917 and 1918 when air combat had become the order of the day and air duelling was a fine art. 'Biggles,' as I have said, did not exist under that name, yet he represents the spirit of the R.F.C.—daring and deadly when in the air, devil-may-care and debonair when on the ground.

To readers who are unfamiliar with the conditions that prevailed in the blue skies of France during the last two years of the War, it may seem unlikely that so many adventures could have fallen to the lot of one man. In those eventful years, every day—and I might almost say every hour—brought adventure, tragic or humorous, to the man in the air, and as we sat in our cockpits warming up our engines for the dawn 'show**', no one could say what the end of the day would bring, or whether he would be alive to see it.

Again, it may seem improbable that any one man could have been involved in so many hazardous undertakings, and yet survive. That may be true; sooner or later most War pilots met the inevitable fate of the flying fighter. I sometimes wonder how any of us sur-

* Royal Flying Corps 1914–1918. An army corps responsible for military aeronautics, renamed the Royal Air Force (RAF) when amalgamated with the Royal Naval Air Service on 1st April 1918.
** Slang: operational flight into enemy-held territory.

vived, yet there were some who seemed to bear a charmed life. William Bishop, the British ace, René Fonck, the French ace and prince of air duellists, and, on the other side, Ernst Udet, and many others, fought hundreds of battles in the air and survived thousands of hours of deadly peril. Every day incredible deeds of heroism were performed by pilots whose names are unknown, and had the Victoria Cross been awarded consistently, hundreds instead of a few would have worn the coveted decoration.

Nowhere are the curious whims of Lady Luck so apparent as in the air. Lothar von Richthofen, brother of the famous ace, shot down forty British machines; he was killed in a simple cross-country flight shortly after the War. Nungesser, the French champion of forty-five air battles, was drowned, and McKeever, Canadian ace of thirty victories, was killed in a skidding motor-car. Captain 'Jock' McKay of my Squadron survived three years air warfare, only to be killed by 'archie*' an hour before the Armistice was signed. Lieutenant A. E. Amey, who fought his first and last fight beside me, had not even unpacked his kit! I have spun into the ground out of control from 6,000 feet, yet I am alive to tell the tale. Gordon, of my Squadron, made a good landing, but bumped on an old road that ran across the aerodrome, turned turtle, and broke his neck.

Again, should the sceptic think I have been guilty of exaggeration, I would say that exaggeration is almost impossible where air combat is concerned. The terrific speed at which a dog-fight took place and the amazing manner in which machines appeared from nowhere, and could disappear, apparently into thin air, was so

* Slang: Anti-aircraft gunfire

bewildering as to baffle description. It is beyond my ability to convey adequately the sensation of being one of ten or a dozen machines, zooming, whirling, and diving among the maze of pencil lines that marked the track of tracer bullets.* One could not exaggerate the stunning horror of seeing two machines collide head-on a few yards away, and words have yet to be coined to express that tightening of the heart-strings that comes of seeing one of your own side roaring down in a sheet of flame. Seldom was any attempt made by spectators to describe these things at the time; they were best forgotten.

It is not surprising that many strange incidents occurred, incidents which were never written down on combat reports, but were whispered 'with wrinkled brows, with nods, and rolling eyes' in dim corners of the hangars while we were waiting for the order to start up or for the 'late birds' to come home to roost. It was 'H', a tall South African S.E.** pilot who came in white-faced and told me that he had just shot down a Camel*** by mistake. It was the Camel pilot's fault. He playfully zoomed over the S.E., apparently out of sheer light-heartedness. 'H' told me that he started shooting when he only saw the shadow; he turned and saw the red, white, and blue circles, but it was too late. He had already gripped the Bowden control† and fired a burst of not more than five rounds. He had fired

* Phosphorus-loaded bullets whose course through the air could be seen by day and by night.
** Scouting experimental single-seater British biplane fighter in service 1917–1920
*** Sopwith Camel, a single-seater biplane fighter with twin machine guns synchronised to fire through the propeller. See front cover for illustration.
† The 'trigger' to fire the guns, usually fitted to a pilot's control column.

hundreds of rounds at enemy aircraft without hitting one, but the Camel fell in flames. He asked me if he should report it, and I, rightly or wrongly, said no, for nothing could bring the Camel back. 'H' went West* soon afterwards.

What of 'T—L—' still in the Service, who was attacked by a Belgian scout? For ten minutes he endeavoured to escape, and then, exasperated, he turned and shot the Belgian down, narrowly escaping court-martial as a consequence. Almost everybody has heard the story told by Boelcke, the German ace — and he was a man to be believed — of how he once found a British machine with a dead crew flying a ghostly course amid the clouds. On another occasion he shot down an F.E.** which, spinning viciously, threw its observer out behind the German lines and the pilot behind the British lines. What of the R.E.8*** that landed perfectly behind our lines with pilot and observer stiff and stark in their cockpits! The R.E.8 was not an easy machine to land at any time, as those who flew it will bear witness.

René Fonck once shot down a German machine which threw out its pilot; machine and man fell straight through the middle of a formation of Spads below without touching one of them! The German pilot was Wissemann, who had just shot down Guynemer, Fonck's friend and brother ace, but he did not know that at the time. The coincidence is worth noting. Madon, another ace, once attacked a German two-seater at point-blank

* Slang: was killed
** British two-seater pusher biplane with the engine behind the pilot and the gunner in the forward cockpit.
*** British two-seater biplane designed for reconnaissance and artillery purposes.

range—his usual method. A bullet struck the goggles off the Boche* observer and sent them whirling into the air; Madon caught them on his wires and brought them home. When Warneford shot down his Zeppelin** one of the crew jumped from the blazing airship, and after falling a distance generally believed to be about 200 feet, crashed through the roof of a convent and landed on a bed which had just been vacated by a nun. He lived to tell the tale. When it comes to pure coincidence the following tale goes rather farther than a fiction writer would dare to venture. It was told to me by the principal actors themselves shortly after they had been led into the prison camp where I was confined. They themselves were still finding the thing difficult to believe.

It came about through Pat Manley losing his propeller. For the benefit of the reader who is not conversant with air jargon, to lose one's propellor does not mean that it fell off, or anything like that. It is said to be 'lost' when it stops turning round.

Pat Manley and Swayze were friends who joined the infantry and came over with the Canadian contingent. They were hit on the same day, went to different hospitals and completely lost touch with each other. A year later Pat, beetling around over the line in a Bristol Fighter***, saw another Bristol going down under a cloud of enemy aircraft. He throttled back and put his nose down in a steep dive to join the party; but he was too late and he saw the other Bristol crash in a field.

* Derogatory term for the Germans
** Airships of rigid construction used by the Germans mainly over Britain for strategic bombing and reconnaissance
*** British two-seater fighter with remarkable manoeuvrability, in service 1917 onwards. It had one fixed Vickers gun for the pilot and one or two mobile Lewis guns for the observer/gunner.

Perceiving that no good purpose could be served by hanging around, Pat was about to make for a healthier quarter of the sky, when, as previously stated, he lost his propeller. Being very low he was unable to dive to get it back so he landed beside the crash, just in time to see Swayze crawl out. Thus, they were both taken prisoner within one minute of each other on the same field in France.

Here is another story which illustrates the sort of thing that could happen to a pilot in those days. It happened I believe to Carter, who told me the story when we were prisoners of war together. I see he is now commanding the Iraqian Air Force. He was a Camel pilot then, and was so tickled to death one day at finding a column of enemy troops on the march that he could not tear himself away from them.

He amused himself for a time by unloading his 20-lb. Cooper bombs on them, and when this began to pall he came lower and sprayed them with his gun. So fascinating did this pastime become, and so vastly entertaining were the antics of the warriors below in their frantic haste to remove themselves from the locality, that he quite failed to notice the telegraph wires which, as so often happens, accompanied the road on its winding way. He hit the wires at the bottom of a zoom and took them, together with a snapped-off post or two, for a short joy-ride. It was a pity he could not have given the troops a treat by taking them all the way home, but the Camel, not being designed for such work, gave up the ghost and spread itself over the landscape.

The tables now being somewhat turned, his erstwhile victims proceeded to amuse themselves by battering him to pulp with their rifle butts, a comparatively tame pursuit from which they were only compelled to desist by the arrival of a senior officer.

Carter was taken to the same hospital as the men he had wounded, where a state of affairs prevailed for the next week or so that can be better imagined than described!

One could go on with such stories indefinitely, but these should be sufficient to show that, in the air at least, truth is stranger than fiction.

Many of the adventures that are ascribed to Biggles did actually occur, and are true in their essential facts. Students of air history will have no difficulty in identifying them. In many cases the officers themselves are still alive and serving in the Royal Air Force.

Finally, I hope that from a perusal of these pages a younger generation of air fighters may learn something of the tricks of the trade, of the traps and pitfalls that beset the unwary, for I fear that many of the lessons which we learned in the hard school of war are being rapidly obscured by the mists of peace-time theory. In air-fighting, one week of war experience is worth a year of peace-time practice. In peace a man may make a mistake—and live. He may not even know of his mistake. If he makes that same mistake in war—he dies, unless it is his lucky day, in which case the error is so vividly brought to his notice that he is never guilty of it again.

No one can say just how he will react when, for the first time, he hears the flack! flack! flack! of bullets ripping through his machine. The sound has turned boys into grey-faced men, and even hardened campaigners who learnt their business on the ground have felt their lips turn dry.

In the following pages certain expressions occur from

time to time in connection with the tactics of air combat which may seem to the layman to be out of proportion to their importance. For instance, he will read of 'getting into the sun.' It is quite impossible for anybody who does not fly to realize what this means and how utterly impossible it is to see what is going on in that direction, particularly when the sun is low and one is flying west. To fly into the face of the setting sun can be uncomfortable at any time, but the strain of trying to peer into the glare, knowing that it may discharge a squadron of death-spitting devils at any moment, becomes positive torture after a time; at least, I found it so.

It should also be remembered that an aeroplane is an extremely small vehicle and difficult to see. When one is on the ground it is the noise of the engine that almost invariably first attracts attention, and but for the unmistakable tell-tale hum few would be seen at all. In the air, the roar of one's own engine drowns all other sound, and one is therefore dependent upon sight alone for detecting the presence of other aircraft. This fact should constantly be borne in mind when reading stories of the air, and particularly of air combat.

Constant reference is also made to 'archie.' Most people know by now that this was not an old friend whom we called by his Christian name. There was nothing friendly about archie. On the contrary, he often bit you when you were least expecting it, but on the whole his bark was worse than his bite. Archie was the war-pilot's nick-name for anti-aircraft gun-fire. During the War archie batteries stretched from the North Sea to the Swiss Frontier;* his appearance in the sky was accepted as a matter of course, and dodging him was

* i.e. along the front line trenches where the opposing armies faced one another.

part of the daily round. After a time one became accustomed to it and ignored it unless it was very bad.

Lingfield, 1932.                                W. E. J.

The word 'Hun' as used in this book, was the common generic term for anything belonging to the enemy. It was used in a familiar sense, rather than derogatory. Witness the fact that in the R.F.C. a hun was also a pupil at flying training school.

                                                W. E. J.

# Chapter 1
# The White Fokker

To the casual observer, the attitude of the little group
of pilots clustered around the entrance of B Flight
hangar was one of complete nonchalance. MacLaren,
still wearing the tartans and glengarry of his regiment,*
a captain's stars on his sleeve, squatted uncomfortably
on an upturned chock. To a student of detail the steady
spiral of smoke from the quickly-drawn cigarette,
lighted before the last half was consumed, gave the lie
to his bored expression. Quinan, his 'maternity'** tunic
flapping open at the throat, hands thrust deep into
the pockets of his slacks, leaning carelessly against the
flimsy structure of the temporary hangar, gnawed the
end of a dead match with slow deliberation. Swayne,
bareheaded, the left shoulder of his tunic as black as
ink with burnt castor oil, seated on an empty oil drum,
was nervously plucking little tufts of wool from the tops
of his sheepskin boots. Bigglesworth, popularly known
as Biggles, a slight, fair-haired, good-looking lad still
in his teens, but an acting Flight-Commander, was
talking, not of wine or women as novelists would have
us believe, but of a new fusee spring for a Vickers***

---

* Officers transferring from the army to the air corps were allowed to
retain their previous regiment's uniform.
** Tunic with a flap across the front which fastened at the side, not in
the middle.
*** Machine gun firing a continuous stream of bullets at one squeeze
of the trigger.

217

gun which would speed it up another hundred rounds a minute.

His deep-set hazel eyes were never still and held a glint of yellow fire that somehow seemed out of place in a pale face upon which the strain of war, and sight of sudden death, had already graven little lines. His hands, small and delicate as a girl's, fidgeted continually with the tunic fastening at his throat. He had killed a man not six hours before. He had killed six men during the past month—or was it a year?—he had forgotten. Time had become curiously telescoped lately. What did it matter, anyway? He knew he had to die some time and had long ago ceased to worry about it. His careless attitude suggested complete indifference, but the irritating little falsetto laugh which continually punctuated his tale betrayed the frayed condition of his nerves.

From the dim depths of the hangar half a dozen tousled-headed ack-emmas* watched their officers furtively as they pretended to work on a war-scarred Camel. One habit all ranks had in common: every few seconds their eyes would study the western horizon long and anxiously. A visiting pilot would have known at once that the evening patrol was overdue. As a matter of fact, it should have been in ten minutes before.

'Here they come!' The words were sufficient to cause all further pretence to be abandoned; officers and men together were on their feet peering with hand-shaded eyes towards the setting sun whence came the rhythmic purr of rotary engines, still far away. Three specks became visible against the purple glow; a scarcely

* Slang: Air Mechanics.

audible sigh was the only indication of the nervous tension that the appearance of the three machines had broken. The door of the Squadron office opened and Major Mullen, the C.O.,* came out. He would not have admitted that he too had shared the common anxiety, but he fell in line with the watchers on the tarmac to await the arrival of the overdue machines.

The three Camels were barely half a mile away, at not more than a 1,000 feet, when a new note became audible above the steady roar of the engines. It was the shrill scream of wind-torn wings and wires. Whoof! Whoof! Whoof! Three white puffs** of smoke appeared high above the now gliding Camels. Bang!—Whoof! Bang!—Whoof!—the archie battery at the far end of the aerodrome took up the story. Not a man of the waiting group moved, but every eye shifted to a gleaming speck which had detached itself from the dark-blue vault above. A white-painted Fokker D.VII*** was coming down like a meteor behind the rearmost Camel. There was a glittering streak of tracer. The Camel staggered for a moment and then plunged straight to earth. At the rattle of guns the other two Camels opened their engines and half-rolled convulsively. The leader, first out, was round like a streak at the Fokker, which, pulling out of its dive, had shot up to 3,000 feet in one tremendous zoom, turned, and was streaking for the line. The stricken Camel hit the ground just inside the aerodrome; a sheet of flame leapt skywards.

From first to last the whole incident had occupied

* Commanding Officer.
** In general, British anti-aircraft fire gave off white smoke and German anti-aircraft fire gave off black smoke.
*** Very efficient German single-seater biplane fighter with two forward firing guns.

perhaps three seconds, during which time none of the spell-bound spectators on the tarmac had either moved or spoken. The C.O. recovered himself first, and with a bitter curse raced towards the Lewis gun* mounted outside his office. Half-way he changed his mind and swung round towards the blazing Camel in the wake of the flying ambulance only to stop dead, throw up his hands with a despairing gesture, and turn again towards the hangar.

'Get out, you fool; where the hell do you think you are going—he's home by now,' he snapped at Bigglesworth, who was feverishly clambering, cap and gogglesless, into a Camel.

As the two surviving Camels taxied in, a babble of voices broke loose. Mahoney, who had led the flight, leaned swaying for a moment against the fuselage of his machine. His lips moved, but no sound came; he seemed to be making a tremendous effort to pull himself together. His eyes roved round the aerodrome to identify the pilot of the other Camel. Manley, half-falling out of the cockpit of the other machine, hurried towards him. 'All right, old lad, take it easy, it wasn't your fault,' he said quickly. Mahoney's lips continued to move as he struggled to speak. 'It was Norman—poor little devil! First time over, too—the damn swine—he didn't give him a chance—not a b—' His voice rose to shrill crescendo.

'Stop that!' cut in the C.O. quickly, and then more quietly, 'Steady, Mahoney.' For a moment the Flight-Commander and his Commanding Officer eyed each other grimly. Mahoney's eyes fell first. Slowly he took

---

* Light machine gun, used both on the ground and also often by the observer/gunner in two-seater aircraft.

off his sidcot* and threw it on the ground with studied deliberation. Cap and goggles followed, leaving that part of his face which they had protected like a white mask.

'Officers in the Orderly Room,** please,' said the C.O., turning on his heel. Mahoney lit a cigarette and followed the little group moving towards the Squadron office.

'Sit down, everybody,' began Major Mullen. 'A bad show. I blame no one. Anybody could have been caught the same way. It might have been me, or it might have been you, Mahoney. From some points of view it was a low-down trick; from others, well, it was a smart piece of work; anyway, the fellow was within his rights. He's done it before, farther north; I've heard about it. He did it three times at 197 Squadron, once as they were taking off. He'll try it again, and if he pulls it off again here it's our own funeral. We've had our lesson. We'll get him; we've *got* to get him. You know the unwritten law about having an officer shot down on his own aerodrome? We can't show our faces in another mess until we *do* get him. You know what Wing*** will say about this. That's all. Go and get a drink, Mahoney. I'll see Flight-Commanders here in half an hour.'

An hour later Major Mullen was running over the result of the conference. 'I think Mahoney's right,' he said. 'The Fokker probably came over the line at eighteen or twenty thousand with his engine off. He must

* A thick, padded garment worn by aircrew.
** A room or office used for day to day Squadron business.
*** The administrative headquarters. Each Wing commanded several squadrons. It was headed by a Lieutenant-Colonel.

have been watching you all the time, Mahoney. He knew that you were at the end of the patrol and hadn't enough juice left to go back after him. All right, then. Mahoney, you'll take the patrol in the morning; come back in the ordinary way when it's over. Bigglesworth, you'll take your Flight to the ceiling*. Hang around over Mossyface Wood until you see Mahoney coming back and then follow him home. Stay as high as you can and don't take your eyes off Mahoney's Flight for a moment. If the Fokker comes down, one of you should get him. If he doesn't show up, we'll keep it up until he does. It means long hours, but we can't help that. All clear? Good. Let's go and eat.'

The following morning Mahoney was bringing his Flight back by way of Mossyface Wood as arranged. His altimeter registered 10,000 feet, Often he leaned back in his cockpit and studied the sky above him long and earnestly for a sign of Bigglesworth's Flight, but a film of cirrus cloud far above concealed everything beyond it. Against that cloud a machine would show up like a fly on a white ceiling; his roving eyes searched it, section by section, from horizon to horizon, but not a speck broke its pristine surface. At 6.30 he turned his nose for home according to plan, maintaining his height until he reached the line and only taking his eyes from aloft to see that Manley and Forrest in the other two Camels were in place. He crossed the line in the inevitable flurry of archie, and started a long glide towards the aerodrome. A cluster of black archie bursts far away to the north showed where some allied machines were moving; there was apparently nothing else in the

* Slang: as high as their power will allow.

sky, yet he felt uneasy. What was the other side of that cloud? He wished he could see. Every fibre of his war-tried airman's instinct reacted against that opaque curtain. He flew with his eyes ever turned upwards. Suddenly he caught his breath. For a fraction of a second a black spot had appeared against the cloud and disappeared again almost before he could fasten his eyes on it. Keeping his eyes on the spot he raised his left arm, shook his wings, opened up his engine, and warmed his guns with a short burst. What was going on up there? He was soon to know. A machine, whether friend or foe he could not tell, wrapped in a sheet of flame, hurtled downwards through the cloud into oblivion, leaving a long plume of black smoke in its wake. Mahoney stiffened in his seat. Next came a Camel spinning wildly out of control. Then another Camel, streaking for home, followed by five Fokkers. Mahoney muttered a curse through his clenched teeth and swung round and up in a wide arc, knowing as he did so that he could never get up to the Fokkers in time to help the Camel, now crossing the line at a speed which threatened to take its wings off. A barrage of archie appeared between the Fokkers and the Camel, and the black-crossed machines, after a moment's hesitation, turned and dived for home. Mahoney raced after the solitary Camel, whose pilot, seeing him coming, throttled back to wait for him.

They landed together and the C.O. ran out to meet them. Bigglesworth, the pilot of the lone Camel, was out first. 'I've lost Swayne and Maddison,' he said grimly, as the others joined him. 'I've lost Swayne and Maddison,' he repeated. 'I've lost Swayne and Maddison, can't you hear me?' he said yet again. 'What the hell are you looking at me like that for?'

'Nobody's looking at you, Biggles,' broke in the C.O. 'Take it steady and tell us what happened.'

Biggles groped for his cigarette case. 'We're boobs,' he muttered bitterly. 'Pilots, eh? We ought to be riding scooters in Kensington Gardens. What did we do? We did just what they damn well knew we'd do, and they were waiting for us, the whole bunch of 'em!' He passed his hand over his face wearily as his passion spent itself. He tossed his flying-coat on to the tarmac and went on quietly. 'I was up 20,000, or as near as I could get, waiting. So were they, but I didn't see 'em at first; must have been hiding in that damn soup. I saw Mahoney coming, heading for Mossy-face, and then I saw the White Fokker, by himself. He wasn't there for you, Mahoney, he was there to get me down. I didn't look up and that's a fact. I saw the Fokker going down and I fell for it. I thought he was cold meat and I went down after him. Where the others came from I don't know. They were into us just before we hit the cloud. The first thing I saw was the tracer, and poor Mad going down in flames next to me. I went after the white bird like a sack of bricks, but I lost him in the cloud. Swayne had gone, so I made for home, and I'm damn lucky to get here. That's all.'

He turned and strode off towards the mess. Major Mullen watched him go without a word.

'I'll have a word with you, Mahoney, and you, Mac,' he said, and together they entered the orderly room. 'We've got to do something about this,' he began briskly. 'We shall all be for Home Establishment* if it goes on. Bigglesworth's going to bits fast, but if he can get that Fokker it will restore his confidence. We've

* Posted home to the UK for a non-combat role.

lost three machines in two days and we are going to lose more if we don't stop that white devil.'

Bigglesworth entered. 'Hullo, Biggles, sit down,' said the C.O. quietly. Biggles nodded.

'I've been trying to work this out, sir,' he began, 'and this is my idea. First of all you'll notice that this Fokker doesn't go for the leaders. He always picks on one of the rear men in the formation; you saw how he got Norman. All right. Tomorrow we'll do the usual patrol of three. Mahoney or Mac can lead and I'll be in the formation. I'll pretend I'm scared of everything and sideslip away from every archie burst. Coming home I'll hang back and the others will go on ahead without me. That should bring him down. If he comes I'll be ready and we'll see who can shoot straightest and quickest. If he gets me—well—he gets me, but if he doesn't, I'll get him. He'll have height of me I know, and that's where he holds the cards. I've got an idea about that, too. Someone will have to take every available machine and wait upstairs to keep the others off if they try to butt in. Don't make a move unless they start coming down; let them make the first move, that should give you height of 'em. I'm having an extra tank put in my machine so that I'll have some spare juice when he'll reckon I've none left, in case I want to turn back.'

The C.O. nodded: 'That sounds all right to me,' he said. 'I've only one thing to say, and that is, I'll take the party up topsides. You can rely on me to keep anybody busy who starts to interfere with your show. Good enough! We'll try it in the morning.'

The pink hue of dawn had turned to turquoise when Mahoney turned for home at the end of the dawn patrol. One machine of his Flight was lagging back, and for the hundredth time he turned and waved for it to close up, smiling as he did so. Biggles had played the novice to perfection. Even now, a bracket of archie* sent him careering wide from the formation. Mahoney's roving eyes were never still; slowly and methodically they searched every section of air around, above, and below. Far above them a Rumpler** was making for home followed by a long line of white archie, but he made no attempt to pursue it. Far to the north-east a formation of 'Nines' was heading out into the blue; high above them he could just make out the escorting Bristols. He gazed upwards long and anxiously. He could see nothing, but he knew that somewhere in the blue void at least one formation of fighters was watching him that very moment. Biggles too was watching; he had pushed his goggles up to see better. Now and then he dived a little to gain speed so that the watchers above might think he was trying to keep in position. They were going home now; if the White Fokker was about today he would soon have to show up. The formation started to lose height slowly; Biggles warmed his gun every few minutes, but still kept up the pretence of bad flying.

They were well over the line now. The two other Camels had dropped to 5,000 feet, but he hung back slightly above them. Once he threw a loop to show his apparent relief at being safely back over his own side of the line. Dash it, why didn't the fellow come? The two other Camels were nearly a mile ahead when Biggles suddenly focussed his eyes upon a spot far above and held it. Was it, or was it not? Yes! Far above

* A bracket is when shells burst on either side of a target.
** German two-seater biplane for observation and light bombing raids.

226

and behind him a tiny light flashed for an instant, and he knew it for the sun striking the planes* of a machine, whether friend or foe he could not tell. He kept his eyes glued to the spot. He could see the machine now, a tiny black speck rapidly growing larger. Biggles smiled grimly. 'Here comes the hawk, I'm the sparrow. Well, we'll see.' The machine was plainly visible now, a Fokker D.VII. There was no sign of archie, so he concluded that the Fokker had shut his engine off and had not yet been seen from the ground. Biggles opened his throttle wide and put his nose down slightly in order to get as much speed as possible without alarming the enemy above. The Fokker was coming down now with the speed of light; a cluster of archie far above it showed that the pilot had cast concealment to the winds. Biggles pushed his nose down and raced for home. Speed—speed—speed—that was all he wanted now to take him up behind the Fokker. How near dare he let him come? Could the Fokker hit him first burst? He had to chance it. At 200 feet a stream of tracer spurted from the Fokker's Spandaus.** Biggles moved the rudder-bar, and, as the bullets streamed between his planes pulled the stick back into his stomach. Half-rolling off the top of the loop and looking swiftly for his adversary, he caught his breath as the Fokker swept by a bare ten feet away. He had a vivid impression of the face of the man in the pilot's seat, looking at him. Biggles was on its tail in a flash. Through his sights he saw it still climbing. Rat-tat-tat—he cursed luridly as he hammered at the gun which had jammed at the

* The wings of an aircraft were also called its planes.
** German machine guns were often referred to as Spandaus, due to the fact that many were manufactured at Spandau, Germany.

critical moment. The Fokker had Immelmanned* and was coming back at him now, but Biggles was ready, and pulled his nose up to take it head-on. Vaguely, out of the corner of his eye he saw another Fokker whirling down in a cloud of smoke and other planes above. The White Fokker swerved and he followed it round.

They were circling now, each machine in a vertical bank not a hundred feet apart, the Fokker slowly gaining height. Biggles thought swiftly, 'Ten more circles and he's above me and then it's goodbye.' There was one chance left, a desperate one. He knew that the second he pulled out of the circle the Fokker would be on his tail and get a shot at him. Whatever he did the Fokker would still be on his tail at the finish. If he rolled, the Fokker would roll too, and still be in the same position. If he spun, the Fokker would spin; there was no shaking off a man who knew his job, but if he shot out of the circle he might get a lead of three hundred feet, and if he could loop fast enough he might get the Fokker from the top of his loop as it passed underneath in his wake. If he was too quick they would collide; no matter, they would go to Kingdom Come together. A feeling of fierce exultation swept over him. 'Come on, you devil!' he cried, 'I'll take your lead,' and shot out of the circle. He shoved his stick forward savagely as something smashed through the root of the nearest centre-section strut,** and then he pulled it back in a swift zoom. A fleeting glance over his shoulder showed the Fokker three hundred feet behind. He

* This manoeuvre consists of a half roll off the top of a loop thereby quickly reversing the direction of flight. It was named after Max Immelmann, successful German fighter pilot 1914–1916 with seventeen victories who was the first to use this turn in combat.

** Rigid supports between the wings and fuselage of a biplane or triplane.

pulled the stick right back into his stomach in a flick loop and his eyes sought the sights as he pressed his triggers. Blue sky—blue sky—the horizon—green fields—where was the Fokker? Ah! There he was, flying straight into his stream of tracer. He saw the pilot slump forward in his seat. He held the loop a moment longer and then flung the Camel over on to an even keel, looking swiftly for the Fokker as he did so. It was rocketting like a hard-hit pheasant. It stalled; its nose whipped over and with the engine racing it roared down in an almost vertical dive. Biggles saw the top plane fold back, and then he looked away feeling suddenly limp and very tired.

A mile away five straight-winged machines were making for the line, followed by four Camels; another Camel was trying to land in a ploughed field below. Even as he watched it the wheels touched and it somersaulted; a figure scrambled out and looked upwards, waving. Biggles side-slipped down into the next field and landed. Major Mullen, the pilot of the wrecked Camel, ran to meet him.

'Good boy,' he cried, 'you brought it off.'

# Chapter 2
# The Packet

'Two no-trumps.' Biggles, newly appointed to Captain's rank since his affair with the White Fokker, made the bid as if he held all the court cards in the pack.

'Two diamonds,' offered Quinan, sitting on his left.

Mahoney, Biggle's partner, looked across the table apologetically. 'No bid,' he said, wearily.

'Hell's bells, don't you ever support your partner?' complained Biggles. 'You've sat there all the afternoon croaking "No bid" like a damned parrot. You ought to have a gramophone record made of it, and keep it with your scoring block.'

'Who the devil are you grousing at?' fired up Mahoney. 'Any fool could sit and chirp no-trumps if they held the paper you do. If you could only play the cards you hold we'd get a rubber sometimes, instead of being a thousand points down.'

'What sort of a game do you call this, anyway?' broke in Batson, the fourth player. 'Why don't you show each other your cards and have done with it?'

Major Mullen entered the ante-room. 'I want you, Biggles, when you've played the hand. Stand by, everybody; it's clearing,' he continued, addressing the othes in the room and referring to the steady drizzle which had washed out flying so far that day.

Biggles looked at the hand which his partner had laid on the table with disgust. The knave to two diamonds was his best suit. 'Clearing, eh?' he said, grimly.

'So am I. Holy smoke, what a mitt.' He was two down on the bid. He rose. 'Tot it up,' he invited his opponents, 'I'll settle when I come back.'

'No you don't, you settle now,' snapped Batson. 'Miller went West owing me seventy francs—you cough it up, Biggles.' Biggles reluctantly counted out some notes. 'Take it and I'll starve,' he grumbled. 'We'll finish this last rubber when I come back.' He followed Major Mullen to the Squadron office, where he found an officer awaiting them, whose red tabs showed that he came from a higher command.

'Captain Bigglesworth—Colonel Raymond,' began the C.O. 'This is the officer I was telling you about, sir.'

Biggles saluted and eyed the stranger curiously. The Colonel looked at him so long and earnestly that Biggles ran his mind swiftly over the events of the last few days, trying to recall some incident which might account for the senior officer's presence. 'Sit down, Bigglesworth,' said the Colonel at last, 'smoke if you like.' Biggles sat and lit a cigarette.

'You are wondering why I've sent for you,' began the Colonel. 'I'll tell you. Frankly, I'm going to ask you to undertake a tough proposition.' Biggles stiffened in his chair.

'First of all,' went on the Colonel, 'what I am going to tell you is secret. Not a word to anybody, and I mean that. Not one word. Now, this is the position. You know, of course, that we have—er—agents—operatives—call 'em what you like—over the line. They are usually taken over by aircraft; sometimes they drop by parachute and sometimes we land them, according to circumstances. Sometimes they come back; more often they do not. Sometimes the pilot who takes them over picks them up at a pre-arranged spot at a subsequent date. Sometimes—but never mind—that doesn't concern you.

'A fortnight ago such an agent went over. He did not come back. We know, never mind how, that he obtained what he went to fetch, which was, to be quite frank, a packet of plans. An officer went to fetch him by arrangement, but the enemy had evidently watched our man and wired* the field. When the F.E. pilot—it was at night—got to the field it was a death trap. The officer was killed landing. The operative bolted, but was taken. We have since received information that he has been shot. Before he was taken he managed to conceal the plans, and we know where they are. We want those plans badly—urgently; in three days they will be useless.'

'I see,' said Biggles slowly, 'and you want me to go and fetch them?'

'If you will.'

'May I ask roughly where they are?' said Biggles.

'You may,' replied the Colonel; 'they are near Ariet.'

'Ariet?' cried Biggles. 'Why 297 and 287 Squadrons are both nearer than we are; why not send them?'

'For two reasons,' replied Colonel Raymond, '297 Squadron is equipped with D.H.9's** and a "nine" could not get down in the field. Obviously, if it were possible, we should send an F.E. over at night, but, unfortunately, a night landing is out of the question. Only a single-seater could hope to get in, and then only by clever flying. A single-seater might just get into the

---

* strung wires across the field at head height so that any aeroplane attempting to land will run into them and crash.

** De Havilland 9—a two-seater British bomber with one fixed forward-firing gun for the pilot plus a mobile gun for the rear gunner/observer.

field, collect the plans, and get off again before the enemy arrived. We photographed the place at once, naturally. Here they are—take a look at them.' He tossed a packet of photographs casually to Biggles. 'The place is about two miles from where the disaster occurred, and the poor devil must have been taken somewhere near that spot.'

One glance showed Biggles that the Colonel had not underestimated the difficulty. 'From what height was this taken?' he asked, holding up a photograph on which was marked a small white cross.

'Six thousand feet,' replied the Colonel. 'The white mark is the position of the packet. When our man knew the game was up he shoved the plans down a rabbit-hole at the foot of a tree in the corner of that field. His last act was to release a pigeon, pin-pointing the position. The bird could not, of course, carry the plans.'

'Stout effort,' said Biggles approvingly. 'So the plans are in the corner of the field I land in. From this photo I should say that the field is about 150 yards long by 50 yards wide. I might just get in, but the wind would have to be right.'

'It is right, *now*,' replied the Colonel, softly but pointedly.

'Now?'

'Now!'

'What about 287 Squadron?' asked Biggles curiously. 'Don't think I am inquisitive, sir, but they've got S.E.5's and they are nearer than we are.'

'If you must know,' returned the Colonel, 'we have already been to them. They have lost two officers in the attempt and we can't ask them for another. Neither of them reached the field; archie got one, and we can only suppose that enemy aircraft got the other. You will pass both crashes on the way.'

'Thanks,' said Biggles grimly. 'I can find my way without them. It's about twenty miles over, isn't it?'

'About that, yes.'

'All right, sir,' said Biggles, 'I'll go, but I'd like to ask one thing.' He turned to Major Mullen. 'Do you mind if I ask for MacLaren or Mahoney to watch me from "upstairs"? If they could meet me on the way home it might help. I shall be low coming home—cold meat for any stray Hun that happens to be about?' He turned to Colonel Raymond. 'What would happen if I had to land with those plans on me?' he asked.

'I expect the enemy would shoot you,*' returned the Colonel. 'In fact, I am sure they would.'

'All right, sir,' said Biggles, 'as long as we understand. If my engine cuts out while I am over the other side those plans are going overboard before I hit the deck. I don't mind dying, but when I die, I'll die sitting down, like an officer and a gentleman—not standing with my back to a brick wall. If I come back, I shall have the plans with me—if they are still there.'

'That's fair enough,' agreed Colonel Raymond.

'May I take Mac and Mahoney with me to look after the ceiling?' he asked the C.O.

'Any objection, sir?' asked Major Mullen.

'None, as far as I am concerned,' replied the Colonel.

'Good; then I'll be off,' said Biggles, rising. 'Going to wait for the plans, sir? I shall be back within the hour, or not at all.'

'I'll wait,' said the Colonel gravely.

---

* Members of the forces captured during the War were entitled to be held prisoner and honourably treated but anyone engaged in spying (which included transporting a spy) was shot by firing squad.

Major Mullen accompanied Biggles to the door. 'Get those plans, Biggles,' he said, 'and the Squadron's name is on the top line. Fail—and it's mud. Good-bye and good luck.' A swift handshake and Biggles was on his way to the sheds.

As he gave instructions for his Camel to be started up, he noticed that the sun was already sinking in the west; he could not expect more than an hour and a half of daylight. He turned towards the Mess*, a burst of song greeting him as he opened the door.

'Mac! Mahoney! here a minute,' he called.

'What's the matter now, you hot-air merchant?' growled Mahoney as they advanced to meet him. 'Can't you—' Biggles cut him short.

'Show on,' he said crisply. 'I'm going to Ariet—to fetch a packet.'

'To Ariet?' said Mahoney incredulously.

'You'll get a packet all right,' sneered MacLaren, 'but why go to Ariet for it?'

'Never mind, I can't tell you,' said Biggles. 'Seriously, chaps, I'm going to land at Ariet. I shall go over high up, but I shall be damned low coming home, right on the carpet most of the way in all probability. Shan't have time to get any height. I'm going straight there and, I hope, straight back. You can help if you will by watching things up topsides. I've got to bring something back besides myself or I wouldn't ask you, and that's a fact. It's a long way over—twenty miles, and I expect every Hun in the sky will be looking for me as I come back. If they spot you they may not see me. That's all,' he concluded.

* The place where the officers eat and relax together.

'What the bl—' cut in Mahoney. Biggles cut him short.

'I'm off now,' he announced, 'may I expect to see you shortly?'

'Of course,' said Mahoney, 'I don't understand what it's all about and it seems a damn-fool business to me.' He glanced up and saw Colonel Raymond and Major Mullen walking towards the Mess. 'Blast these brass-hats*,' he growled. 'Why can't they stay at home on a dud day? Righto, laddie; see you presently.'

Twenty minutes later, well over the line at 12,000 feet, Biggles scanned the sky anxiously. Far away to the right, 3,000 feet above him, a formation of 'Fours**' were heading towards the line after a raid; he hoped that they would prove an attractive lure for any prowling enemy aircraft.

Ariet lay just ahead and below; Biggles put his nose down and dived, his eyes searching for his objective. Two miles west of Ariet, the Colonel had said! Good heavens, there seemed to be hundreds of oblong fields two miles west of Ariet. He looked at the photograph which he had pinned to his instrument board and compared it to the ground below. That must be the field, over there to the right. He spun to lose height more rapidly. Pulling out, he examined the field closely. An encampment seemed dangerously close—perhaps a mile away, not more. There was the field. He noticed two horses idling in a corner and looked anxiously at a row of poplars which stood like a row of soldiers at the far end. 'If I do get into that field I shall be mighty

* Slang: staff officers, (ie very senior officers), referring to the gold braid worn on their caps.
** De Havilland 4s—British two-seater day bomber 1917–1920. W. E. Johns flew a DH4 with 55 Squadron.

lucky to get out of it again,' he mused. Fortunately the wind—as the Colonel had said—was blowing in the right direction, otherwise it would be impossible.

He was only a couple of hundred feet up now and he could see men running about the encampment; some were clustered in little crouching groups, and as he cut his engine off he heard the faint rattle of a machine gun. He winced as something crashed through the fuselage behind him. 'That's too close,' he muttered, and in the same breath, 'Well, here goes.'

He did a swift S turn, then kicked out his left foot and brought the stick over in a steep side-slip. As he levelled out the tops of the trees brushed his undercarriage wheels and he fish-tailed* desperately to lose height.

The poplars at the far end of the field appeared to race towards him; he held his breath as his wheels touched the ground in a tail-wheel landing. 'A molehill now, and I somersault,' he thought, cursing himself for coming in so fast. His tail dropped, the skid dragged, and he breathed again. Without waiting for the machine to finish its run he swung round towards the tree in the corner. That must be the one, he thought. Springing quickly from the cockpit he looked around— ah! there was the rabbit-hole. He was on his hands and knees in a second, arms thrust far down. Nothing!

For a moment he remained stupefied with dismay. 'Must be another hole—or another tree,' he thought frantically, as he sprang to his feet. Realizing that he was on the verge of panicking, he steadied himself with an effort, and ran towards the next tree; his foot caught in an obstruction and he sprawled headlong, but he

* A quick side-to-side movement of the rudder, used when landing to reduce speed by creating extra wind resistance.

was on his feet again in an instant, instinctively glancing behind him to ascertain the cause of his fall. It was
a rabbit-hole—there were a cluster of them all about
him. Of course, there would be, he thought grimly, and
thrust his hand into the nearest. Thank God! His fingers closed around a bulky object—he pulled it out—
it was a thick packet of papers.

He raced towards the Camel. Two hundred yards
away a file of soldiers with an officer at their head were
coming at the double. He tossed the packet into the
cockpit, swung himself into his seat, and the next
instant was racing, tail up, down the field to get into
the wind. His heart sank as he surveyed the poplars;
they seemed to reach upwards to the sky. 'Can't be
done,' he said, bitterly. In one place there was a gap
in the line where a tree had fallen; could he get between
them? He thought not, but he would try.

Already the grey-clad troops were scrambling
through the hedge below the poplars. He opened the
throttle and shoved the stick forward. The tail lifted.
Hop—hop—thank goodness—she was off! He held his
nose down for a moment longer and then zoomed at
the middle of the gap. He flinched instinctively as a
sharp crackling stabbed his ears and the machine shiv-
ered; whether it was gunshots or breaking wings, he
didn't know.

He was through, in the air, and he'd got the plans!
He laughed with relief as he dodged and twisted to
spoil the aim of the marksmen below. Dare he waste
time trying to gain height? He thought not. He would
never be able to get to a safe height—better to stick at
two or three thousand feet just out of range of small
arms from the ground, race for home, and trust to luck.
With every nerve vibrating he looked up, around and

below; most of the time he flew with his head thrown back, searching the sky above and in front of him, the direction from which danger would come. Not a machine was in sight. Half-way home he had climbed to 4,000 feet; tail up, he raced for the line, swerving from time to time when archie came too close to be comfortable. Fortunately the wind had died away; ten minutes now would see him safe over the line. Ten minutes! A lot could happen in the air in ten minutes. His eyes were never still; anxiously they roved the air for signs of enemy aircraft, or for Mahoney or MacLaren's Camels.

Where was the packet? He groped about the floor of the cockpit, but couldn't find it. It must have got under his seat and drifted down the fuselage out of reach. Instinctively he glanced at the rev. counter. If he had to force-land now the enemy would find the packet. Would they! He felt for his Very* pistol and made sure that it was loaded. 'Provided I don't crash I can always set fire to her,' he reflected; 'the plans will burn with the rest.'

His eyes, still searching, suddenly stopped and focussed on a spot ahead. His heart missed a beat and his lips curled in a mirthless smile. Across the sky, straight ahead, moving swiftly towards him, were a line of straight-winged aeroplanes. Fokkers! Six of them.

He looked above the Fokkers for the expected Camels, but they were not there. 'All right,' muttered Biggles, 'I'll take the lot of you; come on, you devils.' For perhaps a minute they flew thus, the Camel, cut

* Short-barrelled pistol for firing coloured flares, used as a signal. Before the days of radio in aircraft different coloured flares were often used to pass messages.

off by the Fokkers, still heading for the line, with the distance rapidly closing between them.

'They'll get me, damn 'em; I can't fight that lot and get away with it,' thought Biggles. Even as the thought crossed his mind the enemy machines made a swift turn and started climbing for more height. A puzzled expression crossed Biggles' face as he watched the manœuvre. 'What's the big idea?' he muttered. 'They're making a lot of fuss about one poor solitary Camel. They behave as if they were scared of me.' Not since the first moment that he had spotted the enemy aircraft had Biggles taken his eyes off them; now, still following the Fokkers round, they stopped abruptly and he started with astonishment. Twenty feet away from his right-wing tip was a Camel. Mahoney, in the cockpit, pushed up his goggles and grinned derisively at him. Biggles looked to the left and saw another Camel; he recognized MacLaren's machine. He glanced behind him and saw two more Camels bringing up the rear.

Biggles almost felt himself turn pale. 'My God!' he breathed, 'where did they come from? And I never saw them. Am I going blind? Suppose they had been Fokkers, it would have been just the same except that I'd be smoking on the floor by now. No wonder the Fokkers swerved when they saw this lot coming. Five against six,' he mused, 'that's better. They'll come in now, but they'll have to be quick to stop us, it isn't four miles to home.' Already he could see the British balloon line.* 'Good old Mac, good old Mahoney,' he thought exultantly.

* Both sides in the First World War used kite or observation balloons, with observers in baskets suspended below the balloon, for spotting guns and enemy troop movements. Their slang name was gas bags or sausages.

The Fokkers were coming in now, the leader dropping on one of the rear Camels which swung round like a whirlwind and nosed up to face its attack head-on. The other Fokkers closely followed the first, and Mac and Mahoney turned outwards to meet them. Biggles' hand gripped the stick in a spasm of impotent rage at the realization that he would have to run for it and leave them to do his fighting for him. Twice he half-turned and checked himself. 'I'll never take on another job like this as long as I live,' he swore.

Two Fokker triplanes passed him to the eastward, making for the dog-fight now ranging behind him. He was low, and against the sun they had not seen him. Thrusting aside the temptation to take advantage of his ideal position for attack, Biggles raced across the line, swearing savagely to himself. He dare not trust himself to look back. Suppose they got Mac or Mahoney—he daren't think of it. Curse that brass-hat and his messenger-boy errands, anyway. Well, he was over the line now—safe—safe with his damned packet. As the aerodrome loomed up he shifted slightly in his seat for a better view. He moved his hand to shift a lump which seemed to have formed in the cushion on his seat and the lump came away in his hand. It was the packet. 'It must have fallen on the seat and I've been sitting on it all the time—too worried to notice it,' he laughed. Then he put his nose down and dived for the aerodrome; 100, 120, 150 ticked up on the speed indicator.

Major Mullen and Colonel Raymond were standing on the tarmac waiting for him; he could see the Colonel's red tabs. He took the joystick in his left hand and the packet in his right—100 feet—50 feet—30—he saw the Colonel duck as he flung the plans at him, and then, after a wild zoom, swung round in a climbing turn for the line.

As he neared the support trenches he saw three Camels coming towards him. He looked anxiously for Mahoney's blue propeller boss; it was not among them. 'They've got old Mahoney'—he swallowed a lump in his throat. The three Camels turned and fell in line with him. Mac, in the nearest, flew closer and waved his hand and jabbed downwards. Looking down Biggles saw a Camel with a smashed undercarriage standing crookedly among the shell holes. By its side was a figure waving cap and goggles. Mahoney! He must have been shot up and just made the line, thought Biggles, as, with joy in his heart, he turned for home.

The C.O. was waiting for him on the tarmac when he landed.

'Don't you know better than to throw things at staff officers?' he said smiling. 'The Colonel has dashed back to headquarters with your billet-doux; he has asked me to thank you and to say that he will not forget to-day's work.'

'You can tell him when you see him that I won't either,' grinned Biggles. 'Come on, chaps, let's go and fetch Mahoney, and finish that rubber.'

# Chapter 3

# J–9982

Biggles hummed contentedly to himself as he circled slowly at 16,000 feet. He looked at his watch; he had been out nearly two hours on a solitary patrol which had so far proved uneventful. 'I'll do another five minutes and then pack up,' he decided.

Below him lay a great bank of broken altocumulus cloud. Detached solid-looking masses of gleaming white mist floated languidly above the main cloud-bank. Not another plane was in the air, at least, not above the cloud, as far as he could see. Every few minutes he turned, and holding his hand before his eyes studied the glare in the direction of the sun long and carefully between extended fingers. If danger lurked anywhere it was from there that it would probably come. He examined the cloud-bank below in detail, section by section. His eyes fell on a Camel coming towards him, far below, threading its way between the broken masses of cloud through which the ground occasionally showed in a blur of bluey-grey.

Biggles placed himself between the sun and the other Camel as he watched it; it would pass about a thousand feet below. 'You poor hoot,' thought Biggles as he watched the machine disinterestedly. 'If I was a Fokker you'd be a dead man by now. Ah! here comes his partner.' The second Camel had emerged from the cloud-bank and was now rapidly overtaking the first. The pilot of the leading Camel was evidently wide-

awake, for he turned back towards the second Camel
and then circled to allow it to overtake him. Biggles
noted that the second Camel was slightly above the
leading one and that instead of putting its nose down
to line up with it, the pilot was deliberately climbing
for more height.

The second Camel was not more than fifty feet
behind the first when its nose suddenly dropped as if
the pilot intended to ram it. 'Silly ass,' thought Biggles;
'what fool's game is he playing? That's how accidents
happen.' He caught his breath in amazed horror as a
stream of tracers suddenly spurted from the guns of the
topmost Camel point-blank into the cockpit of the one
below. The stricken machine lurched drunkenly, a
tongue of flame ran down the fuselage, its nose dropped
and it dived through the cloud-bank out of sight, leaving only a little dark patch of smoke to mark its going.

For a moment Biggles stared unbelievingly, his brain
refusing to believe what his eyes had seen.

'Great God!' he gasped, and then, thrusting the stick
forward, he dived on the murderer out of the sun. But
the other Camel was diving too, the pilot evidently
intending to get below the cloud to watch the result of
his handiwork. Biggles noted that the pilot did not once
look up, and he was barely thirty feet behind it and
slightly to one side when it disappeared into the swirling mist. Biggles pulled up to avoid a collision.
'J–9982,' he muttered aloud, naming the maker's
number which he had seen painted in white letters on
the fin of the diving machine. 'J–9982,' he repeated
again. 'All right, you swine, I'll remember you.'

He circled for a moment and dived through a hole
in the clouds, not daring to risk a collision in the opaque
mist. He looked about him quickly as he pulled out

below the cloud, but the Camel had disappeared. Far below he could see a long trail of black smoke where the fallen machine was still burning. For ten minutes he searched in vain, and then, feeling sick with rage and horror, he headed for the line. He wondered who was in the Camel which had been so foully attacked; he knew it must be either from his own or 231 Squadron, as they were the only Camel Squadrons in that area. He landed, and taxied quickly towards the sheds where a group of pilots lounged.

'Anybody out, Mac?' he almost snapped at MacLaren who had walked over to meet him.

'Yes, Mahoney's out with Forest and Hall on an O.P.*,' replied MacLaren, looking at him curiously. 'Here they come now,' he added, pointing to the sky in the direction of the line. 'Two of 'em, anyway.'

Biggles watched the two machines land, and Mahoney and Forest climbed out of their cockpits. 'Where's Hall, Mahoney?' he asked in a strained voice.

'About somewhere—won't be long I expect—he went fooling off on his own after I'd washed out,' answered the Flight-Commander.

'Towards Berniet?'

'Yes—why?'

'You can pack his kit—he won't be coming back,' said Biggles slowly, with a catch in his voice. He turned on his heel and walked towards the Squadron office.

Major Mullen smiled as he entered. 'Sit down, Biggles,' he said, the smile giving way to a look of anxiety as he noted the expression on the pilot's face.

'What's wrong, laddie?' he asked, coming quickly towards him.

* Offensive patrol, actively looking for something to attack.

245

Biggles told him what he'd seen, while the C.O. listened incredulously. 'Good heavens, Biggles,' he said at the end, 'what a hellish thing to do! What shall we do about it?'

'I am going over to 231 Squadron to see if they know anything about the other machine,' said Biggles shortly. 'It was never one of ours.'

'If it's a Hun we shall have to warn every Squadron along the line,' exclaimed Major Mullen gravely.

'And the Hun will know he is spotted within twenty-four hours,' sneered Biggles. 'You know what their intelligence service is like. At the first word he'll change the number on the machine and then we shall be in a hell of a mess. We have got him taped as it is, and he doesn't know it. No! You leave this to me, sir; we've got to take a chance. We'll get him, don't you worry.'

Twenty minutes later Biggles strode into the anteroom of 231 Squadron. A chorus of salutations, couched according to individual taste, greeted him. 'No, thanks, old man—can't stay now,' he replied curtly to a dozen invitations to have a drink.

'On the water waggon, Biggles?' asked Major Sharp, the C.O.

'No, sir, but I've got several things to do and I don't want to waste time. I have a word for your private ear, sir.'

'Certainly, what is it?' replied the Major at once.

'Have you got a Camel on your strength numbered J–9982?' inquired Biggles.

'I don't know, but Tommy will tell us. Tommy!' he called to the Equipment Officer, 'come here a minute. Do you happen to know if we have a machine numbered J–9982 on the station?'

'Not now, sir; but we had. That was Jackson's

machine; he went West at the beginning of the month, you remember.'

'Anybody see him crash?' asked Biggles.

'Don't think so, but I'll check up on the combat reports if you like. Speaking from memory, he went on a balloon-strafing show and never came back; yes, that was it.'

'So that was it, was it,' said Biggles slowly. 'Righto, Tommy, many thanks.'

Biggles took Major Sharp on one side and spoke to him earnestly for some minutes, the Major nodding his head as if in agreement from time to time.

'Right, sir,' he said at length, 'we'll leave it like that. Goodbye, sir. Cheerio, Tommy—cheerio, chaps,'

Major Mullen looked up as Biggles re-entered his office.

'It was as I thought, sir,' began Biggles. 'A Hun is flying that kite.'

'I can't believe a German pilot would do such a dastardly thing,' said the Major, shaking his head.

'No ordinary officer would, of course,' agreed Biggles, 'I'll bet you anything you like he is in no regular squadron. None of the Richthofen Staffel* would stand for that stuff any more than we would. But you'll find skunks in every mob if you look for 'em. The higher command wouldn't stand in a chap's way if he was low enough to do it. Maybe they've detailed somebody for the job for a special reason; you can never tell. One thing is certain. The pilots over the

---

* German equivalent of a squadron, 12 or 13 planes which fly together, often named after their leader, as here, where it is named after Baron Von Richtofen 'The Red Baron' the top scoring World War One fighter pilot, who shot down 80 Allied planes, before being killed in 1918.

other side know all about it or they'd shoot him down themselves. He's got a private mark somewhere. The archie batteries must know it, too. He drops them a light or throws some stunt occasionally so that they'll know it's him and not open fire.'

'I shall have to report it to Wing,' said the Major seriously.

'Give me forty-eight hours, sir,' begged Biggles, 'and then you can do what you like. Report it to Wing, and it will be known from Paris to Berlin and from Calais to Switzerland before the day's out. There won't be one Hun flying a Camel. Every Camel our archie batteries see will have a Hun in it, and they'll shoot at it. We'll be a blight in the sky—a target for every other pilot in the air to shoot at. A pretty mess that would be. Perhaps that is what the Huns are hoping for. Stand on what I tell you, sir; forget it for twenty-four hours, anyway, and you won't regret it. I'm going to talk to Mac and Mahoney, then I'm going over to look for him. I know his hunting-ground. I just want to see him once more—just once—through my sights.' Biggles, breathing heavily, departed to look for the other Flight Commanders.

He found them in the sheds and called them aside. 'Listen, chaps,' he began, 'there's a Hun flying a Camel over the line. His number is J–9982. J—9—9—8—2, remember it. If you let your imagination play on that for a moment you'll realize just what that means. We've got to get him, and get him quick. It was he who got Hall—I saw him, the dirty cannibal.'

MacLaren turned pale as death. Mahoney, his Celtic temper getting the better of him, spat a burst of profanity. His rage brought tears to his eyes.

'Well,' said Biggles, 'that's that, and it's enough; I'm going to look for him. You coming?'

'We're coming,' said the two pilots together, grimly.

'All right, now look, we've got to be careful. You can't shoot at a Camel like you would at a Hun. I'm going to paint my prop boss, centre-section and fin, blue. Sharp is painting all 231 Squadron machines like that so we'll know 'em. He knows the reason, but none of his officers do. None of our fellows are leaving the ground until we come back. If you see a Camel *without* these markings it may be him. If he is over Hunland and not being archied, it's almost certain to be him; but look for the number on the fin before you shoot. J–9982. If you see a Camel wearing that number, shoot quick and ask questions afterwards. He was working over the Berniet sector when I saw him, and that is where I am going to look for him. I'm off now.'

The sun was low in the western sky; Biggles, patrolling at 14,000 feet, yawned. Lord! he was tired. This was his fourth patrol; he seemed to have been in the sky all day—looking for a Camel without a blue prop-boss. He had seen MacLaren and Mahoney several times; they too were still searching. Biggles had found a Hanoverana* and shot it down in flames at the first burst without satisfying the stone-cold desire to kill which consumed him. He had been attacked by three Tripe-hounds** and had returned the attack with such savage fury and good effect that they acknowledged their mistake by diving for home.

This should have improved his temper, but it did

* German two-seater fighter and ground attack biplane.
** Slang: German fighter with three wings on each side, with two forward-firing guns.

249

not. Biggles wanted a certain Camel, and nothing would satisfy him until he had seen it plunging earthwards in flames, like its victim. He almost hoped that neither Mac nor Mahoney would find it and rob him of the pleasure. Biggles yawned again; he could hardly keep awake, he was so tired. 'This won't do,' he muttered, and leaned out of the cockpit to let the icy slipstream fan his cheeks. Three black spots appeared in front of him and he had warmed his guns before he realized that they were only oil spots on his goggles. He wiped them clean and for the hundredth time began a systematic scrutiny of the atmosphere in every direction.

It would be dark in half an hour. Already the earth was a vast swell of blue and purple shadows. 'It's a washout,' he thought bitterly. 'I might as well be getting home; he's gone to roost.' Without losing height he commenced a wide circle towards his own lines; his eye fell on a tiny speck far over and heading still farther in over the British lines. Small as it was, he recognized it for a Camel. 'Mac or Mahoney going home, I expect,' he said to himself; 'well, I'll just make one more cast.' The outer edge of his circle took him well over enemy lines, and ignoring the usual salvo of archie he looked long and searchingly into the enemies' country. A cluster of black spots attracted his attention. He recognized it for German archie and flew closer to ascertain the reason for it. 'S' turning, he climbed steadily and kept his eye on the bursts. He could see two machines approaching now, and the straight top wings and dihedral-angled lower planes told him they were Camels. A minute later he could see that both had blue prop-bosses. Mac and Mahoney!

Suddenly he stiffened in his seat. Who was it then

that he had seen far over his own lines? He was round in a flash heading for the direction taken by the lone machine. Five minutes later he saw a machine coming towards him. It was a Camel! His heart thumping uncomfortably with excitement, Biggles circled cautiously to meet it. His nostrils quivered when he was close enough to see that the prop-boss was unpainted and the leading edge of the centre-section was painted brown. An icy hand seemed to clutch his heart. Suppose he made a mistake! Suppose it was one of his own boys—out without order—he daren't think about it.

The Camel was close now, the pilot waving a greeting, but Biggles' eyes were fixed on the fin. J-... the numbers seemed to run into each other. Was he going blind? He pushed up his goggles and looked again. J–9982, he read, and grated his teeth.

The Camel closed up until it was flying beside him; the pilot smiling. Biggles showed his teeth in what he imagined to be an answering smile. 'You swine,' he breathed: 'you dirty, unutterable, murdering swine! I'm going to kill you if it's the last thing I do on earth.' Something made him glance upwards. Five Fokker triplanes were coming down on him like bolts from the blue. 'So, that's it, is it?' he muttered. 'You're the bait and I'm the fish. That's your game. Well, they'll get me, but you're getting yours first.'

Swiftly he moved the stick slightly back, sideways, and then forwards. 'Hold that, you rat,' he shouted, as he pressed his triggers. Rat-tat-tat-tat-tat-tat-tat-tat— a double stream of glittering tracer poured into the false Camel's cockpit. The pilot slumped forward in his seat and the machine nosed downwards.

Beside himself with rage, Biggles followed it, the Fokkers forgotten. 'Hold that—AND THAT'—he gritted through his teeth as he poured in burst after burst at point-blank range. 'Burn, you hound!' He laughed aloud as a streamer of yellow fire curled aft along the side of the fuselage. The rattle of guns near at hand made him look over his shoulder; a Fokker was on his tail, Spandaus stuttering. Another Fokker roared past with a Camel apparently glued to its tail; and still another Fokker and Camel were circling in tight spirals above. 'Go to it, boys,' grinned Biggles as he pulled the joystick right back into his stomach, and half-rolling off the top of the loop looked swiftly for the Fokker that had singled him out for destruction. Rat-tat-tat-tat . . . 'Oh! there you are,' he muttered, as the Fokker, which had followed his manœuvre, came at him again. Biggles, fighting mad, flew straight at it, guns streaming lead; the German lost his nerve first and swerved, Biggles swinging round on its tail, guns still going. Without warning, the black-crossed machine seemed to go to pieces in the air, and Biggles turned to look for the others. He saw a Camel spinning—a Tripehound followed it down. He thrust his joystick forward and poured in a long burst at the Fokker, which, turning like lightning and nearly standing on its tail, spat a stream of death at him. It stalled as Biggles zoomed over it.

Where were the others? Biggles looked around for the Camel he had seen spinning and breathed a sigh of relief when he saw it far below streaking for the line. A Fokker was smoking on the ground near the false Camel. Then he discovered another Camel flying close behind him. For the first time since the combat began he realized it was nearly dark. Feeling suddenly limp from reaction he waved to his companion, and together they dived for the line, emptying their guns into the enemy trenches as they passed over. The Camel below had already crossed the line to safety.

Major Mullen was waiting anxiously for them when they landed.

'Have you been balloon-strafing, Biggles?' he asked, looking aghast at bullet-shattered struts and torn fabric.

'No, sir,' replied Biggles with mock dignity, 'but I have to report that I have today shot down a British aircraft numbered J–9982, recently on the strength of 231 Squadron, and more recently the equipment of an enemy pilot, name unknown.'

He broke into a peal of nerve-jarring laughter which ended in something like a sob. 'Get me a drink somebody, please,' he pleaded. 'Lord! I am tired.'

# Chapter 4
# The Balloonatics

Captain James Bigglesworth brought the Headquarters car to a halt within a foot of the Service tender which had just stopped outside the Restaurant Chez Albert in the remote village of Clarmes. As he stepped out of the car, Captain Wilkinson of 287 Squadron leapt lightly from the tender. Biggles eyed him with astonishment.

'Hullo, Wilks!' he cried. 'What the deuce brings you here?'

'What are you doing here?' parried Wilkinson.

'I've come'—Biggles paused—'I've come to do some shopping,' he said brightly.

'What a funny thing, so have I,' grinned Wilkinson, 'and as I was here first I'm going to be served first. You've missed the boat, Biggles.'

'I'm dashed if I have,' cried Biggles hotly. 'Our crowd discovered it—you pull your stick back, Wilks, and let the dog see the rabbit.'

'Not on your life,' retorted Wilkinson briskly. 'First come, first served. You go and aviate your perishing Camel.' So saying he made a swift dash for the door of the estaminet; but he was not quite fast enough. Biggles tackled him low, brought him down with a crash, and together they rolled across the sun-baked earth.

Just how the matter would have ended it is impossible to say, but at that moment a touring car pulled up beside them with a grinding of brakes and Colonel Raymond, of Wing Headquarters, eyed the two belligerent officers through a monocle with well-feigned astonishment.

'Gentlemen! Officers! No, I must be mistaken,' he said softly, but with a deadly sarcasm that brought a blush to the cheeks of both officers. 'Are there no enemy aircraft left in the air that you must bicker among yourselves on the high road? Come, come. Can I be of any assistance?' He left the car, bade his chauffeur drive on, and came towards them. 'Now,' he said sternly, 'what is all this about?'

'That is the point, sir,' began Biggles. 'Yesterday morning Batty—that is, Batson, of my Flight—was coming back this way by road from a forced landing, and dropped in here for—er—well, I suppose, for a drink. During a conversation with the proprietor he learned that M. Albert had, some years ago, laid in a stock of whisky at the request of the staff of an Englishman who had taken the Château d'Abnay for the season. When this man returned to England, Albert had some of the stuff left on his hands, and, as the local bandits do not apparently drink whisky, it is still here. To make a long story short, sir, Batty—that is, Batson—found no less than fourteen bottles of the pre-War article reposing under the cobwebs in the cellar—and going for the pre-War price of five francs fifty the bottle. Unfortunately Batty—I mean Batson—had only enough money on him to bring one bottle back to the Mess, so I slipped along this morning to get the rest. But it appears that Batty—that is, Batson—went to a binge—er—guest night—at 287 Squadron last night and babbled the good news—at least that is presumably what happened since I find Captain Wilkinson here this morning. I think you will agree, sir, that having been found by an officer of 266 Squadron the stuff should rightly belong to them,' concluded Biggles, eyeing the would-be sharer of the spoils in cold anger.

'Well, well,' said the Colonel after a brief pause, 'if that is the cause of the trouble I can settle the matter for you. The whisky has gone.'

'Gone!' cried Biggles aghast—'all of it?'

'Yes, I fear so,' replied the Colonel sadly.

'Can you understand the mentality of a man who would take the lot and leave none for anyone else,' exclaimed Biggles bitterly. 'Do you know who it was, sir?'

The Colonel paused for a moment before replying. 'Well, as a matter of fact, it was me,' he admitted, the corners of his mouth twitching.

Biggles turned red and then white. Wilkinson started a guffaw which he turned to a cough as the Colonel's eye fell on him.

'You see,' went on the Colonel, 'I, too, was a guest at 287 Squadron Mess last night, and fearing that the whisky might fall into unappreciative hands, I collected it on my way home. I have just come to pay for it.'

Biggles breathed heavily, but said nothing. Colonel Raymond eyed him sympathetically, and then brightened as an idea struck him.

'Now, I'll be fair about this; I'll tell you what I'll do,' he began.

'I know! Toss for it, sir,' suggested Biggles eagerly, feeling in his pocket for a coin.

The Colonel shook his head. 'No,' he said, 'I've a better idea than that; do you fellows know the Duneville balloon?'

Biggles showed his teeth in a mirthless smile. 'Do I? I should say I do! When I'm tired of life I am going to fly within half a mile of that sausage. That's all that will be necessary.'

Wilkinson nodded. 'You won't have to go so far as that, Biggles,' he said. 'Go within a mile of that kite and you'll see old man Death waiting with the door wide open.'

'In that case it doesn't 'matter,' said the Colonel, preparing to enter the estaminet.

'Just a moment, sir! What about the balloon?' cried Biggles anxiously.

'Well, what I was going to suggest was this,' replied the Colonel. 'Strictly between ourselves, the infantry are doing a show in the morning. We are moving a lot of troops, and that observation balloon has got to come down and stay down. I'm willing to hand over six bottles of that whisky, free, gratis and for nothing, to the officer who does most to keep that balloon on the floor for the next few hours. To-day is Sunday. Time expires twelve noon to-morrow. We'll score like this. Forcing the ground crew to haul the balloon down counts three points; shooting it down in flames, five points. My observers will have their glasses on the balloon all day. You know as well as I do that if you shoot the balloon down there will be another one up within a few hours. Duneville is an important observation post for the Boche.'

'Did you say just now that you would be *fair*, sir?' asked Biggles incredulously.

Colonel Raymond ignored the thrust. 'Pulled down — a try — three points; down in flames — goal — five points; don't forget.' In the doorway of the estaminet he turned and a broad smile spread over his face. 'Any officer taking the balloon prisoner scores a grand slam and gets the other six bottles. Good-bye.'

For a full minute the two Flight-Commanders stood staring at the closed door as if fascinated; then Biggles started towards his car. With his foot on the running-board he turned to Wilkinson.

'You keep your damned glasshouse out of my way,' he said curtly, referring to the S.E.5, which was, at that time, fitted with a semi-cabin windscreen.

'And you keep your oil-swilling "hump" where it belongs,' snapped Wilkinson, referring to Biggles' Camel.

Inside the estaminet Colonel Raymond was sipping pre-War whisky with the air of a connoisseur; Albert was packing twelve bottles into a case. 'Unless I am very much mistaken,' mused the Colonel, 'that Boche balloon is in for a trying time—a very trying time.'

An hour later Biggles, clad in a leather coat, made his way towards the hangars. In his pocket he carried written orders to strafe the Duneville Balloon; these orders permitted him to carry Buckingham (incendiary) bullets, forbidden on pain of death for any other purpose by the rules of war. Rules were seldom observed during the great struggle, but the order would, at least, protect him from trouble at the hands of the enemy, should he be forced to land on the wrong side of the lines. He halted before a Camel upon which a squad of ack-emmas were working feverishly.

'What are you doing, Flight?' he asked the Flight-Sergeant in charge.

'Just a top overhaul, sir, while you were away,' replied the Flight-Sergeant. 'She'll be ready in an hour.'

Biggles frowned, but said nothing; he was disappointed to find his machine wasn't ready, but he would not say anything to discourage the mechanics. 'Fill the belts with tracer and Buckingham right through in that order,' he said presently as he seated himself and prepared to wait.

'Going balloon strafing, sir?' Biggles nodded. The Sergeant shrugged his shoulders and said no more.

The machine was ready at last. Biggles, fretting with impatience, took off and headed for the line, climbing all the time in the direction of Duneville. It did not take him many minutes to spot his objective. There it was, the mis-shapen beast, four miles away and five thousand feet below him. Circling cautiously towards it he examined the air and ground in its vicinity carefully. He could see nothing, but he knew perfectly well that once let him venture within a mile of that sausage floating so placidly in the blue vault, the air about it would be a maelstrom of fire and hurtling metal. He started. Far above the balloon appeared a tiny black speck surrounded by a halo of black smoke and little darting jabs of flame. Biggles swore and raced towards the scene, watching the machine which he now recognized as an S.E.5, with interest. 'Sweet spirits of nitre,' he muttered, 'What a hell to be flying through, all for a case of whisky. He must be crazy.' The S.E.5 was going down in an almost vertical dive, twisting like a wounded sparrow-hawk, pieces of torn fabric streaming out behind it. Swift as had been its descent the balloon crew were faster, and the sausage was on the ground before the S.E. could reach it. The machine pulled up in an almost vertical zoom, and as it flew past him, Wilkinson, the pilot, pushed up his goggles and then very deliberately, jabbed up three fingers at him.

'Three points, eh,' muttered Biggles. He placed his

thumb against his nose and extended his fingers in the time-honoured manner. Wilkinson grinned, and with a parting wave, turned for home. Biggles climbed away disconsolately.

For an hour he circled around, returning at intervals to see if the balloon had reappeared, but there was no sign of it, and he knew the reason. 'They can see me,' he pondered. 'They know why I'm hanging around; presently they'll send for a Staffel of Huns to drive me away. I'll have to try different tactics.' He returned to the aerodrome, refuelled, and returning to the line crossed over four or five miles from the balloon station. For ten minutes he flew straight into the enemies' country and then circled back to approach the balloon from its own side of the line. Looking ahead anxiously, his heart leapt as his eyes fell on the ungainly gas-bag floating below him. Instinctively he looked upwards to make sure that there were no protecting machines, and caught his breath sharply.

Three Fokker Triplanes were coming down in a steep dive, but not in his direction. Following their line of flight he saw an S.E.5 which, apparently, just realizing its danger was streaking for home. 'That's Wilks,' thought Biggles, 'Wilks for a certainty. He did the same thing as I've done and was just going for the sausage when he saw them coming. They'll get him. They've 3,000 feet of height on him—he'll never reach the line. The Tripehounds have left the coast clear for me though; I'll never get such a chance again. It's Wilks or the balloon—damn the luck—I can't let them get old Wilks.' He put his nose down in the wake of the Fokkers in a wire-screaming dive.

He reached the nearest Fokker almost at the same time as the leading Fokker fired at the S.E.; at that moment the black-crossed machines were too intent on their quarry to look back. Biggles held his fire until his propeller was only a few feet from the nearest enemy machine, and then raked it from tail skid to propeller-boss with one deadly burst. The Triplane slowly turned over on to its back. Hearing the shots, the other two Fokkers whirled round, leaving the S.E. a clear run home. Biggles, cold as ice, was on the tail of the nearest in a flash, and the next instant all three machines were turning in a tight circle. The Fokkers started to outclimb him at once, as he knew they would. 'I'm in a mess now,' he muttered, as the top Fokker levelled out to come down on him, and he pulled the Camel up to take it head-on.

What was that? An S.E.5 was above them all, coming down like a comet on the Fokker, guns streaming two pencil lines of white smoke. The Fokker turned and dived, the S.E. on its tail. 'Good for you, Wilks,' grinned Biggles; 'that evens things up.' He looked for the other Triplane, but it was a mile away far over its own side of the line.

Then he remembered the balloon. Where was it? Great Scott! there it was, still up, less than a mile away. Even as Biggles put his nose down towards it, its crew seemed to divine his intention and started to haul it down. A stabbing flame and a cloud of black smoke appeared in front of him, but he did not alter his course. He was flying through a hail of archie and machine gun bullets now, every nerve taut, eyes on the blurred mass of the balloon. Five hundred feet—three hundred—one hundred, the distance closed between them: 'At least I won't be out for a duck,' he muttered as he pressed his triggers. He had a fleeting vision of the observers' parachutes opening as they sprang from the basket, a great burst of flame, and then he was twisting upwards in a wild zoom in the direction of the line.

He breathed a sigh of relief as he passed over. An S.E.5 appeared by his side, the pilot waving a greeting. Biggles pulled off his gauntlet and jabbed five fingers upwards. 'There will be no more balloons to-day,' he said to himself, glancing towards the setting sun, as he made for home.

As he landed, 'Wat' Tyler, the Recording Officer, handed him a slip. 'Signal for you from Wing, just in,' he said. 'Damned if I know what it means.'

Biggles glanced at the message and grinned. 'Score 5–3 your favour,' he read. The initials were those of Colonel Raymond.

'Tired of life, Biggles?'

Biggles looked up from the combat report to see Major Mullen eyeing him sadly.

'Why, sir?' he asked.

'You've been balloon strafing,' said the C.O.

'That's true, sir, I had a little affair with the Duneville sausage this afternoon,' admitted Biggles.

'I see,' said the C.O. 'Well, if you're in a hurry to write yourself off\*, go right ahead. You get balloon fever and you won't last a week; you know that as well as I do. Don't be a fool, Biggles, let 'em alone. By the way, I see that the wind has shifted; blowing straight over our way for a change. All right, finish your report,

---

\* 'Write-off.' An aeroplane that was so badly damaged as to be of no further use was officially 'written-off' the squadron books. The expression 'write off' was loosely used to infer the complete destruction of anything.

but let those infernal kites alone,' he added, as he left the room.

Biggles remained with his pen poised, as an idea flashed into his mind. The wind was blowing straight over our lines, was it? He hurried to the window and looked at the wind-stocking. 'Lord! so it is,' he muttered, and sat down, deep in thought. What was it Colonel Raymond had said? 'Anybody capturing the balloon scores a grand slam and gets the other six bottles.' 'Great Scott!' he grinned, 'I wonder if it's possible? If I could cut the cable the balloon would drift over to our side. Cables have been cut by shell splinters before to-day. I wonder—!'

He dashed off to the nearest balloon squadron and after spending half an hour asking many questions in the company of a balloon officer, returned to the aerodrome still deep in thought. He sought his Flight-Sergeant.

'What bombs have we, Flight?' he asked.

'Only 20 lb. Coopers, sir,' replied the N.C.O.*, looking at him queerly.

'Nothing bigger?'

'No, sir.'

'I see. Do you think my Camel would carry a 112-pounder?' asked Biggles.

'Carry it all right, sir, if you could get a rack fixed, though you wouldn't be able to throw the machine about much with that lot on,' grinned the Flight-Sergeant.

'Where can we get one?'

'297 Squadron at Arville use them on their "Nines",

* Non Commissioned officer eg a Corporal or a Sergeant.

sir. If you gave me a chit to the E.O.* I could get one and borrow a bomb-rack.'

'Will you do that for me, Flight — and get it fixed to-night. I'm leaving the ground at daylight in the morning. I'd like a five-seconds delay fuse fixed, if you can manage it.'

'I'll have a shot at it, sir.'

Well satisfied with his evening's work, Biggles went to bed early.

At the first streak of dawn Biggles was in the cockpit warming up his engine. The Flight-Sergeant, as good as his word, had hung the bomb under the fuselage just clear of the undercarriage. The change of wind had brought low cloud and Biggles looked at it anxiously. Too much cloud would spoil visibility and the balloon would not go up.

The Camel took a long run to lift its unusual load, but once in the air the difference was hardly noticeable except for a slight heaviness on the controls. 'This is the maddest thing I've ever done in my life,' soliloquized the pilot, as he sped towards the lines. 'If I get away with it I'll sign the pledge.' As he approached Duneville he saw the balloon just going up, but following his tactics of the previous day he circled, crossed the line a few miles lower down, and prepared to attack from the German side. The balloon was straight ahead of him now and Biggles swore as his eye fell on a solitary S.E.5 farther west, trailing a line of archie bursts in its wake. Biggles put the nose of the Camel down and started hedge hopping** in the direction of the sausage, now far above him. Vaguely he heard the

* Equipment Officer.
** Flying very close to the ground, avoiding obstacles.

264

crackle of machine gun fire as he raced across the enemy reserve trenches, but he heeded it not. He was afraid of one thing only, and that was accidentally hitting the balloon cable with his wing; it was only about as thick as his finger and would be difficult to see. The balloon was less than a mile away now, the ground party no doubt looking upwards for any possible danger. With his wheels nearly touching the ground he tore towards the little group at the foot of the cable. He saw them turn in his direction, scatter and dive for shelter, and then he was on them. At the last instant he threw the machine in a bank away from the cable drum, pulled the bomb-toggle, and zoomed, twisting and turning as he dashed towards his own lines. As he reached comparative safety he looked back over his shoulder; a great pillar of smoke marked the spot where the bomb had burst, but the sausage was nowhere in sight.

Ignoring the archie that still followed him, Biggles pushed up his goggles and looked again, an expression of incredulous amazement on his face. A movement far above caught his eye and caused him to look up; an ejaculation of astonishment escaped his lips. The balloon, freed from its anchor, had shot up to ten or eleven thousand feet and was already sailing over no-man's-land! He could see no parachutes, and concluded that the observers, taken unawares, were still in the basket. Far away he saw an S.E.5 diving across the line to where the balloon would normally be. Biggles grinned. 'The bird has flown,' he muttered, as the S.E. pilot swung round in obvious confusion, evidently at a loss to know what had become of it, but when he began climbing, Biggles knew that his balloon had been sighted by the lynx-eyed Flight-Commander.

Biggles reached the balloon first, waved a greeting to the occupants who were busy with something inside the basket, and then fired a warning Very light in the direction of the rapidly approaching S.E.5. The Camel pilot guessed what had happened to the balloon. When the mooring cable had been cut it had shot up until the automatic valve had functioned, and, by releasing the gas, checked the ascent, and incidentally prevented the balloon from bursting. The observers had been too startled to take to their parachutes immediately, and then, seeing that they would in any case drift across the line and be taken prisoners, decided to remain where they were and bring their unwieldy craft to earth.

They were now opening the valve and losing height rapidly, which was exactly what Biggles had hoped would happen. He knew little of ballooning, but enough to understand what the two men in the basket would do. The balloon would drop with increasing rapidity; near the ground the crew would check its descent by throwing ballast overboard and then pull the rip-panel, releasing all the gas from the envelope, which would then collapse and sink lightly to earth. It happened as Biggles anticipated. Close to the ground the fabric spread out like a great mushroom and quietly settled down. Biggles landed in the next field, the S.E.5 landing a moment later. A touring car intercepted them as they crossed the road separating them from the deflated monster. Colonel Raymond greeted them.

'Who did that?' he laughed, pointing towards the balloon.

'My prisoner, sir,' grinned Biggles. 'I claim a grand slam and the twelve bottles. There will be no more balloons up at Duneville to-day.'

'You've won them,' laughed the Colonel. 'Collect them at the Chez Albert. They are paid for.'

'At the where?' said the two pilots together, staring. 'Do you mean to tell us that the whisky was in there all the time?' asked Biggles, with a marked lack of respect.

'Never mind,' said the Colonel soothingly, 'you'll be able to get marvellously drunk to-night.'

'Me! Drunk!' said Biggles disgustedly, 'I never drink whisky.'

Colonel Raymond looked at him in amazement. 'Then why—'

'You see, it's 266 guest-night to-morrow, and I thought we'd give everyone a treat. Will you come, sir? You will, Wilks, I know.'

'You bet I will!' cried both officers together.

# Chapter 5
# The Blue Devil

The summer sun shone down from a sky of cloudless blue. Biggles sat on the doorstep of No. 287 Squadron Mess and watched the evolutions of an aeroplane high overhead with puzzled interest, wondering what the pilot was trying to do.

He was on his way home from an uneventful morning patrol and had dropped in to have a word or two with Wilkinson, only to be told that he was in the air.

Slightly torpid from two hours at 16,000 feet he had settled down in the ante-room to await his return, when the amazing aerobatics of the S.E.5 above had attracted his attention. With several other officers he had moved to the door in order to obtain an uninterrupted view of the performance.

'That's Wilks all right,' observed Barrett, a comparative veteran of six months at the front. 'He's been doing that on and off for the last two days.'

Biggles nodded wonderingly. 'What's the matter with him?' he asked. 'I always thought he was crazy—just look at the fool, he'll break that machine in a minute.'

The evolutions of the S.E.5 were certainly sufficiently unusual to call for comment. The pilot appeared to be trying to do something between a vertical bank and a half-roll. Over and over he repeated the same manœuvre, sometimes falling out of it into a spin and sometimes in a stall.

'Here he comes, you can ask him,' said Barrett, as the engine was cut off and the S.E.5 commenced to glide down to land.

Biggles strolled across the tarmac to meet the pilot.

'How did that look from the ground?' asked Wilkinson, grinning, as he clambered out of the cockpit.

'It looked to me that if you were trying to strip the wings off that kite you must have damn nearly succeeded,' replied Biggles. 'Are you tired of life or something? What's the big idea, anyway?'

'Come across to the mess and I'll tell you,' answered Wilkinson, and together they made their way towards the ante-room.

'Now tell me this,' continued the S.E.5 pilot when they had called for drinks and made themselves comfortable, 'have you ever bumped into that blue and yellow Boche circus* that hangs out somewhere near Lille? I believe they are now on Aerodrome 27.'

'Too true I have,' admitted Biggles. 'What about them?'

'Have you seen 'em lately?'

'No! Come on, cough it up, laddie. Have they turned pink, or what?'

'No, they're still blue, but they've got a new leader, and if you place any value at all on your young life, keep out of his way, that's all,' replied Wilkinson soberly.

'Hot stuff, eh?' inquired Biggles.

'He's hotter than hell at twelve noon on mid-summer's day,' declared Wilkinson. 'Now, let me tell you something else. First of all, as you know, these

* Slang: a formation of German fighter aircraft nicknamed circus by RFC pilots because of the Germans' brightly painted aircraft.

Albatroses* are all painted blue, but there's a bit of yellow on them somewhere.'

'Yes, I've noticed that,' replied Biggles, 'one of them has got yellow elevators, and there's another with a yellow centre-section.'

'That's right,' agreed Wilkinson. 'They've all got that touch of yellow on them somewhere, that is, all except the leader. That's what I'm told by one or two fellows who have seen him and lived to tell the tale. He's blue all over—no yellow anywhere. Blue propeller-boss, wheel discs, everything in fact. That marks him for you. The Huns call him the Blue Devil and they say he's got thirty machines in two months—every machine he's ever tackled. That's pretty good going, and, if it's true, he must be pretty smart. The most amazing thing about it is, though, they say his machine has never been touched by a bullet.'

'Who says?' inquired Biggles curiously.

'Wait a minute, don't be in such an infernal hurry. Now, until a couple of days ago we had only heard rumours about this bloke, but last Thursday I got one of his men, an N.C.O. pilot. I met him over Paschendale and we had a rough house; in the end I got his engine. For once the wind was blowing our way and we had drifted a bit in the scrap. To cut a long story short, he landed under control behind our lines. He managed to set fire to his machine before anybody could get to him, but we brought him back to the mess for a binge—you know. We made a wild night of it and under the influence of alcohol he started bragging, like a Boche will when he's had a few beers. Among other things he told us that this Blue Bird is going to knock

* German single-seater fighter with two fixed machine guns synchronised to fire through the propeller.

down every one of our machines one after the other, just like that. Now listen to this. This Hun has got a new stunt which sounds like the Immelmann business all over again. You remember that when Immelmann first invented his turn, nobody could touch him until we rumbled it, and then McCubbin got him. Everybody does the stunt now, so it doesn't cut much ice. Nobody knows quite what this new Hun does or how he does it. He's tried to explain it to his own chaps, but they can't get the hang of it, which seems damn funny, I'll admit. This lad I got tried to tell me how it was done when he was blotto—that is, the stick and rudder movements, but I couldn't follow how it worked. I've tried to do it in the air; you saw me trying just now. It's a new sort of turn; just when you get on this fellow's tail and kid yourself you've got him cold, he pivots somehow on his wing-tip and gets you. This lad of mine swore that the man who gets on his tail is cold meat—dead before he knows what's hit him. It sounds damned unlikely to me, but then the Immelmann turn probably sounded just as unlikely in its day. Well, that's the story, laddie, and now you know as much about it as I do. The point is, what are we going to do about it?'

Biggles pondered for a few moments. 'The thing seems to be for us to find him and see how he does it,' he observed in a flash of inspiration.

'I thought you'd get a rush of blood to the brain,' sneered Wilkinson. 'You get on his tail and I'll do the watching.'

'Funny, aren't you?' retorted Biggles. 'If I meet him I'll do my own watching and then come back and tell you all about it. Maybe you'll be able to earn your pay and get a Hun or two occasionally. Blue devils go pop at the end, if I remember my fireworks.'

On his way home Biggles thought a good deal about what Wilkinson had told him concerning the blue Albatros. 'Sooner or later I shall meet him,' he reflected, 'so I might as well decide how am I going to act. When he pulls this patent stunt he must reckon on the fellow he's fighting doing the usual thing, making a certain move at a certain time, and up to the present the fellow has always obliged him; but if he happened to do something else, something unorthodox, it might put him off his stroke. Well, we'll see; but it's difficult to know what to do if you don't know what the other fellow's going to do. If I could see the trick once I should know, but apparently he takes care that nobody gets a second chance.'

His curiosity prompted him to spend a good deal of time in the Lille area, but his vigilance was unrewarded; of the blue circus he saw no sign. He saw Wilkinson several times, and each time he learned that the Blue Devil had claimed another victim, but the knowledge only sharpened his curiosity.

By the perversity of fate it so happened that the encounter occurred at a moment when no thought of it was in his mind. He was returning from a lone patrol at 15,000 feet, deliberating in his mind as to whether or not he should have a shot at the new Duneville balloon as he crossed the lines, when his ever-watchful eye saw a grey shadow flit across a cloud far below. It was only a fleeting glimpse, but it was sufficient. It was not his own shadow. What, then? More from instinct than actual thought he whirled round and flung stick and rudder-bar hard over as the rattle of guns struck his ears. An Albatros screamed past him barely twenty feet away. 'Nearly caught me napping, did you?' muttered Biggles, as he swung the Camel in the wake of the enemy machine. He was on its tail in a flash, and only then did he notice its colour.

It was blue! Biggles caught his breath as he ran his eyes swiftly over it, looking for a touch of yellow, but there was none. 'So it's you, is it?' he muttered, as he tore after it, trying vainly to bring his sights to bear. 'Well, let's see the trick.'

He was as cold as ice, every nerve braced taut as a piece of elastic, for unless rumour lied, he was up against a foeman of outstanding ability, a man who had downed thirty machines in as many duels without once having his own machine touched.

Biggles knew that he was about to fight the battle of his life where one false move would mean the end. Neither of them had ever been beaten, but now one of them must taste defeat. In a few minutes either a Camel or an Albatros would be hurtling downwards on its way to oblivion. He tightened his grip on the joystick and warmed his guns with a short burst.

Both machines were banking vertically now, one each side of a circle not a hundred feet across. Round and round they raced as if swinging on an invisible pivot, the circle slowly decreasing in size. Tighter and tighter became the spiral as each pilot tried to see the other through his sights. The wind screamed in his wires and Biggles began to feel dizzy with the strain; he had lost all count of time and space, and of the perpendicular. His joystick was right back in his thigh as he strove to cut across a chord of the circle and place himself in a position for a shot. Always just in front of his nose was the blue tail, just out of range, just far enough in front to make shooting a waste of ammunition. Another few inches would do it; the ring of his sight cut across the blue tail now—God—just for a little more—just another inch. 'Come on, where's your trick?' snarled Biggles, feeling that he was getting giddy.

He was ready for it when it happened, although just how it came about he could never afterwards tell. At one moment his sights were within a foot of the blue cockpit; he saw the Boche turn his head slowly, and the next instant the blue nose was pointing at him, a double stream of scarlet flame pouring from the twin Spandau guns.

Biggles knew that he was caught—doomed. He heard bullets tearing through the fuselage behind him and the sound seemed to send him mad. Unconsciously he did the very thing he had planned to do—the unorthodox. Instead of trying to get out of that blasting stream of lead, thereby giving himself over to certain death, he savagely shoved the stick forward and tried to ram his opponent, pressing his triggers automatically as his nose came in line with the other's.

For perhaps one second the two machines faced each other thus, not fifty feet apart, their tracer making a glittering line between them. Biggles had a fleeting glimpse of the Albatros jerking desperately sideways, at the same instant something snatched at the side of his Sidcot and a hammer-like blow smashed across his face; he slipped off on to his wing and spun. He came out of the spin tearing madly at the smashed goggles which were blinding him, spun again, and then righted the machine by sheer instinct.

Half-dazed he wiped the blood from his eyes and looked around for the machine which he knew must now be coming in for the coup-de-grace. It was nowhere in sight. It was some seconds before he picked it out, half-way to the ground, spinning viciously.

Biggles leaned back in his cockpit for a moment, sick and faint from shock and reaction. When he looked down again the black-crossed machine was a flattened wreck on the ground. Gently he turned the torn and tattered Camel for home. 'That was closish,' he muttered to himself, 'closish. I shall have to be more careful. I wonder how he did that stunt? Pity Wilks wasn't watching!'

# Chapter 6
# Camouflage

From his elevated position in the cockpit of a Camel, Biggles surveyed the scene below him dispassionately. An intricate tracery of thin white lines marked the trench system where half a million men were locked in a life and death struggle, and a line of tiny white puffs, looking ridiculously harmless from the distance, showed the extent of the artillery barrage of flame and hurtling steel.

He turned eastward into enemy country and subjected every inch of the sky to a searching scrutiny. For a few minutes he flew thus, keeping a watchful eye upwards and occasionally glancing downwards to check his landmarks. During one of these periodical inspections of the country below something caught his eye which caused him to prolong his examination; he tilted his wing to see more clearly.

'Well, I'm dashed,' he muttered to himself; 'funny I've never noticed that before.' The object that had excited his curiosity was commonplace enough; it was simply a small church on a slight eminence. His eye followed the winding road to where it crossed the main Lille road and thence to the small hamlet of Bonvillier, which the church was evidently intended to serve. 'I could have sworn the church was in the middle of the village,' he thought. 'Dammit, it is,' he said aloud, as his eye fell on a square-towered building in the market place. 'Two churches, eh? They must have religious mania,' he mused. 'I expect the other is a chapel; funny I've never noticed it before, it's plain enough to see, in all conscience.'

He turned back towards the lines, and after another penetrating examination of the surrounding atmosphere, glanced at his map to pin-point* the chapel. It was not shown. He made a wide circle, wing down, side-slipping to lose height quickly, and, ignoring the inevitable salvo of archie, took a closer look at the building which had intrigued him. Pretty old place, he commented, as he picked out the details of ivy-covered masonry, the crumbling tombstones and the neat flower beds that bordered the curé's residence.

An exceptionally close burst of archie reminded him that he was dangerously low over the enemy lines, and as he was at the end of his patrol he dived for home, emptying his guns into the Boche support trenches as he passed over them.

Arriving back at the aerodrome, he landed and made his way slowly to the Squadron office. Colonel Raymond, of Wing Headquarters, who was in earnest conversation with Major Mullen, the C.O., broke off to nod a greeting.

'Morning, Bigglesworth,' he called cheerfully.

'Good morning, sir,' replied Biggles. 'No more packets for me to fetch, I hope,' he added with a grin.

'No,' responded the Colonel seriously, 'but I'm a bit worried all the same. We can't locate that damned heavy gun the Boche are using against our rest camps. I've had every likely area photographed, but we can't

---

* During the War maps were divided and subdivided into squares. By naming the letters and numbers of the squares, any single spot, almost to the yard, could be named and identified. This was known as pin-pointing.

find the blaze* anywhere. Haven't seen a loose gun anywhere, I suppose?'

Biggles shook his head. 'I haven't seen a damned thing the whole afternoon,' he replied bitterly, 'except a church I didn't know existed.' He took a pencil off the Major's desk and marked the position carefully on his map.

The Colonel, glancing over his shoulder, smiled with superior wisdom. 'You've got that wrong,' he said, 'there's no church there.'

Mahoney and several other officers entered the room to write their combat reports, but Biggles heeded them not.

'What do you mean, sir?' he asked, a trifle nettled. 'I know a church when I see one.'

'What sort of church is it?' asked Colonel Raymond.

Biggles described it briefly.

'Why, that's the church on the hill at Berniet,' smiled the Colonel.

'Berniet!' cried Biggles, 'but I haven't been near Berniet this morning. I beg your pardon, sir, but I saw that church here,' and he indicated the position at Bonvillier, emphatically, with the point of a pencil.

Colonel Raymond shook his head. 'Look,' he said suddenly, and selecting a photograph from a folio on the table, passed it across. 'Those photos were taken yesterday. There is Bonvillier, there are the cross-roads—there's no church, as you can see.' Biggles stared at the photographs in comical amazement, and then frowned.

---

* The line of burnt or flattened grass in front of the muzzle of a gun, caused by the flash. It showed up plainly in air photographs and betrayed many batteries.

'You're wrong, Biggles, there's no church there,' broke in Mahoney.

Biggles wheeled round in a flash. 'Are you telling me that I can't read a map, or that I don't know where I am when I'm flying?' he snapped.

'Looks like it,' grinned the other Flight-Commander, frankly, amid laughter. Biggles sprang to his feet, white with anger. 'Funny, aren't you?' he sneered; 'all right, we'll see who's right.'

He went out and slammed the door behind him.

On a dawn patrol the following morning he flew to Bonvillier, and looked down confidently for the church. His eye picked out the white ribbon of road. 'There's the crossroads—the village—well, I'm damned!' He stared as if fascinated at the spot where, the afternoon before, he thought he had located the sacred building. He pushed up his goggles and examined both sides of the road minutely, but only empty fields met his gaze. 'I'm going crazy,' he told himself bitterly, 'I'll soon be for H.E.* at this rate; I'm beginning to see things. Well, it isn't there. Let's have a look at Berniet.'

Ten minutes later he was circling high above the other village looking for the church, but in vain. 'Ha! ha!' he laughed. 'Damn good, we're all wrong; it isn't here, either.' Suddenly he became serious. 'If it isn't here, where the devil is it?' he mused. 'There must *be* a church, because the others have seen it; the thing can't walk, not complete with churchyard, ivy and gardens.' He was puzzled, and his eyes took on a thoughtful frown. 'I'll get to the bottom of this if it

* Home Establishment.

279

takes me all day,' he promised himself, and settled down for the search.

For an hour or more he flew up and down the line, systematically examining the ground section by section, and was about to abandon his self-appointed task when he came upon it suddenly, and the discovery gave him something like a shock. He was studying a wood, far over the lines, which he suspected concealed an archie battery that was worrying him, when his eyes fell on the well-remembered ivy-clad walls, crumbling tombstones and well-kept rectory gardens. It nestled snugly by the edge of the wood, half a mile from a row of tumbledown cottages.

'So there you are,' he muttered grimly. 'I'll have a closer look at you and then I'll know you next time I see you.' He shoved the stick forward and tore down in a long, screaming dive that brought him to within 1,000 feet of his objective. As he flattened out, his eyes still on the church, he caught his breath suddenly and swerved away. The Camel lurched drunkenly as a stabbing flame split the air and a billow of black smoke blossomed out not thirty yards away. Another appeared in front of him and something smashed through his left wing not a foot from the fuselage. In a moment the air about him was full of vicious jabs of flame and swirling smoke.

'My God!' grunted Biggles, as he twisted like a wounded bird in the sea of flying steel and high explosive. 'What have I barged into?' He put his nose down until the needle of the speed indicator rested against the pin, and then, thirty feet from the ground, sped out of the vicinity like a startled snipe.

'Good Lord,' he said, weakly, as the fusillade died away behind him; 'What a mazurka.' He tore across

the lines amid a hail of machine-gun bullets, and landing on the aerodrome ran swiftly to the Squadron office.
The C.O., he was told, was in the air. He seized the
telephone and called Wing Headquarters, asking for
Colonel Raymond.

'I've found the church, sir,' he called as the Colonel's
voice came over the 'phone.

'What about it? I'll tell you. It isn't at Berniet—I
beg your pardon, sir—I didn't mean to be impertinent,
but it's a fact. It isn't at Bonvillier, either. I spent the
morning looking for it and finally ran it to earth on the
edge of the oblong-shaped wood just east of Morslede.
Funny, did you say, sir? Yes, it is funny; but I've got
something still funnier to tell you. That damn taber-
nacle's on wheels; it moves about after dark—*and the
gun you are looking for is inside it.* Just a moment, sir, I'll
give you the pin-point. What's that, sir? Shoot! Good,
I'll go and watch the fireworks.'

Twenty minutes later, from a safe altitude, he
watched with marked approval salvo after salvo of
shells, hurled by half a dozen batteries of howitzers,*
tearing the surface off the earth and pounding the
'church' and its contents to mangled pulp. An R.E.8**
circled above, doing the shoot***, keeping the gunners
on their mark.

'That little lot should teach you to stay put in future,'
commented Biggles drily, as he turned for home.

---

* A short-barrelled large-bore gun which fires a heavy shell for short-
range firing.
** British two seater biplane, designed for reconnaissance and artillery
observation.
*** An aircraft pin-pointing a target for the artillery below. The pilot
would check how close the shells were falling to the target, then signal
to the gunners below using morse code transmitted by a one-way radio.

# Chapter 7
# The Carrier

Biggles sat shivering in the tiny cockpit of his Camel at rather less than 1,000 feet above the Allied reserve trenches. It was a bitterly cold afternoon; the icy edge of the February wind whipped round his face and pierced the thick padding of his Sidcot suit as he tried to snuggle lower in his 'office'.

The little salient on his right was being slowly pinched out by a detachment of infantry; to Biggles it seemed immaterial whether the line was straightened out or not, a few hundred yards one way or the other was neither here nor there, he opined. He was to change his mind before the day was out. Looking down he could see the infantry struggling through the mud from shell-hole to shell-hole, as inch by inch they drove the enemy back.

Squadron orders for the day had been to help them in every possible way by strafing back areas with machine-gun fire and 20-lb. Cooper bombs to prevent the enemy from bringing up reinforcements. He had been at it all morning, and as he climbed into the cockpit for the afternoon 'show', he anticipated another miserable two hours watching mud-coated men and lumbering tanks crossing no-man's-land, as he dodged to and fro through a venomous fire from small-arms, field guns and archie batteries.

He was flying a zig-zag course behind the British lines, keeping a watchful eye open for the movements of enemy troops, although the smoke of the barrage, laid down to protect the advancing troops, made the ground difficult to see. It also served to some extent to conceal him from the enemy gunners. From time to time he darted across the line of smoke and raked the German front line with bullets from his twin Vickers guns. It was a highly dangerous, and, to Biggles, an unprofitable pursuit; he derived no sense of victory from the performance, and the increasing number of holes in his wings annoyed him intensely. 'I'll have one of those damned holes in *me* in a minute,' he grumbled.

Crash! Something had hit the machine and splashed against his face, smothering his goggles with a sticky substance. 'What the hell has happened now?' he muttered, snatching off the goggles. His first thought was that an oil lead had been cut by a piece of shell, and he instinctively throttled back and headed the Camel, nose down, farther behind his own lines.

He wiped his hand across his face and gave a cry of dismay as it came away covered in blood. 'My God! I'm hit,' he groaned, and looked anxiously below for a suitable landing ground. He had little time in which to choose, but fortunately there were many large fields handy, and a few seconds later the machine had run to a standstill in one of them.

He stood erect in the cockpit and felt himself all over, looking for the source of the gore. His eyes caught sight of a cluster of feathers stuck on the centre section bracing wires, and he sank down limply, grinning sheepishly. 'Holy mackerel,' he muttered, 'a bird! So that was it.' Closer investigation revealed more feathers, and finally he found a mangled mass of blood and feathers on the floor of the cockpit. 'The propeller must have caught it and chucked what was left of it back through the centre-section into my face,' he mused. 'Looks like a pigeon. Oh, well!—'

He made to throw it overboard, when something caught his eye. It was a tiny tube attached to the bird's leg. 'A carrier pigeon, eh?' he whistled. 'I wonder if it is one of ours or a Boche?' He knew, of course, that carrier pigeons were used extensively by both sides, but particularly by the Allies for the purpose of conveying messages from spies within the occupied territory.

Sitting on the 'hump' of his Camel he removed the capsule and extracted a small flimsy piece of paper. One glance at the jumbled lines of letters and numbers was sufficient to show him that the message was in code. 'I'd better get this to Intelligence right away,' he thought and looked up to see an officer and several Tommies regarding him curiously from the hedge.

'Are you all right?' called the officer.

'Yes,' replied Biggles. 'Do you know if there is a field telephone anywhere near?'

'There's one at Divisional Headquarters—the farmhouse at the end of the road,' was the answer.

'Can I get through to 91st Wing from there?'

'I don't know.'

'All right, many thanks,' called Biggles. 'I'll go and find out. Will you keep an eye on my machine? Thanks.'

Five minutes later he was speaking to Colonel Raymond at Wing Headquarters, and after explaining what had happened, at the Colonel's invitation, read out the message letter by letter. 'Shall I hold on?' asked Biggles at the end.

'No, ring off, but don't go away. I'll call you in a minute or two,' said the Colonel crisply.

Five minutes passed quickly as Biggles warmed himself by the office fire, and then the 'phone bell rang shrilly.

'For you, sir,' said the orderly,* handing him the instrument.

'Is that you, Bigglesworth?' came the Colonel's voice.

'Yes, sir.'

'All right, we shan't want you again.'

'Hope I brought you good news,' said Biggles, preparing to ring off.

'No, you brought bad news. The message is from one of our fellows over the other side. The machine that went to fetch him last night force-landed and killed the pilot. That's all.'

'But what about the sp—man?' asked Biggles aghast.

'I'm afraid he is in a bad case, poor devil. He says he is on the north side of Lagnicourt Wood. The Huns have got a cordon of troops all round him and are hunting him down with dogs. He's heard them.'

'My God, how awful!'

'Well, we can't help him, he knows that. It will be dark in an hour and we daren't risk a night landing without looking over the ground. They'll have got him by to-morrow. Well, thanks for the prompt way you got the message to us. By the way, your M.C.** is through; it will be in orders to-night. Good-bye.' There was a click as the Colonel rang off.

Biggles sat with the receiver in his hand. He was not thinking about the decoration the Colonel had just mentioned. He was visualizing a different scene from the one that would be enacted in mess that night when his name appeared in orders on the notice board. In

* Private or non-commissioned officer detailed to assist senior officers.
** Military Cross, a medal.

his mind's eye he saw a cold-bleak landscape of leafless trees through which crawled an unkempt, mud-stained, hunted figure, looking upwards to the sky for the help that would never come. He saw a posse of hard-faced grey-coated Prussians holding the straining hounds on a leash, drawing ever nearer to the fugitive. He saw a grim, blank wall against which 'stood a blindfolded man—the man who had fought the war his own way, without hope of honour, and had lost.

Biggles, after two years of war, had little of the milk of human kindness left in his being, but the scene brought a lump into his throat. 'So they'd leave him there, eh?' he thought. 'That's Intelligence, is it? No, by God,' he ground out aloud through clenched teeth, and slammed the receiver down with a crash.

'What's that, sir?' asked the startled orderly.

'Go to hell,' snapped Biggles. 'No, I didn't mean that. Sorry,' and made for the door.

He was thinking swiftly as he hurried back to the Camel. 'North edge of Lagnicourt Wood the Colonel said; it's damn nearly a mile long. I wonder if he'd spot me if I got down. He'd have to come back on the wing—it's the only way, but even that's a better chance than the firing party'll give him. We'll try it, anyway, it isn't more than seven or eight miles over the line.'

Within five minutes Biggles was in the air heading for the wood, and ten minutes later, after being badly archied, he was circling over it at 5,000 feet.

'They haven't got him yet, anyway,' he muttered, for signs of the pursuit were at once apparent. Several groups of soldiers were beating the ditches at the west end of the wood and he saw hounds working along a hedge that ran diagonally into its western end. Sentries were standing at intervals on the northern and southern sides.

'Well, there's one thing I can do in case all else fails. I'll lay my eggs first,' he decided, thinking of the two Cooper bombs that still hung on their racks. He pushed the stick forward and went tearing down at the bushes where the hounds were working.

He did a vertical turn round the bushes at fifty feet, levelled out, and, as he saw the group just over the junction of his right-hand lower plane and the fuselage, he pulled the bomb toggle, one—two. Zooming high, he half rolled, and then came down with both Vickers guns spitting viciously. A cloud of smoke prevented him from seeing how much damage had been done by the bombs. He saw a helmeted figure raise a rifle to shoot at him, fall, pick himself up, fall again, and crawl into the undergrowth. One of the hounds was dragging itself away. Biggles pulled the Camel up, turned, and came down again, his tracer making a straight line to the centre of the now clearing smoke. Out of the corner of his eye he saw other groups hurrying towards the scene, and made a mental note that he had at least drawn attention to himself, which might give the spy a chance to make a break.

He levelled out to get his bearings. Left rudder, stick over, and he was racing low over the wood towards the northern edge. At thirty feet from the ground he tore along the side of the wood, hopping the trees and hedges in his path. There was only one field large enough for him to land in; would the spy realize that, he wondered, as he swung round in a steep climbing turn and started to glide down, blipping* his engine as he came.

He knew that he was taking a desperate chance. A

* Opening and closing the throttle, to alter the sound of the engine, often used as a signal.

bad landing or a single well-aimed shot from a sentry when he was on the ground would settle the matter. His tail-skid dragged on the rough surface of the field; a dishevelled figure, crouching low, broke from the edge of the wood and ran for dear life towards him. Biggles kicked on rudder and taxied, tail up, to meet him, swinging round while still thirty yards away, ready for the take-off.

A bullet smashed through the engine cowling; another struck the machine somewhere behind him. 'Come on!' he yelled frantically, although it was obvious that the man was doing his best. 'On the wing—not that—the left one—only chance,' he snapped.

The exhausted man made no answer, but flung himself at full length on the plane, close to the fuselage, and gripped the leading edge with his bare fingers.

'Catch!' cried Biggles, and flung his gauntlets on the wing within reach of the fugitive.

Bullets were flicking up the earth about them, but they suddenly ceased, and Biggles looked up to ascertain the reason. A troop of Uhlans* were coming down the field at full gallop, not a hundred yards away. Tight-lipped, Biggles thrust the throttle open and tore across the field towards them. His thumbs sought the Bowden lever of his Vickers guns and two white pencil lines of tracer connected the muzzles with the charging horsemen.

A bullet struck a strut near his face with a crash that he could hear above the noise of his engine, and he winced. Zooming high he swung round towards the lines. 'I've got him—I've brought it off!' hammered exultantly through his brain. 'If the poor devil doesn't

* German cavalry.

freeze to death and fall off, I'll have him home within ten minutes.' With his altimeter needle touching 4,000 feet he pulled the throttle back and leaning out of the cockpit yelled at the top of his voice, 'Ten minutes!' A quick nod told him that the spy had understood.

Biggles pushed the stick forward and dived for the line. He could feel the effect of the drag* of the man's body, but as it counterbalanced the torque** of his engine to some extent it did not seriously interfere with the performance of the machine.

He glanced behind. A group of small black dots stood out boldly against the setting sun. Fokkers! 'You can't catch me, I'm home,' jeered Biggles, pushing the stick further forward. He was down to 2,000 feet now, his air speed indicator showing 150 m.p.h.; only another two miles now, he thought with satisfaction.

Whoof! Whoof! Whoof! Three black clouds of smoke blossomed out in front of him, and he swerved. Whoof!—Spang! Something smashed against the engine with a force that made the Camel quiver. The engine raced, vibrating wildly, and then cut out dead. For a split second Biggles was stunned. Mechanically he pushed his stick forward and looked down. The German support trenches lay below. 'My God! what luck; I can't do it,' he grated bitterly. 'I'll be three hundred yards short.' He began a slow glide towards the Allied front line, now in sight.

At 500 feet, and fast losing height, the man on the wing twisted his head round, and the expression on his face haunted Biggles for many a day. A sudden thought struck him and an icy hand clutched his heart. 'By

* Wind-resistance.
** The reaction of a propeller which tends to turn an aeroplane in the opposite direction to which the propeller is turning.

heavens! I'm carrying a professed spy; they'll shoot us both!'

The ground was very close now and he could see that he would strike it just behind the Boche front line. 'I should think the crash will kill us both,' he muttered grimly, as he eyed the sea of shell-holes below. At five feet he flattened out for pancake landing*; the machine started to sink, slowly, and then with increasing speed. A tearing, ripping crash and the Camel closed up around him; something struck him on the head and everything went dark.

'Here, take a drink of this, young feller—it's rum,' said a voice that seemed far away.

Biggles opened his eyes and looked up into the anxious face of an officer in uniform and his late passenger.

'Who are you?' he asked in a dazed voice, struggling into a sitting position and taking the proffered drink.

'Major Mackay of the Royal Scots, the fust of foot, the right of the line and the pride of the British Army,' smiled his *vis-à-vis*.

'What the hell are you doing here—where are the Huns?'

'We drove 'em out this afternoon,' said the Major, 'luckily for you.'

'Damned lucky for me,' agreed Biggles emphatically.

* Instead of the aircraft gliding down to land, it flops down from a height of a few feet after losing flying speed.

# Chapter 8
# Spads and Spandaus

Biggles looked up from his self-appointed task of filling a machine-gun belt as the distant hum of an aero engine reached his ears; an S.E.5 flying low, was making for the aerodrome. The Flight-Commander watched it fixedly, a frown deepening between his eyes. He sprang to his feet, and loose rounds of ammunition falling in all directions.

'Stand by for a crash!' he snapped at the duty ambulance driver. 'Grab a Pyrene*, everybody,' he called, 'that fellow's hit; he's going to crash!'

He caught his breath as the S.E. made a sickening flat turn, but breathed a sigh of relief as it flattened out and landed clumsily. The visiting pilot taxied to the tarmac and pushed up his goggles to disclose the pale but smiling face of Wilkinson, of 287 Squadron.

'You hit, Wilks?' called Biggles anxiously.

'No.'

Biggles grinned his relief and cast a quick, critical glance at the machine. The fabric of the wings was ripped in a dozen places; an interplane strut was shattered and the tail unit was as full of holes as the rose of a watering-can.

'Have you got a plague of rats or something over at your place?' he inquired, pointing at the holes. 'You want to get some cats.'

---

* Hand-held fire extinguisher.

'The rats that did that have red noses, and it'll take more than cats to catch 'em,' said Wilkinson meaningly, climbing stiffly out of the cockpit.

'Red noses, did you say?' said Biggles, the smile fading from his face. 'You mean—'

'The Richthofen crowd have moved down, that's what I mean,' replied Wilkinson soberly. 'I've lost Browne and Chadwicke, although I believe Browne managed to get down just over our side of the line. There must have been over twenty Huns in the bunch we ran into.'

'What were they flying?'

'Albatroses. I counted sixteen crashes on the ground between Le Cateau and here, theirs and ours. There's an R.E.8 on its nose between the lines. There's a Camel and an Albatros piled up together in the Hun front line trench. What are we going to do about it?'

'Pray for dud weather, and pray hard,' said Biggles grimly. 'See any Camels on your way?'

Wilkinson nodded. 'I saw three near Mossyface Wood.'

'That'd be Mac; he's got Batty and a new man with him.'

'Well, they'll have discovered there's a war on by now,' observed Wilkinson. 'Do you feel like making Fokker fodder of yourself, or what about running down to Clarmes for a drink and talk things over?'

'Suits me,' replied Biggles, 'I've done two patrols to-day and I'm tired. Come on; I'll ask the C.O. if we can have the tender.'

Half an hour later they pulled up in front of the Hôtel de Ville, in Clarmes. In the courtyard stood a magnificent touring car which an American staff officer had just vacated. Lost in admiration, Biggles took a step towards it.

'Thinking of buying it?' said a voice at his elbow.

Turning, Biggles beheld a Captain of the American Flying Corps. 'Why, are you thinking of selling it?' he asked evenly.

As he turned and joined Wilkinson at a table, the American seated himself near them. 'You boys just going up to the line,' he asked, 'because if you are I'll give you a tip or two.'

Biggles eyed the speaker coldly. 'Are you just going up?' he inquired.

'Sure,' replied the American, 'I'm commanding the 299th Pursuit Squadron. We moved in to-day—we shall be going over to-morrow.'

'I see,' said Biggles slowly, 'then I'll give *you* a tip. Don't cross the line under fifteen thousand.'

The American flushed. 'I wasn't asking you for advice,' he snapped; 'we can take care of ourselves.'

Biggles finished his drink and left the room.

'That baby fancies himself a bit,' observed the American to Wilkinson. 'When he's heard a gun or two go off he won't be so anxious to hand out advice. Who is he?'

'His name's Bigglesworth,' said Wilkinson civilly. 'Officially, he's only shot down twelve Huns and five balloons, but to my certain knowledge he's got several more.'

'That kid? Say, don't try that on me, brother. You've got a dozen Huns, too, I expect,' jibed the American.

'Eighteen, to be precise,' said Wilkinson, casually tapping a cigarette.

The American paused with his drink half-way to his

lips. He set the glass back on the table. 'Say, do you mean that?' he asked incredulously.

Wilkinson shrugged his shoulders, but did not reply.

'What did he mean when he said not to cross the line under fifteen thousand?' asked the American curiously.

'I think he was going to tell you that the Richthofen circus had just moved in opposite,' explained Wilkinson.

'I've heard of that lot,' admitted the American, 'who are they?'

Wilkinson looked at him in surprise. 'They are a big bunch of star pilots, each with a string of victories to his credit. They hunt together, and are led by Manfred Richthofen, whose score stands at about seventy. With him he's got his brother, Lothar—with about thirty victories. There's Gussmann and Wolff and Weiss, all old hands at the game. There's Karjus, who has only one arm, but shoots better than most men with two. Then there's Lowenhardt, Reinhard, Udet and—but what does it matter? A man who hasn't been over the line before, meeting that bunch, has about as much chance as a rabbit in a wild beast show,' he concluded.

'You trying to put the wind up me?'

'No. I'm just telling you why Biggles said don't cross under 15,000 feet. You may then have a chance to dive home if you meet 'em. That's all. Well, cheerio, see you later perhaps.'

'It's a damn shame,' raved Biggles, as they drove back to the aerodrome. 'Some of these Americans are the best stuff in the world. One of two of 'em have been out here for months with our own squadrons and the French Lafayette and Cigognes Escadrilles.* Now their

* French fighter and bomber squadrons.

brass-hats have pulled 'em out and rolled 'em into their own Pursuit Squadrons. Do they put them in charge because they know the game? Do they—Hell! No. They hand 'em over to some poor boob who has done ten hours solo in Texas or somewhere, but has got a command because his sister's in the Follies; and they've got to follow where he leads 'em. Bah! It makes me sick. You heard that poor prune just now? He'll go beetling over at five thousand just to show he knows more about it than we do. Well, he'll be pushing up the Flanders poppies by this time to-morrow night unless a miracle happens. He'll take his boys with him. that's the curse of it. Not one of 'em'll ever get back—you watch it,' he concluded, bitterly.

'We can't let 'em do that,' protested Wilkinson.

'What can we do?'

'I was just thinking.'

'I've got it,' cried Biggles. 'Let them be the bait to bring the Huns down. With your S.E.'s and our Camels together, we'll knock the spots off that Hun circus. How many S.E.'s can you raise?'

'Eight or nine.'

'Right. You ask your C.O. and let me know to-night. I'll ask Major Mullen for all the Camels we can get in the air. That should even things up a bit; we'll be strong enough to take on anything the Huns can send against us. I'll meet you over Mossyface at six. How's that?'

'Suits me. I hope it's a fine day,' yawned Wilkinson.

The show turned out to be a bigger one than Biggles anticipated. Major Mullen had decided to lead the entire Squadron himself, not so much on account of the possibility of the American Squadron being massacred, as because he realized the necessity of massing his machines to meet the new menace.

Thus it came about that the morning following his conversation with Wilkinson found Biggles leading his flight behind the C.O. On his right was 'A' Flight, led by Mahoney, and on his left 'B' Flight, with MacLaren at their head. Each Flight comprised three machines, and these, with Major Mullen's red-cowled Camel, made ten in all. Major Sharp, commanding the S.E.5 Squadron, had followed Major Mullen's example, and from time to time Biggles looked upwards and backwards to where a formation of nine tiny dots, 6,000 feet above them, showed where the S.E.'s were watching and waiting. A concerted plan of action had been decided upon, and Biggles impatiently awaited its consummation.

Where were the Americans? He asked himself the question for the tenth time; they were a long time showing up. Where was the Boche circus? Sooner or later there was bound to be a clash, and Biggles thrilled at the thought of the coming dog-fight.

It was a glorious day; not a cloud broke the serenity of the summer sky. Biggles kept his eyes downwards, knowing that the S.E.'s would prevent molestation from above. Suddenly, a row of minute moving objects caught his eye, and Biggles stared in amazement. Then he swore. A formation of nine Spads* was crossing the line far below. 'The fools, the unutterable lunatics,' he growled, 'they can't be an inch higher than four thousand. They must think they own the sky, and they

---

* A French-made fighting biplane Scout which first appeared in 1916, top speed 132 m.p.h. armed with one or two Vickers machine guns. It was used by the US when they formed their own squadrons.

haven't even seen us yet. Oh, well, they'll wake up presently, or I'm no judge.'

The Spad Squadron was heading out straight into enemy sky, and Biggles watched them with amused curiosity, uncertain as to whether to admire their nerve or curse their stupidity. 'They must think it's easy,' he commented grimly, as his lynx-eyed leader altered his course slightly to follow the Americans.

Where were the Huns? He held his hand, at arm's length, over the sun, and extending his fingers squinted through the slits between them. He could see nothing, but the glare was terrific and might have concealed a hundred machines.

'They're there, I'll bet my boots,' muttered the Flight-Commander; 'they are just letting those poor boobs wade right into the custard. How they must be laughing!'

Suddenly he stiffened in his seat. The Major was rocking his wings — pointing. Biggles followed the out-stretched finger and caught his breath. Six brightly painted machines were going down in an almost vertical dive behind the Spads. Albatroses. He lifted his hand high above his head, and then, in accordance with the plan, pushed the stick forward and, with Batson and Healy on either side, tore down diagonally to cut off the enemy planes. He knew that most of the Hun circus was still above, somewhere, waiting for the right moment to come down. How long would they wait before coming down, thus bringing the rest of the Camels and S.E.'s down into the mix-up with them? Not long he hoped, or he might find his hands full, for he could not count upon the inexperienced Spad pilots for help.

The Spad Squadron had not altered its course, and

Biggles' lip curled as he realized that even now they had not seen the storm brewing above them. Ah! they knew now. The Albatroses were shooting, and the Spads swerved violently, like a school of minnows at the sudden presence of a pike. In a moment all formation was lost as they scattered in all directions. Biggles sucked in his breath quickly as a Spad burst into flames and dropped like a stone. He was among them now; a red-bellied machine appeared through his sights and he pressed his triggers viciously, cursing a Spad that nearly collided with him.

A green Albatros came at him head-on, and as he charged it, another, with a blue and white checked fuselage sent a stream of tracer through his top plane. The green machine swerved and he flung the Camel round behind it; but the checked machine had followed him and he had to pull up in a wild zoom to escape the hail of lead it spat at him. 'Hell!' grunted Biggles vigorously, as his wind-screen flew to pieces, 'this is getting too hot. My God, what a mess!' A Spad and an Albatros, locked together, careered earthwards in a flat spin. A Camel, spinning viciously, whirled past him, and another Albatros, wrapped in a sheet of flame, flashed past his nose, the doomed pilot leaping into space even as it passed.*

Biggles snatched a swift glance upwards. A swarm of Albatroses were dropping like vultures out of the sky into the fight; he had a fleeting glimpse of other machines far above and then he turned again to the work on hand. Where were the Spads? Ah, there was one, on the tail of an Albatros. He tore after it, but the Spad pilot saw him and waved him away. Biggles

* Very few pilots carried parachutes during the First World War so to leap from a plane meant certain death.

grinned. 'Go to it, laddie,' he yelled exultantly, but a frown swept the grin from his face as a jazzed machine darted in behind the Spad and poured in a murderous stream of lead. Biggles shot down on the tail of the Hun. The Spad pilot saw the danger and twisted sideways to escape, but an invisible cord seemed to hold the Albatros to the tail of the American machine. Biggles took the jazzed machine in his sights and raked it from end to end in a long deadly burst. There was no question of missing at that range; the enemy pilot slumped forward in his seat and the machine went to pieces in the air.

The Spad suddenly stood up on its tail and sent two white pencils of tracer across Biggle's nose at something he could not see. A Hun, upside down, went past him so closely that he instinctively flinched. 'My God!' muttered Biggles, 'he saved *me* that time; that evens things up.'

His lips closed in a straight line; a bunch of six Albatroses were coming at him together. Biggles fired one shot, and went as cold as ice as his gun jammed. Bullets were smashing through his machine when a cloud of S.E.'s appeared between him and the Hun, and he breathed again. 'Lord, what a dog-fight,' he said again, as he looked around to see what was happening. Most of the enemy planes were in full retreat, pursued by the S.E.'s. Two Camels and two Albatroses were still circling some distance away and four more Camels were rallying above him. Biggles saw the lone Spad flying close to him. Seven or eight crashed machines were on the ground, two blazing furiously, but whether they were Spads or Camels he couldn't tell.

He pushed up his goggles and beckoned to the Spad

pilot, whom he now recognized as his acquaintance of the previous day, to come closer.

The American waved gaily, and together they started after the Camels, led by Major Mullen's red cowling, now heading for the line . . . Biggles landed with the Spad still beside him; he mopped the burnt castor oil off his face and walked across to meet the pilot. The American held out his hand. 'I just dropped in to shake hands,' he said. 'Now I must be getting back to our field to see how many of the outfit got home. I'd like to know you better; maybe you'll give me a tip or two.'

'I can't tell you much after what you've seen to-day,' laughed Biggles, turning to wave to an S.E.5, which had swung low over them and then proceeded on its way.

'Who's that?' asked the American.

'That's Wilks, the big stiff you saw with me yesterday,' replied Biggles. 'He's a good scout. He'll be at the Hôtel de Ville to-night for certain; so shall I. Do you feel like coming along to tear a chop and knock a bottle or two back?'

'Sure,' agreed the Spad pilot enthusiastically.

# Chapter 9
# The Zone Call

> Oh, my batman awoke me from my bed,
> I'd had a thick night and I'd got a sore head;
>    So I said to myself,
>    To myself, I said,
> Oh, I haven't got a hope in the mo—orning.
>
> So I went to the sheds to examine my gun.
> And then my engine I tried to run,
>    But the revs she ga-ve
>    Were a thousand and one.
> So I hadn't got a hope in the mo—orning.

The words of the old R.A.F. song, roared by forty youthful voices to the tune of 'John Peel', drowned the accompaniment of the cracked mess piano in spite of the strenuous efforts of the pianist to make his notes audible.

Biggles pushed the hair off his forehead. 'Lord, it's hot in here; I'm going outside for a breath of air,' he said to Wilkinson of 287 Squadron, who had come over for the periodical binge.

The two officers rose and strolled slowly towards the door. It was still daylight, but a thick layer of thundercloud hung low in the sky, making the atmosphere oppressive.

> Oh, we were escorting 'twenty-two,'
> Hadn't got a notion what to do,
>    So, we shot down a Spa-a-d,

And an F.E. too,
For we hadn't—

'Stop!' Biggles had bounded back into the centre of the room and held up his arms for silence. 'Hark!' At the expression in his face a sudden hush fell upon the assembly and the next instant forty officers had stiffened into attitudes of tense expectancy as a low vibrating hum filled the air. It was the unmistakable 'pour-vous, pour-vous' of a Mercédès aero-engine, low down, not far away.

'A Hun!' The silence was broken by a wild yell and the crash of fallen chairs as Biggles darted through the open door and streaked like a madman for the sheds, shouting orders as he went. The ack-emmas had needed no warning, a Camel was already on the tarmac; others were being wheeled out with feverish speed. Capless and goggleless, tunic still thrown open at the throat, Biggles made a flying leap into the cockpit of the first Camel, and within a minute, in spite of Wilkinson's plaintive 'Wait for me,' was tearing down-wind across the sun-baked aerodrome in a cloud of dust.

He was in the air, climbing back up over the sheds, before the second machine was ready to take off. The clouds were low, and at 1,000 feet the grey mist was swirling in his slipstream. He could no longer hear the enemy plane for the roar of his Bentley Rotary drowned all other sound. He pushed his joystick forward for a moment to gather speed and then pulled it back in a swift zoom. Bursting into the sunlight above he literally flung the machine round in a lightning right-hand turn to avoid crashing into a Pfalz scout,* painted vivid scarlet with white stripes behind the pilot's seat.

* Very successful German single-seater biplane fighter, fitted with two or three machine guns synchronised to fire through the propeller.

'My God!' muttered Biggles, startled. 'I nearly rammed him.' He was round in a second, warming his guns as he came. The Pfalz had turned too and was now circling erratically in a desperate effort to avoid the glittering pencil lines of tracer that started at the muzzles of Biggles' guns and ended at the tail of the Boche machine. The German pilot made no attempt to retaliate, but concentrated on dodging the hail of lead, waving his left arm above his head. Biggles ceased firing and looked about him suspiciously, but not another enemy machine was in sight.

'Come on, let's get it over,' he muttered, as he thumbed his triggers again, but the Boche put his nose down and dived through the cloud, Biggles close behind him.

They emerged below the cloud bank in the same relative positions, and it at once became obvious that the German intended to land on the aerodrome, but a brisk burst of machine-gun fire from Lewis guns in front of the mess caused him to change his mind; instead, he hopped over the hedge and made a clumsy landing in the next field. Biggles landed close behind him and ran towards the pilot, now struggling to get a box of matches from his inside pocket to fire the machine.

Biggles seized him by the collar and threw him clear.

'Speak English?' he snapped.

'Yes.'

'What's the matter with you? Haven't you got any guns?' sneered the British pilot, noting the German's pale face.

'Nein, no guns,' said the German quickly.

'What?'

The German shrugged his shoulders and pointed. A

swift glance showed Biggles that such was indeed the case.

'My God!' he cried aghast. 'You people running short of weapons or something? We'd better lend you some.'

'I vas lost,' said the German pilot resignedly. 'I am to take a new Pfalz to Lille, but the clouds—I cannot see. The benzine is nearly finished. You come—I come down, so.'

'Tough luck,' admitted Biggles as a crowd of officers and ack-emmas arrived on the scene at the double. 'Well, come and have a drink—you've butted into a party.'

'Huh! no wonder your crowd score if you go about shooting at delivery pilots,' grinned Wilkinson, who had just landed.

'You go and stick your face in an oil sump, Wilks,' cried Biggles hotly. 'How did I know he hadn't any guns?'

Biggles sprang lightly from the squadron tender and looked at the deserted aerodrome in astonishment. It was the morning following his encounter with the unarmed Pfalz. For some days a tooth had been troubling him, and on the advice of the Medical Officer he had been to Clarmes to have the offending molar extracted. He had not hurried back, as the M.O. had forbidden him to fly that day, and now he had returned to find every machine except his own in the air.

'Where have they all gone, Flight?' he asked the Flight-Sergeant.

'Dunno, sir. The C.O. came out in a hurry about an hour ago and they all went off together,' replied the N.C.O.

'Just my luck,' grumbled Biggles, 'trust something to happen when I'm away for a few hours! Oh, well!'

He made his way to the Squadron Office where he found Tyler, commonly know as 'Wat,' the Recording Officer,* busy with some papers.

'What's on, Wat?' asked Biggles.

'Escort.'

'Escorting what?'

'You remember that Hun you got yesterday?'

Biggles nodded.

'Well, apparently he was three sheets in the wind when Wing came and fetched him. He blabbed a whole lot of news to the Intelligence people. This is what he told 'em. He said that three new Staffels were being formed at Lagnicourt. A whole lot of new machines were being sent there; in fact, when he was there two days ago, over thirty machines were being assembled.'

'Funny, him letting a thing like that drop,' interrupted Biggles. 'He didn't strike me as being blotto, either. He drank practically nothing.'

'Well, Wing says he was as tight as a lord, and bragged that the three new circuses were going to wipe us off the map, so they decided to nip the plot in the bud. They've sent every machine they can get into the air with a full load of bombs to fan the whole caboodle sky-high—all the Fours, Nines, and Biffs** have gone, and even the R.E.8's they can spare from Art. Obs.*** Two-eight-seven, two-nine-nine and our people are escorting 'em.'

'Well, they can have it,' said Biggles cheerfully. 'Escorting's a mouldy business, anyway. Thanks, Wat.'

* The officer designated to supervise all the Squadron records.
** Slang: Bristol Fighters.
*** Artillery observation.

He strolled out on to the aerodrome, gently rubbing his lacerated jaw, and catching sight of the German machine now standing on the tarmac, made his way slowly towards it. He examined it with interest, for a complete ready-to-fly-away Boche machine was a *rara avis*. He slipped his hand into the map case, but the maps had been removed. His fingers felt and closed around a torn piece of paper at the bottom of the lining; it was creased as if had been roughly torn off and used to mark a fold in a map. Biggles glanced at it disinterestedly, noting some typewritten matter on it, but as it was in German and conveyed nothing to him he was about to throw it away when the Flight-Sergeant passed near him.

'Do you speak German, Flight?' called Biggles.

'No, sir, but Thompson does; he used to be in the Customs office or something like that,' replied the N.C.O.

'Ask him to come here a minute, will you?' said Biggles.

'Can you tell me what that says?' he asked a moment later, as an ack-emma approached him and saluted.

The airman took the paper and looked at it for a minute without speaking. 'It's an extract from some orders, sir,' he said at length. 'The first part of it's gone, but this is what it says, roughly speaking: "With effect"—there's a bit gone there—"any flieger"—flyer, that is—"falling into the hands of the enemy will therefore repeat that three Jagdstaffels are being assembled at Langi—" can't read the place, sir. "By doing so, he will be doing service by assisting"—can't read that, sir. It ends, "Expires on July 21st at twelve, midnight. This order must on no account be taken into the air." That's all, sir.'

'Read that again,' said Biggles slowly.

After the airman had obeyed Biggles returned to the Squadron office deep in thought. He put a call through to Wing Headquarters and asked for Colonel Raymond.

'That you, sir? Bigglesworth here,' he said, as the Colonel's crisp voice answered him. 'About this big raid, sir. Do you mind if I ask whether you know for certain that these Boche machines are at Lagnicourt?'

'Yes, we made reconnaisance at dawn, and the observer reported several machines in various stages of erection on the tarmac. Why do you ask?'

'I've just found a bit of paper in the Pfalz the Boche brought over. I can't read it because it's in German, but I've had it translated, and it looks as if that Hun had orders to tell you that tale. Will you send over for it?'

'I'll send a messenger for it right away, but I shouldn't worry about it; the Huns are there, we've seen them. Good-bye.'

Biggles hung the receiver up slowly and turned to Wat, who had listened to the conversation.

'You'll get shot one day ringing up the Wing like that!' he said reprovingly.

'It would be a hell of a joke to send forty machines to drop twenty thousand quid's worth of bombs on a lot of obsolete spare parts,' mused Biggles; 'but there's more in it than that. The Boche want our machines out of the way. Why? That's what I want to know. Lagnicourt lies thirty miles north-west of here. I fancy it wouldn't be a bad idea if somebody went and had a dekko what the Huns were doing in the north-east. Even my gross intelligence tells me that when a Hun

307

is told what he's got to say when he's shot down, there's something fishy about it.'

'The M.O. says you're not to fly to-day,' protested the R.O.

'Rot! What the hell does he think I fly with, my teeth?' asked Biggles sarcastically. 'See you later.'

Within ten minutes Biggles was in the air, heading into the blue roughly to the north-east of the aerodrome. An unusual amount of archie marked his progress and he noticed it with satisfaction, for it tended to confirm his suspicions. 'What ho,' he addressed the invisible gunner, 'so you don't want any Peeping-Toms about to-day, eh? Want to discourage me.' The archie became really hot, and twice he had to circle to spoil the gunner's aim. He kept a watchful eye on the ground below, but saw nothing unusual.

He passed over an R.E.9 spotting for the artillery, manfully plodding its monotonous figure-of-eight 3,000 feet below, and nodded sympathetically. Presently he altered his course a little westerly and the archie faded away. 'Don't mind me going that way, eh? Well, let's try the other way again,' he muttered. Instantly the air was thick with black, oily bursts of smoke, and Biggles nodded understandingly. 'So I'm getting warm, am I?' he mused. 'They might as well say so; what imaginations they've got.'

Straight ahead of him, lying like a great dark green stain across the landscape, lay the forest of Duvigny. Keeping a watchful eye above for enemy aircraft, Biggles looked at it closely, but there was no sign of anything unusual about its appearance. 'I wonder if that's it?' he mused, deep in thought. 'I could soon find out; it's risky, but it's the only way.' He knew what all old pilots knew, a trick the German pilots had learned early in the War, when vast numbers of Russian troops were concealed in forests along the north-German frontier, and that was, that if an enemy plane flew low enough, the troops, no matter how well hidden, would reveal their presence by shooting at it. Not even strict orders could prevent troops from firing at an enemy aeroplane within range.

He pushed his stick forward and went roaring down at the forest. At 1,000 feet he started pulling out, but not before he had seen several hundred twinkling fire-flies amongst the greenery. The fireflies were, of course, the flashes of rifles aimed at him. In one place a number of men had run out into a clearing and started firing, but an officer had driven them back. 'So that's it, is it?' muttered Biggles, thrilling with excitement. 'I wonder how many of them there are.'

Time and time again he dived low over different parts of the forest and each time the twinkling flashes betrayed the hidden troops. His wings were holed in many places, but he heeded them not. It would take a lucky shot from a rifle to bring him down. 'My God!' he muttered, as he pulled up at the far end of the forest, after his tenth dive, 'the wood's full of 'em. There must be fifty thousand men lying in that timber, and it's close to the line. They're massing for a big attack. What did those orders say? July 21st? Great God, that's to-morrow. They'll attack this afternoon, or at latest to-night. I'd better be getting out of this. So that's why they didn't want any of our machines prowling about.'

He made for the line, toying with the fine adjustment to get the very last rev. out of his engine. He could see the R.E.8 still tapping out its 'G.G.' (fire) signal to the gunners and marking the position of the falling shells, and the sight of it gave him an idea. The R.E.8 was fitted with wireless; he was not. If only he could get the pilot to send out a zone call on that wood, his work was done.*

Biggles flew close to the R.E.8, signalling to attract attention. How could he tell them, that was the problem. He flew closer and gesticulated wildly, jabbing downwards towards the wood, and then tapping with his finger on an invisible key. The pilot and observer eyed him stupidly and Biggles shrugged his shoulders in despair. Then inspiration struck him. He knew the morse code, of course, for every pilot had to pass a test in it before going to France. He flew close beside the R.E.8, raised his arm above his head and, with some difficulty, sent a series of dots and dashes. He saw the observer nod understandingly and grab a notebook to take down the message. Biggles started his signal. Dash, dash, dot dot—Z, dash, dash, dash—O, dash, dot—N, dot—E. He continued the performance until he had sent the words, 'Zone Call, Wood,' and then stabbed viciously at the wood with his forefinger. He saw the observer lean forward and have a quick,

* A Zone Call was a special call from an aircraft to the artillery and was only used in very exceptional circumstances. When the zone call was tapped out by the wireless operator it was followed by the pin-point of the target. Military maps were divided into squares and smaller squares, each square numbered and lettered. By this means it was possible to name any spot on the map instantly. When a zone call was sent out, every weapon of every calibre within range directed rapid fire on the spot, and this may have meant that hundreds of guns opened up at once on the same spot. The result can be better imagined than described. Obviously such treatment was terribly expensive, costing possibly £10,000 a minute while it lasted, and only exceptional circumstances, such as a long line of transport, or a large body of troops, warranted the call. There was a story in France of a new officer who, in desperation, sent out a zone call on a single archie battery that was worrying him. He was court-martialled and sent home.

difficult conversation with the pilot, who nodded. The observer raised both thumbs in the air and bent over his buzzer. Biggles turned away to watch the result.

Within a minute he saw the first shell explode in the centre of the wood. Another followed it, then another and another. In five minutes the place was an inferno of fire, smoke, flying timber and hurtling steel, and thousands of figures, clad in the field-grey of the German infantry, were swarming out into the open to escape the pulverizing bombardment. He could see the officers attempting to get the men into some sort of order, but there was no stemming that wild panic. They poured into the communication trenches, and others, unable to find cover, were flinging away their equipment and running for their lives.

'Holy mackerel, what a sight!' murmured Biggles. 'What a pity the Colonel isn't here to see it.' A Bristol Fighter appeared in the sky above him, heading for the scene of carnage. The observer was leaning over the side and the pilot's arm was steadily moving up and down as he exposed plate after plate in his camera. 'He'll have to believe me when he sees those photographs though,' thought Biggles.

'Well, I should think I've saved our chaps in the line a lot of trouble,' he soliloquised, as he turned to congratulate the R.E.8 crew, but the machine was far away. Biggles' Camel suddenly rocked violently and he realized the reason for the R.E.8's swift departure. He was right in the line of fire of the artillery and the shells were passing near him. He put his nose down in a fright and sped towards home in the wake of the R.E.8.

He landed on the aerodrome to find the escorting

Camels had returned, and the pilots greeted him noisily.

'Had a nice trip, chaps?' inquired Biggles.

'No,' growled Mahoney, 'didn't see a Hun the whole way out and home. These escorts bore me stiff. What have you been doing?'

'Oh, having a little fun and games on my own.'

'Who with?'

'With the German army,' said Biggles lightly.

# Chapter 10
# The Decoy

Biggles landed and taxied quickly up to the sheds. 'Are Mr Batson and Mr Healy home yet?' he asked the Flight-Sergeant, as he climbed stiffly from the cockpit. 'We got split up among the clouds near Ariet after a dog-fight with a bunch of Albatros.'

'Mr Healy came in about five minutes ago, sir; he's just gone along to the mess, but I haven't seen anything of Mr Batson,' replied the N.C.O.

Biggles lit a cigarette and eyed the eastern sky anxiously. He was annoyed that his flight had been broken up, although after a dog-fight it was no uncommon occurrence for machines to come home independently. He breathed a sigh of relief as the musical hum of a Bentley Rotary reached his ears, and started to walk slowly towards the mess, glancing from time to time over his shoulder at the now rapidly-approaching Camel. Suddenly he paused in his stride and looked at the wind-stocking. 'What's the young fool doing, trying to land cross-wind,' he growled, and turned round to watch the landing.

The Camel had flattened out rather too high for a good landing, and dropped quickly as it lost flying speed. The machine bumped—bumped again as the wheels bounced, and then swung round in a wide semicircle as it ran to a standstill not fifty yards away.

Biggles opened his mouth to shout a caustic remark at the pilot, but his teeth suddenly closed with a snap, and the next instant he was running wildly towards the machine, followed by the Flight-Sergeant and several ack-emmas. He reached the Camel first, and, foot in the stirrup, swung himself up to the cockpit; one glance, and he was astride the fuselage unbuckling the safety belt around the limp figure in the pilot's seat.

'Gently, Flight-Sergeant, gently,' he said softly, as they lifted the stricken pilot from his seat and laid him carefully on the grass. Biggles caught his breath as he saw an ugly red stain on his hand that had supported the wounded pilot's back. 'How did they get you, kid?' he choked, dropping on to his knees and bending close over the ashen face.

'I—got—the—bus—home—Biggles,' whispered Batson eagerly.

'Sure you did,' nodded Biggles, fighting back a sob and forcing a smile. 'What was it, laddie—archie?'

The pilot looked at his Flight-Commander with wide open eyes. 'My own fault,' he whispered faintly . . . 'I went down—after Rumpler—with green—tail. Thought I'd—be—clever.' He smiled wanly. 'Alba-troses—waiting—upstairs. It was—trap. They got me—Biggles. I'm going—topsides.'

'Not you,' said Biggles firmly, waving away Batson's mechanic who was muttering incoherently.

'It's getting dark early; where are you—Biggles—I can't see you,' went on the wounded man, his hand groping blindly for the other pilot.

'I'm here, old boy. I'm with you, don't worry,' crooned Biggles like a mother to an ailing child.

'Not worrying. Get that—Rumpler—for me—Biggles.'

'I'll get him, Batty, I'll get the swine, never fear,' replied Biggles, his lips trembling.

For a minute there was silence, broken only by the sound of a man sobbing in the distance. The wounded pilot opened his eyes, already glazed by the film of death.

'It's getting—devilish—dark—Biggles,' he whispered faintly, 'dev—lish—da—ark—'

The M.O. arrived at the double and lifted Biggles slowly, but firmly to his feet. 'Run along now, old man,' he said kindly after a swift glance at the man on the ground. 'The boy's gone.'

For a moment longer Biggles stood looking down through a mist of tears at the face of the man who had been tied to him by such bonds of friendship as only war can tie.

'I'll get him for you, Batty,' he said through his teeth, and turning, walked slowly towards the sheds.

The Rumpler with the green tail was an old menace in the sky well known to Biggles. Of a slow, obsolescent type, it looked 'easy meat' to the beginner, unaware of its sinister purpose, which was to act as a tempting bait to lure just such pilots beneath the waiting Spandau guns of the shark-like Albatroses. Once, many months before, Biggles had nearly fallen into the trap. He was going down on to an old German two-seater when a premonition of danger made him glance back over his shoulder, and the sight that greeted his eyes sent him streaking for his own side of the line as if a host of devils were on his tail—as indeed, they were.

Such death-traps were fairly common, but they no longer deceived him for an instant. 'Never go down after a Hun,' was the warning dinned into the ears of every new arrival in France by those who knew the pitfalls that awaited the unwary—alas, how often in vain.

So the old pilots, who had bought their experience, went on, and watched the younger ones come and go, unless, like Biggles, they were fortunate enough to escape, in which case the lesson was seldom forgotten.

And now the green-tailed Rumpler had killed Batty, or had led him to his doom—at least, that was what it amounted to; so reasoned Biggles. That Batson had been deceived by the trap he did not for one moment believe. The lad—to use his own words—'tried to be clever,' and in attempting to destroy the decoy, had failed, where failure could have only tragic results; and this was the machine that Biggles had pledged himself to destroy.

He had no delusions as to the dangers of the task he had undertaken. Batson's disastrous effort was sufficient proof of that. First, he must find the decoy; that should not be difficult. Above it, biding their time, would be the school of Albatroses, eyes glued downwards, waiting for the victim to walk into the trap.

Biggles sat alone in a corner of 'C' Flight hangar and wrestled with the problem, unconscious of the anxious glances and whispered consultations of his mechanics. The death of Batson had shaken him badly, and he was sick; sick of the war, sick of flying, sick of life itself. What did it matter, anyway? he mused. His turn would come, sooner or later, that was certain. He didn't attempt to deceive himself on that point. He made up his mind suddenly and called the Flight-Sergeant to him in tones that brooked no delay.

'Let's go and look at Mr Batson's machine,' he said tersely.

'I have examined it, sir,' said the N.C.O. quickly.

'It's still O.K. Hardly touched; just one burst, through back of the fuselage, down through pilot's seat and through the floor.'

'Good. I'll take it,' said Biggles coldly. 'Come and give me a swing.'

'But you're not going to—not going—'

'Do what you're told,' snapped Biggles icily. 'I'm flying that machine from now on—until—' Biggles looked the Flight-Sergeant in the eyes—'until—well—you know—' he concluded.

The N.C.O. nodded. 'Very good, sir,' he said briskly.

Five minutes later Biggles took off in the dead pilot's Camel; the Flight-Sergeant and a silent group of ack-emmas watched his departure. 'Mad as a bleedin' 'atter. Gawd 'elp the 'Un as gets in 'is way to-day,' observed a tousle-headed cockney fitter.

'Get to hell back to your work,' roared the Flight-Sergeant. 'What are you all gaping at?'

Major Mullen hurried along the tarmac. 'Who's just taken off in that machine, Flight-Sergeant?' he asked curtly.

'Mr Bigglesworth, sir.'

The C.O. gazed after the rapidly-disappearing Camel sadly. 'I see,' he said slowly, and then again, 'I see.'

The finding of the green-tailed Rumpler proved a longer job than Biggles anticipated. At the end of a week he was still searching, still flying Batson's machine, and every pilot within fifty miles knew of his quest. Major Mullen had protested; in fact, he had done everything except definitely order Biggles out of the machine; but, being a wise man and observing the high pressure under which his pilot was living, he refrained from giving an order that he knew would be broken. So Biggles continued his search unhindered.

The Rumpler had become an obsession with him. For eight hours a day he hunted the sky between Lille and Cambrai for it, and at night, in his sleep, he shot it down in flames a hundred times. He had become morose, and hardly even spoke to Mac or Mahoney, the other Flight-Commanders, who watched him anxiously and secretly helped him in his search. He was due for leave, but refused to accept it. He fought many battles and, although he hardly bothered to confirm his victories, his score mounted rapidly. His combat reports were brief and contained nothing but the barest facts.

No man could stand such a pace for long. The M.O. knew it, but did nothing, although he hoped and prayed that the pilot might find his quarry before his nerves collapsed like a pack of cards.

One morning Biggles had just refuelled after a two-hour patrol and was warming up his engine again, when a D.H.9 landed, and the observer hurried towards the sheds. Dispassionately, Biggles saw him speak to the Flight-Sergeant and the N.C.O. point in his direction. The observer turned and crossed quickly to the Camel.

'Are you Bigglesworth?' he shouted above the noise of the engine.

Biggles nodded.

'I hear you're looking for that green-tailed Rumpler?'

Biggles nodded again eagerly.

'I saw it ten minutes ago, near Talcourt-le-Château.'

'Thanks,' said Biggles briefly, and pushed the throttle open.

He saw the Rumpler before he reached the lines, at least he saw the wide circles of white archie bursts that followed its wandering course. The British archie was white, and German archie black, so he knew that the plane was a German and from its locality suspected it to be the Rumpler. A closer inspection showed him that his supposition was correct. It was just over its own side of the lines, at about 8,000 feet, ostensibly engaged on artillery observation. Biggles edged away and studied the sky above it closely, but he could see nothing. He climbed steadily, keeping the Boche machine in sight, but making no attempt to approach it, and looked upwards again for the escorting Albatroses which he knew were there, but he was still unable to discover them.

'If I didn't know for certain that they were there, I should say there wasn't a Hun in the sky,' he muttered, as he headed south-east, keeping parallel with the trenches. With his eye still on the Rumpler he could have named the very moment when the Boche observer spotted him, for the machine suddenly began to edge towards him as though unaware of his presence, and seemingly unconsciously making of itself an ideal subject for attack by a scout pilot.

To an old hand like Biggles the invitation was too obvious, and even without his knowledge of the trap the action would have made him suspiciously alert. Unless he was the world's worst observer, the man in the back seat of the black-crossed machine could not have failed to have seen him, in which case he should have lost no time in placing as great a distance as possible between himself and a dangerous adversary, for the first duty of a two-seater pilot was to do his job and get home, leaving the fighting to machines designed for the purpose. Yet here was an old and comparatively unmanœuvrable machine deliberately asking for trouble. 'Bah!' sneered Biggles, peeved to think he had been taken for a fool. ' "Will you step into my parlour?" said the spider to the fly. Yes, you hound, I will, but it won't be through the front door.' He looked upwards above the Rumpler, but the sun was in his eyes, so he held on his way, still climbing, and had soon left the Boche machine far below and behind him.

At 15,000 feet Biggles started to head into enemy sky, placing himself between the sun and the Rumpler, now a speck in the far distance. His roving eyes suddenly focused on a spot high over the enemy plane. 'So there you are,' he muttered grimly, 'how many?— One—two—three'—he shifted his gaze still higher— 'four—five—six—seven. Seven, in two layers, eh? Ought to be enough for a solitary Camel. Well, we'll see.'

He estimated the lowest Albatroses to be at about his own height. The other four were a couple of thousand feet higher. With the disposition of the trap now apparent he proceeded in accordance with the line of action upon which he had decided. He had already placed himself 'in the sun,' and in that position it was unlikely that he would be seen by any of the enemy pilots. He continued to climb until he was above the highest enemy formation, and then cautiously began to edge towards them, turning when they turned, and keeping in a direct line with the the sun.

He felt fairly certain that the crew of the Rumpler would ignore the possibility of danger from above on account of the escorting Albatroses, and the pilots of the enemy scouts would have their eyes on the machine below. Upon these factors Biggles planned his attack. If he was able to approach unseen he would be able to make one lightning attack almost before the Huns were aware of his presence. If he was seen, his superior altitude should give him enough extra speed to reach the lines before he was caught.

He knew he would only have time for one burst at the Rumpler. If he missed there could be no question of staying for a second attempt, for the Albatroses would be down on him like a pack of ravening wolves. The Rumpler was now flying almost directly over no-man's-land, and Biggles edged nearer, every nerve quivering like the flying wires of his Camel.

The decoy, confident of its escort, was slowly turning towards the British lines, and this was the moment for which Biggles had been waiting, for the end of his dive would see him over his own lines—either intact or as a shattered wreck. His lips were set in a straight line under the terrific strain of the impending action as he swung inwards until the Albatroses were immediately between him and the Rumpler, and then he pointed his nose downwards. 'Come on, Batty, let's go,' he muttered huskily, and thrust the stick forward with both hands.

The top layer of Albatroses seemed to float up towards him. Five hundred feet, one hundred feet, and still they had not seen him; he could see every detail of the machines and even the faces of the pilots. He went through the middle of them like a streak of lightning—down—down—down—he knew they were hard on his heels now, but he did not look back. They would have to pull out as he went through the second layer— or risk collision. 'Come on, you swine,' he gritted through his set teeth, and went through the lower Albatroses like a thunderbolt. The Rumpler lay clear below; he could see the observer idly leaning over the side of the fuselage watching the ground. He took the machine in his sights, but held his fire, for he was still too far off for effective shooting. Down—down—down—a noise like a thousand devils shrieking in his ears, his head jammed tight against the head-rest under the frightful pressure.

At 200 feet he pressed his triggers, and his lips parted in a mirthless smile as he saw the tracers making a straight line through the centre of the Boche machine. The observer leapt round and then sank slowly on to the floor of the cockpit. The nose of the Rumpler jerked upwards, an almost certain sign that the pilot had been hit.

He held his fire until the last fraction of a second, and only when collision seemed inevitable did he pull the stick back. His under-carriage seemed to graze the centre section of the Rumpler as he came out, and he bit his lips until the blood came as he waited for the rending crash that would tell him that his wings had folded up under the pressure of that frightful zoom. Before he had reached the top of it he had thrust the stick forward again and was zig-zagging across his own lines.

For the first time since he had started the heartbursting dive he looked back. The Rumpler was nowhere in sight, but an involuntary yell broke from his lips as his eyes fell on two Albatroses, one minus its top plane, spinning wildly downwards; whether as the result of a collision or because they had cracked up in the dive, he neither knew nor cared. The five remaining Albatroses were already turning back towards their own lines, followed by a furious bombardment of archie.

Where was the Rumpler? He looked downwards. Ah! He was just in time to see it crash just behind the

British front-line trench. Tiny ant-like figures were already crawling towards it, some looking upwards, waving to him. Biggles smiled. 'Given the boys a treat, anyway,' he thought, as he pushed up his goggles and passed his hand wearily over his face. A sound like a sob was drowned in the drone of the engine. 'Well, that's that,' he said to himself, and turned his nose for home.

The following morning, as the Sergeant-Major in charge of the burying party at Lavricourt Cemetery entered the gate, his eye fell on a curious object that had been firmly planted on a new mound of earth, at the opposite end to the usual little white cross.

'What the devil's that thing, corporal?' he said, 'It wasn't there yesterday, I'll swear.'

The corporal took a few steps nearer.

'That's where they planted that R.F.C. wallah last week, Sergeant-Major,' he replied. 'Looks to me like a smashed aeroplane propeller.'

'All right, let it alone. I expect some of his pals shoved it there. For-ward—ma-arch!'

# Chapter 11
# The Boob

Mahoney, on his way to the sheds to take his Flight off for an early Ordinary Patrol, paused in his stride as his eye fell on Biggles leaning in an attitude of utter boredom against the door-post of the Officers' mess.

'Why so pensive, young aviator?' he smiled. 'Has Mr. Cox* grabbed your pay to square up the over-draft?' he added, as he caught sight of an open letter in the other's hand.

'Worse than that; much, much worse,' replied Biggles. 'Couldn't be worse, in fact—What do you think of this?' He held out the letter.

'I haven't time to read it, laddie. What's the trouble?'

'Oh, it's from an elderly female relative of mine. She says her son—my cousin—is in the R.F.C. on his way to France. She's pulled the wires at the Air Board for the Pool** to send him to 266, as she feels sure I can take care of him. She asks me to see that he changes his laundry regularly, doesn't drink, doesn't get mixed up with the French minxes, and a dozen other "doesn'ts." My God! it's a bit thick; what the hell does she think this is—a prep. school?'

'What's he like?'

'I don't know; it's years since I saw him; and if he's anything like the little horror he was then, God help

* Cox's were the army's official bank.
** A depot to which officers were posted until assigned to an active service squadron.

us—and him. His Christian names are Algernon Mont-gomery, and that's just what he looked like—a slice of warmed-up death wrapped in velvet and ribbons.'

'Sounds pretty ghastly. When's he coming?'

'To-day, apparently. His name's on the notice board. The old girl had the brass face to write to the C.O., and he's posted him to my Flight—in revenge, I expect.'

'Too bad,' replied Mahoney sympathetically. 'We'll go and get the letter done, telling her how bravely he died, and forget about it. There comes the tender now—see you later.'

Biggles, left alone, watched the tender pull up and discharge two new pilots and their kit; he had no diffi-culty in recognizing his new charge, who approached eagerly.

'You're Biggles—aren't you? I know you from the photo at home.'

The matured edition of the youth was even more unprepossessing than Biggles expected. His uniform was dirty, his hair long, his face, which wore a perma-nent expression of amused surprise, was a mass of freckles.

'My name's Captain Bigglesworth,' said the Flight-Commander coldly. 'You are posted to my Flight. Get your kit into your room, report to the Squadron office, and then come back here; I want to have a word with you.'

'Sorry, sir,' said Algernon apologetically; 'of course, I forgot.'

A few minutes later he rejoined Biggles in the mess. 'What'll you have to drink?' invited Biggles.

'Have you any ginger ale?'

'I shouldn't think so,' replied Biggles; 'we don't get

much demand for it. Have you any ginger ale, Adams?'
he asked the mess waiter—'I'll have the usual.'

'Yes, sir, I think I've got one somewhere, if I can
find it,' replied the waiter, looking at the newcomer
curiously.

'Sit down and let's talk,' said Biggles, when the
drinks had been served. 'How much flying have you
done?'

'Fourteen hours on Avros* and ten on Camels.'

'Ten hours, eh?' mused Biggles; 'ten hours. So
they're sending 'em out here with ten hours now. My
God! Now listen,' he went on, 'I want you to forget
those ten hours. This is where you'll learn to *fly*—they
can't teach you at home. If you live a week you'll begin
to know something about it. I don't want to discourage
you, but most people that come out here live on an
average twenty-four hours. If you survive a week you're
fairly safe. I can't teach you much, nobody can; you'll
find things out for yourself.

'First of all, never cross the line alone under 10,000
feet—not yet, anyway. Never go more than a couple of
miles over unless you are with a formation. Never go
down after a Hun. If you see a Hun looking like easy
meat, make for home like hell, and if that Hun fires a
Very light, kick out your foot and slam the stick over
as if somebody was already shooting at you. Act first
and think afterwards, otherwise you may not have time
to act. Never leave your formation on any account—
you'll never get back into it if you do, unless it's your
lucky day; the sky is full of Huns waiting to pile up
their scores and it's people like you that make it possible. Keep your eyes peeled and never stop looking for

* Avro 504, used extensively for training. Originally used in 1914 as a
bombing aircraft.

326

one instant. Watch the sun and never fly straight for more than two minutes at a time if you can't see what's up in the sun. Turn suddenly as if you've seen something—and you may see something. Never mind archie—it never hits anything. Watch out for balloon cables if you have to come home under 5,000. If a Hun gets on your tail, don't try to get away. Go for him. Try and bite him as if you were a mad dog; try and ram him—he'll get out of your way then. Never turn if you are meeting a Hun head-on; it isn't done. Don't shoot outside 200 feet—it's a waste of ammunition. Keep away from clouds, and, finally, keep away from balloons. It's suicide. If you want to commit suicide, do it here, because then someone else can have your bus*. If you see anything you don't understand, let it alone; never let your curiosity get the better of you. If I wave my hand above my head—make for home.** That means everybody for himself. That's all. Can you remember that?'

'I think so.'

'Right. Then let's go and have a look at the line and I'll show you the landmarks. If I shake my wings it means a Hun—I may go for it. If I do, you stay upstairs and watch me. If anything goes wrong—go straight home. When in doubt—go home, that's the motto. Got that?'

'Yes, sir.'

They took off together and circled over the aerodrome, climbing steadily for height. When his altimeter showed 6,000 feet Biggles headed for the line. It was not an

* Slang: aeroplane
** No aeroplanes had radio communicaton so messages between pilots were passed by hand or aeroplane movements.

ideal day for observation. Great masses of detached cumulus cloud were sailing majestically eastward and through these Biggles threaded his way, the other Camel in close attendance. Sometimes through the clouds they could see the ground, and from time to time Biggles pointed out salient landmarks—a chalk pit—stream—or wood. Gradually the recognizable features became fewer until they were lost in a scene of appalling desolation, criss-crossed with a network of fine lines scarred by pools of stagnant water.

Biggles beckoned the other Camel nearer and jabbed downwards. Explanation was unnecessary. They were looking down at no-man's-land.* Suddenly Biggles rocked his wings violently and pointed, and without further warning shot across the nose of the other Camel and dived steeply into a cloud. He pulled out underneath and looked around quickly, but of his companion there was no sign. He circled the cloud, climbing swiftly, and looking anxiously to right and left, choked back a furious curse as his eye fell on what he sought. Far away, almost out of sight in the enemy sky were five straight-winged machines; hard on their heels was a lone machine with a straight top wing and lower wings set at a dihedral angle—the Camel.

'The crazy fool,' ground out Biggles, as he set off in pursuit; but even as he watched, the six machines disappeared into a cloud and were lost to view. 'I should say that's the last anyone will see of Algernon Montgomery,' muttered Biggles philosophically, as he climbed higher, scanning the sky in the direction taken by the machines, but the clouds closed up and hid the earth from view, leaving the lone Camel the sole

* The land between the opposing armies at the front line trenches.

occupant of the sky. 'Well, I might as well go home and write that letter to his mother, as Mahoney said,' mused the pilot. 'Poor little devil! After all I told him, too. Well—!' He turned south-west and headed for home, flying by the unfailing instinct some pilots seem to possess.

Major Mullen, MacLaren and Mahoney were standing on the tarmac when he landed. 'Where's the new man, Biggles?' said Major Mullen quickly.

'He's gone,' said Biggles slowly as he took off his helmet. 'I couldn't help it, God knows. I told the young fool to stick to me like glue. We were just over the line when I spotted the shadows of five Fokkers on the clouds; I gave him the tip and went into the cloud, expecting him to follow me. When I came out he wasn't there. I went back and was just in time to see him disappearing into Hunland on the tails of the five Fokkers. I spent some time looking for him, but I couldn't find him. Could you believe that a—bah!—it's no use talking about it. I'm going for a dr—Hark!' The hum of a rotary engine rapidly approaching sent all eyes quickly upwards.

'Here he comes,' said Biggles frostily. 'Leave this to me, please, sir. I've something to say to him.'

The Camel landed and taxied in. The pilot jumped out and, with a cheerful wave of greeting, joined Biggles on the tarmac.

'I've—'

'Never mind that,' cut in Biggles curtly. 'Where the hell do you think you've been?'

'I saw the Huns—I was aching to have a crack at them—so I went after them.'

'Didn't I tell you to stay with me?'

'Yes, but—'

'Never mind "but"; you do what you're damn well told or I'll knock hell out of you. Who do you think you are—Billy Bishop or Micky Mannock*, perhaps?' sneered Biggles.

'The Huns were bolting—'

'Bolting be damned; they hadn't even seen you. If they had you wouldn't be here now. Those green and white stripes belong to von Kirtner's circus. They're killers—every one of 'em. You poor boob.'

'I got one of them.'

'*You what*!'

'I shot one down. I don't think he even saw me, though. I got all tangled up in a cloud, and when I came out and looked up his wheels were nearly on my head. I pulled my stick back and let drive right into the bottom of his cockpit. He went down. I saw the smoke against the clouds.'

Biggles subjected the speaker to a searching scrutiny. 'Where did you read that tale?' he asked slowly.

'I didn't read it, sir,' said the new pilot flushing. 'It was near a big queer-shaped wood. I think I must have been frightfully lucky.'

'Lucky!' ejaculated Biggles sarcastically. 'Lucky! Ha, ha! Lucky! You don't know how lucky you are. Now listen. If ever you leave me again I'll put you under close arrest as soon as your feet are on the ground. Whatever happens, you stick to me. I've other things to do besides write letters of condolence to your mother. All right, wash out for to-day.'

Biggles sought Major Mullen and the other Flight-

* Billy Bishop was a Canadian fighter pilot with 72 victories to his credit; Micky Mannock was an Irish fighter pilot with 73 victories, the highest scoring British pilot. He was killed in 1918.

Commander in the Squadron office. 'That kid got a Hun, or else he's the biggest liar on earth.'

'The liar sounds most likely to me,' observed MacLaren.

'Oh, I don't know; it has been done,' broke in Major Mullen, 'but it does seem a bit unlikely, I'll admit.'

The new pilot entered to make his report, and Biggles and MacLaren sauntered to the sheds. 'Wait a minute,' said Biggles suddenly. He swung himself into the cockpit of the Camel which had been flown by the new pilot. 'Well, he's used his guns anyway,' he said slowly, as he climbed out again. 'I'll take him on the dawn patrol with Healy in the morning. He's not safe alone.'

Biggles, leading the two other Camels, high in the pearly morning sky, pursed his lips into a soundless whistle as his eyes fell on a charred wreck at the corner of Mossyface Wood. 'So he got him all right,' he muttered; 'the kid was right. Well I'm damned!' A group of moving specks appeared in the distance. He watched them closely for a moment, then he rocked his wings and commenced a slow turn, pointing as he did so to the enemy machines which were coming rapidly towards them. He warmed his guns, stiffened a little in his seat, and glanced to left and right to make sure that the other two Camels were in place. He saw a flash of green and white on the sides of the enemy machines as they swung round for the attack, and he unconsciously half-glanced at the new pilot. 'You'll have the dog-fight you were aching for yesterday,' was his unspoken thought. The Fokkers, six of them, were slightly above, coming straight on. Biggles lifted his nose slightly, took the leader in his sights, and waited. At 200 feet, still holding the Camel head-on to the

331

other machines, he pressed his triggers. He saw the darting, jabbing flame of the other's guns, but did not swerve an inch. Metal spanged on metal near his face, the machine vibrated, and an unseen hand plucked at his sleeve. He clenched his teeth and held his fire. He had a swift impression of two wheels almost grazing his top plane as the first Fokker zoomed.

Out of the corner of his eye he saw Healy's tracer pouring into the Fokker at his right, and a trail of black smoke burst from the engine. Neither machine moved an inch. There was a crash which he could hear above the roar of his own engine as the Camel and the Fokker met head-on. A sheet of flame leapt upwards.

'Healy's gone—that's five to two now—not so good.' He did a lightning right-hand turn. Where was Algernon? There he was, still in position at his wing-tip. The Huns had also turned and were coming back at them. 'Bad show for a kid,' thought Biggles, and on the spur of the moment waved his left hand above his head. The pilot of the other Camel was looking at him, but made no move. 'The fool, why doesn't he go home?' Biggles muttered, as he took the nearest Fokker in his sights again and opened fire. The Hun turned and he turned behind it, and the next second all seven machines were in a complete circle. Out of the corner of his eye Biggles saw the other Camel on the opposite side of the circle on the tail of a Hun. 'Why doesn't he shoot?' Biggles cursed blindly. He pulled the stick back into his right side and shot into the circle, raking the Fokker that had opened fire on the other Camel. It zoomed suddenly, and as Biggles shot past the new pilot he waved his left arm.

He saw Algernon make a turn and dive for the line. A Fokker was on his tail instantly and Biggles raked it until it had to turn and face him. He half-rolled as a stream of lead ripped a strip of fabric from the centre section and went into a steep bank again to look at the situation.

He was alone, and there were still four Fokkers. For perhaps a minute each machine held its place in the circle, and then the Fokkers began to climb above him. Biggles knew that he was in an almost hopeless position, and he glanced around for a cloud to make a quick dash for cover, but from horizon to horizon the sky was an unbroken stretch of blue. The circle tightened as each machine strove to close it. The highest Fokker turned suddenly and dived on him, guns spitting two pencil lines of tracer. Biggles crouched a little lower in the cockpit. Two more of the Fokkers were turning on him now, and he knew that it was only a question of time before a bullet got him or his engine in a vital part.

Already the Camel was beginning to show signs of the conflict. 'God! What's that?' Biggles almost stalled as another Camel shot into the circle. It did not turn as the others, but rushed across the diameter, straight at a Fokker which jerked up in a wild zoom to avoid collision. The Camel flashed round—not in the direction of the circle, but against it, and Biggles stared open-eyed with horror as the other Fokkers shot out at a tangent to avoid disaster. 'My God! What's he doing?' he muttered, as he flung his own machine on its side to pass the other Camel. He picked out a Fokker and blazed at it. Where were the others? They seemed to be scattered all over the sky. The other Camel was circling above him. 'We'll get out of this while the going's good,' he muttered grimly, and waved his hand to the other pilot. Together they turned and dived for the line.

Biggles landed first and leant against the side of his machine to await the new pilot. For a moment he looked at him without speaking.

'Listen, laddie,' he said, when the other had joined him, 'you mustn't do that sort of thing. You'll give me the nightmare. You acted like a madman.'

'Sorry, but you told me to go for 'em like a mad dog. I thought that's what I did.'

Biggles looked at the speaker earnestly. 'Yes,' he grinned, 'that's just what you did; but why didn't you do some shooting? I never saw your tracer once.'

'I couldn't.'

'Couldn't?'

'No—my gun jammed.'

'When?'

'It jammed badly with a bulged cartridge in that first go, and I couldn't clear it.'

Biggles raised his hand to his forehead. 'Do you mean to say you came back into that hell of a dog-fight with a jammed gun?' he said slowly.

'Yes. You said stick with you.'

Biggles held out his hand. 'You'll do, kid,' he said; 'and you can call me Biggles.'

# Chapter 12
# The Battle of Flowers

The summer sun was sinking in the western sky in a blaze of crimson glory as Biggles, with his flying kit thrown carelessly over his arm, walked slowly from the sheds towards the Officers' mess. At the porch he paused in his stride to regard with wonderment the efforts of a freckled-faced youth, who, regardless of the heat, was feverishly digging up a small square patch of earth some thirty feet in front of the mess door.

'What the hell are you doing, Algy?' he called cheerfully. 'Making a private dugout for yourself?'

'No,' replied Algernon Montgomery, straightening his back with an obvious effort and wiping the perspiration off his brow with the back of his hand. 'I'm making a garden. This dust-smitten hole wants brightening up.'

'You're what?' cried Biggles incredulously.

'Making a garden, I said,' responded Algy shortly, resuming his task.

'Good God! What are you going to sow, or whatever you call it?'

'I've got some sunflowers,' replied Algy, nodding towards a newspaper package from which some wilted, sickly, green ends protruded.

'Sunflowers, eh?' said Biggles, curiously, advancing

towards the scene of action. 'They ought to do well. But why not plant some bananas or pineapples, or something we could eat?'

'It isn't hot enough for bananas,' said Algy, between breaths. 'They were all I could get, anyway.'

'Not hot enough?' answered Biggles. 'Holy mackerel! It feels hot enough to me to grow doughnuts.'

Algy dropped his spade and drew one of the seedlings gently from the package.

'Do you mean to tell me that you are going to stick that poor little devil in that pile of dust? I thought you said you were going to brighten things up,' said Biggles slowly.

'That'll be ten feet high presently,' said Algy confidently, scratching a hole in the earth and dropping the roots in.

'Ten feet! You mean to tell me that little squirt of a thing's got a ceiling of ten feet? Why, he's stalling already. Bah! You can't kid me. Straighten him up. You've got him a bit left wing low.'

'You push off, Biggles; I want to get these things in before dark,' cried Algy hotly. 'They've got to have some water yet.'

'They look to me as if a damn good double-Scotch would do them more good,' retorted Biggles as he turned towards the mess. 'So long, kid—see you later. You can lie up in the morning. I'll take Cowley and Tommy on the early show.'

Three hours later Biggles pushed his chair back from the card table in the anteroom. 'Well, I'm up five francs,' he announced, 'and now I'm going to roost. I'll—' A voice from the doorway interrupted him. It was Algy.

'Here, chaps,' he called excitedly, 'come and look at this—quick, before it goes.'

'He wants us to go and watch his posies sprouting in the moonlight, I expect,' grinned Biggles at Mahoney and McLaren, who were leaning back in their chairs. He turned towards the door, but as his eye fell on a window which had been flung wide open to admit as much air as possible, he stopped abruptly. 'What the hell!' he ejaculated, and sprang towards the door. The crash of falling chairs announced that the others were close behind him.

At the open doorway he stopped and looked up. A hundred feet above, a brilliant white light was sinking slowly earthwards, flooding the mess and the surrounding buildings with a dazzling radiance. A faint whistling sound, increasing in volume, became audible.

'Look out!' screamed Biggles and covering twenty yards almost in a bound dived headlong into a trench which surrounded a near-by Nissen hut. The whistle became a shrieking wail. 'Look where the hell you are coming,' yelled Biggles, as a dozen bodies thudded into the trench, one landing on the small of his back. 'Where's—' His voice was lost in a deafening detonation; a blinding sheet of flame leapt upwards.

'If they've knocked my drink over—' snarled Mahoney, struggling to get out of the trench.

'Come back, you fool,' yelled Biggles, hanging on to his foot. 'Here comes another—get down.'

Bang! Another terrific explosion shook the earth and falling debris rattled on to the tin roof beside them. The roar of an aero-engine almost on their heads, but swiftly receding, split the air.

'All right, chaps, he's gone,' said Biggles, scrambling out of the trench. 'Don't step on my cigarette case, anybody; I've dropped it somewhere. Hell's bells, he nearly caught us bending! Damn these new parachute flares, they don't give you a chance.'

'I hope he hasn't knocked our wine store sideways, like somebody did to 55 the other day,' grumbled Mahoney. 'Hullo! the searchlights have got him. Just look at that stinking archie; I wouldn't be in that kite for something.'

All eyes were turned upwards to where a black-crossed machine was twisting and turning in the beams of three searchlights which had fastened upon it. The air around was torn with darting, crimson jets of flame.

'He'll get away; they always do,' said MacLaren with deep disgust, making his way towards the mess.

'Well, I hope he does; he deserves to. I'd hate his job,' observed Biggles philosophically.

'Where's Algy?'

'I expect the kid's gone to see if his plantation's all right,' replied Mahoney. 'Well, good-night, chaps — good-night, Biggles.'

'Cheerio, laddie.'

Ten minutes later there was a knock on Biggles' door, and in reply to his invitation a wild-eyed, freckled-faced youth thrust his head inside. He seemed to be labouring under some great emotion.

'What — what was that?' he gasped.

Biggles grinned. 'Hanoverana — didn't you see it in the beam?' he replied. 'There's no harm done.'

'Where did that dirty dog come from, do you think?' choked Algy.

'Aerodrome 29, I expect, they are the only Hanovers near here. Must have crossed the line at twenty thousand and glided down with his engine off,' replied Biggles.

'Where's Aerodrome 29?'

'On, go to the map-room and find out; it's time you knew. There are some photos there, too. Push off, I'm tired and I'm on the early show.'

Algy stood for a moment breathing heavily, staring at his Flight-Commander, and then abruptly slammed the door.

II

Biggles scarcely seemed to have closed his eyes when he was awakened by the ear-splitting roar of an engine. It was still dark. He grabbed his luminous watch and looked at the time—it was 3.30. 'What the devil—' he croaked, springing out of bed. He reached the window just as the dim silhouette of a Camel passed overhead. He flung on a dressing-gown and raced along the sun-baked path to the sheds. 'Who's that just gone off?' he called to a tousled-headed ack-emma who was still staring upwards with a vacant grin on his face.

'Alger—sorry, sir—Mr—'

'Never mind,' snapped Biggles, overlooking the breach of respect, 'I know. Where's he gone—did he say?'

'No, sir, but I saw him marking up his map. He took eight Cooper bombs.'

'What did he mark on his map?' snapped Biggles.

'Aerodrome 29, sir.'

Biggles swung on his heel and tore back towards the huts. He shook and pummelled the life into Cowley and Thomas. 'Come on,' he said tersely, 'jump to it. Algy's gone off his rocker—he's shooting up 29 alone. Let's get away.'

Sidcots were hastily donned over pyjamas, and

339

within five minutes three machines were in the air heading for the line. The sun was creeping up over the horizon when Biggles, at 5,000 feet, waved to the other two pilots and leaning over the side of his cockpit, pointed downwards. Far below, a tiny moving speck was circling and banking over a line of hangars. A cloud of white smoke arose into the air. Tiny ant-like figures were running to and fro.

'The fool, the crazy lunatic,' gasped Biggles, as he pushed the stick forward and went roaring down with the others behind him. At 500 feet a row of holes appeared like magic in his wing and he sideslipped violently. He levelled out and poured a stream of tracer at a group of figures clustered around a machine-gun. A green machine was taking off cross-wind; he swung down behind it and raked it with a stream of lead. The gunner in the rear seat dropped limply and the machine crashed into the trees at the far end of the aerodrome. The air was full of the rattle of guns and an ominous flack! flack! flack! behind warned him that it was time to be leaving.

He looked around for Algy, and, spotting him still circling, zoomed across his nose, frantically waving his arm above his head. 'If he doesn't come now he can stay and get what he deserves,' muttered Biggles, as he shot over the edge of the aerodrome. He looked behind. To his relief three Camels were on his tail, so, climbing swiftly for height, he headed back towards the lines.

'I'll see him back home and then go straight on with the morning show,' he mused a few minutes later as they raced across the lines in a flurry of archie. He landed and leaned against the side of the Camel while he waited for the others to come in. Another Camel touched its wheels gently on the aerodrome and finished its run not twenty yards away. Algy sprang out of the cockpit and ran towards him. 'I got it—I got it!' he shouted exultantly as he ran.

'Who do you think you are?' snapped Biggles, 'Archimedes?'

'I got four hits out of eight,' cried Algy joyously.

'You got nothing—I had a good look. You didn't touch a single hangar,' growled Biggles.

'Hangar—hangar—' replied Algy stupidly, 'who's talking about hangars?'

'I am, what else do you suppose?'

'Hangars be damned!' cried Algy, 'I mean their geraniums!'

'Germaniums—germaniums—my God, am I going crazy—what are you talking about—germaniums?'

'Raniums—raniums—N—N—! Good Lord! Did you never hear of geraniums? They had a bed full of geraniums and calceolarias.'

'Calcium—calcium—' Biggles took a quick step backwards and whipped out his Very pistol. 'Here, stand back you or I'll shoot. You're daft.'

'Daft be damned! I mean flowers—I've scattered their blinking geraniums all over the aerodrome.'

Biggles stared at him for a moment, his jaw sagging foolishly. 'Do you mean to tell me you've been to that hell-hole, and dragged me there to bomb a ruddy flowerbed?'

'Yes, and I've made a salad of their lettuce patch,' added Algy triumphantly.

'But why? What have the lettuces done to you?'

'Done to me? Haven't you seen what that damn swine did to my sunflowers last night?'

Biggles swung round on his heel as enlightenment burst upon him. At the spot where Algy's flower-bed had been yawned a deep round hole.

# Chapter 13
# The Bomber

Biggles, cruising along the line on a dawn patrol, pressed on the rudder-bar with his left foot as his ever-searching eyes fell on a line of white archie bursts to the south-east, far over the British lines. The colour of the bursts told him at once that the shells were being fired by British guns, for German anti-aircraft gunfire was usually black. It could only mean that one or more enemy machines were in the vicinity, an event sufficiently unusual to intrigue him immensely. 'I must look into this,' was his unspoken thought as he headed his Camel along a course which would intercept the target of the rapidly-lengthening line of archie bursts.

A small, black speck, well in front of the foremost bursts, soon became visible and his curiosity increased, for the machine was of a type unknown to him. As he drew nearer a puzzled frown lined his forehead.

'I don't believe it; it can't be true,' he murmured at last, when only a few hundred yards separated him from his objective. The anti-aircraft fire ceased when the gunners observed his presence, and Biggles closed rapidly with the other machine, which with sublime indifference continued on its way without paying the slightest attention to him. Large Maltese crosses on the tail and fuselage left no doubt as to its nationality.*

It was the largest aeroplane Biggles had ever seen.

* Some German aeroplanes in the First World War were painted with the Maltese Cross (see front cover of *Biggles of the Fighter Squadron*).

He noted two engines, one on each side of the fuselage, and raked his memory for some rumour or gossip by which he could identify it. 'It isn't a Gotha*,' he mused; 'damned if I know what it is; but I'll bet she carries a tidy load of eggs.' Almost unconsciously he had been edging nearer to the nose of the big machine as he inspected it, but a sudden burst of fire from the gunner in the nacelle**, and an ominous flack! flack flack! behind warned him that the crew were on the alert and well prepared to receive him. He made a lightning right-hand turn, and as he flashed back past the bomber a murderously accurate burst of fire from the rear gunner startled him still further. 'Hell's bells!' swore Biggles, 'this is a bit hot.'

The big machine had not moved an inch from its course, and to be thus treated with contempt annoyed him intensely. They were rapidly approaching the lines and if he was to prevent the return of the bomber to its aerodrome, something would have to be done quickly.

Biggles swept to the rear of the machine, swearing again as the Camel bumped violently in the slipstream of the two engines. 'All right, let's see how you like this one,' he snapped angrily, and put his nose down in a steep dive. He was following the usual practice of attacking a two-seater, judging his speed and distance to bring him up under the elevators of the enemy machine, out of the field of fire of both gunners.

The attack was perfectly timed and the Camel soared up like a bird immediately under the big fuselage. Biggles glanced through the sights and took the bomber

* German twin-engined biplane with a crew of three, which carried 14 bombs weighing a maximum total of 1100 lbs.
** The crew section placed on or between the wings.

at where he judged the pilot's seat to be, withholding his fire until the Camel was almost at stalling point in order to make certain of his aim. What happened next occurred with startling rapidity. The muzzles of a pair of twin Parabellum guns slid out of a trap door in the floor of the bomber and the next instant a double stream of lead was shooting the Camel to pieces about him. Flack! flack! Whang! whang! sang the bullets as they bored through fabric and metal. Biggles, shaken as never before in all his flying experience, kicked out his left foot spasmodically and flung the stick over and back into his stomach. The Camel whirled over and fell into a dive; the 150 h.p. Bentley Rotary coughed once—twice—and then cut out altogether. The propeller stopped dead and the thoroughly alarmed pilot started to glide earthwards with the rapidly-diminishing hum of the bomber's engines in his ears.

Biggles pushed up his goggles and looked downwards, and then up at the fast disappearing Boche machine.

'Phew! My God' he muttered soberly, 'that'll stop me laughing in church in the future. What a hell-trap. Who would have guessed it? Well, we live and learn,' he concluded bitterly, and turned his attention to the inevitable forced landing. He anticipated no difficulty, for he had ample height from which to choose a landing ground. 'Thank goodness I'm over my own side of the line,' he mused philosophically, as he slowly lost height.

He could not get to his own aerodrome, at Maranique, but 287 Squadron might just be reached, and although he did not look forward with any degree of pleasure to the inevitable jibes of the S.E.5 pilots, it was better than risking damaging the machine in an open field.

He made a good landing in the middle of the aerodrome and sat up on the 'hump' of the Camel to await the arrival of the mechanics to tow the machine to the tarmac, where a group of cheering pilots awaited him.

'Get stung, Biggles?' yelled Wilkinson, the good-natured Flight Commander.

'I got stung all right,' acknowledged Biggles ruefully. 'That kite's got more stings than a hornet's nest. What the hell is it, anyway?'

'That's our pet Friedrichshafen.* Come and have a drink while we ring up your old man and tell him you're O.K., and I'll tell you about it,' said Wilks, linking his arm through that of the Camel pilot's.

'Have you had a go at it?' inquired Biggles.

'Me? We've all had a go at it. It comes over just before dawn nearly every day, lays its eggs, and beetles home about this time.'

'And do you mean to say that you can't stop it?' exclaimed Biggles incredulously.

Wilkinson shrugged his shoulders. 'You didn't do a hell of a lot yourself, did you. The only thing that did any stopping was your cowling by the look of it. It's as full of holes as a colander. It'd be easier to sink a battleship than that flying arsenal. There isn't a blind spot anywhere that we've discovered; the usual weak spots aren't weak any longer. They just plaster you whichever way you come—oh!—I know. Twin mobile guns'll beat fixed guns any day. I'm not aching to commit suicide, so I let it alone, and that's a fact. There was a rumour that Wing had offered three pips to anybody who got it. Lacie of 281 had a go, and went down in flames. Crickson of 383 had a stab at it in one

* Twin-engined biplane bomber with a crew of three. It could carry a bomb-load of 3000 lbs.

346

of the new Dolphins*, and it took a week to dig him out of the ground. Most people keep their distance now and watch archie do its daily dozen, but *they* couldn't hit a damn Zeppelin at fifty yards. Guns** reckons that the Friedrichshafen costs our people who are paying for the War, five thousand pounds a day for archie ammunition, and I reckon he isn't far out.'

'I see,' said Biggles thoughtfully. 'Well, I'll be getting back if you can find me transport. I'll come back for the Camel later on. Cheerio, Wilks.'

'Cheerio, Biggles. Keep away from that Hun till the first of the month. I'll send you a wreath, but I'm broke till then.'

'Yes? Well, don't chuck your money away on losers. What you'll need is a pair of spectacles next time I meet that Hun.'


After seeing the damaged Camel brought home, and the ignition lead which had caused the engine failure repaired, Biggles spent the evening with a lead pencil and some paper, making drawings of the big bomber as he remembered it. He marked the three guns and drew lines and circles to represent the field of fire covered by each. He quickly discovered that what Wilkinson had told him concerning the guns covering all angles of approach was correct, and ordinary attack was almost useless, and certainly very dangerous.

The old weakness in the defence of all big machines, which was underneath the fuselage, did not exist. The only possible spot which could be regarded as 'blind'

* British Sopwith Dolphin — biplane fighter armed with two machine guns, in service 1917. Not as popular as the Camel — it was only used by 4 RAF squadrons.
** Guns was the usual squadron nickname for the gunnery officer.

was immediately under the nacelle, and even so he would be exposed to the fire of at least one of the gunners while he was manoeuvring into that position. He considered the possibility of dropping bombs, but discarded it as impraticable. If he dropped the bombs over his own side of the line and missed, the people down below would have something to say about it, and it was hardly likely that he would be allowed to go about it unmolested over the German side.

No! The only chance was the spot under the nacelle and then to use a Lewis gun which fired upwards through his centre section. He did not usually carry this weapon, as he infinitely preferred head-on tactics with his double Vickers guns; not entirely satisfied with the result of his calculations, he gave instructions for the Lewis gun to be fitted, told his batman* to call him an hour before dawn, and went to bed.

It was still dark when, with his flying coat and boots over his pyjamas, he climbed into the cockpit of his Camel the following morning. He felt desperately tired and disinterested in the project, and half regretted his decision to pursue it, but once in the air he felt better.

It was a glorious morning. A few late stars still lingered in the sky; to the east the first gleam of dawn was lightening the horizon. He pointed his nose and cruised steadily in the direction of his encounter of the preceding day, climbing steadily and inhaling the fresh morning air. As he climbed, the rim of the sun, still invisible to those below, crept up over the skyline and bathed the Camel in an orange glow. Around and below him the earth was a vast basin of indigo and deep purple shadows, stretching, it seemed, to eternity.

*An attendant serving an officer. A position discontinued in today's RAF.

He appeared to hang over the centre of it, an infinitesimal speck in a strange world in which no other living creature moved. The sense of utter loneliness and desolation, well known to pilots, oppressed him, and he was glad when six D.H.9's, that had crept up unseen from the void beneath, gleamed suddenly near him like jewels on velvet as the rays of the sun flashed on their varnished wings. He flew closer to them and waved to the observers, leaning idly over their Scarff rings.* The Nines held on their way and were soon lost in the mysterious distance. Biggles idly wondered how many of them would come back. The dome above him had turned pale green, and then turquoise, not slowly, but quickly, as if hidden lights had been switched on by the master of a stage performance.

'And this is war!' mused the pilot. 'God! it's hard to believe—but unless I'm mistaken here it comes,' he added, as his eye caught a cluster of tiny sparks in the far distance at about his own height. 'Good morning, Archibald, you dirty dog,' he muttered, as he eyed the approaching flashes at the head of which he could now discern the silhouette of the big bomber. He swiftly closed the distance between them, warming his guns as he went, and the answering stream of tracer from the forward guns of the bomber brought a faint smile to his lips. There was no chance of approaching unobserved and he had not attempted it. He circled slowly 500 feet above the big machine and looked down; the gunner in the rear cockpit gave him a mock salute, and he waved back.

He wasted no further time on pleasantries, but dived steeply, still well outside effective range. Down and

*The gun mounting which completely encircled the gunner's cockpit. Around this ring the gun could slide to point in any direction.

down he went until he was well below the bomber and then slowly pulled the stick back; the bomber seemed to be dropping out of the sky on to him. He was coming up under the nacelle and his eyes were glued to the trap door through which he could see the crouching gunner. A spurt of flame leapt outwards towards him and the ominous tell-tale flack! flack! flack! behind and on each side told that the gunner was making good shooting. A moment later he was flying on even keel not more than twenty feet below the nacelle and in the same direction as the other machine.

Something seemed to drop off the bomber and whizz past him; he looked upwards with a start in time to see another bomb swing off the bomb-rack and hurtle past dangerously near. He looked along the line of racks, but could see no more bombs, which relieved him greatly, for he had entirely overlooked the fact that the bomber might not have laid all its eggs. He could see the face of the forward gunner peering over the side, looking at him, and a quick glance astern revealed spasmodic bursts of tracer passing harmlessly under the tail of the Camel. Satisfied that the gunner could not reach him, he took the joystick between his knees and seized his top gun, left hand grasping the spade-grip and right forefinger curled around the trigger. Rat-tat—he cursed luridly as he struggled to clear the jammed gun. Why did guns always jam at the crucial moment?

The bomber was turning now and he had to grab the stick with one hand to keep his place. He stood up in the cockpit and hammered at the ammunition drum with his fist. He tried the trigger, found the gun was working and, dropping back into his seat, just had time to push the stick forward as the bomber came down on him as its pilot tried to tear his wing off with its undercarriage. He sideslipped in a wild attempt to keep in position, but his windscreen flew to pieces as a stream of tracer from the rear gun caught him. He dived frantically away, kicking alternate feet as he went to spoil the gunner's aim.

Safely out of range he pushed up his goggles and wiped his forehead. 'Damn this for a game,' he moaned, 'but for that jam I'd have had him then.' He glanced down and was horrified to see that they were already over the enemy lines. He tested his top gun to make sure that it was working and then savagely repeated his manoeuvre to come up underneath the bomber. He held his breath as he ran the gauntlet of the gunners again, and then at point-blank range he dropped the stick, seized the gun and pressed the trigger.

There was no mistake this time. He held the burst until the Camel began to fall away from under him and then he dropped back into his seat grabbing wildly at the stick as the machine went into a spin, bracing himself with all his strength against the sides of the cockpit to prevent himself being thrown out.

'My God! That's all I want of that,' he muttered, as he got the machine under control and looked around for the bomber.

It was steering an erratic course for the ground, obviously in difficulties. He dived after it and noticed that the rear gunner's cockpit was empty. 'I've hit the pilot and the observer is trying to get the machine down,' he decided instantly, and a closer view confirmed his suspicions, for he could see the observer holding the joystick over the shoulder of the limp figure of the pilot.

'I hope he manages it,' thought Biggles anxiously,

and held his hand up to show that they had nothing more to fear from him, afterwards circling round to watch the landing. It was a creditable effort; the big machine flattened out, but failed to clear a line of trees; Biggles almost fancied he could hear the crash as it settled down in a pile of torn fabric and splintered wood.

'I'll have to go and tell Wilks about this,' said the elated pilot to himself, as he steered a course for the S.E.5 aerodrome; 'he'll be tickled to death!'

# Chapter 14

# On Leave

Captain Bigglesworth glanced up carelessly at the notice-board in passing; a name caught his eye and he took a step nearer. The name was his own:

*Captain J. C. Bigglesworth. Posted to 69 F.T.S.\**
*Narborough. W./48 P./1321.*

he read. For a full minute he looked at the notice uncomprehendingly, and as its full significance dawned upon him, swore savagely and hurried to the Squadron office.

'Yes, Biggles,' said Major Mullen glancing up from his desk, 'do you want to see me?'

'I see I'm posted to Home Establishment,' replied Biggles. 'May I ask why?'

The C.O. laid down his pen, crossed the room and laid a fatherly hand on the Flight-Commander's shoulder. 'I'm sorry, Biggles,' he said simply, 'but I've got to send you home. Now listen to me. I've been out here longer than you have. I know every move in the game; that's why I'm commanding 266. I know when a man's cracking up; I saw you start weeks ago; when Batson went West you were at breaking point. Now, remember I'm telling you this for your own good—not to hurt your feelings. I think too much of you for that.

---

\* Flying Training School, based in the UK.

If I thought less of you, why, I'd leave you here to go on piling up the score in the Squadron "game book." If you did stay here, you'd be a sot in a month. Already you're drinking more than you used to; that's the beginning of the end. You'll be caught napping; you'll stall taking-off, or you'll hit a tree coming in. Cleverer pilots than you have gone out that way. You can't help it and you can't stop it. No one can stand the pace for ever. This game makes an old man of a young one without him knowing it. That's the truth, Biggles. You've got to have a rest. If you don't rest now you'll never be able to rest again. You are more use to us alive than dead; put it that way if you like. That's why I put your posting through.'

'But can't I have a rest without being posted?' said Biggles bitterly.

'No, I have asked you to take some leave. The M.O. has asked you, and I've heard Mac and Mahoney telling you to—they've both been on leave and it's done them a power of good.'

'All right, sir. I'll go on leave if you'll cancel the posting. It would kill me to hang about an F.T.S.'

'Very well. Fill in your application. Ten days with effect from to-morrow. I'll send it to Wing by hand right away. You stay on the strength of 266.'

'I've only one other thing to ask, sir. May I fly home?'

'There you go, you see. You can't leave it alone. Well, you might get a lift with a ferry pilot from Bourget. How's that?'

'Not for me,' said Biggles firmly. 'I'm not trusting my life to any ferry pilot. I'll fly myself in a Camel.'

'How am I going to account for the Camel if you break it up?'

354

'Break it! I don't break machines up.'

'You might.'

'Well, send one back for reconditioning. I'll take it.'

'All right,' said the C.O. after a brief pause. 'It's against regulations and you know it. Don't come back here without that Camel, that's all.'

'Very good, sir.'

Biggles saluted briskly and departed.

Major Mullen turned to 'Wat' Tyler, the Recording Officer, who had been a witness of the scene, and deliberately winked. 'You were right, Tyler,' he smiled. 'That posting worked the trick; that was the only way we would have got him to take some leave.'

Early the following morning Biggles, in his best uniform, took off and steered a course for Marquise, where he proposed to refuel before crossing the Channel. He eyed the enemy sky longingly, but true to his word to the C.O., held firmly to his way. The trip proved uneventful, and midday found him lunching in the officers' mess at Lympne. He reported to the officer commanding the station, presented his movement order, saw his machine safely in a hangar, and went on to London by train.

Arriving home, he discovered the house closed; he telephoned a friend of the family, only to find out that his father and brother, his only living relations, were in the Army and 'somewhere in France.' 'Well, that's that,' said Biggles as he hung up the receiver. 'I might have known they would be.'

For a week he hung about town, thoroughly bored, doing little except drift between his hotel, the Long Bar at the Trocadero, the American Bar at the Alhambra, or anywhere he thought he might strike somebody he knew, home on leave from the Front. The weather was cold and wet and he looked forward joyfully to his return to the Squadron. And then, walking down Shaftesbury Avenue, he met Dick Harboard, his father's greatest friend and business associate. Over a drink Biggles briefly explained his position, bitterly lamenting the time he was wasting when he might be doing something useful in France. 'I'm sick of loafing about here,' he concluded. 'London is getting me down fast. I hate the sight of the place, but there's nowhere else to go.'

'Why not come down to my place for the rest of your time. I've a shooting party down for the week-end. Mixed crowd, of course— some funny people have got the money these days, but it can't be helped. What about it?'

'Where is your place?'

'Felgate, in Kent—near Folkestone.'

'Folkestone is near Lympne, isn't it?'

'Next door to it. Why?'

'Oh, I just wondered,' said Biggles vaguely. He did not think it worth while explaining that he had a machine at Lympne and had visions of putting in a few hours' flying-time if the weather improved.

'Good enough,' said Harboard as they parted. 'I shall expect you to-night in time for dinner.'

'I'll be along,' agreed Biggles. 'I'll come down in mufti* I think, and forget the war for a bit. Cheerio— see you later.'

Biggles, clad in grey flannels and a sweater, deep in a Sabatini novel from his host's library, paused to pull

* Out of uniform.

his chair a little nearer to the hall fire. It was bitterly cold for the time of the year; lowering skies and a drizzle of rain had put all ideas of flying out of his head, and he settled down for a comfortable spell of reading.

He frowned as the door opened to admit a party of men and girls whose heavy boots and macintoshes proclaimed them to be a shooting party, bound for the fields. At their head was Frazer, a big, florid, middle-aged man to whom Biggles had taken an instant dislike when they had been introduced the previous evening. Biggles did not like the easy air of familiarity with which he had addressed him. His loud overbearing manner, particularly when there were women present, irritated his frayed nerves. He had noticed on arrival that none of the party were in uniform, and he wondered vaguely why a man of such obviously splendid physique as Frazer was not in the Army; to save any possible embarrassment he had asked to be introduced as Mr Bigglesworth. He was not left long in wonder, for Frazer, tapping his chest ruefully with his forefinger, complained at frequent intervals of the weak heart that kept him at home and thus prevented him from showing in actual practice how the War could be ended forthwith.

The fact that he was obviously making a lot of money out of the War did nothing to lessen Biggles' irritation, and these were the reasons why he had decided to remain in the hall with a book rather than have to suffer the fellow's society with the shooting party.

'Well, well,' observed Frazer in affected surprise with his eyes on the slippers on Biggles's feet. 'Not coming out with the guns?'

'No, thanks,' replied Biggles civilly.

357

'Huh! I should have thought a bit of exercise would have done you good; a shot or two at the birds will get your eye in for when you join the Army.' The sneer behind the words was unmistakable.

'It's too confoundedly cold, and I hate getting my feet wet,' said Biggles quietly, keeping his temper with an effort.

'I can't understand you young fellows,' went on Frazer, when the snigger that had followed Biggles' words had subsided. 'Anyway, I should have thought there were plenty of things you could do with a War on besides rotting over a fire.'

Again the inference was obvious, and Biggles choked back a hot retort. 'Bah! Why argue,' was his unspoken thought. The man was in his element, holding the floor; well, let him. He eyed Frazer coldly, without answering, and it may have been something in his eye that caused Frazer to shift uneasily and turn to the outside door.

'Well, let's get along, folks,' he said loudly. 'Somebody has got to keep the home fires burning, I suppose,' was his parting shot as the door closed behind them.

Biggles, left alone, smiled to himself for a moment, and then settled down to his book. The telephone in the next room shrilled noisily—again, and yet again, and Biggles breathed a prayer of thankfulness when he heard Lea, the butler, answer it. He was half-way through the first chapter of his book when the 'phone again jarred his nerves with its insistent jangle. He laid down his book with a weary sigh. 'My God! I can't stand this infernal racket,' he muttered, and looked up to see Lea standing white-faced in the doorway.

'What's the matter, Lea?' he asked irritably, 'is the house on fire or something?'

'No, sir; but Mr. Harboard is out. He is the Chief Constable you know, and they say that two German seaplanes are bombing Ramsgate.'

'What!' Biggles leapt up as if he had been stung by a hornet. 'Say that again.'

'Two German seaplanes—'

Biggles made a flying leap to the window and cast a critical eye at the sky. The rain had stopped and small patches of blue showed through the scudding clouds.

'Quick!' he snapped, every nerve tingling with excitement, 'get the car round.'

The butler, shaken from his normal sedate bearing by the brisk command, departed almost at a run.

'Get me to Lympne as quickly as you can; put your foot down and keep it down,' he told the chauffeur a few minutes later, as, with flying coat, cap and goggles over his arm, he jumped into the big saloon car.

For fifteen minutes Biggles fretted and fumed with impatience as the car tore through the narrow Kentish lanes. 'Go on,' he shouted, when they arrived at the aerodrome, 'straight up to the hanger.'

The guard at the gate challenged him, but Biggles yelled him aside with a swift invective.

'Get that Camel out of No. 3 shed,' he snapped at a group of idling mechanics. 'Number 9471—jump to it!' and then he burst into the C.O.'s office.

'Captain Bigglesworth, 266 Squadron, on leave from overseas, sir. You remember I reported last week?'

'Oh, yes, I remember,' said the C.O. 'What's the hurry?'

'Two Huns are bombing Ramsgate—I'm going for them. I've got ammunition—I had two belts put in in case I ran into anything coming over.'

'But—'

Biggles was already on his way; he took a flying leap into the cockpit.

'Switches off, petrol on,' sang out the ack-emma.

'Petrol on,' echoed Biggles.

'Contact!'

'Contact!'

The Bentley started with a roar and sent a cloud of smoke whirling aft in the slipstream. He adjusted his goggles, waved the chocks away, and a few minutes later was in the air heading N.N.E. with the coastline cutting across the leading edge of his starboard wing. He had no maps, but he estimated the distance to Ramsgate to be about fifteen to twenty miles, not more; with the wind under his tail he should be there in less than ten minutes. Deal was on his starboard quarter now, and Sandwich loomed ahead; in the distance he could see the sweep in the coast where the North Foreland jutted out.

He had been flying low in order to watch the landmarks, but now he pulled the joystick back and climbed through a convenient hole in the clouds. Above, the cloud-tops were bathed in brilliant sunshine, and still climbing, he looked eagerly ahead for the enemy machines. The only machine he could see was an old F.E. circling aimlessly some distance inland, so he pointed his nose north-west and headed out to sea in an endeavour to cut the raiders off should they have started on the homeward journey.

For a quarter of an hour he flew thus, peering ahead and around him for the hostile machines. Doubts began to assail him. Suppose the whole thing was a wild rumour? What a fool he had been not to get some reliable information before he started. His altimeter was registering 10,000 feet, the clouds, through which he could occasionally see patches of grey sea, were far below.

He commenced a wide circle back towards land, noting that he had already ventured much too far away to be safe should his engine give trouble. He throttled back to three-quarter and for a few minutes cruised quietly in a due easterly direction, touching his rudder-bar from time to time to permit a clear view ahead.

A movement—or was it instinct—made him glance to the north. Far away, flying close together were two machines—seaplanes. He was round in an instant heading north-west to cut them off. Five minutes later he could see that he would catch them, for they were appreciably nearer. He could tell the moment they saw him, for they turned in a more northerly direction away from him and put their noses down for more speed. A few minutes later he could see the black crosses and the gunners standing up waiting to receive him. 'Well, mused Biggles, 'this is no place to mess about in a Camel. If I run out of fuel, or if they get a shot in my tank, I'm sunk. I must have been crazy to come right out here. It's neck or nothing if I'm going to do any-thing. Here goes.'

He pushed his nose down for speed and then pulled up in a steep zoom under the elevators of the nearest machine; but the pilot had seen his move and swung broadside on and exposed him to the full view of his gunner who at once opened fire; but his shooting was wild, and Biggles could see his tracer passing harm-lessly some distance away. The Camel pilot deliberately hung back until the other had emptied his drum of ammunition and started to replace it with a new one; then he zoomed in to point-blank range, and, knowing that he might not get such another opening, held his fire until his sights were aligned on the forward cockpit, and then pressed his triggers.

The nose of the Brandenburg* seaplane tilted sharply upwards, and then dropped; the machine made an aimless half-turn that quickly became a spin as the nose dropped, and then whirled downwards with the engine still at full throttle.

Biggles fell off on to his wing and peered through his centre section for the second seaplane. For a moment he could not see it and when he did spot it, it was going down in a steep dive towards the clouds. 'Looks as if he's lost his nerve,' muttered the Camel pilot as he pushed his stick forward and went down like a thunderbolt in the wake of the diving German.

He opened fire some distance away at a range which he knew quite well could not be effective unless a lucky shot found its mark, but he did it with the deliberate intention of rattling an obviously nervous foe.

The Brandenburg dropped tail-up into the cloud-bank and Biggles carefully followed it; he found it again just below the clouds and resumed the chase. Just ahead, a wide patch of blue sky showed through a gap in the cloud and Biggles closed in quickly, but the German swung round in obvious indecision. 'The fool can't be thinking of trying to land,' thought Biggles in astonishment, and fired a series of short bursts to confuse his opponent still more. But the German had had enough, and apparently having no wish to share the fate of his companion, cut off his engine and commenced to glide down towards the water. A new possibility occurred to Biggles. 'If he gets that kite down on the water safely the gunner might be able to hold me

* German two-seater seaplane used for reconnaissance and light bombing.

off until my petrol ran out,' he thought. He also knew that a floating target was more difficult to hit than one in the air, for he dare not risk overshooting his mark. 'Well, I've got to cramp his style,' thought Biggles, and he dived recklessly at the seaplane, guns streaming tracer, to which, to his surprise, the enemy gunner made no reply.

'What a gutless hound,' he thought. 'Hullo—there he goes!'

The Brandenburg pilot, in his haste to get out of that withering blast of lead, had tried to land too fast; the floats struck the surface of the sea with a terrific splash, the nose buried itself under the water and the tail cocked high into the air. Biggles watched both occupants climb along to the elevators, and, circling low, pointed in the direction of the shore, in the hope that they would realize that he had gone for help.

'You are wanted on the 'phone, sir,' said Lea, the butler, apologetically.

It was late in the afternoon. Biggles put down his book and hurried to the instrument, for he was expecting the call, and anxious to hear the fate of the two German airmen. He picked up the receiver.

'Major Sidgrove speaking, from Lympne,' said a voice.

'Captain Bigglesworth here, sir,' replied Biggles.

'Good show, Bigglesworth; we found both machines in the sea. The crew of the first were both dead—gunshot wounds, but the others were all right except for shock and exposure. Rather funny; the pilot had a brace of beautiful black eyes that the observer had given him. The pilot was an N.C.O. under the command of an officer in the rear seat; the Germans fly like that, you know.'

363

Biggles knew well enough, but he made no comment.

'Apparently it was the pilot's first show,' went on the Major, 'and when you started shooting he went to bits. He made for the water with the officer beating hell out of him and yelling for him to get into the clouds. He was swiping him over the nut instead of shooting at you. I've never seen a man so peeved in my life. Well, that's all. I thought you'd like to know. I've forwarded your report to the Ministry. They've been on the phone wanting to know what the dickens you were doing at Lympne, where you got the Camel, who gave you instructions, and God knows what else! They seem more concerned about that than about the two Huns—they would be! I expect they'll send for you during the next day or two; where can I get hold of you if they do?'

'Maranique,' replied Biggles shortly. 'I'm going back to-morrow. Many thanks, Major; good-bye.'

Biggles hung up the receiver and returned to the hall. The door opened and the shooting party, covered with mud, entered. Frazer looked at Biggles in undisguised disgust.

'Still keeping the fire warm,' he sneered. 'You should have been with us, we've had great sport.'

'So have I,' said Biggles softly.

'I got in some pretty shooting,' continued Frazer.

'Funny, so did I,' said Biggles smiling faintly.

'You! Why you haven't been out. I can't understand why some people are so careful about their skins.'

One of the girls came forward.

'There,' she said, 'I've brought you a little souvenir.' She laid a small white feather* on the table.

* A symbol of cowardice.

'Thanks,' said Biggles evenly, 'I've always wanted a feather in my cap. I've got one to-day.'

Mr. Harcourt bustled into the room.

'What's that—what's that—feather in your cap? I should say it will be. I shouldn't be surprised if you got the D.S.O.* Well done, my boy, you deserve it.'

'D.S.O.—D.S.O.—' echoed Frazer stupidly, 'What the devil for?'

'Haven't you heard?'

'Oh, cut it out, sir,' protested Biggles.

'Cut it out, be damned. I'm proud to have you under my roof and I want everybody to know it.' He turned to the others. 'He's just shot down a couple of Hun bombers in the sea, after they had bombed Ramsgate.'

A silence fell that could almost be felt.

'Who—who is he?' blurted out Frazer, at last, nodding towards Biggles, who was lighting a cigarette. 'He's not *the* Bigglesworth—the fellow we read about in the papers—the flyer—is he?'

'Of course he is; who else did you think he was?' cried Harcourt in astonishment.

'Well,' said Frazer quietly, 'I'll be getting along. I've just had a phone call calling me up to Newcastle in the morning. I'll have to start to-night to catch my train.'

'That's all right,' said Biggles cheerfully. 'Stay the night and I'll fly you up in the morning. I can get a Bristol from Lympne.'

'No, thanks,' replied Frazer firmly.

'I can't understand some people,' said Biggles softly, as he turned towards the library, 'being so careful about their skins.'

* Distinguished Service Order, a medal.

# Chapter 15
# Fog!

Fog, mist, and still more mist. Biggles crouched lower in his cockpit as the white vapour swirled aft, and wished he had taken Major Sidgrove's advice and waited at Lympne until it had lifted.

'It will clear as the sun comes up,' he had told the Major, optimistically, as he took off. He was anxious to get back to the Squadron, and although visibility on the ground had not been good, he did not think it was so bad as it proved to be in the air. At 500 feet the ground was completely hidden from view, but a glance at the compass told him that he was heading towards the French coast. 'What a hell of a day!' he muttered, and climbed steadily to get above the opaque curtain. At 5,000 feet the mist began to thin and the sun showed wanly as a pale white orb; when his altimeter told him that he was 6,000 feet above the earth, he emerged into clear sunshine with a suddenness that was startling.

'I've a damn poor chance of finding the aerodrome if this stuff doesn't lift,' he told himself as he skimmed along just above the pea-soup vapour. For an hour he followed his course, peering below anxiously for a break in the mist to show him his whereabouts, but in vain. 'Well, I'd better go down and see where I am,' he muttered; he throttled back and slid once more into the bank of clammy moisture. He was flying blind now, hoping against hope that the mist would thin out before he reached the ground; if it didn't, well, he would probably crash, that's all there was to it; but sooner or later he would have to come down, and he preferred to do it now rather than when he was getting short of fuel.

He kept a watchful eye on the altimeter; 2,000—1,000—500—he muttered a curse. 'I'll be into the damn carpet in a minute,' was his unspoken thought. He went into a shallow glide, peering below anxiously, praying that his altimeter was functioning properly and that he would not crash into a church tower or a tree. Something dark loomed below and for a minute he could not make out what it was. 'My God! It's the sea,' he ejaculated, and thrusting the throttle wide open he began climbing swiftly.

For a moment the discovery left him stunned. 'Where the devil have I got to?' he said to himself, half in anger and half in fright; 'I ought to have crossed the coast half an hour ago; this damn compass is all wrong, I expect.' He climbed above the mist and for another fifteen minutes flew south and then dropped down again. Something dark reared up in front of him and he zoomed swiftly to avoid hitting a tree, but an exclamation of relief escaped his lips as he saw that he was, at least, over terra firma. 'What a hell of a day!' he muttered again, and once more climbed up above the swirling fog, realizing that if conditions did not improve he would be lucky to get down without damaging the machine and possibly himself. In all directions the fog stretched in an unbroken sea of glistening white. 'This is no use,' he mused; 'I'd better find out where I am—it might as well be now as later on.'

He throttled back once more and commenced another slow glide towards the ground. At 500 feet he could just see what appeared to be open fields below.

He S-turned, almost at stalling point, keenly alert for any possible obstruction. When he was satisfied that all was clear he tipped up his wing and sideslipped down; he levelled out, switched off the ignition, and a moment later ran to a standstill not ten yards from a thick hedge. For a few moments he sat contemplating his predicament, and then climbed slowly out of the cockpit. 'I suppose all I can do is to walk until I find a house or somebody who can tell me where I am,' he reflected ruefully, as, pushing up his goggles and loosening his throat-strap, he set off at a steady pace across the field. He was glad of his short, leather coat, for the ground-mist was cold and clammy.

A hedge loomed up in front of him and he faced it blankly. 'Which way now?' he asked of himself. He thrust his hand in his trouser-pocket and pulled out a coin. 'Heads left, tails right,' he muttered. 'Heads, eh, left it is then'; and he once more set off parallel with the hedge. A hundred yards and another hedge appeared dimly in front of him and he swore luridly. 'Let's have a look what's over the other side,' he muttered, as he took a flying leap and landed on top of it. A sunken road, or rather a cart track, lay before him. 'I wish this blasted mist would clear,' he muttered petulantly, as he set off down the road. 'Hullo! Here's signs of life anyway.' On his right was a row of poles which reminded him of the hop fields he had often seen in Kent; a thick layer of greenery was spread over the tops of the wires that connected them. 'Hell, don't tell me I'm back home again,' he said, aghast. 'No, by God; it's camouflage!' He paused in his stride to survey what was the finest and certainly the largest piece of camouflage he had ever seen. Below it the ground fell away suddenly into a steep dip, and across the intervening valley stretched row after row of posts, criss-crossed at the top with wires, and the whole covered with a layer of drab green canvas and imitation grass.

'Whew!' he whistled; 'whatever's under that would take a bit of spotting from the air.' He bent down and peered below the concealing canopy, but could only see what appeared to be a number of grey cisterns and cylinders. 'Beats me,' he muttered, as he continued his walk. 'Well, here's someone coming, anyway, so we'll soon know.' On the left a gate opened into the field he had just left, and he leaned against it carelessly awaiting the arrival of the owners of the approaching footsteps. 'It sounds like troops,' was his unspoken thought as he lit a cigarette and gazed pensively into the grey mist that hung like a blanket over the field. The footsteps of marching men were close now, and he turned casually in their direction.

The sight that met his eyes seemed to freeze his heart into a block of ice. The shock was so great that he did not move, but stood rigid as if he had been transformed into a block of granite. Out of the mist, not ten yards away, straight down the middle of the road, marched a squad of grey-clad steel-helmeted German soldiers, an N.C.O. at their head. Biggles looked at them with a face of stone, praying that they would not hear the tumultous beating of his heart. There was a sharp word of command; as in a dream he saw the N.C.O.'s hand go up in salute, and his return of the salute was purely automatic. Another word of command and the troops had disappeared into the mist.

For a full minute Biggles gazed after them, utterly and completely stunned, and then a thousand thoughts flooded into his brain at once. Nauseating panic seized him, and he ran to and fro in agitated uncertainty. Never before had he experienced anything like the sensation of helplessness that possessed him now. 'Steady, steady, you fool!' he snarled, as he fought to get a grip on himself. 'Think—think!' Sanity returned at last and he listened intently. In the distance someone was hammering metal against metal. 'Clang! clang! clang! boomed the sound dully through the enveloping mist. 'They took me for one of their own pilots—of course they would. Why should they expect a British pilot to be standing gaping at them? Thank God I had my coat on,' were thoughts that rushed through his mind.

A little father down the road a large notice faced him, and he wondered how he had failed to see it before.

> ACHTUNG! LEBENSGEFAHR
> CHLORGASANSTALT
> EINTRITT STRENG
> VERBOTEN*

Chlorgasanstalt! Gas! In an instant he understood everything; the camouflage covered a Hun gas manufacturing plant. 'I'll be getting out of this,' he muttered, and vaulting over the gate set off at a run across the field in the direction of the Camel. Another hedge faced him; he struggled through it and found himself in a field of roots. 'This isn't it,' he muttered hoarsely, and realized with horror that he had lost his sense of direction. He clambered back into the field he had just left

---

* Danger! Public warning:
Gas plant
Entrance strictly forbidden.

and raced down the side of the hedge, pulling up with a cry of despair as the edge of a wood suddenly faced him. He knew he was lost. 'Damn and blast this fog; where the hell am I?' he groaned out viciously. It was suddenly lighter and he glanced upwards; the mist was lifting at last, slowly, but already he could see the silvery disc of the sun. 'The Boche'll see the Camel as soon as I shall,' he pondered, hopelessly, 'and the farther I go now the farther I shall get away from it. If they spot it, I'm sunk. Oh, hell!' Another thought occurred to him—what of his discovery? Quite apart from saving his own skin he was now in possession of information which the Headquarters Staff would willingly give fifty officers to possess—the whereabouts of the German gas supply dump.

'If I do get away I can't tell them where it is,' he mused; 'I don't know where I am to within a hundred miles. Blast that compass!' He started; someone was coming towards him. He dived into the undergrowth and crouched low, scarcely daring to breathe. The new-comer was a Belgian peasant, garbed in the typical garments of a worker on the land; in his hand he carried a hedger's hook. He was a filthy specimen of his class, dirty and unshaven, and Biggles watched him anxiously as he plodded along muttering to himself, glancing from time to time to left and right. 'I wonder if I dare risk speaking—if he would help me?' thought Biggles. But the risk was too great and he dismissed the idea from his mind. The peasant was opposite him now, snivelling and wiping his nose on the back of his hand; he stopped suddenly and listened intently.

'Where are you?'

The words, spoken in English in a quick sibilant hiss from somewhere near at hand, stunned Biggles into a frozen state of immobility for the second time within a quarter of an hour. His heart seemed to stop beating and he felt the blood drain from his face. Who had spoken? Had anybody spoken—or had he imagined it? Were his nerves giving out? He didn't know, but he bit his lip to prevent himself crying out.

'Where are you?'

Again came the words in a low penetrating whisper, but in an educated English voice.

'Here,' said Biggles involuntarily.

The peasant swung round on his heel and hurried towards him. 'Your machine is in the next field,' he said quickly; 'hurry up, you've no time to lose. Fifty yards—Look out—get down!'

Biggles flung himself back into the undergrowth and pressed himself into the bottom of the ditch that skirted the wood. The peasant's hook flashed above him and a tangle of briars covered him. Through them Biggles could just see the Belgian lopping at the hedge unconcernedly, muttering to himself as he did so. Gutteral voices jarred the silence somewhere near at hand and a group of German soldiers, carrying mess tins, loomed into his field of vision. Without so much as a glance at the hedge trimmer they passed on and were swallowed up in the mist.

'Quick now,' said the voice again, 'run for it. There's an archie battery fifty yards down there—you were walking straight into it; I saw you land, and I've been chasing you ever since.'

'What about the gasworks?' said Biggles irrelevantly.

The pseudo-Belgian started violently. 'What gasworks?' he said, in a curiously strained voice.

'The Hun gas dump,' replied Biggles.

'Where is it?'

'Just across there at the corner of the wood, it's well camouflaged.'

'God Almighty! You've stumbled on the thing I've been looking for for three weeks. Get back and report it in case I am taken before I can loose a carrier pigeon. Here comes the sun—turn right down the hedge, fifty yards, then get through the hedge and you will see the machine in front of you.'

'Where am I now?' inquired Biggles.

'Thirty kilos north-west of Courtrai—one mile due east of Berslaade.'

'Aren't you coming, I can take you on the wing?'

'No, I'll stay here and see what damage the bombers do.'

'What's your name?' asked Biggles quickly.

'2742,' replied the other with a queer smile.

'Mine's Bigglesworth—266 Squadron. Look me up sometime—good-bye.'

A swift handshake and Biggles was sprinting down the side of the hedge in the direction indicated by his preserver.

'God! What jobs some people have to do. I wouldn't have that fellow's job for a million a year and a thousand V.C.s,' thought Biggles, as, fifty yards down the hedge, he crawled through a convenient gap. As he sprang erect the mist rolled away as if a giant curtain had been drawn, and the sun poured down in all its autumnal glory. There, ten yards away, stood the Camel, and beside it two German soldiers. They carried mess tins, and were evidently two of the party he had seen a few moments before.

With a bound, almost without pausing to think, Biggles was on them. The Germans swung round in alarm as they heard his swift approach, but Biggles held all the advantages of surprise attack. The first went down like a log before he had time to put his hands up as his jaw stopped a mighty swing from Biggles's right; the iron mess-tin rolled to one side as he fell. Biggles snatched it up by the strap and swung it with all his force straight at the head of the other German. It caught the man fairly and squarely on the temple and he dropped with a grunt like a pole-axed bullock. The whole thing was over almost before Biggles had realized the danger. With feverish speed he sprang to the cockpit of the Camel, switched on, turned the petrol on, and opened the throttle a fraction. Dashing back to the front of the machine he paused to feel the cylinders of the Bentley engine. They were not yet cold. He seized the propeller and whirled it with all his strength, almost falling backwards as it started with a roar. He tore madly round the wing and literally fell into the cockpit; once there, all his old confidence returned in a flash and he looked eagerly around. Behind him the field stretched open for a take-off; in the far corner some men were running, pointing at him as they ran. He blipped the engine with the rudder hard over almost swinging the Camel round on its own axis, and for the first time since he realized he was in enemy country, he breathed freely. He pushed the throttle open and tore across the field like a blunt-nosed bullet; a moment later he was in the air heading for the line, with the landscape lying clear and plain below him.

A stab of orange flame and a cloud of black smoke blossomed out in front of him, another, and another, and Biggles twisted like a snipe to throw the archie gunners off their mark. Strings of flaming onions* shot

* Slang: a type of incendiary anti-aircraft shell only used by Germans.

past him and the sky was torn with fire and hurtling metal.

'Hell's bells! they're taking damn good care no one comes prowling about here for long,' he observed, as he kicked out first one foot and then the other to maintain his erratic course in order to confuse the batteries below. He was glad when the storm died down behind him. He surveyed the sky ahead intently. 'They saw me take off and they'll phone every damn aerodrome between here and the line to be on the look-out for me,' he swore to himself. With his nose slightly down and engine at full throttle he sped onwards.

An aerodrome appeared ahead; he could see little ant-like figures running around the black-crossed machines which stood on the tarmac. Something struck the Camel with a vibrating sprang—g—g, and he knew the machine-gunners were busy. He put his nose down in a fury and swept across the hangars with his guns spurting a double stream of tracer, and laughed as he saw the figures below sprinting for cover. He zoomed up and roared on without waiting to see what damage he had done.

A Fokker triplane, looking like a Venetian blind, flashed down on his flank and the sight sent him fighting mad. The Camel made the lightning right-hand turn for which it was famous and the twin Vickers guns on the cowling poured a stream of bullets through the Fokker's centre section. The Boche machine lurched drunkenly and plunged down out of sight below, and Biggles continued his way without another glance. Far away to his left he could see a formation of straight-winged machines heading towards him, and he swept still lower, literally hopping the trees and hedges that stood in his path. The pock-marked desolation of the trenches appeared below and Biggles thrilled at the sight; he shot across them at fifty feet, wondering vaguely where all the bullets that were being fired at him were going.

He was over his own side of the lines now, and he sagged lower in the cockpit with relief as he passed the balloon line. Ten minutes later he landed at Maranique. Major Mullen was standing on the tarmac and came to meet him as he taxied in.

'You've got back then, Biggles—had a good leave?'

'Fine, sir, thanks,' responded Biggles.

'It's been pretty thick here. What time did you leave this morning?'

'Oh, about sixish.'

'Then you must have called somewhere on the way—I hope they gave you a good time?'

'They did that,' grinned Biggles as he climbed out of the cockpit.

Major Mullen eyed his mud-plastered boots and coat with astonishment. 'Good God!' he cried, 'where the devil have you been?'

'On leave, sir,' smiled Biggles innocently, 'but I've got an urgent message for H.Q.'

In a few words he described his adventures of the morning, and ten minutes later his written report was on its way by hand to Headquarters. One thing only he omitted—his finding of the gas plant. He reported its position, but the credit for that discovery he left to '2742.' 'That's the least I can do for him,' decided Biggles.

# Chapter 16
# Affaire De Cœur*

Biggles hummed cheerfully as he cruised along in the new Camel which he had just fetched from the Aircraft Park. 'Another five minutes and I shall be home,' he thought, but fate willed otherwise. The engine coughed, coughed again, and with a final splutter, expired, leaving him with a 'dead' prop. He swore softly, pushed the joystick forward, and looked quickly around for the most suitable field for the now inevitable forced landing.

To the right lay the forest of Clarmes. 'Nothing doing that way,' he muttered, and looked down between his left wings. Ah! there it was. Almost on the edge of the forest was a large pasture, free from obstruction. The pilot, with a confidence born of long experience, side-slipped towards it, levelled out over the hedge and made a perfect three-point landing.

He sat in the cockpit for a minute or two contemplating his position, then he yawned, pushed up his goggles and prepared to take stock of his immediate surroundings. He raised his eyebrows appreciatively as he noted the sylvan beauty of the scene around him. Above, the sun shone from a cloudless blue sky. Straight before him a low lichen-covered stone wall enclosed an orchard through which he could just perceive a dull red pantiled roof. To the right lay the forest, cool and

* French: an affair of the heart.

inviting. To the left a stream meandered smoothly between a double row of willows.

'Who said there was a war on?' he murmured, lighting a cigarette, and climbing up on to the 'hump' of his Camel, the better to survey the enchanting scene. 'Well, well, let's see if anyone is at home.' He sprang lightly to the ground, threw his leather coat across the fuselage and strolled towards the house. An old iron gate opened into the orchard; entering, he paused for a moment, uncertain of the path.

'Are you looking for me, monsieur?' said a voice, which sounded to Biggles as musical as ice tinkling in a cocktail glass.

Turning, he beheld a vision of blonde loveliness wrapped up in blue silk, smiling at him. For a moment he stared as if he had been raised in a monastery and had never seen a woman before. He closed his eyes, shook his head, and opened them again — the vision was still there, dimpling.

'You were looking for me, perhaps?' said the girl again.

Biggles saluted like a man sleep-walking.

'Mademoiselle,' he said earnestly, 'I've been looking for you all my life. I didn't think I'd ever find you.'

'Then why did you land here?' asked the girl.

'I landed here because my mag. shorted,' explained Biggles.

'What would have happened if you had not landed when your bag shorted?' inquired the vision, curiously.

'Not bag — mag. Short for magneto, you know,' replied Biggles grinning. 'Do you know, I've never even thought of doing anything but land when a mag. shorts; if I didn't, I expect that I should fall from a great altitude and collide with something substantial.'

'What are you going to do now?'

'I don't know—it takes thinking about. It may be necessary for me to stay here for some time. Anyway, the War will still be on when I get back. But, pardon me, mademoiselle, if I appear impertinent; are you English? I ask because you speak English so well.'

'Not quite, monsieur. My mother was English and I have been to school in England,' replied the girl.

'Thank you, Miss—er—'

'Marie Janis is my name.'

'A charming name, more charming even than this spot of heaven,' said Biggles warmly. 'Have you a telephone, Miss Janis? You see, although the matter is not urgent, if I do not ring up my Squadron to say where I am, someone may fly around to look for me,' he explained.

The thought of Mahoney spotting his Camel from the air and landing, did not, in the circumstances, fill him with the enthusiasm one might normally expect.

'Come and use the telephone, m'sieur le Capitaine,' said the girl, leading the way. 'May I offer you *un petit verre*\*?'

'May you?' responded Biggles, warmly. 'I should say you may!'

Five hours later Biggles again took his place in the cockpit of the Camel which a party of ack-emmas had now repaired. He took off and swung low over the orchard, waving gaily to a slim blue-clad figure that looked upwards and waved back.

Rosy clouds drifted across the horizon as he made the short flight back to the aerodrome.

'That girl's what I've been reading about,' he told

\*French: a little glass of something.

himself. 'She's the "Spirit of the Air," and she's going to like me an awful lot if I know anything about it. Anyway, I'd be the sort of skunk who'd give rat poison to orphans if I didn't go back and thank her for her hospitality.

Biggles, a week later, seated on an old stone bench in the orchard, sighed contentedly. The distant flickering beam of a searchlight on the war-stricken sky meant nothing to him; the rumble of guns along the line seemed very far away. His arm rested along the back of the seat; a little head, shining whitely in the moonlight, nestled lightly on his sleeve. In the short time that had elapsed since his forced landing, he had made considerable progress.

'Tell me, Marie,' he said, 'do you ever hear from your father?'

'No, m'sieur,' replied the girl sadly. 'I told you he was on a visit to the north when war was declared. In the wild panic of the Boche advance he was left behind in what is now the occupied territory. Communication with that part of France is forbidden, but I have had two letters from him which were sent by way of England by friends. I have not even been able to tell him that maman is—dead!'

Tears shone for a moment in her eyes, and Biggles stirred uncomfortably.

'It is a hell of a war,' he said compassionately.

'If only I could get a letter to him to say that maman—*est mort\**, and that I am looking after things until he returns, I should be happy. Poor Papa!'

---

\* French: is dead.

'I suppose you don't even know where he is?' said Biggles sympathetically.

'But yes,' answered the girl quickly, 'I know where he is. He is still at our friend's château, where he was staying when the Boche came.'

'Where's that?' asked Biggles in surprise.

'At Vinard, near Lille; le Château Boreau,' she replied, 'but he might as well be in Berlin,' she concluded sadly, shrugging her shoulders.

'Good Lord!' ejaculated Biggles suddenly.

'Why did you say that, monsieur?'

'Nothing—only an idea struck me, that's all,' said Biggles.

'Tell me.'

'No. I'm crazy. Better forget it.'

'Tell me—please.'

Biggles wavered. 'All right,' he said, 'say "please Biggles," and I'll tell you.'

'Please, Beegles.'

Biggles smiled at the pronunciation. 'Well, if you must know,' he said, 'it struck me that I might act as a messenger for you.'

'Beegles! How?'

'I had some crazy notion that I might be able to drop a letter from my machine,' explained Biggles.

'Mon dieu*!' The girl sprang to her feet in excitement, but Biggles held her arm and pulled her towards him. For a moment she resisted, and then slipped into his arms.

'Beegles—please.'

'Marie,' whispered Biggles, as their lips met. Then, his heart beating faster than archie or enemy aircraft

* French: My God!

381

had ever caused it to beat, he suddenly pushed her aside, rose to his feet and looked at the luminous dial of his watch. 'Time I was getting back to quarters,' he said unsteadily.

'But, Beegles, it is not yet so late.'

Biggles sat down, passed his hand over his face and then laughed. 'My own mag. was nearly shorting then,' he said.

They both laughed, and the spell was broken.

'Tell me, Beegles, is it possible to drop such a letter to papa?' said the girl presently.

'I don't know,' said Biggles, a trifle anxiously. 'I don't know what orders are about that sort of thing, and that's a fact. There wouldn't be any harm in it, and they wouldn't know about it, anyway. You give me the letter and I'll see what I can do.'

'Beegles—you—'

'Well?'

'Never mind. Come to the house and we will write the letter together.'

Hand in hand they walked slowly towards the house. The girl took a writing pad from a desk and began to write; the door opened noiselessly and Antoine, Marie's elderly man-servant appeared.

'Did you ring, mademoiselle?' he asked.

'Merci, Antoine.'

'Do you know,' said Biggles, after the man had withdrawn, 'I don't like the look of that bloke. I never saw a nastier-looking piece of work in my life.'

'But what should I do without Antoine and Lucille, his wife. They are the only two that stayed with me all the time. Antoine is a dear, he only thinks of me,' said the girl reproachfully.

'I see,' said Biggles. 'Well, go ahead with the letter.'

The girl wrote rapidly.

'Look,' she smiled when it was finished. 'Read it and tell me if you do not think it is a lovely letter to a long-lost father.'

Biggles read the first few lines and skipped the rest, blushing. 'I don't want to read your letter, kid,' he said.

Marie sealed the letter, addressed it, and tied it firmly to a small paper weight. 'Now,' she said, 'what can we use for a banner?'

'You mean a streamer,' laughed Biggles.

'Yes, a streamer. Why! Here is the very thing.' She took a black and white silk scarf from the back of a chair and tied the paper-weight to it. 'There you are, *mon aviateur**,' she laughed. 'Take care, do not hit papa on the head or he will wish I had not written.'

Biggles slipped the packet into the pocket of his British 'warm'** and took her in his arms impatiently.

Arriving at the aerodrome he went to his quarters and flung the coat on the bed, and then made his way across to the mess for a drink. As the door of his quarters closed behind him, two men—an officer in uniform and a civilian—entered the room. Without a moment's hesitation the civilian picked up the coat and removed the letter from the pocket.

'You know what to do,' he said grimly.

'How long will you be?'

'An hour. Not more. Keep him until 11.30, to be on the safe side,' said the civilian.

'I will,' replied the officer, and followed Biggles into the mess.

* French: my pilot.
** Slang: Thick padded jacket.

Biggles, humming gaily, headed for home. His trip had proved uneventful and the dropping of Marie's letter ridiculously simple. He had found the château easily, and swooping low had seen the black and white scarf flutter on to the lawn. Safely back across the line he was now congratulating himself upon the success of his mission. 287, the neighbouring S.E.5 Squadron, lay below, and it occurred to him to land and pass the time of day with them.

Conscious that many eyes would be watching him, he side-slipped in and flattened out for his most artistic landing. There was a sudden crash, the Camel swung violently and tipped up on to its nose. Swearing savagely he climbed out and surveyed the damage.

'Why the devil don't you fellows put a flag or something on this sunken road?' he said bitterly to Wilkinson and other pilots who had hurried to the scene; and pointing to the cause of his misadventure, 'Look at that mess.'

'Well, most people know about that road,' said Wilkinson. 'If I'd have known you were coming I'd have had it filled in altogether. Never mind; it's only a tyre and the prop. gone. Our fellows will have it right by to-morrow. Come and have a drink; I'll find you transport to take you home. The C.O.'s on leave, so you can use his car.'

'Righto, but I'm not staying to dinner,' said Biggles emphatically. 'I'm on duty to-night,' he added, thinking of a moonlit orchard and an old stone seat.

It was nearly eight o'clock when he left the aerodrome, seated at the wheel of the borrowed car. He had rung up Major Mullen and told him that he would be late, and now, thrilling with anticipation, he headed for the home of the girl who was making life worth living and the war worth fighting for.

The night was dark, for low clouds were drifting across the face of the moon; a row of distant archie-bursts made him look up, frowning. A bomb raid, inter-rupting the story of his successful trip, was the last thing he wanted. His frown deepened as the enemy aircraft and the accompanying archie drew nearer. 'They're coming right over the house, blast 'em,' he said, and switching off his lights raced for the orchard. 'God! they're low,' he muttered, as he tore down the road, the roar of the engines of the heavy bombers in his ears. 'They're following this road, too.' He wondered where they were making for, trying to recall any possible objective on their line of flight. That he himself might be in danger did not even occur to him. He was less than five miles from the house now, and taking desperate chances to race the machines. 'The poor kid'll be scared stiff if they pass over her as low as this.'

With every nerve taut he tore down the road. He caught his breath suddenly. What was that! A whistling screech filled his ears and an icy hand clutched his heart. Too well he knew the sound. Boom! Boom! Boom! Three vivid flashes of orange fire leapt towards the sky. Boom! Boom! Boom!—and then three more.

'My God! what are they fanning, the fools? There is only the forest there,' thought Biggles, as, numb with shock, he raced round the last bend. Six more thunder-ing detonations, seemingly a hundred yards ahead, nearly split his eardrums, but still he did not pause. He tried to think, but could not; he had lost all sense of time and reason. He seemed to have been driving for ever, and he cursed as he drove. Searchlights probed the sky on all sides and subconsciously he noticed that the noise of the engines was fading into the distance.

'They've gone,' he said, trying hard to think clearly. 'God! If they've hit the house!' He jammed on his brakes with a grinding screech as two men sprang out in front of the car as he turned in the gates, but he was not looking at them. One glance showed him that the house was a blazing pile of ruins. He sprang out of the car and darted towards the conflagration, but a hand closed on his arm like a vice. Biggles, white-faced, turned and struck out viciously. 'My girl's in there, blast you,' he muttered.

A sharp military voice penetrated his stunned brain.

'Stand fast, Captain Bigglesworth,' it said.

'Let me go, damn you,' snarled Biggles, struggling like a madman.

'One more word from you, Captain Bigglesworth, and I'll put you under close arrest,' said the voice harshly.

'You'll what?' Biggles turned, his brain fighting for consciousness. 'You'll what?' he cried again incredulously. He saw the firelight gleam on the fixed bayonets of a squad of Tommies; Colonel Raymond of Wing Headquarters and another man stood near them. Biggles passed his hand over his eyes, swaying.

'I'm dreaming,' he said, 'that's it, dreaming. God! what a hell of a nightmare. I wish I could wake up.'

'Take a drink, Bigglesworth, and pull yourself together,' said Colonel Raymond passing him a flask. Biggles emptied the flask and handed it back.

'I'm going now,' said the Colonel, 'I'll see you in the morning. This officer will tell you all you need to know,' he concluded, indicating a dark-clad civilian standing near. 'Good-night, Bigglesworth.'

'Good-night, sir.'

'Tell me,' said Biggles, with an effort, 'is she—in there?'

The man nodded.

'Then, that's all I need to know,' said Biggles, slowly turning away.

'I'm sorry, but there are other things you will have to know,' returned the man.

'Who are you?' said Biggles curiously.

'Major Charles, of the British Intelligence Service.'

'Intelligence!' repeated Biggles, the first ray of light bursting upon him.

'Come here a moment.' Major Charles switched on the lights of his car. 'Yesterday, a lady asked you to deliver a message for her, did she not?' he asked.

'Why—yes.'

'Did you see it?'

'Yes!'

'Was this it?' said Major Charles, handing him a letter.

Biggles read the first few lines, dazed. 'Yes,' he said, 'that was it.'

'Turn it over.'

Unconsciously Biggles obeyed. He started as his eyes fell on a tangle of fine lines that showed up clearly. In the centre was a circle.

'Do you recognize that?'

'Yes.'

'What is it?'

'It is a map of 266 Squadron aerodrome,' replied Biggles, like a child reciting a catechism.

'You see the circle?'

'Yes.'

'The Officers' mess. Perhaps you understand now.

The letter you were asked to carry had been previously prepared with a solution of invisible ink and contained such information that, had you delivered it, your entire squadron would have been wiped out to-night, and you as well. The girl sent you to your death, Captain Bigglesworth.'

'I'll not believe it,' said Biggles distinctly. 'But I did deliver the letter, anyway,' he cried suddenly.

'Not this one,' said Major Charles smiling queerly. 'You delivered the one we substituted.'

'Substituted!'

'We have watched this lady for a long time. You have been under surveillance since the day you force-landed, although your record put you above suspicion.'

'And on the substituted plan you marked her home to be bombed instead of the aerodrome?' sneered Biggles. 'Why?'

Major Charles shrugged his shoulders. 'The lady was well connected. There may have been unexpected difficulties connected with an arrest, yet her activities had to be checked. She had powerful friends in high places. Well, I must be going; no doubt you will hear from Wing in the morning.'

Biggles walked a little way up the garden path. The old stone seat glowed dully crimson. 'Bah!' he muttered, turning, 'what a fool I am. What a hell of a war this is.'

He drove slowly back to the aerodrome. On his table lay a letter. Ripping it open eagerly he read:—

'CHÈR*,

'I have something important to ask you—some-

* French: Dear.

thing you must do for me. To-night at seven o'clock I will come for you. It is important. Meet me in the road by the aerodrome. I will be very kind to you, my Biggles.

MARIE.'

Biggles, with trembling hands, sat on the bed and reread the letter, trying to reason out its purport. 'She timed the raid for eight,' he said to himself, 'when all officers would be dining in mess. She knew I should be there and wrote this to bring me out. She knew I'd never leave her waiting on the road—that was the way of it. She must have cared, or she wouldn't have done that. When I didn't come she went back home. She didn't even know I hadn't seen her letter—how could she? Now she's dead. If I hadn't landed at 287 I should be with her now. Well, she'll never know.' He rose wearily. Voices were singing in the distance, and he smiled bitterly as he heard the well-remembered words:—

> Who minds to the dust returning,
>   Who shrinks from the sable shore,
> Where the high and haughty yearning
>   Of the soul shall be no more?
>
> So stand by your glasses steady,
>   This world is a world of lies;
> A cup to the dead already,
>   Hurrah! for the next man who dies.

A knock at the door aroused him from his reverie. An orderly of the guard entered.

'A lady left this for you,' he said, holding out a letter.

'A lady?—when?' said Biggles, holding himself in hand with a mighty effort.

'About ten minutes ago, sir. Just before you came in. She came about eight and said she must see you, sir, but I told her you weren't here.'

'Where is she now?'

'She's gone, sir, she was in a car. She told me to bring the letter straight to you when you returned, sir.'

'All right—you may go.'

Biggles took the letter, fighting back a wild desire to shout, opened it, and read:

'Good-bye, my Biggles.

'You know now. What can I say? Only this. Our destinies are not always in our own hands—always try and remember that, my Biggles. That is all I may say. I came to-night to take you away or die with you, but you were not here. And remember that one thing in this world of war and lies is true: my love for you. It may help you, as it helps me. Take care of yourself. Always I shall pray for you. If anything happens to you I shall know, but if to me, you will never know. My last thought will be of you. We shall meet again, if not in this world then in the next, so I will not say good-bye.

'Au revoir,

'MARIE.'

'And they think she's dead,' said Biggles softly. 'She risked her life to tell me this.' He kissed the letter tenderly, then held it to the candle and watched it burn away.

He was crumbling the ashes between his fingers

when the door opened, and Mahoney entered. 'Hullo! laddie, what's wrong; had a fire?' he inquired.

'Yes,' replied Biggles slowly, 'foolish of me; got my fingers burnt a bit, too.'

# Chapter 17
# The Last Show

In the days that followed his tragic *affaire*, Biggles flew with an abandon and with such an utter disregard of consequences, that Major Mullen knew that if he persisted it could only be a matter of time before he failed to return. The C.O. had not mentioned the affair of the girl to him, but Biggles knew that he must be aware of the main facts of the case, or he would certainly have asked him why he had been called to Headquarters.

However much the Major knew he said nothing, but he watched his Flight-Commander's behaviour with deep-rooted anxiety. He called McLaren and Mahoney into his office to discuss the matter with them.

Mahoney nodded sympathetically as he listened to the C.O.'s plaint. 'Biggles is finished unless he takes a rest,' he said. 'He's drinking whisky for his breakfast, and you know what that means—he's going fast. He drank half a bottle of whisky yesterday morning before daylight, and he walked up to the sheds as sober as I was. A fellow doesn't get drunk when he's in the state Biggles is in. It's no use talking to him—you know that as well as I do. He's got to the stage when he takes advice as a personal affront against his flying. It's a pity, but most of us go that way at the end I suppose. Newland, of 287, told me confidentially the other day that a blue pigeon follows him in the air wherever he goes, and he meant it.'

'Well, I shall have to send him home, whether he likes it or not,' went on the Major, 'but it will break his heart if I don't find a good excuse. Now look, you fellows. I've got to send somebody home to form a new Squadron—of Snipes*, I believe—and bring it over. You are both senior to Bigglesworth; you are both due for promotion. I shall be going to Wing in a week or two I hear, so one of you will have to take over 266. Do you mind if I send Bigglesworth home for the new Squadron?' added the C.O., looking at the two Captains apologetically.

'Not me, sir,' said Mahoney instantly.

'Nor I, sir,' echoed McLaren.

'Thank you. That's what I wanted to know,' said the Major. 'I'll send him home, then. Where is he now?'

'He's in the air,' replied Mahoney, 'he's never on the ground. God knows where he goes, it must be miles over; I never see him on patrol.'

The C.O. nodded. 'Well, he can't get away with that much longer. They're bound to get him. By the way, there's a big show tomorrow—it will be in orders tonight. You'd better have a good look round your machines.'

Biggles, cruising at 18,000 feet, turned in the direction of Lille without being really conscious of the fact. He surveyed the surrounding air coldly and dispassionately for signs of enemy aircraft, but except for a formation of Bristol Fighters homeward bound, far below, the sky was empty. His thoughts wandered back to the girl who had come into his life. Where was she now? Where

* Sopwith Snipe – a development of the Sopwith Camel, with slightly better performance.

had she gone on that tragic night of disillusionment? Had she been caught? That was the thought that made the day a torture and night a hell. He visualized her in the cold-grey of dawn with a bandage over her eyes facing a firing party in some gloomy French prison.

A volley of shots rang out, something jerked the rudder-bar from his feet and brought him back to the realities of life with a start.

He half-rolled and looked around; a Hannoverian was rapidly receding into the distance. He frowned at it in surprise and consternation. 'Good Lord! I must have nearly flown into it without seeing it, and the observer had a crack at me as he went by,' he mused. 'If it had been a D.VII'—he shrugged his shoulders. What did it matter—what did anything matter?

He looked downwards to pick up his bearings; the landscape was familiar, for he had seen it a dozen times during the past week. To the left lay Lille, the worst hot-bed of archie in the whole of France. On his right a narrow, winding road led to the village of Vinard and the Château Boreau—his only link with Marie. She might even be there now—the thought occurred to him for the first time. How could she have reached it? Spies went to and fro across the line, he reflected, nobody knew how, except the chosen few whose hazardous business it was. He looked around the sky, but could see nothing; he put the stick forward and commenced to spiral down in wide circles.

At 5,000 feet he hesitated. Dare he risk losing more height? He looped, half-rolled, came out and looped again, half-rolling off the top of it. Then he spun. He came out at 2,000 feet and studied the château intently. No one was in sight—yes—his eye caught a movement at the end of the garden and he glided lower. He knew that he was taking a foolish risk, but his curiosity overcame his caution.

Someone was waving—what? He put his nose down in a swift dive and then zoomed upwards exultantly, his heart beating tumultuously. Had his eyes betrayed him or had he seen a blue-clad figure waving a blue and white scarf. He looked back; the blue and white scarf was spread on the lawn. He turned the Camel in the direction of the lines and raced for home, his mind in a whirl. 'I'm mad,' he grated between his clenched teeth. She must be a spy or she wouldn't be there. The thought seemed to chill him, and only then did he realize that he still hoped the authorities were mistaken in their belief that she was engaged in espionage.

Doubts began to assail him. Had he really seen her—or had it been a trick of the imagination? It might have been someone else; he was too far away to recognize features. 'She's a spy, anyway. I must be stark, staring mad,' he told himself, as he dodged and twisted away from a close salvo of archie.

Half-way home he had the good fortune to fall in with a formation of S.E.5's to which he attached himself. Safely over the lines he waved them farewell and was soon back at Maranique. He made his way to the mess and thrust himself into a group of officers clustered around the notice board.

'What's on, chaps?' he asked.

'Big show tomorrow, Biggles,' replied Mahoney.

'What is it?'

'Escort—a double dose. Eighteen "Nines" are bombing aerodrome 27 in the morning and the same lot are doing an objective near Lille in the afternoon. We and 287 are escorting. 287 are up in the gallery, and we're sticking with the formation. Rendezvous over Mossy-face at 10,000 feet at ten ack-emma.'

'Good God! have they discovered the German Head-quarters Staff or something?'

'Shouldn't be surprised. Must be something import-ant to do the two shows. The aerodrome 27 show was on first—and the second show came through later. They must be going to try and blot something off the map; the idea's all right if the bombers could only hit the thing.'

Biggles nodded moodily, for the show left him unmoved. Escort was a boring business, particularly in his present state of mind. Later in the evening another notice was put on the board which was greeted with loud cheers. Biggles forced his way to the front rank of the group and read:

*Promotions*
*Act. Cpt. J. Bigglesworth, M.C., to Major W.E.F.\**
10.11.18. (*Authority*) P.243/117/18.
*Postings*
*Major J. Bigglesworth, from 266 Squadron to Command 319 Squadron. H.E., W.E.F.\*\* 11.11.18. P.243/118/18.*

Biggles looked at the notice, unbelievingly. He turned to Major Mullen, who had just entered.

'So I'm going home, sir,' he said in a strained voice.

'Yes, Bigglesworth. Wing wants you to fetch 319 out. I believe you're getting Snipes—you'll be able to make rings round Camels.'

'Camels are good enough for me,' protested Biggles. 'That's the trouble with this damn war; people are

\* With Effect From.
\*\* Home Establishment (i.e. England) With Effect From.

never satisfied. Let us stick to Camels and S.E.'s and the Boche have their D. Sevens—damn all this chopping and changing about. I've heard a rumour about a new kite called a Salamander* that carries a sheet of armour plate. Why? I'll tell you. Some brass-hat's got hit in the pants and that's the result. What with sheet iron, oxygen to blow your guts out, and electrically heated clothing to set fire to your kidneys, this war is going to bits.'

'You'll talk differently when you get your Snipes,' laughed the Major.

'Orders say I'm to move off tomorrow.'

'Yes, that's right.'

'Good. You can give my love to the Huns at aerodrome 27 and—what's the name of the other target they're going to fan down?'

'Oh, it's a new one to me,' replied the Major. 'Place near Lille, Château Boreau or something like that—cheerio—see you later.'

It was as well that he did not pause to take a second glance at his Flight-Commander's face, or he might have asked awkward questions. For a full minute Biggles remained rooted to the spot with the words ringing in his ears. 'Château Boreau, eh?' he said, under his breath. 'So they know about that. My God! how the devil did those nosey-parkers on Intelligence find that out,' he muttered bitterly.

Mahoney slapped him on the back. 'Have a drink, Biggles?' he cried.

Biggles swung round with a curse. 'No, I didn't mean that, old lad,' he said quickly. 'I was a bit upset at

---

* Sopwith Salamander. British single seat biplane, designed for use against infantry, fitted with two machine guns and protective armour to the cockpit.

leaving the Squadron. Sorry—what are you having, everybody?' he called aloud. 'Drinks are on me tonight.'

Dinner was a boistrous affair; the usual farewell speeches were made and everybody was noisily happy. Biggles, pale-faced, with his eyes gleaming unnaturally, held the board.

'So tomorrow I am doing my last show,' he concluded.

The C.O. looked up quickly. 'But I thought you were going in the morning,' he exclaimed in surprise.

'In the afternoon, if you don't mind, sir,' answered Biggles, 'I must do one more show with 266.'

Major Mullen nodded. 'All right,' he said, 'but don't take any chances,' he added. 'I ought to pack you off in the morning, really.'

Biggles spent a troubled and restless night. Why he had asked to be allowed to fly with the morning show he hardly knew, unless it was to delay departure as long as possible. He racked his brain to find an excuse to postpone it until the evening in order to learn the result of the bombing of the Château. If he was unable to do that, he had decided to ask Mac or Mahoney to try to send him copies of the photographs of the bomb bursts.

Thinking things over, he realized that his first fears that the Château was to be bombed because Intelligence had learned that Marie had made her way there, were unfounded. It was far more likely that they had known for some time that the building housed certain members of the German Headquarters or Intelligence Staff, and the recent trouble had simply served to expedite their decision to bomb it.

What could he do about it? Nothing, he decided despairingly, absolutely nothing. It crossed his mind that he might drop a message of warning, but he dismissed the thought at once, because such an act would definitely make him a traitor to his own side. The thought of returning to England and leaving the girl to her fate without lifting a finger to save her nearly drove him to distraction. After all, the girl had tried to save him when the position had been reversed!

He was glad when his batman brought him his early morning tea and he arose, weary and hollow eyed. Ten o'clock found him in the air heading for the line and the Boche aerodrome at Lille. Behind him were Cowley and Algernon Montgomery. On his left were the bombers, the sun flashing on their varnished wings, the observers leaning carelessly on their Scarff rings. Beyond was Mahoney and A Flight. Somewhere in the rear was McLaren and B Flight, while two thousand feet above he could see the S.E.5's. 'What a sight,' thought Biggles, as his eyes swept over the thirty-six machines; 'it will take a Hun with some nerve to tackle this lot.'

The observer in the nearest 'Nine' waved to him, crossed his fingers and pointed; Biggles following the direction indicated, saw a half-a-dozen Fokker Triplanes flying parallel with them. Presently they turned away and disappeared into the distance. The observer waved and laughed and held out his hands with the thumbs turned up.

'Yes,' agreed Biggles mentally, 'they spotted the S.E.'s up top. They've thought better of it, and I don't wonder.' He was sorry that the Huns had departed, for he was aching for action. For three-quarters of an hour they flew steadily into enemy sky, and then the leader of the bombers conspicuous by his streamers, began to turn. 'He's coming round into the wind,' thought Biggles; 'we must be over the objective.'

He looked down and beheld the aerodrome. He looked up again just in time to see the leader fire a green Very light; eighteen 112-lb. bombs swung off their racks into space.

A moment later a second lot of eighteen bombs followed the first. Keeping a watchful eye on his position in the formation Biggles snatched quick glances at the earth below. What a time it seemed to take the bombs to reach the ground. 'Damn it, they can't all be duds,' he muttered. 'Ah! there they go.' A group of smoke-bursts appeared on the aerodrome, and a moment later, another group.

The second lot were better than the first. One bomb had fallen directly on to a hangar, one had burst among the machines on the tarmac, and another had struck some buildings just behind. The rest of the bombs had scattered themselves over the aerodrome. 'There will have to be a lot of spade work there before anybody will try any night-landings,' grinned Biggles, as he visualized the havoc the bombs had caused to the surface of the aerodrome.

The faint crackle of guns reached his ears above the noise of the engines; he looked quickly over his shoulder and caught his breath as his eyes fell on a mixed swarm of Fokker D.VII's and triplanes coming down almost vertically on the rearmost 'Nines.' The gunners in the back seats were crouching low behind their Lewis guns. For a brief moment, as the enemy came within range, the air was full of sparkling lines of tracer, and then the Fokkers disappeared through and below the bombers.

He saw McLaren's machine wallow for a moment like a rolling porpoise, and then, with the rest of his

Flight, plunge down in the wake of the enemy machines.

'God! There must be thirty of them, and they mean business, coming in like that,' thought Biggles, as he rocked his wings and roared down into the whirling medley below. A red-painted machine crossed his sights and he pressed his triggers, but had to jerk round in a steep bank to avoid colliding with the first of the S.E.'s which were coming down from above. He glanced around swiftly. The air about him was full of machines, diving, zooming and circling; the bombers had held on their course and were already a mile away.

He flung his Camel on the tail of a blue-and-white Fokker, and the same instant there was a splintering jar as something crashed through his instrument board. A burning pain paralysed his leg, and he twisted desperately to try to see his opponent. Huns were all around him shooting his machine to pieces. He pulled the joystick back into his stomach and zoomed wildly. A Fokker flashed into his sights; he saw his tracer pour straight through it; the pilot slumped forward in his seat and the nose of the machine went down in an engine stall as the withering blast of lead struck it.

Something lashed the Camel like a cat-o'-nine-tails; he felt the machine quiver, and the next moment he was spinning, fighting furiously to get the machine on an even keel. A feeling of nauseating helplessness swept over him as he realized the Camel was not answering to the controls.

Something strange seemed to be whirling on the end of his wing-tip, and he saw it was an aileron*, hanging by a single wire. He kicked the opposite rudder and

* Usually a part of the trailing edge of a wing, made to turn the aircraft to left or right by means of a control column.

401

the nose of the Camel came up. 'God!—If I can only keep her there,' was the thought that flashed through his brain; but another burst of fire from an unseen foe tore through his centre section and he instinctively kicked out his right foot. The Camel spun again at once. He was near the ground now and he fought to get the nose of the machine up again, but something seemed to have gone wrong with his leg. He could not move it.

Biggles knew his time had come. He knew he was going down under a hail of lead in just the same way as he had seen dozens of machines going down, as he himself had sent them down. He knew he was going to crash, but the knowledge left him unmoved. A thousand thoughts crowded into his mind in a second of time that seemed like minutes; in that brief moment he thought of a dozen things he might do as the machine struck.

The nose of the Camel half came up—slowly—and the machine stopped spinning.

The Camel was side-slipping steeply to the right now, nose down, on the very verge of another spin that would be the last. The joystick was back in his left thigh and he unfastened his belt and twisted in his seat to get his right foot on the left side of the rudder, but it had no effect. A row of poplars appeared to leap upwards to meet him; he switched off the ignition with a lightning sweep of his hand, lifted the knee of his unwounded leg to his chin, folded his arms across his face and awaited the impact.

There was a splintering, rending crash, like a great tree in a forest falling on to the undergrowth. With the horror of fire upon him he clawed his way frantically out of the tangled wreck and half-rolled and half-crawled away from it. He seemed to be moving in a ghastly nightmare from which he could not awake. He became vaguely aware of the heat of a conflagration near him; it was the Camel, blazing furiously. Strange-looking soldiers were running towards him and he tore off his blood-stained goggles and stared at them, trying to grasp what had happened and what was happening. 'I'm down,' he muttered to himself in a voice which he hardly recognized as his own. 'I'm down,' he said again, as if the sound of the words would help him to understand.

The German soldiers were standing in a circle around him now, and he looked at them curiously. One of them stepped forward; 'Schweinhund flieger*!' he grunted, and kicked him viciously in the side. Biggles bit his lip at the pain. The man raised his heavy boot again, but there was a sudden authoritative word of command and he stepped back hastily. Biggles looked up to see an officer of about his own age, in a tight-fitting pale-grey uniform, regarding him compassionately. He noted the Pour-le-Merite Order at his throat, and the Iron Cross of the First Class below.

'So you have had bad luck,' he said, in English, with scarcely a trace of accent.

'Yes,' replied Biggles with an effort, forcing a smile and trying to get on to his feet. 'And I am sorry it happened this morning.'

'Why?'

'Because I particularly wanted to see a raid this afternoon,' he answered.

'Yes? But there will be no raid this afternoon,' replied the German smiling.

* German: Pilot swine!

'Why not?'

The German laughed softly. 'An armistice* was signed half an hour ago—but of course, you didn't know.'

* Peace, the end of the War. Signed 11 o'clock, 11 November 1918. Remembered today by Poppy Day.

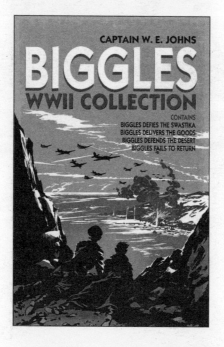

# ENJOY MORE DARING FIRST WORLD WAR BIGGLES ADVENTURES!

## EBOOKS ALSO AVAILABLE

# MORE BIGGLES STORIES
# FROM BETWEEN THE WARS

## EBOOKS ALSO AVAILABLE